The Riddle of Solomon

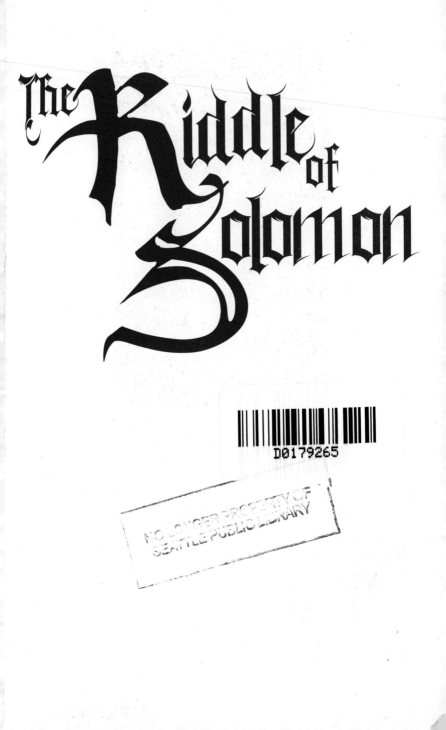

"Like a sandstorm roaring out of the Judean Desert, *The Riddle of Solomon* rips readers out of the familiar world, dropping them breathless in a place where ancient kings still keep their secrets. D. J. Niko's storytelling carries the grit of desert dust and the seductive scent of incense on every page as Sarah Weston races with a madman to save the treasures that King Solomon left behind."

—Mary Anna Evans, award-winning author of
Artifacts and *Wounded Earth*

Reviews from *The Tenth Saint*

"The characters are lively, and the story is fast-paced and exciting, especially for inveterate fans of the genre."

—David Pitt, *Booklist*

"Interesting, intricate, and intriguing, *The Tenth Saint* is an archeological puzzle the reader can't wait to solve."

—James O. Born, author of *Burn Zone*

"Like *The Da Vinci Code*, *The Tenth Saint* takes you to a place you have never been, creating an adventure you will not soon forget."

—Laurence Leamer, *New York Times* best-selling author of
The Kennedy Women, *The Kennedy Men*, and *Sons of Camelot*

The Riddle of Solomon

D.J. Niko

MEDALLION
P R E S S

Medallion Press, Inc.

Printed in USA

Published 2013 by Medallion Press, Inc.

The MEDALLION PRESS LOGO
is a registered trademark of Medallion Press, Inc.

Names, characters, places, and incidents are the products of the author's
imagination or are used fictionally. Any resemblance to actual events, locales,
or persons, living or dead, is entirely coincidental.

Typeset in Adobe Garamond Pro
Printed in the United States of America

ISBN 978-1605425-29-0
10 9 8 7 6 5 4 3 2 1

First Edition

For Peter

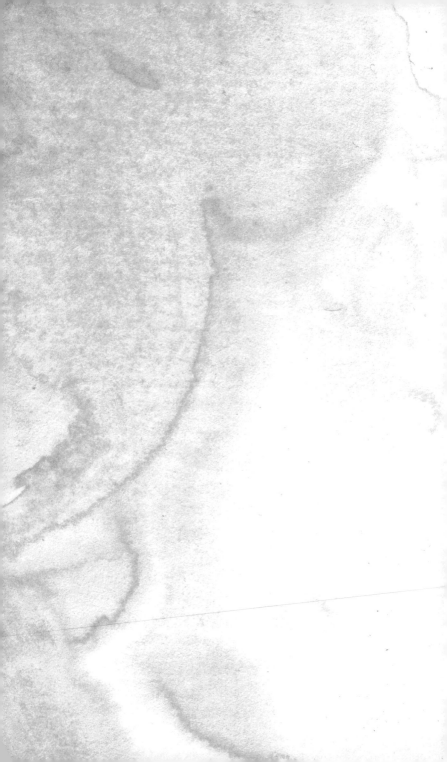

Prologue

City of David

Tenth century BCE

The old priest Zadok stood at the edge of the spring and gazed upon the face of the moon reflected on the still waters. It was pregnant with light and more intense than usual—the perfect moon for what he was about to do. He lifted his gaze to the sky. There was nary a cloud.

He regarded the royal city sprawled across the valley. The structures stretching like stone fingers toward the very edge of the desert were bathed in brilliant pewter light, interrupted only by the shadows of the date palms that sprouted from the rocky soil. Rising above the squat, flat-roofed houses was the royal citadel, built by the shepherd who had united the twelve tribes of Israel into one monarchy. Terraces of stone led to a fortified platform on which stood a palace built by Phoenician masons, the highest point in the city and the closest to heaven.

Behind Zadok, the orchards of Siloam clung to the verdant hillside. Ripe figs hung from the boughs, releasing their honeyed fragrance into the night air. He closed his eyes and inhaled the sweet scent that embraced him, a balm to still his mind. He felt the breath of the desert summer warm his face. He stood in that manner until all thought passed from his consciousness and he was an empty vessel, ready to receive. He turned to his disciple.

"It is time, my king."

The young king, who had scarcely completed his third year on the throne, lowered his head before the high priest of his court and of his father's before him. Zadok was pleased with the humble nature of his sovereign. It had been only twenty-one years since his mother bore him, but Solomon already was wise enough to know when to be king and when to be pupil.

Zadok slipped off his robes and stepped into the pool. It was water from this very spring that anointed the kings of Judah, and now the same water would purify his body, and that of Solomon, for the rite they were preparing to perform. He filled an earthen bowl with the water and held it high above his head, as if offering it to the sky.

"O wise and most powerful God, this servant comes before thee with pure intent, asking for nothing but grace. With this sacred water I cleanse this wretched body and wash away my trespasses so as to be unsoiled in thy presence."

He tipped the bowl and let the water run over his crown, drenching the straight, silver-streaked black hair that hung to the middle of his back and the wiry gray beard that covered his face and throat. He filled the bowl again and let the water cleanse the brown skin that clung loosely to his old bones. And when he was satisfied with his cleanliness, he dried himself and slipped on a robe of freshly woven white linen embroidered by the needle of a virgin.

Solomon felt his heart pound like the drumbeat of an army march as he slipped out of his royal blue garment and released his luxurious black curls from the gold band that encircled his head like a halo. He stood naked before his god, the same god who had granted him wisdom to lead the tribes of Israel with fairness and justice, and stepped into the pool. The frigid water made his body tingle with a pleasant chill. He thought of his father. King David was but a memory now, but in Solomon's mind he remained a giant. He recalled the promise he'd made to his father just hours before his death.

My father, go in peace, for I, your son Solomon, vow to build the one and magnificent sacred sanctuary and fill it with the holy vessels, just as God has commanded and the prophecies have foretold.

Tonight he would take the first step toward fulfilling that promise.

Clothed in vestment of pure white linen, Solomon followed Zadok up the stone steps to a clearing inside the orchard, where the priest had placed a carved cedar altar expressly for this purpose. Among the shadows cast by the fruit trees, they kneeled before the altar and prayed for guidance, for what they were about to do was reserved for only those whose souls were immaculate before heaven. Zadok rose first and offered the king his hand to kiss, which Solomon did dutifully and without reservation.

Zadok approached the assembly of objects on the altar and stopped before the one in the center. He slipped off a white sheath woven of spun spider's silk to reveal a stone censer, then poured into his palm the contents of a small white pouch embroidered with a golden lion. He rubbed the nuggets together so that the warmth of his hands could release their oil, placed them inside the censer, and lit them by scraping together two pieces of flint. The vessel issued a tentative thread of smoke.

"Let this perfume fumigate your humble servants, O Great One, so that their minds are laid open for what visions may come." With both hands, Zadok coaxed the fragrant smoke toward his face and inhaled deeply. He then waved the censer in front of Solomon and let the fumes of burning myrrh and mastic enter the king.

The night was so still that even the leaves on the fig and pomegranate trees did not quiver. Solomon was as calm as the air that hung over his father's city and regarded the ritual without eagerness or expectation. He had let go completely, trusting the divine to grant him everything he was ready for and deny him what he could not yet fathom.

For all the rituals and ceremonies that governed his kingship, he had never participated in anything like this. Conjurations of spirits and communication with the beyond realms were the dominion of Zadok, the kingdom's priest and seer. Solomon had absolute faith in Zadok. It was he, after all, who had helped him ascend to the throne that was not rightfully his. The old priest had proven his loyalty many times over, most notably when convincing King David that it was Solomon, not David's elder son Adonijah, who should rule over Israel and build the holy temple. And so it was done.

Zadok carefully unfolded layers of an unsullied white textile, woven by the women of the court using the silk of thousands of spiders, to reveal a slab of limestone carved in a round shape, the width and weight of a man's head. On it was etched the divine circle, symbolic of all creation, and in the center was engraved the most sacred and unutterable name of Yahweh.

The priest's voice tore at the veil of stillness draped over the orchard. "O David, most powerful and just ruler and father of King Solomon, I summon thee by the name which cannot be spoken and which strikes fear in the hearts of the unholy. I invoke thy presence by the two tablets on which is inscribed the sacred covenant of our people and by the holy tabernacle in which the almighty dwells, and by the holy of holies into which the high priest alone can enter. Show thyself, O David, and guide thy successor so that he may be worthy of the legacy which he has inherited."

The silence was complete. Zadok reached toward the earth and picked up a handful of soil. He held it toward the heavens and, turning in a clockwise circle, he sprinkled a little in each direction until all the soil was gone. Then he dropped to his knees, and with hands outstretched and head back, he said: "Tranquil and most gentle spirit of David, I bid thee come in peace. By the most sacred name of the one who dwells in the heavens, who has supreme power over creatures great and small, who has chosen the people of Israel to be the bearers and witnesses of his word, and who is the divine authority over the souls of men living and not, I summon thee, O David. Come forth and reveal the secrets of the angels who have spoken unto thee so that the Lord's will may be done."

A breeze whispered through the fruit trees, making the leaves tremble for a moment no longer than a man's heartbeat. The sign was not lost on Solomon. He felt his father's presence, sheer and amorphous as the *sharav*, as surely as he felt his own breath rise and fall. He inhaled the perfumed vapors issuing forth from the censer until his head felt light, his mind open and pliable. He had a singular mission this night: to receive the key for building the holy temple on Mount Moriah, a monumental task that had been entrusted to him alone.

"My son, everything I have done during my life on this earth—every battle I have waged, every victory I have won, every edifice I have built—has been in preparation for the one true task, and that is to build a temple to the Lord our God, to replace the tattered tabernacle that has long accompanied our people on their journey, and establish the permanence of our people on this land," his father had told him. "For many years, I thought this task was my calling. But the Lord appeared to me in a dream and said, 'David, do not build my house, for much bloodshed has marked thy reign. One of thy sons will become king, and in his days Israel will know peace. He alone will be worthy of carrying out so glorious a task.' It has been ordained, my son. It is you who must build this temple."

Solomon had watched as King David, recognizing his son's youth and inexperience, made provisions for the execution of this divine ordinance. In the final days of his life, the old king had ordered his masons to cut stones for the purpose of building, ordered cedar logs to be transported from the lands to the north, and amassed great stores of gold, copper, iron, and bronze.

When his father lay dying, Solomon received from him the most prized gift of all: a volume of parchments containing the plans for building the temple complex, which were revealed to David by the angels descending from the heavens. The plans mapped out the vestibule and the inner chambers, the courts and the treasuries, the rooms for the priests and the Levites, the vessels and the altars necessary for performing the holy rites, the pillars named Boaz and Jachin, the awesome brazen sea, and the holy of holies that was to house the Ark of the Covenant.

But to young Solomon's frustration, David did not reveal all. The old king had feared the plans might fall into the hands of the unwise, so he gave the dimensions for each chamber in a mysterious measuring unit, saying the angels had instructed him to keep the truth hidden from Solomon until it was time to execute the vision. So the knowledge had died with him.

In the early days of his reign, Solomon had studied the plans every day and night, convinced in his adolescent arrogance he would come to understand them. He did not.

Then, one night, as the flame of his candle expired in a pool of wax, he closed his eyes and heard a voice thunder in the space between his ears.

"I will grant you one thing. What is it you want more than anything else?"

Solomon dropped to his knees and touched his forehead to the ground. No sooner had he done so than he felt a force pull him upright.

"Stand before me a king. What is your one wish?"

Though there was no one with Solomon in his chamber, he understood at that moment he would never be alone. He would forever be guided: it was written.

"Grant me wisdom, O Lord," he whispered.

Everything changed that night. The new king no longer bristled with impatience. He rolled up the scrolls and placed them inside an alabaster box in his private chamber.

The box remained sealed for three years.

Now, surely as he knew the sun would rise in the east, Solomon knew his time had come. But he needed his father one last time.

Zadok nodded to his king, a signal that the spirit was among them. He handed Solomon the single object wrapped in red silken cloth and backed away from the altar. He had done all he could; the rest was up to the young king.

Solomon slowly peeled away the protective covering and beheld a knife with handle made from ram's horn and a curved blade like a sickle. He held it to the heavens, and its cutting edge gleamed in the moonlight. Then, without emotion or hesitation, he brought its point to the inside of his left forearm and made a diagonal incision on the taut, caramel-colored skin. He did not flinch at the sting of the puncture or the throbbing ache as the hot, dark red contents of his veins welled and streamed down his forearm, over the bony mound of his wrist, and into the valley of his palm. He let the blood pool in his hand for a few seconds before guiding it across his middle finger and letting it drip into a bowl carved of pure white marble and polished to a slippery smoothness. When it was filled, he stepped away from the altar and spilled the blood onto the earth, forming a circle around himself.

"O spirit of my father, come forth and recognize your own blood." Solomon's deep voice sounded across the orchard. "Enter this circle which can be penetrated only by those who share the same royal blood, and reveal the secret the angels granted to thee, for the time has come to venerate the name of the Lord our God by building his temple on the holy mound. Reveal, O noble spirit, the key to the treasure belonging to the children of Israel, and help your humble son become the instrument the Lord intended him to be."

Solomon stood motionless inside the circle of blood, waiting. He was in a deeply meditative state, his mind like fertile soil ready to receive the seeds of inspiration. He thought of nothing, resisting the urge to let thoughts intrude upon the perfect stillness that enveloped him.

For a long time, there was silence. He knew he was being tested; he expected no less from his shrewd and sage father. If he could harness the wild horses of the young mind and bend them to his will, then he was deemed ready. This was no easy feat for the king of whom so much was expected, so early in his reign and in the dawn of manhood.

Solomon felt weakness seep through the walls of his

spiritual fortress and stand before him, wearing the cloak of doubt. The thoughts floated in the ether of his mind, threatening his peace. *Will he come? Is he angry with me? Am I truly ready?* He focused on his breath and became aware of its rhythms as it swelled and expired like the waves of a distant sea. Every inhale was laced with the perfume of myrrh, a vaguely sweet scent redolent of musk and spice. He let the moment embrace him and shield him from the intruders, and soon any power they claimed over him diminished like the last breaths of winter.

He felt a single rush of wind blow upon his face and tousle his curls.

I am here.

The voice of David reverberated inside the young king's head like a clarion call, filling even the darkest corners. At that moment, Solomon was completely effaced and all that existed was a conduit for the message.

That which is four really is five. That which is five really is one. Look beyond that which you can see and feel, and you will have your answer.

The air suddenly became tomb still, and silence filled Solomon's head. He opened his eyes slowly and looked to the heavens. A single star shot across the cloudless indigo sky, disappearing almost as quickly as it came. He felt the coolness of the earth beneath his bare feet and became keenly aware of his duty to both the upper and lower heavens. He looked down and noticed a shining red object peer through the soil inside the blood circle. He brushed the dirt aside and saw a ring forged of iron, with four stones embedded inside a perfect circle. He recognized their significance: ruby for fire, aquamarine for water, tiger's eye for earth, and diamond for wind.

The four elements. *That which you can see and feel.*

Solomon turned the ring to examine it from all sides and noticed the tiny hinge. He lifted the gem-encrusted iron lid and beneath it found a circle of gold etched with a five-pointed star—the symbol of the heavens and the quintessence of all things, the fifth element seen only by the chosen few. He knew the key he sought lay within the symbol.

That which is five really is one.

A faint smile crossed the wise king's lips as he realized the meaning of his father's message. He slipped the ring on his left index finger, still smeared with his own blood, and clenched his fist. The knowledge and the power were his and his alone. And so it would remain through the ages, until someone worthy came forth to claim it.

Chapter 1

Northwestern edge of the Rub' al Khali Desert
Saudi Arabia

The sheer sandstone cliffs of the Tuwaiq Escarpment rose like rocky stalagmites from the sandy expanses of central Arabia, casting long shadows on the parched wasteland below. The morning sun made the landscape glow like the gold of pharaohs and gave definition to the softly sculpted dunes beneath the gaze of the escarpment. In the distant horizon, the crests and valleys of the sand sea dissolved into an umber fog.

Sarah Weston halted her horse and surveyed the terrain. Through the fine mist of sand that hung in the air, the massifs to the east appeared slightly hazy, as if reflected in an antique mirror. She knew why. This part of the Rub' al Khali Desert was subject to the *shamal* winds, at times harmless and other times annihilating everything in their path. All but the hardiest nomads steered clear of this place, where gales rose without warning—and without mercy.

Sarah felt a whisper of a breeze flutter her white gauze turban, which warded off the cruel July sun that baked the land at temperatures often exceeding a hundred and twenty degrees. She used the end of the turban to wipe the cocktail of perspiration and fine sand from her face. The tiny grains scratched at her fair skin, a familiar sensation.

The conditions couldn't have been more different than those of her privileged British upbringing. The house parties at her family's country manor, the banal company, her father's notoriety and influence, her mother's tragic end, her own brief career among the learned men of her alma mater, Cambridge University—all were ruins from a distant past. And that was the way she liked it.

She took in the vastness of the remote, inhospitable place she had come to love. She was awed by the vast wilderness of sand and rock that held so many secrets of early civilization and was humbled by the impermanence of the desert, which shifted and drifted like a capricious nymph who could be captured briefly but never possessed.

In this harsh terrain, she had worked for seven months as the lead archaeologist in a dig jointly funded by Rutgers and King Saud universities to excavate Qaryat al-Fau, the ancient Kindite city lost in the shifting sands of the Rub' al Khali. She was brought on board by cultural anthropologist Daniel Madigan, who'd put together the expedition seven years ago and had uncovered significant new sections of this once-great commercial center that had thrived in the first through fourth centuries of the Common Era.

Today, however, they had strayed from the site. The al-Fau expedition was operating with a pared-down crew for only two hours a day due to the heat, so they had time on their hands. At the beginning of the summer, Sarah and Daniel had quietly begun digging two miles north of al-Fau, in the desolate place known to Bedouin nomads as Valley of the Wind.

Their foray here was prompted by a blip in their satellite imagery, which suggested the possibility of a debris field buried beneath the sands. As it happened, their timing was fortuitous: a few months ago, a vicious sandstorm had howled through the valley. The ferocious *shamal* had blown away huge dunes, scattering the sand to all points of the compass. It was how the desert regenerated itself.

And how it revealed its secrets.

Daniel rode next to Sarah. He shifted the black baseball cap covering his shoulder-length mahogany waves streaked with just enough gray to hint at his forty-three years. He looked at his partner through dark green aviators and spoke in a musical Tennessee accent. "Pretty hot out here for an English girl. You doing all right?"

"I could do without the sauna. Otherwise, never better."

"Well, all right. Ready to collect some specimens?"

"Let's do it."

It was the first time since they'd uncovered the bones,

strewn across a good half mile of desert, that they were ready to take up some specimens for study. There were hundreds of them—porous, broken, half-buried in sand. Some were cameloid, some human, all remarkably well preserved in the dry, bacteria-free environment of their desert tombs.

Was it a caravan or an army? The questions swirled in Sarah's head, ratcheting up her excitement as they began to piece together a theory.

They dismounted in unison. Daniel reached inside his saddlebag and pulled out a pair of two-way radios, their only means of communication with each other and with the two crew members at the main camp. He tossed one to Sarah.

She stroked the neck of her gray Arabian mare and clipped the radio to the waistband of her army-green expedition pants, which she had tucked into weathered leather riding boots.

The plan was to walk south, where the cliff passage narrowed to form a sort of trough. It was there that most of the bones lay. She could envision the camels and their riders, trapped in the passage as great columns of sand rose, stamping out their cries of desperation and devouring them without mercy. It had been the way of the desert for eons, this ruthless claim over all creatures that walked its sands. It was a showdown no man could win—not then, not now.

Inside the natural hollow surrounded by limestone massifs, the sand had been blown into ripples by the incessant winds. So symmetrical and evenly spaced a draftsman could not have drawn them with more precision, the ripples undulated across a flattened piece of desert whose hardened crust yielded with a crunch underfoot. Sarah glanced behind her at her footprints, regretting her imprint on the perfection of nature.

From the sand sprouted the occasional clump of tumbleweed, the lone life-form clinging to the arid badlands. One plant, separated from its roots, tumbled across the golden expanse as a hot breeze blew through. Sarah tasted the slightly salty grit between her teeth.

When they arrived at the study site, Daniel slipped off his backpack and tossed it onto the ground. "I reckon we don't have much time. Looks like the wind's picking up." He gestured toward the pit they'd dug to contain a cache of excavated human bone fragments. They had already reconstructed the majority of a male arm. "I'll finish up here if you want to work on the saddle."

A few days before, they'd spotted a wooden knob, barely darker than the desert itself, peeking out from the sand about fifty feet away from the bone pit. They had brushed enough of the sand away to expose the back of an acacia saddle frame with a piece of black rope still attached.

Daniel had examined the frayed rope end, sand falling away as he ran his thumb across the plaits. Goat hair, he'd proclaimed. It was their first clue that the caravan was centuries old. Goat hair rope, which took an inordinate time to weave, had not been used by desert dwellers for generations.

Today, Sarah's mission was to expose a larger section of the gray woven cloth attached to the frame. Like the bones, it was preserved as if it'd been buried yesterday. She kneeled in front of the object and removed her brushes and trowel from her backpack.

The camel wool felt coarse. The fibers were thick and the weave tight, as if the fabric was meant to support weight. A row of red embroidery decorated the gray wool. The color was vivid and the designs were rather complicated, leading her to believe this wasn't a caravan of common nomads.

By Daniel's evaluation, the textile was Sabaean. He was an expert on the people of southern Arabia and had recognized the stitch as one used by highly trained embroiderers, perhaps ladies of the court, before the Common Era. Sarah did not question his insight. There was no doubt something about it looked regal.

A gust of wind hissed through the passage. Sarah held on to her turban and shifted her gaze downward, avoiding the assault of sand granules. Daniel was right: their time here was limited.

She picked up the pace, brushing away the sand until she found what she was hoping for: a flap made of the same fabric, indicating a saddlebag. A bulge beneath told her the cargo was still inside. Her pulse quickened.

She brought the radio to her mouth and clicked it on. "Danny, you ought to see this."

"On my way." His voice crackled on the other end.

She reached inside. Her hand came across a round object whose surface felt porous and pockmarked. She pulled it out and held it in the palm of her hand. It was a clay pot, coated with a red slip and no bigger than a man's fist, with tiny rolled handles and a thin neck into which was stuffed a stopper made of the same clay. She turned it slowly and noticed a faded imprint on the earthen surface.

Daniel squatted beside her. "Looks like you've struck gold."

"Look at this." She turned the imprint toward him.

He removed his glasses and squinted at the image. "Human-headed, winged lions . . . the cherubim of antiquity. I'll be damned."

"If we needed more proof this is an ancient caravan, here it is."

"The shape of this pot is Canaanite," he said, the word dancing across his tongue. "Probably something they traded for."

She weighed the pot by slightly bouncing her hand. "It's rather heavy for its size. Perhaps there's something inside."

He winked. "One way to find out."

Sarah pulled the stopper, but it was tightly wedged.

She twisted it alternately clockwise and counterclockwise until it gave way. She looked down the pot's dark throat. "Can't see anything." She brought it to her nose and sat upright when she inhaled the unexpected scent.

She turned to Daniel. "It's sweet." She sniffed again, taking in a perfume redolent of fig blossom. It was so unmistakable she could imagine the taste of it. "Honey. Definitely honey."

Daniel extended a hand, and she placed the pot in it. He sniffed too, then tipped the pot until a small bead of golden, viscous liquid appeared on the rim. He smiled at her. "A brilliant discovery, Dr. Weston."

"Yes, it is." A deep voice thundered behind them.

They both jerked their heads toward the voice.

Behind them stood four men on camelback, dressed in long, black, high-collared *thobes* with sarongs beneath and sleeveless woolen *kibr* coats belted twice around the waist. Red-checkered keffiyeh scarves covered their heads and shoulders. The two men in the back held rifles and the reins of Sarah and Daniel's horses. Daniel's horse, a spirited black stallion, reared in protest.

"You have no business here," the leader said in Arabic. He raised a hand, and the marksmen pointed their weapons at the perceived intruders. "These lands are ours. And so is everything in them."

Daniel stood slowly and addressed the man in Arabic. "The Al Murrah are peace-loving people. Why do you threaten us?"

"We are protecting our heritage."

"But we're scientists. We can help you identify the origin and chronology of these remains."

"We don't need you. We know what we need to know." He and another of the men dismounted. "Your science will never reveal the whole truth. Now kneel next to her."

Daniel dropped to his knees.

"Put your hands behind your head. Both of you."

Sarah glanced at the two marksmen, whose weapons were still trained on them, and then at Daniel. His face was tight, his jaw clenched. Perspiration trickled down his temple, carving a river through the sandy film covering his tanned skin. She watched as the two tribesmen hoisted the saddle, groaning.

Clumps of sun-baked sand fell away as the saddle emerged from its sandy grave. They stuffed the honey pot inside the saddlebag and lifted the saddle onto one of the camels.

"This is criminal," Sarah said. "This is not yours to take. It belongs to the people."

The leader pierced her with his glare and pointed a brown, dust-caked finger at her. "In this country, women speak only when spoken to. Do not ever question the authority of a man. You are not worthy."

Her face flushed. Though she knew the rules of the

land, she had trouble playing the role of the submissive female. It was the kind of injustice she could not stomach. She opened her mouth to speak.

The tribesman clenched his fists. She harbored no illusions: he would do it.

She closed her mouth, biting her lip so hard she could taste the metallic tang of her own blood. She cast a furtive glance at Daniel. He was looking straight ahead, expressionless, seemingly oblivious to her plight.

The tribesman turned to Daniel. "Take nothing else from this place. Or we will be back . . . with more than a warning."

He mounted his camel and gave the departure sign to the rest of his crew. They rode away in haste, horses in tow. The hooves of the animals raised great plumes of dust as they galloped across the sandy plains toward the massifs to the east.

Daniel stood and exhaled loudly. "What the hell was that, Sarah? You know better than to irritate these guys."

"I know what women can and can't do here. Speaking is not a crime."

"You and I know that, but they're old school. They could have killed you."

She could debate all day about Saudi Arabia's marginalization of women, but it wasn't an argument she could win. She let it go. "Who were they, anyway?"

"Al Murrah. They're nomads. Camel herders." He

shook his head. "Al Murrah descended from Bedouin nobility and are, usually, honorable people. My guess is these guys are part of a clan, some sort of militant faction. There's one in every tribe."

Sarah watched them disappear behind the cliffs, the cloud of dust suspended behind them. "Do you think this was the caravan of some of their ancestors?"

"Those brutes couldn't care less." He spat on the ground. "Probably selling the stuff and using the money to fund weapons."

Sarah stood. Her loose chambray shirt whipped like a flag in the gathering wind. "How far did you get at the bone pit?"

"Maybe we ought to call it a day." He pointed a thumb at the cliffs behind which the camel riders had disappeared. "I suggest we avoid pissing them off."

"I'm not leaving here without those bones. Besides, your friends at King Saud won't be happy if we come home empty-handed."

He gave her a tight-lipped smile, the lines around his eyes deepening. "One of these days your stubbornness will get you into a lot of hot water."

She took his comment as an acquiescence. She repacked her bag and slung it over her shoulder. "Let's go, then. Our specimens await."

"As a matter of fact," he said as they walked, "I had just located the phalanges when you called. They were surprisingly intact. Such small bones usually scatter."

"The beauty of preservation in sand. I wonder what else is buried in this valley."

At the dig site, the larger arm bones were already unearthed and classified, ready to take back to the lab. The rest—the metacarpals and phalanges—lay in situ, encrusted in the amber-colored sand.

"Let's just bag what we have and head back." Daniel radioed to the main camp and asked one of his crew to pick them up at the edge of the valley, which was as far as a vehicle could go. He clipped the radio onto his belt and began collecting the prepared specimens.

Sarah stared at the sand pit containing the hand bones. Something caught her eye: a faint glimmer of white, its shape vaguely suggesting a corner. "Wait a minute." She waved him over. "Did you see this?"

He came for a look. "Those are the phalanges I was telling you about."

"No." She kneeled and wiped the area with a brush, revealing a flat, white surface. "This is no bone."

Another gust blasted through the valley, blowing the sand upward in violent swirls. Sarah's eyes stung from the assault. She pulled the end of her turban across her face and continued working as the wind whipped.

"Sarah, we have to get out of here." He looked at the ominous cloud of dust being raised around them. "Things could get ugly."

"Not without this," she said, still digging.

"I mean it, Sarah."

"Why don't you grab a tool and help? It could go faster."

He huffed. "Damn you, Sarah Weston. How do you talk me into these things?"

"You'll thank me later."

Daniel took up another brush and helped her expose more and more of the white object.

"There it is! It's alabaster. An alabaster box."

"Leave it," he shouted over the wind. "We'll come back for it."

"No way. It may not be here then. Are you willing to risk that?"

As the *shamal* hissed in her ears, Sarah brushed furiously to reveal the full span of the lid. And there it was, as sure and solemn as a promise: the same winged lion insignia that was stamped on the pot of honey.

Daniel looked at her, wild eyed.

Without another word, they quickly scraped away the rest of the sand with hand trowels. They worked together in a dance so seamless it bordered on telepathy. It pleased Sarah to know he was beside her, even if he sometimes seemed so far away.

At last, the box revealed itself. It was no bigger than a pencil case, its tranlucent brilliance barely masked by the film of sand that still clung to its surface after all those years.

Sarah picked up the box and shook it gently. "There is something in this." Though she knew it wasn't an option, her every nerve pulsed with the desire to open the box.

Daniel held up a specimen bag. "Put it in."

She clutched the box, reluctant to let it go, even temporarily.

"Sarah . . ."

He was right. With a reverence that bordered on obsession, she placed the box inside the bag and watched him tuck the package into his backpack, which was custom segmented and padded for artifact collection.

She knew it was unorthodox to do things this way, but in her mind there was no other choice. If they didn't act, the object could be lost forever, either to looters or to the voracious maws of the ever-shifting desert.

And so could the knowledge it potentially held.

She got to her feet despite the wind's better efforts to keep her hunched down and threaded her arms through the straps of her backpack. She pressed down on her turban and gave Daniel the thumbs-up.

With heads lowered, the two walked against the violent gusts and driving sand toward the edge of the valley.

Chapter 2

 *S*arah ran her long, slim fingers across the surface of the box. It was smooth and cold to her touch. The corners were still sharp, as if it had been newly chiseled.

The light of the kerosene lamp made the alabaster glow with a pale golden hue and revealed the specks and veins of the translucent stone. She had intentionally turned off the fluorescent lights in the lab and worked under the lamplight to let the stone speak to her. She saw nothing extraordinary about the alabaster itself, other than the stamp on the lid.

The shape was faded but unmistakable: two lions in profile, their anthropomorphic heads facing each other, not in confrontation but rather in apparent reverence of the empty space between them. From their backs sprouted wings, outstretched in readiness for flight. These were the ancient world's cherubim—not the angelic creatures of Christianity but hybrid beasts representing spiritual beings or guardians.

She moved an errant curl away from her eyes and tucked it behind her ear.

She looked over at Daniel. The flickering flame danced upon the hard angles of his face, pronouncing the creases around his eyes that were testament to the years he'd spent in the field.

"All right, Sarah," he said. "You've flirted with this thing long enough. Time to see what's inside."

The anticipation had been mounting inside Sarah for days as she studied and recorded the box from every perspective. She'd had to stifle the urge to get to the contents quickly, for haste could mean lost information that could help them interpret the find. Now the maddening exercise in patience had at last found its reward.

She slowly lifted the lid. It didn't give way easily; a crust of sand had formed inside the grooves, acting as a natural seal. She twisted gently, and it yielded. She removed the lid, feeling the familiar churning inside her core, a combination of excitement and intrigue.

Daniel sat back and rubbed the back of his neck. "That's just about the last thing I'd expect to find in the middle of this desert."

Sarah scanned the length of the rolled-up papyrus, noting the tightness of the fibers. She had seen many scrolls during her career, but most were in tatters. This specimen was both well constructed and well preserved.

She could not take her eyes off it.

"It's highly unusual to find papyrus here," he continued. "I've seen plenty of parchment made of animal skins, but this . . . this is extraordinary."

"I'm with you. This likely isn't local. Perhaps this was from a caravan of traders."

"Maybe. It's too early to tell." He stared at the scroll for a long moment. "Let's see what the scribe had to say. That'll give us a clue."

After photographing and recording the dimensions and characteristics of the scroll, Sarah slipped off the dirty twine wrapped three times around its belly and laid the fragile document onto a tray. Taking extreme care not to crack or damage the ancient paper, she unrolled it with gloved hands.

The papyrus was thick, which probably explained why it had suffered so little damage. She suspected whoever pounded this was an expert. The edges were ragged and there were some small tears, but otherwise the scroll was intact, which would facilitate the interpretation of the long-form script.

Sarah examined the characters rendered in black ink. "Hieratic. Practically every word is legible. It's almost too good to be true."

"That's odd," Daniel said. "Hieratic was used almost exclusively in Egypt for sacred texts. What would something like this be doing here?"

Sarah recalled the close proximity of the box to the phalanges. "Whatever it is, someone was holding onto it as he died. That's rather telling, don't you think?"

"Right. I'll be curious to see what the C-14 looks like. There's a lab in Arizona that can date papyrus with AMS. All we need is a tiny sample."

Though she hadn't had occasion to use it, she knew all about the accelerator mass spectrometry used by the University of Arizona, the same facility that dated the Dead Sea Scrolls and other old biblical texts by counting carbon-14 atoms rather than measuring their decay. It had become one of the most important resources in archaeology.

She shifted her focus to the hieratic script. The characters were so fluid and elegant she suspected they were penned by a highly skilled scribe—someone from a royal court, perhaps, or the priesthood. "What about translating the text? Have you got any ideas?"

"I will send it to the top linguist at King Saud, who's an expert in ancient languages. She's good, and she's fast. I'll bet she can have it done in a couple of months."

Considering the potential magnitude of the find, two months seemed like an eternity. But it was the archaeologist's reality: the rigors of the process were the ultimate exercise in patience.

Patience, however, never had been one of Sarah's virtues. She had her own plan.

Chapter 3

My son,
The dusk of my life is upon me.
I wander shoeless in the desert, searching for my beloved.
I have been blessed with riches and wisdom and wives aplenty,
But now, as my youth withers and my powers fail me,
I seek solace in her breast.
What good is knowledge if thou art the only keeper of it?
What good is a divine secret if thou must take it to the grave?
Hear me, O my son, and make thyself worthy of what I grant thee,
For it will bloom and bear fruit for all the ages of ages.

The orchard is profuse with fig, the vines heavy with grape.
When my lover's face appears from the shadows,
All mysteries are revealed.
Her beauty illuminates the path and the dark stones,
And I follow, powerless to resist.

What power hast thou over me, O fair nymph?
And she saith, All that is hidden I will show thee,
All that thou hunger for I will feed to thee,
But only if thou art faithful.
Come with me now to the ramparts, under the gaze of the mountain,
And partake of my love, for when the rooster crows I will be gone,
But thou will have all that thou desire.
Our love is a perfect circle forged of earthly matter
But anointed by celestial grace.
Its mystery unfolds and, lo, there is rapture in the heavens.
Give to me thy chest of treasure and I will give thee the key that unlocks it.

Under the darkest cloak of night, the temptress appears.
She is redolent of balsam and good spices and her fingers are dusted with gold.
Mortal men are defenseless against her beauty,
And they are drawn to her like moths to the fire.
Beware, brethren, for she will trap thee and feed thee to her army of beasts.
Her lions will stretch out their claws and rip at thy flesh.
Her oxen will gore thee and her eagles will deafen thee with their cries.
Her demons will stab thee with their forked tongues,
And her serpents will coil themselves around thy foot and

paralyze thee.
Only he who is pure of heart and gentle of manner
Can tame her beasts and possess the fruit of her womb.
But if thou art the chosen one,
She will reward thee with a treasure unlike any other,
Forged by the whispers of angels and guarded by kings for
all eternity.

This, my son, is thy father's gift to thee.
Open thy palm and receive it with grateful heart.
Open thy mind and thou shall know its value.
Seek always the divine in the midst of the earthly
And go in the direction of the bright star
Whose five rays of light point to the one divine truth
That will guide thee in turmoil and deliver thee in thy
darkest hour,
Just as it has your father and his father before him.

Sarah read and reread the translated passages, haunted by the weight of the words whose meaning she did not yet fully comprehend. She crossed her arms and sank into the black leather, button-tufted armchair that was as deep and high-backed as a throne.

The conference room at King Saud University looked more like a corporate boardroom, with a long, gleaming walnut table around which were arranged twenty-four of the leather chairs. The walls were painted gray and devoid of art, save for a portrait of the king, giving the room a clinical feel in spite of the richness of the furnishings.

She looked across the conference table at Daniel. He rested his square jaw, dusted with two-day growth, on his hand, and his bronzed face was hardened by thought as he tried to make sense of what he was reading.

At the end of the table, their host was seated. Mariah Banai, the head of the linguistics program at King Saud's College of Languages and Translation, and one of academia's leading scholars in ancient Hebraic studies, was bent over her phone, tapping on the screen.

Mariah, originally from Israel, wore a floor-length turquoise djellaba with a coordinating hijab loosely draped over her head. As she sat cross-legged, her four-inch heels peeked beneath the fabric in quiet defiance. She looked to be in her early forties, though her taut, golden honey-toned skin made it hard to tell. Her nose was as straight and sharp as a Roman statue's, and her mahogany hair was cropped like a boy's and tousled around her face as if she had just come in from a windstorm. Her deep-set brown eyes were framed by angled brows that looked like thick black brushstrokes.

Mariah put her phone down and studied Sarah. "You seem puzzled, Dr. Weston. Is there anything I can explain?"

Her gaze was so hypnotic that Sarah was compelled to look away. "There is one thing I don't understand. Why would a papyrus scroll written in Egyptian hieratic end up in the middle of the desert? There has been nothing else to suggest the language was spoken or written here."

"First of all, let me correct you," Mariah said. "The language is late Egyptian hieratic, specifically the high form. There were several forms of hieratic in ancient Egypt, and the differences among them are material."

Sarah heard a barb in Mariah's voice. She seemed to enjoy correcting her a little too much.

She brushed it off. "All right, then. Late Egyptian hieratic. That was prevalent, in written form, starting in the fourteenth century BCE."

"Up to about 600 BCE, yes."

"During that time frame, Egyptians waged several campaigns in the Near East but did not venture down this far. So this scroll was likely taken from the Holy Land. Question is, why?"

"I'm a linguist, not an historian," Mariah said. "That's your job."

Daniel weighed in. "The Valley of the Wind was part of a trading route. My guess is these were people from the South, Sabaeans most likely, returning home from a trading mission in the Near East—Canaan, Israel, Assyria, Phoenicia. The items we found, which may or may not be of Egyptian origin, were probably part of a trade."

"It's highly unlikely someone would trade for a scroll," Sarah interrupted, "unless it contained significant knowledge."

Daniel addressed Mariah. "Sarah's right. This was obviously written by a father to his son. Writing was such a big deal back then that nobody would have done that for the hell of it. There is something important within this text—a set of instructions, perhaps—but it is obscured in the language. That's significant, because not everyone was educated enough to hide a message in verse—or to write prose this sophisticated. Whoever wrote this had a high place in society. I'm convinced of it."

"If this scroll dates from the late Bronze or Iron Age, as the script suggests," Mariah said, "the only society capable of something like this at the time was Egypt."

"I don't buy it."

Daniel and Mariah both turned to look at Sarah. There was a deep silence in the room.

Sarah folded her arms on the table and leaned forward. "There was a reference to angels in the text. Egyptians didn't believe in angels. People of Mesopotamia did. Sumerians . . . Israelites . . ."

Mariah glared at her coldly. "There are plenty of winged beings in early Egyptian iconography. They may not have been angels the way we perceive them, but they were deities."

"But you specifically used the word *angels*. Are you saying that is not entirely accurate?"

Mariah turned to Daniel, as if Sarah were not in the room. "I happen to be an expert in ancient Hebrew and in Judaic studies. I can assure you the scribal tradition of ancient Israel and its neighbors was neither this sophisticated nor did it include expression in an Egyptian tongue. In my estimation, it's an open-and-shut case. This is an Egyptian document."

Sarah had more to say but kept her thoughts to herself. She was sure this wasn't the time, or the company, for it. She caught Daniel's gaze and held it for a long moment. She could tell by the penetrating look in his caramel-colored eyes he was trying to read her mind—and couldn't.

Mariah looked at her watch. "Perhaps we ought to continue this another day. I am delivering a lecture in five minutes on the other side of campus." She stood and gathered her stack of books and folders. She extended a hand to Daniel. "This has been a fascinating exchange. Do keep me in the loop about the dating of the scroll. Perhaps that will provide the missing piece of information that will help us identify the author."

"And the meaning," Daniel added, shaking her hand.

She smiled at him; then, assuming a serious expression, she glanced briefly at Sarah and walked out of the room.

Daniel turned to Sarah. "What was that all about?"

She listened as Mariah's footsteps echoed down the hallway. "I'll explain later."

That night, the Qaryat al-Fau site looked like a city of wraiths as its cold stones took on the silver hue of the waxing moon rising over the flat tops of the Tuwaiq Escarpment. The roofless chambers lay exposed before the moon's interrogating light, like beehives that had long since been stripped of their purpose but not of their dignity. By day, the complex, with its ramparts and towers and boundaries outlined with stones, was akin to a child's sand castle, frozen in a desiccated landscape by the long fingers of a punishing sun. In the ghostlight, it took on a strange new dimension as the black shadows lengthened and the night wind whispered through the hollows.

It was on nights like these that Sarah liked to sit alone and imagine the ancient inhabitants of al-Fau to life. In her mind's eye she saw their routines—their daily ambles through the marketplace to buy oil for their lamps and spices for their stews, the tending of their flocks in distant pastures fed by the rivers of antiquity, their spirited negotiations with the Himyarites and Sabaeans and other tribesmen traveling northward to Mesopotamia.

It was September and, as the temperatures became slightly more bearable, the project was again in full swing. This season, the crew worked on the souk and two burial sites beyond the boundaries of the city, uncovering new remnants of magnificent wall art, painted in red iron ore on peeling gypsum by tomb artists in the dawn of the Common Era.

That night, however, she wasn't thinking of the expedition as she usually did. She lay on her side, propped on her right elbow, on an old kilim spread out by the campfire. A white gauze shawl was draped across her shoulders to ward off the night chill. She took off the bandana that covered her head and let her mane of loose curls tumble haphazardly around her face. She gazed absently into the belly of the ebbing flames, her thoughts consumed by the contents of the papyrus scroll.

"A riyal for your thoughts."

Daniel's voice startled her out of her reverie and she jerked upright.

"Sorry, sweetheart," he said with a singsong twang. "Didn't mean to scare you."

She waved off his apology. "Nonsense. Come. Join me."

Daniel stoked the fire to coax a few more flames and sat next to her. They both stared at the fire, a silent space between them.

He spoke first. "You haven't said two words all night. Now go on. Spill it."

She gave him a half smile. "I think you know what I'm thinking about."

"I know. It's been on my mind too."

"Do you really believe that text was written by an Egyptian?"

"It's a theory; that's all. Why? You got a better one?"

"I just don't think we should dismiss the possibility that it came from the Euphrates Valley or perhaps even the Negev. Plenty of Canaanite and Israelite ostraca containing hieratic characters have been found."

"True. But Mariah is right. The scribal tradition of the ancient Near East was nothing compared to Egypt's. I have no reason to doubt what she's saying."

She shrugged. "I'm not as convinced about her as you are."

He shot her a look of surprise. His face—unshaven and encircled by long, undulating sweeps of dark hair— looked almost primitive in the firelight. "Mariah is on our side, Sarah. She is on the faculty of our partner university. If she knew something that was material to our cause, she would tell us."

Sarah didn't mention the rest of her reservations, but there was something about Mariah she didn't trust. Maybe it was an emotional reaction to Mariah's condescending attitude toward her. She checked herself, granting the Israeli professor the benefit of the doubt. Besides, Daniel obviously trusted her, and his instincts were not often off-target.

Sarah had come to respect Daniel far more than she'd ever expected to. When they'd met in Aksum, Ethiopia, a little more than a year ago, he'd come across as a pompous American with a hokey Southern accent and a bigger-than-life personality. At the time she was guarded toward him, unsure of his intentions. But he systematically broke down all her barriers.

She recalled the exact moment she'd relinquished

all doubts. They were alone in the Simien Mountains, marched there and left for dead by a hired gun during their contested pursuit of Ethiopia's tenth saint. After a few days struggling for survival in the desolate wilderness, she'd come down with dysentery and could not continue.

"Go on without me," she'd told him and had meant it.

"Even if I have to hoist your corpse out of here," he'd said, "I'm not leaving you."

Not only did he not leave; he carried her ailing body across sloping cliffs and craggy ridges, where one misstep could mean a fall into a steep gorge. His actions sent a clear message: *We're doing this together.* And it had been that way since.

When he invited her to join his expedition in Saudi Arabia, she couldn't refuse. After all they had been through in Ethiopia and beyond, she had come to regard him as a kindred spirit and a true partner. And if she were to admit the stirrings in the depths of her heart, she longed to be near him.

"You're right, Danny. Why would she hold something back?" She directed the question as much to herself as to him. "I'll play along with her theory—for now."

He flashed a bright smile. "That's more like it." He stood and offered her his hand. "Come on; let's turn in. We have a big day ahead."

The next morning, Sarah worked with a small crew on

one of the tomb sites on the outer edges of the city. A dry, saunalike heat had settled into the valley as the sun traveled toward the apex of the sky. At that time of day, not a single shadow was cast on the endless stretches of sand. In this unforgiving terrain, there was no trace of anything green for miles. The only living things were the scorpions and the scarabs, and even they hid deep beneath the scorched surface.

Sarah wore a long-sleeved T-shirt and cargo pants, both in desert khaki, and a wide-brimmed hat over the red bandana wrapped around her head. It was too hot for so many clothes, but showing skin was a grave offense in rural Saudi Arabia. The crewmen were country or tribal folk who were entrenched in the rules of their patriarchal society. It had taken several months and a great deal of diplomacy to get them to accept orders from her, the only woman in the expedition, let alone respect her.

The raven-haired, brown-skinned men working alongside Sarah gossiped harmlessly about her. One of the men pointed at her and whispered something to another, who issued a hearty laugh, revealing tobacco-stained teeth. She shook her head and smiled, happy they'd accepted her enough to make fun of her.

Daniel's white Land Rover, coated permanently with dust, arrived noisily on the scene. He stepped out and said something to the men in Arabic, which prompted another round of guffaws.

She approached him. "Are they laughing at your Arabic?"

"Nah," he said. "I just told them I was taking you to town for your daily hammam appointment."

"Nice."

"Thought you'd like that one. Come on. I have something to show you."

Sarah got into the seventies-vintage Rover and slipped off her hat. "Turn on the air conditioner in this thing, will you?" She used her most snobbish English accent, figuring he would be amused by it.

"It's on," he said, pointing at the open windows and the ventilation holes in the floorboard. "Not very fancy for a girl used to private jets and Bentleys, is it?"

She was taken back by the comment. She'd spent her entire career escaping the stigma of the little rich girl, devoting her life to fieldwork. She worked harder than she had to in order to earn the respect of her colleagues and separate herself from the myth of her family name.

Daniel knew this—all the more reason his comment felt like a slap. Her eyes clouded, and she searched his face for an explanation.

His sunny expression turned somber. "Sarah, I'm kidding. Lighten up." He shook his head and chuckled. "You Brits have no sense of humor."

Perhaps he was right. She took everything so seriously these days. She didn't say another word about it, snuffing out the whispers in the back of her mind.

He opened his titanium laptop case and punched away at the keyboard, then turned the screen toward her. "Here. Take a look at this."

She saw the familiar logo on the cover of the PDF document: a red-bordered white box with the word *BETA*. Her dissonance evaporated, making way for the delicious feeling of anticipation. "The report from the radiocarbon lab. Finally."

"Open it."

She clicked on the first page of the American lab's report on the human humerus. She continued until she saw the familiar chart outlining the C-14 activity of the sample. She did an initial scan, then leaned into the screen to make sure she had read it correctly.

She turned to Daniel. "Twenty-nine hundred years before the present?" She did a quick calculation in her head, subtracting the figure from the present, which in radiocarbon dating terms referred to the year 1950. "That would put us somewhere in the tenth century BCE."

"That's consistent with the language." He paused. "I also got the report on the papyrus from the University of Arizona."

"And?"

"Same thing. They dated it to 920 BCE, plus-minus forty." He called up another screen on the laptop. "See for yourself."

She read through it. There were no surprises. It was consistent with her suspicions, which she'd slowly confirmed through experiments she was conducting on her own.

She looked out the window, absently observing the men digging at the tomb site. She tried to imagine what the place must have looked like at the time the scroll was written—and if this was the desert to which the author referred. Though there had been evidence of dried up riverbeds strewn with date pits, indicating the existence of both water and a food source on the fringes of the Empty Quarter, she knew the desert itself was a notoriously harsh, inhospitable environment and always had been.

"Who would wander here, looking for his beloved? The place was barely inhabited." Her thoughts traveled to places north. "Unless . . ."

"Unless?"

"Unless this wasn't the desert he was referring to."

Daniel pressed into the back of his seat and looked absently at the top of the cracked windshield. "True. There are other deserts in the Middle East. Al-Dahna . . . Maranjab . . . the Negev."

"Judea . . ."

He closed the laptop case. "It will be interesting to see what Mariah has to say about it."

"You've sent this to her?"

"No. I wanted you to be the first to see it. But I'm going to."

Sarah felt a vague ripple of anxiety but quickly

dismissed it. She knew keeping the players informed was an integral part of university procedure. She looked at her Timex. It was going on noon; time to call it a day.

"Do what you need to do," she said, opening the door of the Rover. "I'm going to call the crew in before they die of heatstroke. I'll see you back at camp."

Nights in the desert were profoundly still, with nothing—no voices, no man-made contraptions, not even any trees to rustle in the wind—to puncture the cloak of quiet. For all the silence surrounding her, Sarah could not find that space of inner calm. She lay in bed, unable to sleep. She looked out the single window of her sleeping hut, which was nothing more than a closet-sized mud brick building with a corrugated tin roof, and marveled at the night sky above the inky outline of the Tuwaiq. Without any light pollution to impede the panorama, the stars clustered in vast colonies, floating in clouds of astral dust and winking like distant fireflies in the blackness. The only thing that moved outside was the pageant of shooting stars, which darted across the sky every few seconds in a spectacle that rivaled any fireworks display man could conjure.

Sarah's sleepless mind was a revolving door for thoughts she typically liked to suppress from her consciousness. She thought of her father, from whom she was estranged after their dueling prides had exploded into a full-scale war, and wondered if she should be the first to wave the olive branch. Though he had hurt her deeply by marginalizing and manipulating her, he was her only living family. She had no siblings, and her mother, whom she adored, had taken her own life all those years ago.

She thought she would never forgive her father for what she saw as the last straw in a pile of indignities— buying, behind her back, her way into the helm of the Aksum expedition, and then making her feel like she was too mediocre to ever have earned it on her own—but now, more than a year after their confrontation, she was really feeling the loss. Though she had become accustomed to, and even fond of, being alone, it was the first time in her almost thirty-seven years she felt truly lonely.

She gazed at the prayer beads wrapped three times around her left wrist. She rolled the tiny bone spheres between her fingers and remembered the day Daniel had given her the strand, which he'd received as a gift from a Buddhist monk in the Himalayas.

"These are supposed to bring good luck," he'd told her as she prepared to ascend a leather rope to a cliff-top monastery in Ethiopia. "Keep them with you—just in case."

She sighed. Perhaps it was a fool's hope, but she had anticipated her relationship with Daniel would fill part of the void left by the abrupt departure of her father. That was not quite the case. They certainly shared a mutual respect and trust and worked together seamlessly. But, for reasons unclear to her, any physical intimacy they had shared during their time in Ethiopia and Europe had vanished into thin air the moment she'd arrived on Saudi soil. She'd considered every theory—from deference to local moral codes to lack of interest.

They hadn't discussed it, leaving all her questions hanging. She'd often come to the brink of asking, but she feared the answer. Whatever the reasons, they had evolved into friends and work partners and nothing more. It stung, but she didn't dwell on it, instead letting the whispers of antiquity stir her soul, just as they always had. That much she could count on.

Sarah felt a chill enter through the open window and raised the woolen blanket to her bare shoulders. Something crawled on her hand, and she instinctively jerked her arm. The tiny, hairy legs of a creature she could not identify in the dark continued to crawl toward her shoulder. She sat upright and flicked it off, noting its hard shell. She felt more legs on her back and tried to shake the intruders off her camisole.

She threw off the blanket and sprang off the bed, crushing another hard shell under her foot. She haphazardly groped for the flashlight on her bedside table and turned it on. Her eyes widened in shock as she moved the spotlight across the room. Scarab beetles with black heads and striated red backs crawled on the bed and along the floor. There must have been hundreds of them.

They began crawling up her legs more quickly than she was able to brush them off. Her heart galloped, spurred by adrenaline. She lunged toward the door. Though she had not locked it, the door would not open. Gritting her teeth, she pulled hard at the knob. It didn't budge. She didn't have time to ponder why it was stuck; she had to get out.

The window.

She bolted across the beetle-strewn floor, crushing several of the insects with her bare feet. She punched out the wire screen and, using the ledge for leverage, hurled her body into the square opening that measured no more than two feet on each side. She dove headlong onto the ground, breaking her fall with her hands.

Scarabs still crawled on her arms, legs, and head. With spasmodic movements, she flicked the remaining creatures off her body. She charged barefoot across the cool ground of hardened sand and crumbled limestone as the sun ascended on the lavender horizon.

She ran until her anxiety dislodged and she regained her composure. Calmed by the stillness of dawn, she stopped and caught her breath. Heart still racing, she rested her hands on her knees and looked back at her hut.

She recognized evil intent when she saw it. Someone was sending her a message.

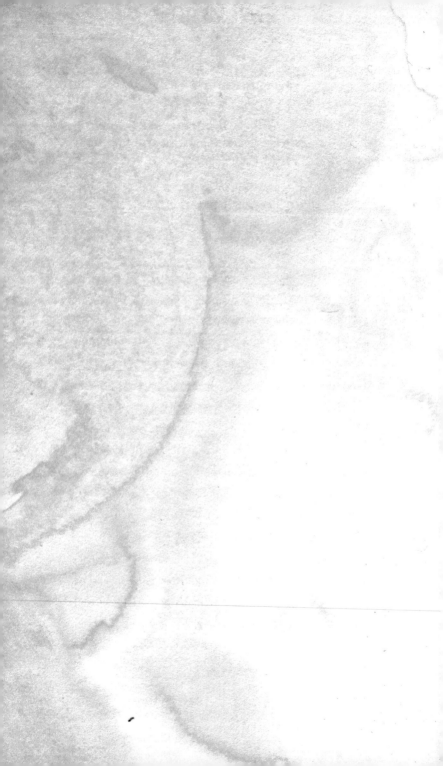

Chapter 4

By late morning the next day, the sun was the hottest it had been since Sarah's arrival. Nothing stirred in the valley. Without so much as a gentle breeze, the heat settled in like a heavy velvet cloak. A shimmering effect distorted the range of limestone mountains east of the site, seeming to liquefy the cliffs into the sandy expanses of the Empty Quarter. Sarah was not surprised at the thermometer reading. The air temperature was a hundred and eighteen degrees, four degrees higher than it had been half an hour ago.

She was supervising the souk site, working with the crew on excavating a new mound that likely housed an annex building or a storage facility. Everything had to be done by hand to preserve the artifacts potentially buried inside. They chiseled and scraped at the hardened sand mound, raising clouds of dust that lingered in the still air like the aftermath of an explosion.

The men, with turbans wrapped around their faces to repel the haze, were quieter than usual. On a typical day, they incessantly shared stories and jokes to make the time pass quickly. Part of it was their culture, and part was their attempt to forget about the working conditions. Today, the meaningless chatter was replaced by the rhythmic tap-tap-tap of chisels.

Sarah had gotten so accustomed to the constant murmur that today she missed it. The relative quiet, in combination with the sweltering temperature, the veil of dust, and her own sleeplessness, weighed down her eyelids. She took a drink from her water bottle and was pleasantly surprised the contents were still cool. She poured a little onto her hands and splashed it on her face, savoring the sensation for the few seconds before the water evaporated into a fine mist that was sucked up by the insatiable heat.

She stood and walked to the research hut, a makeshift structure of three walls covered by a sheet of rusted tin, to enter some data into her laptop. She thought the shade and the change of scenery would help her escape her fatigue, but they didn't. Exhausted from the intensity of the past few days, which was compounded by her predawn encounter with the scarabs, she sat on the dirt floor and leaned against the mud wall, which felt cool against her sweat-soaked back. She shut her eyes.

In the transcendent space between wakefulness and slumber, images came and went unchecked. She saw hands, perhaps her own, with dark crescents of dirt under the fingernails brushing sand away from a potsherd, revealing a relief of vines and grapes rendered on turquoise glaze. The image melted into a turquoise pool of water, from which surfaced black scarabs, one by one exiting the liquid and forming a single file on the cracked, sun-baked sand, like an army marching to war. They kept coming . . . and coming . . . and coming, their hard shells clicking and echoing like voices from a distant realm. She thought she heard them calling to her with an Arabic accent— "Miss Sarah . . . Miss Sarah . . ."—and she jolted awake.

"Miss Sarah."

She removed her oversized black aviators. With tired, stinging eyes, she met the gaze of Abdullah, one of the men from her crew. The stout Arab stood at the doorway of the hut, waiting for permission to enter. His head was wrapped with a white turban, but his fleshy, tobacco-colored face was exposed. Sarah recognized the look of concern in his ebony eyes, which stared at her from beneath a jet-black, bushy unibrow.

She stood. "What is it, Abdullah?"

"It's the men. They are not well."

"What do you mean?"

"Muhammad and Haydar are . . ." He gestured to indicate the act of vomiting, too polite to say the word out loud. "And the others . . . not so good."

Sarah exited the hut and looked toward the site. The

work had all but stopped, and most of the crew were either lying on the stones or sitting with heads bent.

Alarmed, she turned to Abdullah. "Is it the heat?"

He shrugged. "It's not so hot," he said, oblivious to the understatement. "Maybe eat something bad."

Sarah wasn't taking any chances. "Let's get them all on the bus. We'll go back to the camp and have them seen to. Quickly."

At the camp, Sarah escorted her crew to the infirmary, which already was packed with others with similar symptoms. About a dozen men were sitting on the floor, their brown faces awash in a gray pallor. Violent heaving sounds came from behind the curtain separating the clinic from the rudimentary lavatory.

She walked to Nasser, the medic. "Have you seen Dr. Madigan?"

A blush ruddied his café au lait cheeks, and he shifted his gaze downward. He ignored her question and busied himself retrieving bottles of medication from a storage cabinet. Sarah knew he heard her but chose not to answer. She read his attitude as passive aggressive, an unspoken disrespect toward her merely because she was a woman. She had three options: to disregard him and walk away, to confront him and assert her authority, or to stroke his ego by magnifying his importance. She chose the latter.

"Doctor"—she addressed Nasser with an honorific

even though he was only a nurse—"I know you're very busy, but I do need to find Dr. Madigan, stat. Have you seen him?"

Without looking up, he gestured toward the mess hut and went back to work.

Sarah rolled her eyes in reluctant acceptance of the misogyny that was still ingrained in parts of this society. It wasn't the first time she'd encountered it, and she was sure it would not be the last.

Sarah walked to the kitchen hut and found Daniel inside, rifling through the rations. "Danny, what's going on? The entire crew has fallen ill."

His jaw was tight. "I know. I'm not feeling so hot myself. It's got to be the food. Something we ate last night or this morning had to be dodgy."

"It must have been breakfast," she said. "I didn't eat anything this morning, and I'm feeling just fine."

"All we had was fried cheese, olives, and flatbread." He examined the stacks of bread for signs of mold, but there was nothing. He opened the tub of cheese in the fridge and smelled it. "I don't see anything wrong with this."

"Try the spices."

The cooks liked to brush the bread with olive oil, then sprinkle a spice mixture—their "mother's recipe," they called it—on it and sear it in the hot pan. Daniel spilled the contents of the spice box onto the table and picked up some of the powder with his fingers. He sniffed it, then tasted it. "That's strange. It smells kind of sharp, almost like paint."

She smelled it too and turned her face away in repulsion. "That's not paint. That's pesticide. It smells exactly like the powder we've been using to control sand rats."

A look of horror flashed on Daniel's face. He checked the cabinet where the rat poison was usually stored. He pulled out the box and shook it. "Good God. This thing's empty. I opened it myself just two days ago."

Sarah helped him sweep the spice mix off the table and dump it in the trash. She watched as he went through the rest of the provisions to make sure nothing else had been contaminated.

"Why don't we just toss everything?" she said. "We can drive to al-Khamasin right now and pick up new provisions—and some medicine."

He released a strained laugh. "Now I know why they say two heads are better than one. You're right, Sarah. Not sure why it didn't occur to me. Too agitated, I guess." He reached in his pocket for the keys to the Rover. "Would you mind going? I'd like to stay here with the guys, make sure everybody's all right. Problem is, I don't know if anyone's well enough to drive you."

It was one of the most frustrating aspects of life in Saudi Arabia: women were not allowed to drive. But in the desert and rural areas, where roads were not nearly as crowded with men, the rule was relaxed. The rural police turned a blind eye to a woman behind the wheel—so long as she was sufficiently covered—in the event of an emergency. This certainly qualified.

She held out a palm. "I'll take my chances."

He reluctantly handed her the keys. "Just be careful."

"Of course I will." She looked deep into his eyes. They were dull behind a veil of exhaustion and malaise. "Danny . . ."

"I know what you're going to say."

"Do you?"

"You're thinking this whole thing is a little odd. First the bugs, and now this."

"It just doesn't seem like a coincidence."

"I know it doesn't, Sarah, but we can't jump to conclusions. Not yet. I have to believe this was an accident, until I can prove otherwise."

"I'm also thinking—"

"That it has something to do with the scroll."

"Spot on."

"We'll have to deal with it later. Right now, I have a mess on my hands. And you have a shopping trip to take."

She turned to leave.

"Don't forget my case of whisky."

She smiled. "Heathen. Ten lashes for you just for uttering the word."

By the time Sarah left al-Khamasin, about ninety miles from the dig site, night had fallen. The road leading south to al-Fau was nearly deserted and scantily lit, and Sarah fought to concentrate on the task of driving. Her head was heavy, and her eyes burned from the dry air and lack of sleep. She turned on the radio and dialed into a station that played Saudi rock 'n' roll, a combination of western guitar riffs and traditional Middle Eastern percussion. It broke the monotony and kept her awake.

When she was twenty minutes away, she tried calling Daniel, but he didn't pick up. She didn't leave a message.

Ten minutes later, she redialed and again got voice mail. He always carried his phone with him and knew she'd be checking in. She recalled him saying that he, like the others, wasn't feeling well. Had he taken a turn for the worse? She stepped on the gas pedal. All she wanted was to make it back to camp safely, ensure everyone was okay, and get a good night's sleep, putting the day behind her.

As she approached the campsite, a cloud rose above the peaks of the Tuwaiq. It had a curious golden hue, and it billowed softly toward the indigo sky. *Bloody sandstorm*, she thought. *That's all we need.* Anxiety burned in the pit of her stomach. Most of the crewmen were too infirm to take cover from a rising tsunami of sand.

She tried Daniel again. No answer. Shimmers of gold light flashed in the cloud above the flat tops of the escarpment.

"No. It can't be."

She hammered the accelerator, but the Rover, weighed down with supplies, lumbered ahead. The moments it took to round the corner felt eternal.

When the Qaryat al-Fau site came into full view, her worst fears were confirmed. She smelled the smoke first: thick, pervasive, and acrid with the scent of gasoline.

Then she saw the flames. Great tongues of fire engulfed the transport bus and reached for the nearby camp buildings. The infirmary blazed.

Sarah pulled off the road and shut down the engine abruptly. The vehicle jolted and growled. She sprinted toward the fire. Her hijab fell away, leaving her hair exposed and whipping around her face.

As she closed the distance to the camp, the sight became more and more gruesome. Men ran out of buildings like ants under attack. One of them—she could not tell who—fell to the ground to smother the flames engulfing him. The smoke carried his frantic screams downwind. These men were her colleagues. Seeing them harmed pushed a scream to her throat.

This was not an accident. The scarabs and the poisoning were not accidents. This was not the act of a higher power. What had begun as a string of threats was now a full-blown attack.

Sarah ran faster, adrenaline taking the place of fear as she headed directly into the belly of the infernal beast. Daniel was somewhere out there, and she would not back away until she was sure he was safe. She was close now, close enough to feel the blistering heat from the wall of flames that attacked the campsite like an unchained pred-ator hungry for blood. Her skin burned with the intensity of a deadly tropical fever as the fire raged all around her in great copper swirls. She stopped, unable to go farther, and looked frantically for any sign of him.

"Danny," she shouted over and over again, trying des-perately to be heard over the crackle of flames, but there was no answer.

The smoke assaulted her from all directions, so heavy and profuse she felt like she was trying to breathe under-water. She untied the bandana from around her wrist and used it to cover her nose and mouth, but her lungs filled with the insidious vapors. She went into a violent cough-ing fit, her eyes watering, and everything grew hazy and surreal, like images in a dream. She ran in the opposite direction, still searching for him through the curtain of black smoke.

She stumbled and fell to her side as a horse galloped in front of her at full speed. She looked up to see the hind end of her gray mare and a blur of black fabric whipping behind the rider.

They were back.

She followed the rider's path with her gaze and saw him dismount in front of the lab. She gasped as all the pieces fell into place. *They set the fire. They are creating a diversion.*

They are after the scroll.

She sprang to her feet and ran toward the lab.

The Al Murrah horseman removed the rifle slung across his back, raised it to his shoulder, and aimed at the lock. A shot thundered, then another.

Closing in behind him, Sarah could now see the lock had been compromised. Her eyes grew wide as she realized she had only seconds to act.

The black-robed stranger twisted the mangled door handle. It didn't give way easily. He laid the gun down and pulled with both hands. The door cracked open.

His lapse in judgment was her window. Like a lioness protective of her territory, she lunged at him and threw him off-balance. As they tumbled to the ground, she ripped his black *redan* robe from shoulder to hip, exposing a gray *thobe* beneath. A silver-sheathed curved knife—the Bedouin *khanja*—was slung around his waist.

He snapped his head toward her, his onyx eyes glistening, his skin the color of burnt caramel, his head tightly wrapped with a black turban. He uttered a string of profanities in Arabic as he clawed at her.

She was too quick and athletic for him, fueling his ire.

He looked around for his rifle, which lay a few feet away.

Sarah heard the scream of a siren ebb and flow and turned to see the approaching column of flashing red lights. She felt a wave of relief.

The horseman scrambled to his feet, scooped up his rifle, and mounted the horse. With a gunshot aimed at the sky, he spurred the mare to a gallop and rode away from the scene, toward the desert. Two other horsemen followed him.

Sarah stood on shaky legs. She was breathless, and her mouth was dry.

Then she saw him.

Daniel emerged from the smoke cloud, covered in soot and exhausted as he carried an unconscious man to safety. Abdullah.

She summoned whatever energy she had left and rushed to Daniel's side. She picked up Abdullah's heavy, motionless feet. Together they hurried away from the ferocious inferno. They heaved Abdullah onto the ground in front of one of the paramedic trucks that had just arrived.

His face pallid and twisted with anguish, Daniel staggered away. He walked a few yards before collapsing to his knees.

Social convention be damned. She kneeled beside him and put her arms around his shoulders. "You need help."

"It's my fault, Sarah."

She had never seen him more distraught.

"I should have seen this coming."

Her eyes welled as she held him, unsure of what she could possibly say to ease his agony. She breathed in the miasma of smoke and charred earth as the firemen attempted to extinguish the flames. Familiar dread stabbed her as she considered why they had come under such violent attack.

As the flames parted, capitulating to the onslaught of thundering water, she received part of the answer. Almost as if in a trance, she rose and regarded the words that were branded onto the sand.

"Danny," she said, unable to take her eyes off the spectacle.

He stood beside her. "Good God," he whispered.

The message, written in Arabic, was laid down like a gauntlet, at once a proclamation and a warning.

The army is coming. Let no man stand in the way of the judgment.

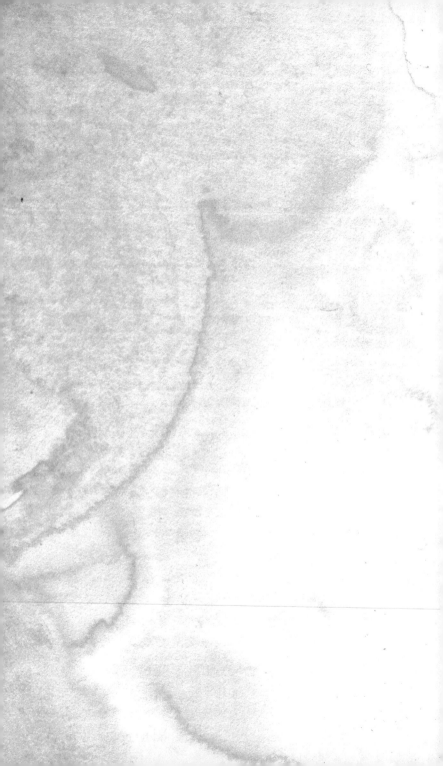

Chapter 5

The temple platforms on the banks of the River Ganges were outlined with rows of candles, their flames trembling as the first breaths of autumn whispered across the water. The floodlights hanging above the platforms reflected off the inky Ganges like streams of molten gold. Incense smoke ribboned skyward, releasing the scent of sandalwood and plumeria into the damp night air. Low tables swathed in orange satin with gold-embroidered borders held the instruments of ritual, foreshadowing the ceremony that would soon be held before thousands of faithful.

Trent Sacks sat alone in a wooden rowboat with the word *Gangaram* written in Hindi across the peeling blue paint. Every night since he'd come to the Indian holy city of Varanasi, it had been his habit to observe the evening *puja*, a temple ritual performed by Hindu priests as an offering to their deities.

He was not a Hindu. A British man of Jewish

ancestry, he believed in one god. His purpose in Varanasi was not one of worship or spiritual purification, as it was for the millions of Hindus who made the pilgrimage to the three-thousand-year-old city to be cleansed in the sacred Ganges or to live out their final days so they could be cremated in one of the burning ghats. For many a pious Hindu, dying here was the ultimate end, for it was said that a Varanasi funeral pyre could absolve them of their earthly sins and release them from the wretched cycle of reincarnation.

Sacks was there not to be among the living but rather among the dead.

A priest dressed in a white sarong and oxblood silk T-shirt, with a gold sash tied at the waist and across his chest, blew into a conchlike clay *shankh*, and its melancholy wail brought the *puja* to life.

Sacks closed his eyes and let the mournful echo of the instrument resonate within his being. His countenance was serene as he willed himself to concentrate on the beauty of the ceremony unfolding before him, but thoughts of the events he had set into motion thousands of miles away muscled their way into his consciousness.

A hint of a smile crossed his pursed lips as he considered the work being carried out by his emissaries at that very moment. He looked at his stainless steel Rolex. It was just after eight in the evening.

Soon, he thought. *Very soon.*

He licked his lips. A stiff breeze blew across the water. He raised the hood of his Windbreaker and ran his hand along the right side of his neck, stroking the head of the serpent tattoo. The mythical creature with slate-colored scales and emerald eyes was coiled around his hairless chest and back, its tail resting above his tailbone and its head commanding the nape of his neck and peering around the side, as if hissing in his ear.

The seven identically robed *pujaris* sat in lotus position on the platforms in front of Dasaswamedh Ghat, moving brass bells to and fro with slight motions of their wrists. The bells rang in practiced unison, their clear, melodic sounds imploring the heavens. They faced the Ganges, directing their worship to the goddess of the river rather than to the thousands of dark faces crowding the stepped stone terraces behind the platforms or spilling out of the windows of the ornate Nagar buildings.

With movements as synchronized and fluid as the rhyme of a poem, the priests stood and took up brass *diya* lamps filled with burning incense coals. The tolling of the bells persisted, now joined by drumming, deliberate as a heartbeat, and a soft monotone chant. The *pujaris* mirrored one another as they waved the lamps like slowly swinging pendulums, raising great clouds of smoke that glowed copper under the golden lights. The faithful bowed their heads as the smoke wafted toward them, anointing them with the sweet fragrance of sandalwood.

Sacks shifted his gaze downriver. A cow, open-eyed and bloated with death, floated past, and he regarded it with indifference. In the distance a plume of smoke rose from Manikarnika Ghat, and arousal stirred within him. Another cremation, another soul being released unto the ether. Funeral pyres were lit hundreds of times every day, from early morning until well into the night. In a country whose population exceeded a billion, there was no shortage of demand for the services of the burning ghats, nor for the delivery from suffering.

The harnessing of ascending souls was precisely his reason for being there. That and the chaos of Varanasi—the streets teeming with an unruly mob of vehicles and ox carts and bicycle rickshaws, the animals wandering through the streets and alleys unchecked, the ubiquitous street musicians strumming their *dotaras* for a handful of rupees, the emaciated sadhus with dreadlocks and whiteface, the throngs of pilgrims performing rites by the river.

In that bedlam, he could be anonymous, his work unquestioned. He could hide in his lair, deep within a derelict old building in a nameless alley, and carry out rituals of his own, conscripting newly purified souls in his search for answers to ancient conundrums. Soon his life's mission would be realized and the entire world—a world steeped in suffering and wickedness—would know his name.

Messiah.

He was so close now. So close he could touch the crown of the anointed king.

Women, their heads covered by saris in colors brilliant as jewels, released small leaf bowls carrying flower petals and tea lights into the quivering waters of the Ganges. The river accepted the offering, inviting the precious cargo of wishes and prayers into its dark heart. The chanting grew louder as the *pujaris* waved brass fire lamps with flames spilling out of seven tiers and leaving streaks of white light and a fine mist of smoke in their wake.

Sacks' phone vibrated in his pocket. A smile crept across his lips. He retrieved the phone and read the text.

It has been done.

Beaming, he sat back and absorbed the symphony of sounds as the night *puja* reached its crescendo. The steady drumming grew frantic and the bells rang with new urgency. The chanting became louder and faster.

The priests, still as columns and aglow with a divine serenity, tossed marigold flowers into the river with slow, fluid movements, seemingly detached from the riotous liturgy that had exploded around them. They brought their palms together and bowed to the river, and the throbbing cadence came to an abrupt end.

A sudden and complete silence descended upon the ancient city. Sacks released his own wishing candle onto the softly breathing black membrane that was the Ganges. The flickering flame slowly drifted away like a soul marching toward an eternal darkness.

Chapter 6

Two days after the fire, against the wishes of the doctors who treated him for smoke inhalation, Daniel returned to the site. He couldn't stay away. He needed to assess the damage and figure out how and when to rebuild. And he needed answers.

Though the police report was slow in coming, he had no doubt it was arson. The perpetrators had doused the interior of the transport bus with gasoline and poured more on the ground between the bus and the infirmary, ensuring the flames would spread quickly and cause the most destruction possible in a short time. Daniel could tell this by the stench of gasoline that night; it was embedded in his olfactory memory. The burn line was another telltale sign. The fire had burned in a single sheet as it stretched its blazing fingers toward the infirmary, obviously coaxed into spreading.

Daniel had seen the Al Murrah horsemen ride away

from the inferno. They clearly had heard about the scroll and were trying to reclaim it, or at least to deal him and Sarah a warning. But who would have tipped them off— and why? Those were answers he was determined to find, and he vowed to do so at any cost.

He parked the Land Rover and walked toward the wreckage of the bus. His lungs were still compromised from the smoke, and he felt a tightness in his chest after just a few steps. He ignored the pressure and kept walking.

Though he knew roughly what to expect, the sight of the charred bus was shocking. The entire top was a hollow cage of mangled metal. All the gray paint had melted in the blaze, leaving an expanse of raw steel blackened by the flames. The windows had been blown out; all that remained were jagged teeth of glass clinging to the window frames. The glass crunched under Daniel's feet as he made his way to the door, which hung on one hinge, and into the cockpit. He was assaulted by the lingering smell of gasoline and the chemical odor from the ashen piles of burnt vinyl and fiberglass foam of the seat cushions.

He held on to the cockpit pole and clutched his chest, struggling for breath. The sensation brought him back to the maelstrom of emotions of the night of the fire. His mind replayed the primal screams of his crewmen as they struggled to flee the blaze and the look of panic frozen on their dark faces.

Most had managed to escape with minor injuries

and smoke inhalation issues, a few still hospitalized with third-degree burns. Two, however, hadn't made it. Mustafa and Azhar, brothers from a nearby village who had recently joined the dig as field technicians, chose against the mad dash for their lives. They oriented themselves toward the east and bowed in prayer as the white-hot flames blazed around them.

Daniel yelled for them to save themselves. When they refused to move, he bolted toward them but was too late. He watched the scene unfold in slow motion as the fire's blistering fingers clawed at the brothers until they were engulfed completely. Daniel could not even hear his own screams through the roar of the blaze as he watched in horror, powerless to do anything. The two remained on the ground in a deep bow, motionless as the beast swallowed them into its infernal maws.

A knot rose in Daniel's throat as his mind dwelled on the memory. He had always viewed the safety of his crew as his personal responsibility. He had failed them. And though Mustafa and Azhar chose their own fate, it would not have happened if there never was a fire in the first place. He had not been vigilant enough; he had not seen the arsonist before it was too late. He'd let down his guard, and that was unforgivable.

He stepped outside the bus and walked past the cinders of the infirmary. The tin roof lay in a mangled pile on the ground, and what remained of the walls was charred and reeked of smoke. He looked around at the surrounding buildings. A couple of them had been damaged but not completely destroyed, while others, in the distance, were miraculously intact. He was relieved to see the archaeological site had not been impacted.

He stood in front of the scorched building for a long time, letting the full scope of what had happened sink in. His crew had been decimated. Two were dead, a dozen or so were injured, and most of the rest were too spooked to come back. From Sarah's texts while he was in the hospital, he knew four of the men reported for work the next day, as if nothing had happened.

They are loyal to the project, she had texted. *Loyal to you.*

He made his way toward the lab on the far side of the camp. Because it housed the bulk of the artifacts and the expedition computers, this was the most permanent of all the structures, built of concrete block with a watertight flat roof, with a heavy gauge steel door and no windows.

Even that was almost breached. *Thank heavens for Sarah*, he thought. Had she not accosted the intruder, he surely would have gained entry. That singular display of courage and dedication reminded him why he had chosen her as his partner in the first place.

He delivered a rapid-fire knock, which he knew Sarah would recognize. Within a few moments, the door cracked open. She was like a lighthouse in a storm. He wanted so much to hold her, to inhale the scent of her hair, to feel her warmth.

Sarah smiled and held the door open for him, her eyes darting over his shoulder as he entered. She closed and double bolted the door.

She looked him up and down, and he was suddenly self-conscious of his three-day facial growth and the clothes he had been wearing since the day of the fire. He realized in that instant his black T-shirt and desert-sand camo pants smelled like the inside of a smokestack.

"Sorry," he said, stepping back. "Not exactly a sight for sore eyes, am I?"

"Well, you do look a bit of a fright. But I am happy to see you."

He tried to assume a light tone, though his heart felt heavy. "So what's going on around here? Where is everybody?"

"At the moment, everybody consists of Abdullah, Abdul-Qadir, Rasul, and Walid. They insisted on coming back to work. Walid is in the mess hut, preparing some lunch. The other three are at the tomb site, clearing away one of the burial chambers." She looked at her watch. "They should be coming in shortly."

"So, business as usual."

"I wouldn't quite say that. But we're doing what we can, given the circumstances."

He looked up and exhaled loudly.

"I'm sorry, Danny," she said softly. "I'm so sorry."

He looked into her clear blue eyes. "Yeah, me too.

This is a major setback."

"We can rebuild. I have already looked into a replacement bus, and there's a team of construction workers on standby—"

"We can't do a thing until the cops finish their investigation. This is Saudi Arabia. It could take months."

"Can't someone from King Saud intervene? Make things go faster?"

He shrugged. "It's a crapshoot. Anyway, most of these guys aren't coming back. And it's not just because of the fire. Everyone knows something's up. It's hard to ignore a message like that inscribed on the ground."

He walked to the lab table, where pottery fragments and flint spearheads lay waiting to be classified. He picked up a particularly fine piece of Nabatean pottery painted with black scrollwork and held it to the fluorescent light. That single shard of decorated ancient clay, which likely had come to Qaryat al-Fau by way of Canaan or Moab, was testament to al-Fau's status as a crossroads between north and south.

He thought of the scroll. Just like the pottery and other objects from the north, it had found its way into the Empty Quarter, whether by trade or chance. He couldn't shake the feeling that by unearthing it, they had unearthed an ancient conflict whose resolution was being played out before them.

Sarah walked to him. "Tell me you're not thinking of

suspending operations for this season."

"We may be foreclosed into it, Sarah. We can't work without a crew." He put the potsherd down and regarded the collection of artifacts wistfully. "We've gained so much momentum in the past seven years. It'd be a crying shame to stop now."

"Exactly. But somebody wants us to do just that."

Daniel turned to her. Under the fluorescent light, her skin glowed like alabaster and her eyes looked like pools of ultramarine. There was a challenge in her eyes, a kindling of sorts. If he knew one thing about Sarah Weston, it was this: she would not cower in the face of injustice.

"I know you don't want to let them win, Sarah, and I don't either. But the people who did this will strike again. I'm sure of it."

"Speaking of the people who did this . . . the man I confronted wore the formal dress of highborn Bedouins. And he carried an engraved silver *khanja*." She looked away. "There might have been a jewel on the handle. I couldn't tell."

"That's very interesting. The black *redan* and silver *khanja* are usually worn by the amir. Or his eldest son and heir."

"This lad was on the young side. I'm guessing he's the latter."

"If they have the amir's blessing, it means they're pretty organized. We might have our hands full."

"I agree. I've hired a guard to watch the place overnight. I figured that extra bit of security couldn't hurt."

He nodded toward the vault, where the mysterious scroll was locked away. "Our best bet is to send that thing to Riyadh for safekeeping."

"No, I'm not finished with it."

He studied her determined features. "Do you have anything?"

"I do, actually. Come and have a look."

He followed her to the computer, where she was examining a three-dimensional image of the scroll. She called up the screen showing the underside and zoomed in on a faint mark on the parchment. "I've been working on this for weeks. I'm sorry I hadn't said anything. I wanted to be sure there was something before I told you. Now I know there is."

He leaned in for a closer look. "Looks like a smudge of some sort."

"That's what I thought at first. But look closer. The mark is along the centerline, about where the scroll was tied with the cord." She zoomed in. "Now. Do you see that?"

There was another, barely discernible, mark along the edge.

"Interesting. Put up the grid."

"Already have." She clicked the keys and laid a grid over the image of the scroll. "The two marks align perfectly. And for the pièce de résistance"—she clicked the computer's commands to simulate the rolling of the parchment and then turned the image three hundred sixty degrees—"we have this."

In this three-dimensional view, it was clear that the two marks made up a single stamp on the scroll.

"Have you tested the cord?" he said.

"I put it under the microscope, yes. There are particles on it, but our scope is not strong enough to give the proper breakdown. I've already sent it out."

His pulse quickened as he realized how close they were to learning the truth about the ancient missive. "Are you thinking what I'm thinking?"

"That it's a type of seal?"

"Yes, the imprint of a bulla. A document like this would almost certainly have been sealed with a small piece of clay placed on the cord. The scribe's stamp would identify himself and the post he held."

"So the analysis will be important. If there are indeed traces of clay on the cord, the lab should be able to identify the origin of that clay."

He clasped his hands on the back of his head. Sarah was right: the molecular analysis of the cord would confirm the material used to seal it and likely point to the source of that material. They would have to extrapolate the rest.

It was a start, but it was not enough. The one thing that haunted him—the identity of the scroll's author, which was central to deciphering the cryptic text—would be almost impossible to pinpoint without the bulla itself.

"That bulla is probably buried in a pile of sand somewhere," he said. "Chances are good we'll never see it."

She did not reply. She was staring at the computer screen, her chin resting on her left fist.

"Sarah?"

She didn't take her eyes off the screen. "Maybe we don't need the bulla, after all. Take a look at this."

Chapter 7

*S*arah zoomed in on the mark and enhanced the resolution. The impression was faint to begin with, and pinpointing an image within it was nearly impossible. Still, she was sure something was there.

Daniel leaned in over her shoulder. "What do you have?"

"I know it doesn't look like much, but I think there's a pattern here."

"Looks like a random blotch to me. You sure you're not chasing ghosts?"

She looked at him. She knew he was distraught over the events of the last few days, and such agitation could easily turn to disillusionment. She was determined to keep things moving forward. "Of course I'm chasing ghosts," she said. "It's what I do."

She turned to the screen and continued to refine the image. There were areas where the impression read a shade darker, and she was convinced those areas represented the stamp of a seal. There was no clearly discernible pattern, only a jumble of slightly darker marks that could be anything—or nothing.

"Let's try something else," Daniel said. "Go ahead and mark every dark spot and then isolate it in a separate layer. Maybe that will give us a clearer picture."

Sarah nodded and went to work on the laborious task of creating a digital map of the darker areas. They were close to finding another clue. Adrenaline pumped through her veins, and she savored the sweet moment of near discovery.

She checked the image carefully to ensure she had marked every relevant area. Satisfied with her work, she demarcated the map and clicked it onto another screen. She sat back and viewed the image with fresh eyes. *Yes,* she thought. *There's a definite pattern.*

"Do you see what I see?" Daniel said.

She turned to him. "Letters."

"Bingo. Let's try to connect the dots."

It was easier said than done. The map was so indistinct the connection could be made in several different ways. She tried to make out the characters of the hieratic script, which had evolved from hieroglyphs. Some were easy to trace; others were impossible and would have to be deduced by context.

"It's a mix of letters and determinatives. This, for example, appears to be the determinative of man." She shook her head. "It's the best I can do, I'm afraid."

"You're doing great." He placed a hand on her shoulder and his thumb gently grazed her neck.

She trembled ever so slightly with the sensation of his touch. He must have felt it, because he abruptly pulled his hand away. Too self-conscious to look at him, she returned to her work.

"I'm going back in," she said, keeping her eyes on the screen. "I've got an idea."

She worked backwards by marking the spaces between the dark spots. She thought that would give her a second reference point for the purpose of comparison. Together, those two maps might just produce something more legible.

Her method proved correct. Though she could still not make out all the words, she could clearly read the first set of characters. It was only a partial resolution, but she saw it as a breakthrough.

"Here it is," she said. "Seshet."

"The ancient Egyptian goddess of writing," Daniel said with the most excitement he'd shown in days.

"Also the name assigned to female scribes, full stop. There were so few female scribes in history. It shouldn't be hard to figure out who penned this."

"It's a great start. We can also get Mariah's take on it. She should be here in a few hours."

"I beg your pardon?"

"I'm sorry, Sarah. I should have mentioned it before, but it slipped my mind. I haven't exactly been . . . She called to ask if she could join us for a few days. She says she has some viable theories about the scroll but needs to see it first. I told her she could come. Figured her input could be valuable to us."

"Danny, do you think that's a good idea? I mean . . . given everything that's happened."

"She's an ally. Right now we need all of those we can get. We don't have to have this conversation again, do we?"

"No. We don't." She closed the document and stood to leave. "This is your show."

Mariah arrived in the early afternoon, when the sun was at its zenith and the temperature in the shade exceeded a hundred degrees. She stepped out of the passenger side of a black Mercedes-Benz SUV. She wore a dazzlingly white button-down shirt with the sleeves rolled just above her wrist and a long straight skirt. A linen ikat hijab was loosely draped over her head and crossed at the shoulders.

Daniel offered a hand in greeting. "Welcome to Qaryat al-Fau. We arranged a warm day just for you."

She shook his hand firmly, holding it a little longer than necessary. "Oh, I don't mind the heat. It's just good to be out in the field for a change. We don't get to do much of that in academia."

"Well, we'll do our best to make it a pleasant

experience for you. Right now, though, we're down to a skeleton crew. I'm sure you heard."

"I did. I'm very sorry about the fire. You must be devastated."

The last thing he wanted was to show emotion, or to admit defeat, to someone from the university. "We'll be all right. Work is continuing, and eventually we will rebuild. Setbacks happen in this business."

"Did the police ever say if it was arson?"

"No, not yet. The investigation hasn't been closed."

"But you suspect it was arson. Perhaps the work of those tribal thieves?"

He looked at her, somewhat taken aback by her directness. He waited for a few seconds to see if she would, out of politeness, retract her comment, but she kept her gaze on him.

"I don't know what I think," he said. He didn't want to have that discussion. "Why don't we head over to the lab? Sarah is waiting for us there."

At the lab, Sarah sat behind the computer, still working on deciphering the seal stamp.

"Sarah, you remember Mariah," Daniel said.

Sarah collapsed the screen and stood. "Of course. How are you?"

"Very well, thanks," Mariah said, her gaze wandering around the room. "So this is it. The famous Qaryat al-Fau research center."

"This is where it all happens," Daniel said. "Including what you came out here to discuss."

"Have you made any inroads?"

"Perhaps," Daniel said. "What do you know about female Egyptian scribes?"

"Well . . . they were extremely rare. We know of only a few instances where female scribes were identified. Even so, their recordings were minor compared to those of men. The women of ancient Egypt generally weren't literate, as you know. Why do you ask?"

Daniel glanced at Sarah.

She gave him an icy look and turned away.

He knew Sarah didn't approve of Mariah's presence among them, but for him it was an important next step, and not only because of the skill the professor brought to the table. University funding for the expedition didn't allow for missteps. Per his agreement with King Saud, everything had to be disclosed, and there could be no rogue missions.

And there certainly could be no personal involvements. As much as it pained him to be so close to Sarah and keep an emotional distance, he knew any contact between them would be hara-kiri. Not only would the university fathers not approve, but his men would lose all respect for him and view her as a common trollop—or worse.

Daniel had been warned. When he presented Sarah as his choice to replace the lead archaeologist who had left the expedition for health reasons, Professor Rashid al-Said, head of the archaeology department at King Saud, had expressed his skepticism.

"This woman," he said. "You say she is qualified?"

"If she wasn't qualified, I would not recommend her, Professor," Daniel said. "She trained at Cambridge and spent her entire career working for the university. You and I both know how high Cambridge standards are."

"This is true. But what of this Aksum expedition? That was—how do you Americans say?—a train wreck."

"Circumstances beyond her control. I was there—"

"The press paints her as a bit of a maverick. You know that will never do here."

"I'm aware. You don't have to worry. She knows the rules, and anyway, I'm in charge."

"Yes . . . yes, you are. If you think she is best for the job, then I trust your judgment."

"Yes, sir. I will not disappoint you." Daniel stood to leave.

The professor looked over his reading glasses. "Daniel? There is . . . one more thing."

"Yes, sir."

"In another of our field expeditions, outside of Mecca, we had a French woman on the crew. She ended up—how to put this delicately?—becoming friendly with one of her fellow crew members. They kept it a secret, but someone saw them and . . . since that day, she was the expedition whore. To make my story brief, the crew had some time off and went into town, and this poor girl was gang-raped by a group of workers." He pursed his lips and shook his head in pity. "She had to return to France for treatment, and her friend was immediately dismissed from his duties. It's not a pleasant thing to bring up, but in our country, it's a reality, I'm afraid."

Daniel chuckled. "Rest assured, Professor. There will be no such incidents on my watch."

Al-Said stood. "This conversation must not go beyond this room. If it ever did, there would be serious consequences. I would hate for anyone's career to be damaged." He extended a hand. "Do I have your word?"

Daniel heard the implication loud and clear. It was an unveiled threat to him and, worse, a betrayal to Sarah. But it was the only way he could have her beside him. He shook the professor's hand firmly. "You have my word."

As was obvious by Sarah's chilly reaction to Mariah's presence, his silence on the matter had a cost. But he counted on the unspoken bond between them to keep their relationship intact and the project moving forward.

Daniel turned to Mariah. "Sarah has found faint traces of what we think was a clay bulla on the parchment. We haven't had the substance tested yet, but that's almost certainly what we're looking at."

"That wouldn't be at all surprising," Mariah said. "Bullae were very commonly used to seal scrolls and manuscripts. I should like to see it. May I?"

He nodded toward the safe. "Sarah, would you mind?"

She eyed Mariah, then gave a half smile. "Of course."

Mariah put on gloves and accepted the scroll from Sarah. She unrolled it slowly and studied the characters. With a pinkie, she brushed one of the letters. She turned to Daniel. "Have you had the ink tested?"

"According to the radiocarbon lab, it's definitely a charcoal ink."

"Interesting."

Daniel knew what she was getting at. In the tenth century BCE, inks were typically carbon based and likely to rub off. This ink was fast. "We're doing some further testing on it. We suspect the addition of a substance."

She turned the scroll over and looked for the smudge along the centerline. "I see what you're talking about. This definitely could be a bulla impression."

"The interesting thing," Daniel said, "is that we think we have a partial reading on the name of the person who sealed the document."

Mariah looked at him, her deep brown eyes wide. "You're kidding."

"Sarah found it," he said. "She's an expert on computer analysis of ancient texts."

Sarah walked to the computer to pull up the digital map of the magnified impression. "We can't make all of it out," she said. "But this portion is fairly clear."

Mariah leaned in and read. "*Seshet*. Remarkable . . ."

Her arms were wrapped tightly around her chest, as if she were protecting herself from something. Her thick black brows were pinched together, and she bit her fleshy bottom lip.

"So," Daniel said. "Any idea who this might be?"

She shook her head. "*Seshet* is the female derivative of *sesh*, the Egyptian word for scribe."

"How likely is it that a male, presumably of high ranking, would have a female scribe?" Sarah asked.

"Not likely but not impossible," Mariah said. "The Egyptians of the New Kingdom were an enlightened lot."

"There are a few depictions of Seshet on Egyptian burial chambers or stelae, but they are not identified," Sarah said. "Only a couple of names of female scribes have been recorded in history, but the dates don't match."

Mariah turned to Daniel. "Leave this part to me. I have some ideas, but I don't want to say anything until I am certain. I should have an answer for you in the morning."

"Fair enough," Daniel said. "Why don't we all take a break from this? Go and relax a little bit, and we'll catch up again during dinner."

"Until then," Mariah said, walking out of the lab.

Daniel collected the scroll, carefully rolling it up and securing it with the cord before placing it inside the safe. He looked at Sarah, who was still working on the computer.

"Sarah, you should rest. You've been at this for days."

She didn't look up. "I'm quite all right."

He walked to the computer station and kneeled beside her, looking at her for a long moment. Sweeps of soft blonde curls fell haphazardly around her face, but she seemed to not notice as she continued to work with a singular focus. Her long fingers commandeered the keyboard with the mesmerizing rhythm and grace of a concert pianist's. She finally stopped and looked at him.

"I don't want to fight," he said.

Her face softened. "Neither do I. I'm sorry for . . ."

He put his hand on her forearm and squeezed lightly. "No. It's my fault. But no more said, okay?"

She nodded.

"Good. I'll see you at dinner."

Sarah watched Daniel exit the room and, when the door closed behind him, she opened the e-mail from the lab, which had come in just prior to Mariah's arrival. The clay particles clinging to the twine had been identified. Though they did not have enough material to date the clay, analysts could pinpoint its origin with a fair amount of precision. In this case, the answer was unambiguous.

Jerusalem.

She was not surprised.

She called up another screen with a digital map far more detailed than the version she showed Mariah. She had worked through the morning and early afternoon perfecting this but kept her findings to herself. Not even

Daniel was clued in.

She had every intention of telling him, but not until Mariah had gone. She did not trust her enough to show all her cards. Besides, if Mariah were the expert she claimed to be, she would figure this out on her own. To some extent, it was Sarah's way of testing her to see whether she would offer reliable information or try to throw them off the scent.

She studied the image on the screen. The words stared back at her, bristling with a life of their own.

Seshet Irisi, in service to the queen.

She closed her eyes and tried to play the image in her mind: the beautiful, black-haired scribe placing a small ball of moist clay onto the cord and branding it with her personal seal, leaving no doubt as to who etched the letters onto the papyrus. But whose words were they? Who was this queen—and who was her king?

Sarah was almost certain she knew. If her theory proved to be correct, the ramifications would be earth-shattering. Every inch of her body pulsed with the sweet agony of anticipation as she considered the scroll in their possession could be an unprecedented link between legend and history.

She needed one more piece of information to be absolutely sure. And she knew exactly who could deliver it.

Chapter 8

"Do you mind if I join you?"

Daniel turned to see Mariah standing behind him. He forced a smile and gestured to her to sit next to him on the faded old kilim. He put another log into the dying fire and stoked the pile to enliven the flames. With a crackling sound, the red-hot cinders flew upward like fireflies in the moonless night. He inhaled the sweet spice of the Yemeni mesquite wood as the fire once again took hold.

"Glad I'm not the only one who can't sleep," she said. "So what's keeping you up at two in the morning?"

He shrugged. "Just thinking, I guess."

"Maybe this will help." She pulled a small silver flask out of the front pocket of her backpack and offered it to him. "Talisker single malt. I lived in Scotland years ago and built a real taste for whisky. This one is my favorite. I smuggled it in during a recent trip."

He accepted and took a swig. The scotch burned his

throat and left a pleasant smoky aftertaste.

"I have to admit," she said, "this scroll is the reason I can't sleep. I have been obsessing over the language, trying to make sense of it. There is so much symbolism in it. Trying to unravel it is like finding your way out of a bog in the dark."

"Have you been able to come up with anything?"

"Just bits and pieces, I'm afraid." She pulled a notebook out of her backpack. "I was going to wait until tomorrow to share this, but since we're here . . ." She winked. "One thing you'll find about me is that I believe in the magic of the moment."

The shadows cast by the firelight danced upon the contours of her face, giving her an almost Byzantine beauty. Her deep-set eyes were like shining onyx orbs inside darkened hollows. There was something provocative about her gaze that he didn't want to give play to. He looked away.

She opened the notebook to a page with handwritten notes and diagrams. "Upon close examination, it's obvious nothing is as it seems. Take this passage, for example. 'Beware, brethren, for she will trap thee and feed thee to her army of beasts.' That is obviously not literal. The beasts mentioned in this text were used as symbols in ancient Egypt. The lion, for example, was symbolic of nobility and strength in ancient times. The pharaohs regarded them as protectors."

"And the serpent was a symbol of evil and darkness."

"That's right. But it was also a symbol of protection. In the Old Kingdom, Renenutet, the guardian deity, was depicted as a snake-headed goddess. A cobra, to be precise."

"In this context, of course, the serpent refers to something wicked since it was wielded by a temptress."

"Ah, the temptress." She lowered her gaze, then raised it slowly. "Here's where it gets interesting. In the ninth century BCE, which is in the periphery of the radiocarbon dating for the scroll, there was a figure who was referred to as a temptress." She paused. "She was a queen. A Phoenician of Egyptian ancestry who became queen of Israel."

Daniel studied Mariah's gaze, which burned with intensity. He knew what she was getting at. "Jezebel."

"It makes perfect sense. Jezebel came from a line of Egyptians, so it would not be unlikely for her to have an Egyptian female scribe. And this would be consistent with your evaluation of the pottery you found on the site. You mentioned the honey pot looked Canaanite or possibly Phoenician."

He mulled her words. His thoughts turned to the clay bulla whose impression lingered on the papyrus, and he recalled the lab results were due in that day. Pinpointing the origin of the clay particles would be a major clue as to the provenance of the artifacts. He made a mental note to ask Sarah about it.

She continued. "Think about it: redolent of myrrh and good spices and fingers dusted with gold. That alludes to royalty. The beasts mentioned are symbolic of her nature. Jezebel was vilified for worshipping her own version of God, the Phoenician god Baal, and was therefore portrayed as a harlot and a heathen in the Kings books of the Bible. It makes sense that such an evil woman would have a metaphorical menagerie of demons and serpents and oxen that would inflict pain on those who did not do her bidding. Or it could be a reference to her army of Baal worshippers, who supposedly were sent by her to kill the prophets of the Jews."

Daniel's face hardened as he contemplated Mariah's theory. What she was saying made sense, though it seemed too easy. But interpreting the nuances of ancient languages was not his forte—he relied on experts like Mariah for that—so he had to defer to her professional capability.

"If what you say is true, then what is this treasure the scribe is referring to? The one forged by the whispers of angels and guarded by kings for all eternity."

She pressed her full lips into a smile. She sought his gaze and held it captive. "You mean the fruit of her womb?"

Daniel recognized the subtle advance but ignored the double entendre. "My guess is the writer of the scroll does not mean that in its traditional interpretation."

She resumed a professional tone. "According to legend, Jezebel was a priestess in the Phoenician kingdom of her father. There has never been evidence of this, but some scholars have interpreted passages in the Bible to argue that she was a sorceress of a kind. During her reign as queen, she and her husband, Ahab, condoned idolatrous worship of other deities and allowed sacrifices of every type, even of young children." She paused, putting weight on her next words. "There is a legend that Jezebel had a book of magic, sort of like the anti-Bible. This scroll's reference to treasure may indeed be a reference to that book."

"Go on."

"Now, if you look at the other verse, it all comes together. The writer speaks of a key to a chest of treasure. Assuming that treasure is the book, it most likely is well hidden . . . and there is a key that unlocks it."

"I suppose you have a theory about that too."

She smiled slyly. "How did you guess? Years ago, when I was working for the antiquities department in Israel, a construction worker tried to sell me a bulla fragment for the national collections. He said he had found it while digging for the foundation of a house in the West Bank. On it were the letters *YZBL* and three figures: a serpent, a winged solar disc, and"—she paused—"a winged lion."

"And you thought this might be authentic, even though it was unprovenanced?"

"Of course not. But I was intrigued enough to have it tested. The first thing we noted was the angle of the impression. The lower part was deeper than the top. With a typical seal, the weight would be evenly distributed and the impression would be uniform. This angle suggested the impression might have been made by a ring. If you recall, the scroll referenced a perfect circle forged of earthly matter. This ring could be the key."

He dismissed the inference as too big a stretch. He was accustomed to thinking like a scientist, not jumping to conclusions. "And the rest of the tests?"

She shook her head. "We never got to that. The guy suddenly changed his mind about selling the bulla and demanded it back. I had no choice but to give it to him. I never heard from him again."

Daniel took another swig of the scotch, swirling it around his mouth to get the full effect. The smooth, smoky flavor seemed out of place in the desert, where any consumption was purely for function and survival, not pleasure. Though he never missed the taste of civilization, when it was before him, he enjoyed the fleeting moment of delight.

"So let me get this straight," he said, enumerating the points with his fingers. "You have an unauthenticated, unprovenanced bulla given to you by a construction worker, a tall tale from the Old Testament, and an obscure legend about some book of magic." He chuckled. "Sorry . . . I don't mean to laugh, but you're building a theory around a bunch of fiction."

Her expression turned hard. "Obviously, you are not a believer."

"Prove it to me and I'll believe it. I don't go on faith."

"Let me remind you that around here faith is everything."

He started to say something but his phone sounded with the familiar beep of an incoming text. "That's strange," he said, fumbling inside the side pocket of his cargo pants to retrieve the phone, curious about who could be texting him so late.

He looked at the number. "Sarah," he said, surprised and slightly alarmed.

"What's the matter?" Mariah's tone was haughty and more than a little barbed. "Does she need you to tuck her in?"

The comment made his face burn with indignation. "You are way out of line, lady." He sprang to his feet. "I've got to go."

Someone is in the lab.

Sarah's text sent up all sorts of red flags in Daniel's mind. Still reeling from the events of the past week, he was not ready for yet another attack. For a moment he considered Sarah might be mistaken, but he knew better. There was no uncertainty in her words. And she wasn't one to exaggerate or be given to drama. If she said someone was in the lab, he could bank on it.

He picked up the pace as he walked toward the building housing the expedition's artifacts and most sensitive information. The lab was the hub of field scientists, the place where all the testing, classification, storage, and study took place. The thought of someone breaching the storage facilities or, worse, the brain—the research computers—filled him with an anger that fortified him. He was on red alert mode: strong, aware, and ready to face down anyone.

Sarah was standing outside the building, shivering in her gray tracksuit. She was calm and composed, but there was uneasiness in her gaze.

He spoke softly. "What's happened?"

"I was out for a walk and when I passed behind the lab, I heard the click of a key in the door. I came around to have a look and saw the door closing behind someone. The guard was nowhere." She wrapped her arms around herself. "After I texted you, I had a bit of a look around and saw him over there"—she tilted her head toward the ruins—"lying in a heap. I've called the police."

"Good girl. I'm going in."

"Not alone, you're not."

"Listen to me. I need you to stay here in case things get ugly in there."

"I don't think it's a good—"

"You'll have my back better this way. Trust me."

Finally, she nodded, and he could see the disappointment in her eyes. It was hard to keep Sarah Weston out of the thick of things. But he needed at least one of them to be safe should things escalate. He was about to confront a perpetrator unarmed.

He gave Sarah a tight-lipped smile and, careful not to make a sound, unlocked the door, leaving it slightly open behind him.

The room was pitch black. He put his hand on the light switch but stopped short of illuminating the space. He stood for a moment in the complete darkness. There was dead silence. All he could hear was his own breath. He felt a drop of perspiration trickle down his temple.

Daniel heard the faintest rustle of fabric and could tell the intruder was on the move. There was no sound of footfall; the intruder had probably taken off his shoes. There was a soft click, then another—five times, once for each number of the combination on the push-button lock.

There was a muted sigh as the pneumatic safe door yielded.

Daniel flicked on the fluorescent lights.

The figure on the far end of the room raised a forearm to shield his eyes. He was dressed in a *thobe*, trousers, and *taqiyah*, the traditional Saudi skullcap—all in black.

Daniel walked toward him. "Show yourself," he said in Arabic.

The man slowly lowered his forearm but looked straight down.

Daniel started. "Abdul-Qadir? What the hell are you doing here?"

Abdul-Qadir, a research technician hired only two

months ago, was the quietest member of the al-Fau crew. A slight man of no more than thirty years, he had tawny skin and soft, almost feminine features. He had dark, mournful eyes. A whisper of a black moustache brushed his upper lip. He always kept to himself as he worked, and he spent his off hours reading. He was the last person Daniel expected to see in the lab in the middle of the night, cracking open the expedition safe.

"Answer me," Daniel barked.

Abdul-Qadir shrank, his gaze darting about the room. He muttered something incomprehensible in Arabic.

"Look, Abdul, I'm losing my patience here. Now, you have two choices. You can talk to me, or I can turn you over to the authorities. What's it gonna be?"

The man trembled. "Okay . . . okay. I can explain."

Daniel crossed his arms and waited. At six feet, he towered over Abdul-Qadir, who was no taller than five-five.

"The scroll has . . . has brought nothing but trouble. It sh-should not be here."

"So you were going to destroy it. Is that it?"

He hesitated.

Daniel raised his voice a notch. "Has it crossed your mind, Abdul, that this manuscript is a piece of human history? For God's sake, man, you are on an archaeological expedition. We are here to preserve artifacts, not randomly destroy them because of some misguided superstition."

"You have stolen this. It belongs to my people." Abdul-Qadir kicked Daniel in the jaw, knocking him off his feet. Abdul reached inside the safe and grabbed the scroll, jumping over Daniel as he dashed for the door.

Daniel rolled over and grabbed Abdul-Qadir's ankle, yanking his leg forcefully until the young man lost his balance and fell on his side. Abdul-Qadir kicked wildly in a mad attempt to inflict damage, but his physical strength was no match for his opponent's. Daniel grabbed the other ankle and held both his legs down.

Sarah stood at the doorway, her eyes wide.

Daniel drove an elbow into Abdul-Qadir's midsection, forcing him to release the scroll.

"Sarah, take the scroll."

She reclaimed the artifact, and he heard her hurried footsteps toward the safe.

The diminutive Arab slipped out of Daniel's grip.

Daniel sprang up and clutched Abdul's arms, whipping him around. He wrapped his hand around Abdul's neck and, when he had a firm grasp, slammed him into the wall, tightening his grip on his throat.

Abdul-Qadir struggled for air.

"You piece of shit," Daniel said through clenched teeth. "You are one of them. You tipped them off. Two men died because of you."

He spoke over his shoulder. "Sarah, tell the cops we have possession of the Qaryat al-Fau arsonist and thief."

He fixed his gaze on Abdul-Qadir and spoke slowly. "We will prosecute to the full extent of Saudi law."

Abdul-Qadir's eyes widened with horror. "I will never confess to it," he said, his voice so strained it was barely audible. He spat, and the saliva dribbled down his chin and onto Daniel's hand.

Daniel bore down on Abdul's throat until the young man's face turned magenta and his eyes protruded.

"Danny, no," Sarah said. "It's not worth it."

He ignored her pleas and spoke in Arabic. "You are unclean in the eyes of Allah. He will be your ultimate prosecutor."

The distant wail of a police siren floated in the night air. Abdul-Qadir's eyes clouded. Daniel wasn't sure if he had finally gotten to him or if it was an act. He released his hold on his throat enough to let him talk.

"Okay," the Arab croaked. "If you don't let them take me, I will tell you the truth."

"He's a liar," Sarah said. "Let the police deal with him."

Daniel kept his eyes on Abdul-Qadir. "I'm listening."

"My loyalty is with the Al Murrah," Abdul said, pride flashing in his eyes. "They are my people. Long ago, we forged a partnership with a British man. He paid us handsomely for any artifacts found in the valley. Everything we found we turned over to him."

"So you were planted here to spy on us. Why?"

He looked down. "The scroll . . . He wants that more

than anything. He offered two million US to the one who could deliver it to him."

"Why does he want it?"

"It is a map. That's all I know."

Daniel tightened his grip. The sound of the siren grew louder.

Abdul-Qadir nodded, communicating his intent to spill more.

Daniel let him talk.

"It shows the location of the treasure of Jezebel."

"What did you say?"

"The treasure of Jezebel. Please. You must believe me. I know nothing more."

The sirens shredded the night's silence as police arrived on the scene.

A pitiful look crossed Abdul-Qadir's face. "Don't let them take me."

Daniel was still computing the impossibility that Abdul's claim matched Mariah's theory. There was something to this. "This British guy. Where is he?"

"India . . . Varanasi, I think. I was there for my training."

The vague outline of a plan began to take shape in Daniel's mind. With a single powerful move, he hurled the traitor onto the floor. "I will give you one chance to redeem yourself. Cross me again, and I will crush you."

Chapter 9

It was four in the morning. Sacks felt energized and alert, though he had not slept at all in twenty-four hours and had consumed only rice and water for three days. It was part of the ritual cleansing required of him prior to an important ceremony.

He stood in the middle of the bathing room before a porcelain tub custom made to accommodate a man's full height. White pillar candles, arranged in a circle around the tub, filled the room with the scent of cloves, which he found most pleasing. The room was devoid of any other objects, yet it was far from stark. Glazed clay tiles depicting traditional mandala patterns in primary colors lined the walls from the blue mosaic floor to the twelve-foot ceiling. A glass and iron light fixture in the shape of a three-dimensional star hung above the tub, casting a warm saffron glow onto the bathwater.

Sacks untied the sash of his white silk robe and let

the garment slip off his shoulders onto the floor. His sculpted, hairless, thirty-two-year-old body looked like a marble statue in the soft light. Silken black ribbons of hair hung past his pecs. He sprinkled salt crystals into the bath and intoned a prayer.

"The blessing of the Father almighty be upon this bath drawn of the two elements that are essential to all life. May this body be cleansed of all its impurities and trespasses that this servant may stand immaculate before his master."

He stepped inside the bath. The water was on the cold side of tepid, just as he liked it. The freshness of the water awoke his senses and helped him focus. He lay supine and let the water buoy him, his hair spilling around his head like Medusa's snakes. He thought about the text he had received earlier in the evening.

There is trouble, his informant had dispatched.

His reply was clear. *Get out*.

He did not worry. His plan was merely delayed. The scroll would soon enough be his. He was certain of it.

It was the last piece of the puzzle he had been trying to assemble since sixth form in boarding school. During a school project in which students were to trace their ancestry, he learned his forebears were wealthy landowners in Israel. He was fascinated by the parallel—his father, an oil and energy baron in northern England, owned thousands of hectares in the Lake District.

When Sacks turned eighteen, he dipped into his trust fund to commission an ancient genealogy expert in London. That was when he traced his bloodline to the ancient Judahite kings and added it all up: he was the heir to the biblical throne long defunct and awaiting resurrection, the one who would fulfill the prophecies and redeem the world from its wickedness.

He confided in his father, as he had about everything else, and together they hatched a plan. Moving in clandestine fashion, young Trent would amass, at any cost, the proof a haggard and faithless world required to believe he was God's chosen, while his father forged an ironclad machine to back his promises—and thrust the family into global dominion.

The al-Fau scroll and the treasure it described were pivotal to his plan. The scroll was his birthright and his inheritance, and no one else had a right to it. The thought of it being sullied in the hands of nonbelievers repulsed him, and a chill ran up his spine like an electrical current.

Sacks submerged himself completely in the bath and stayed beneath the water's surface for several minutes, holding his breath until his heart pounded desperately against his rib cage and his temples throbbed. He felt lightheaded, and consciousness began to slip away. He entered a dream state where thoughts melted into incoherence, replaced by random visions of light and shadow and inchoate forms.

In the split second before blacking out, he exited the water with a loud gasp. He smiled, satisfied with the results of his experiment.

Pushing himself so close to death made him feel alive.

He stepped out of the tub and slowly dried himself, then slipped a hooded white habit over his head and donned a pair of brown leather sandals. It was time to go to work.

The basement of the building, hidden behind two sets of heavy security doors, was transformed into a ritual chamber. It was dark save for a single blue light beaming over a carved wooden altar in the center of the room. In front of the altar was a four-by-six rug of pure white lamb's wool, its two long ends oriented toward east and west.

On one end of the room was a gate, flanked by two six-foot-high pillars on whose capitals sat brass bowls of fire; on the other end was a shallow, round pool decorated with a glass tile mosaic depicting the head of the Serpent of Wisdom—the same image that was tattooed on Sacks' neck and torso. A wall-mounted fountain poured fresh water into the pool and filled the room with a gentle murmur.

His head covered by the hood of his garment, Sacks bowed before his five disciples, and they bowed back. He turned to one and said, "Bring forth the flame of the fire."

The young Indian man walked to the pillars and placed a lighting stick inside one of the bowls of fire, coaxing the flame that would light the guiding candle. He walked back to the altar and, with lowered head, offered his gift. "Let this flame guide the work of the master," he said with a thick northern Indian accent.

Sacks nodded to another disciple, signifying it was time to mix the perfumes and spices for the fumigation. The boy placed crystals of cedar, sandalwood, and wisteria inside a censer and lit the coal rocks beneath it. As the censer delivered its first wisps of fragrant smoke, he spoke with the voice of a child. "Let these vapors purify the master and his disciples before the sacred work."

Sacks opened the dark wood case on the altar and revealed three medallions rendered in copper. On the first was carved the Star of David and five ancient Hebrew words, each symbolizing the sacred and mystical names of his one Lord and master. The second contained a cross. On each arm was written in Hebrew the name of the ruler of each of the four elements. The third medallion, which he deemed the most powerful, was inscribed with mystical characters from the language of angels.

He turned to his first and most trusted disciple, a fair-haired British man with milky skin and glacier-blue eyes. With a look of adoration, he handed him the one key. "Let the seal come forth."

The young man bowed deeply and kneeled before a carved cedar chest beneath the altar. He gently pulled out a box of hollowed rock crystal, stood, and opened it before Sacks. The object inside gleamed in the blue light like a talisman from antiquity. Its four stones, arranged in the shape of a diamond, emitted a radiance that dazzled Sacks' eyes and caused him to momentarily avert his gaze.

He lifted the ring out of its crystal case. The iron was heavy in his hand, reminding him of the gravity of the object in his possession. He could feel his loins move beneath his habit as he placed the ring on the middle finger of his right hand. He closed his eyes and emitted a faint exhale, like the whisper of an ebbing ocean wave.

In that instant he felt invincible.

Sacks had gone to great pains and considerable expense to acquire the ring of the king. Though history painted it as legend, he had always been convinced of its existence. He spent hour upon hour, day upon day at the British Museum, poring over ancient Hebrew manuscripts, looking for any clue. When the research yielded nothing but false starts, he traveled to Tel Aviv and Jerusalem to forge alliances with archaeologists, historians, scholars, and anyone who would give him audience in exchange for a handsome contribution in the form of a research grant.

It wasn't until he discovered the dark arts that he had a true revelation. The moment was indelible in his mind. He stood on a remote hilltop in the Lake District countryside and, as his forebear did before him, offered a sacrifice to God. In a fire he built with fragrant woods he threw a living goat with its fore and hind legs bound. He still recalled without emotion the animal's pathetic bleating as the fire overcame it and the nauseating smell of singed fur and flesh.

It was the first time he had deliberately killed, and he was surprised at how easy it was. In the name of the almighty, no sacrifice was too great.

He was soon rewarded for his offering. The following week he got a tip from his informant in Israel that led him to the most unlikely of places—a small, unassuming temple in the Polish countryside. And there it was, embedded in the masonry, as told in the stories passed down through the oral tradition: the iron and gold ring worn by history's most influential king. It was, according to the mystical texts, the ultimate weapon of power.

Legend had it the ring enabled its owner to perform miracles and to communicate with spirits. Now that privilege belonged to him. With the ring as his guardian and guide, Sacks was certain he would rise as the rightful heir to the Davidic throne—the one the Jews had been awaiting for nearly three millennia.

With the ring on his middle finger, he faced east and raised his hands to the blue light, which represented the heavens.

"Agla, Agla, Agla, Agla," he said, his voice loud as he repeated the mystical word that meant *Thou art great forever, my Lord*. "O God almighty, whose rule is supreme over the whole of the universe, impart wisdom on your humble servant as Elijah's mantle was passed to Elisha. Lend a potent portion of your spirit unto this soul, O Lord, so that your glory may be venerated on the lower heavens."

Sacks stepped onto the rug and felt the soft lamb's wool beneath his feet. One of his disciples handed him a sword with a cabochon ruby encrusted on the tip of the handle. Sacks used it to carve a circle around the carpet on the painted concrete floor. The boy charged with the fumigations approached, waving a hanging censer over the carpet. The perfumed smoke clung to the stale air of the windowless room, and the wisteria vapors gave Sacks a slight high.

As Sacks held his arms out and lifted his head, another disciple pinned the three copper medallions onto his garment: the one bearing the Star of David on his breast and the other two on his back along his spine.

"I give myself fully to thee, O Most Holy Adonai." His voice boomed. "Remove the veil from my eyes so that I may see what has been hidden from me. Grant me the vision of thy prophets and the wisdom of thy chosen so that truth may speak to my ears."

With heads bowed beneath their hoods, the five disciples stood around the sacred circle, chanting medieval hymns. He lay prostrate on the rug, legs and arms outstretched like da Vinci's *Vitruvian Man*.

Aided by the incense and the monotone chanting,

Sacks entered a deeply meditative state. He was an observer rather than an occupant of his mind, watching without judgment or sentiment as images passed in and out of his altered consciousness.

Shrieking demons taunted him. A faceless, elderly figure was bent over a parchment, inscribing letters with a pheasant's quill and blood ink. Black crows squawked hideously as they flew into gathering storm clouds. Angels stood on high mountains, trumpeting as the clouds parted and a great earthquake ripped the earth asunder. Out of the thundering rubble came a voice:

Ascend the throne, and the plan of the master mason will be revealed.

Sacks opened his burning, bloodshot eyes. In the eleven years since he had been practicing the dark arts, he had not once heard the voice of the almighty. He knew with all certainty that at last he had and this was his appointed mission.

All that remained now was to find the throne of which the Great One spoke. The answer was in the scroll, hidden behind the clever king's parables and riddles. He had but to spill the blood of his adversaries and claim the legacy of his ancestors. He salivated as he considered the next phase of his plan.

To war.

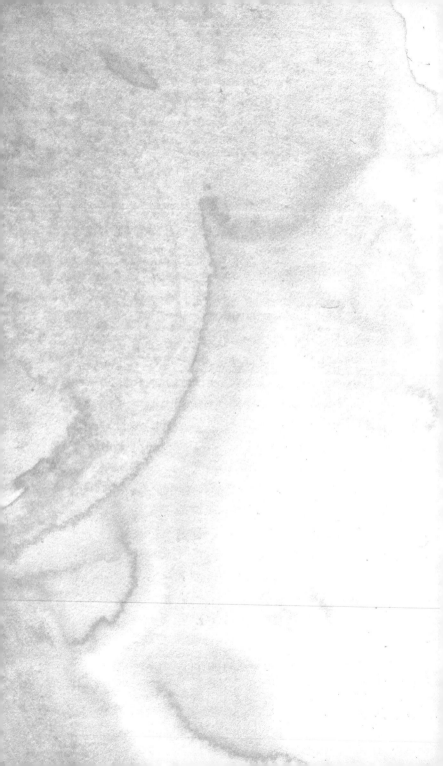

Chapter 10

*S*arah sat on the bed in her hut with her phone on one hand and a cigarette in the other. It had been months since she last lit up, and this local version of Marlboro did not deliver the welcome brume of spicy tobacco she'd expected. It was dry and bitter, like hemlock-laced hay. She put it out in a makeshift ashtray—a tea glass filled with sand. Maybe this time, she thought, she would quit and stick to it.

She touched her phone to display the time. It was just past six in the morning. She wondered if it was too early to place the call. But something told her if he saw her number on the caller ID, he would pick up. She unfolded a small piece of paper with a phone number and tapped the keys.

The ring was distant, like she was calling another world. In a way, she was.

"Allo." The voice sounded alert and confident, the

way she remembered him.

"Ezra," Sarah said. "It's been an absolute age. How are you?"

He hesitated. "Sarah Weston. I don't believe it. We haven't spoken since grad school. Where on earth are you?"

"Not too far from you, actually. Saudi Arabia, the Qaryat al-Fau project."

"Qaryat al-Fau? What's that have to do with Cambridge?"

"I'm no longer working for the university, Ezra. Long story."

"Let me guess. Sourpuss Simon finally ran his fingernails up your chalkboard." He chuckled. "Can't say I blame you. But seriously, what happened?"

She sighed as the tide of memories rose. Stanley Simon, the professor under whom Sarah and Ezra had both read during their doctoral studies, and a longtime Weston family friend, had recommended her to lead the Aksum expedition in Ethiopia two years ago. She thought he'd believed in her abilities when in reality he was answering to her father, who'd made a large gift to the university. The strings attached: a major post, as far away from England as possible, for his nonconformist daughter.

But that hadn't surfaced until much later. The friction began when the Aksum project took a controversial turn: an Ethiopian linguist Sarah and Daniel had consulted for the translation of some obscure inscriptions was murdered. The archaeologists were implicated, and the Cambridge expedition was shut down by the ministry of culture.

As eager to solve the mystery as to clear her name, Sarah vowed to stay and fight. Outraged, Simon ordered her to fly home. The clash escalated as the secret of Ethiopia's tenth saint unfolded—and was rejected by the university fathers as a load of bunk. Sarah disagreed, pressing on despite their warnings, and for that she was deemed a pariah. Ultimately, she was given a choice: her job or her convictions.

"It appears I'm not enough of a follower for Cambridge," she said. "Let's just say our parting was by mutual agreement. They don't like me, and I don't respect them."

"Hmm. Those pseudopatrician bores were never good for you anyway. You should come up this way, do some real work."

She smiled. It was just like Ezra Harel to make a comment like that. He was an Israeli through and through. Though he was the star archaeology student at Cambridge and had the opportunity to work anywhere, he never questioned his return to his homeland. He had a singular focus: to pursue biblical archaeology and separate myth from history. And he had indeed made headway. He was the one who proved definitively that the LMLK seals found in Palestine were connected to King Hezekiah of Judah. He was on the latter-day excavation team for Tell es-Safi, near Hebron, and put forth the now commonly accepted theory that it was the site of Gath, a Philistine city-state. His list of accomplishments went on and on—from discoveries of bullae linked to biblical characters to sniffing out fakes that had fooled even the most learned experts—and had earned him a just reputation as one of Israel's most gifted archaeologists.

Sarah had gotten to know him during the last two years of her doctoral program at the university, when they attended many of the same lectures. At the time, she was impressed by his brilliance and resolve, and had admired his intensity.

Ezra had an attraction to Sarah that bordered on obsession. For two years he did not relent in pursuing her, trying everything from late-night phone calls to writing poetry. She always resisted his advances, albeit in a friendly way. She wanted him on her side, just not on those terms. He kept calling for a while, even after they'd left Cambridge for their respective postdoctoral fieldwork—she in Egypt, he in Jordan—but eventually work responsibilities took over and they lost touch. It had easily been seven years since they last spoke.

"Actually, that's why I'm calling," she said. "I have stumbled onto something that's more up your alley."

"Really? I'm fascinated."

Sarah was hesitant to say much over the phone. If the events of the past few days were any indication, there were ears all around her. "I can't. But I can show you. Are you busy tomorrow?"

"You, coming to me? I do believe my prayers have

been answered. Shall I book us at the Dan?"

"Oh, stop. This is business. And it's rather serious."

"Tsk. As usual, you have no sense of fun. All right. Come on up. You know I wouldn't miss an opportunity to have you in my debt."

"We'll see about that. You might just owe me, rather than the other way around. Good-bye, Ezra."

Sarah walked into the lab with two mugs of thick black coffee. Daniel, who'd spent the night in the lab, guarding against another break-in, was leaning back on a chair with his feet up and eyes closed. He quickly opened his eyes.

"Had a lot of rest, did you?" Sarah said as she handed him one of the mugs.

He rubbed the back of his neck and grimaced. "I've slept more comfortably on rock piles. What about you?"

She shrugged. "The usual."

"Got it. What's the rest of camp looking like? Haven't checked on our friend yet this morning."

"I just brought him some breakfast. He was rather ill-tempered. Clearly, he doesn't enjoy having his hands bound and being locked away in a tiny hut."

"He'll get used to it. Could have had it much worse."

"Do you really think it was wise to keep Abdul here?"

"I think he can be more useful to us on this side of prison. Besides, he's still got some singing to do."

Sarah took a sip of her coffee. "I also checked on Mariah."

"Probably fast asleep, right?"

"Wrong. She was gone." She reached inside a pocket and handed him a page torn from a notebook. "This was on the bed."

Daniel unfolded it and read the note aloud: "'Sorry—had to leave before dawn. I was summoned back to the university for an emergency faculty meeting. Think about what I said. Mariah.'"

"Interesting timing," Sarah said. "I wonder if this meeting has anything to do with us."

"We'll soon find out. You can bet on that."

Sarah studied Daniel's face. By all accounts, he should have looked exhausted. Though his tanned complexion was unusually sallow and his facial hair growth was several days unchecked, his eyes were fierce with purpose. She was familiar with that expression. It meant he had a plan and every intention of putting it into motion.

"What are you thinking of doing with Abdul-Qadir?"

He rubbed the black stubble that had crept across his jawline and throat. "I'm not sure. I have some thoughts, but nothing has gelled yet. One thing I do know. I want to find out more about this British joker who has his eye on the scroll. Not sure what his motives are, but he's sure hell-bent on sabotaging this expedition. I don't take that lightly."

"He's done a pretty good job of it. Look around. We have four crew members left, and one of them is a traitor." She paused before adding, "One that we know of."

"Right." He stood. "He's got to be stopped."

"The only way to stop him is by deciphering the riddle first. And beating him to this treasure, whatever it is." She put her mug down. "By the way, what did Mariah mean by 'Think about what I said'?"

"Abdul-Qadir's comment about the treasure of Jezebel . . . That wasn't the first time I'd heard that. Earlier that night, I was talking with Mariah and she put forth the same theory. She went line by line on the scroll text, explaining her rationale. There were lots of holes in it . . . but hearing the same thing from Abdul made me sit up, you know?"

"Let me give you another bit of information. The analysis of the clay particles came back from the lab. It was Judean clay, sourced specifically to Jerusalem."

"Jerusalem? So the Jezebel theory could have legs."

"Maybe. But I've got a different one."

"The famous Sarah Weston instinct. Tell me what you're thinking."

"Sometime back, in Ethiopia, I read something in the original Coptic version of the Kebra Nagast. It spoke of a royal caravan vanishing in a sandstorm. It didn't say when or what, but the insinuation was that it belonged to the Queen of Sheba."

"Sarah, the Kebra Nagast is not a reliable historic source. Sheba and Solomon . . . their love child . . . the smuggling of the Ark of the Covenant into Ethiopia. The whole thing reads more like a fairy tale."

"I don't disagree. But what if it isn't? Look, you can't deny the facts. A tenth-century caravan, a Sabaean saddle, Judean artifacts, a scroll penned by a royal scribe . . ." Her tone was confident. "Think about it, Danny. Who married an Egyptian princess and made her his queen? Who wandered in the desert at the dusk of his life? Who had a knack for enigmatic, proverbial writing?"

Daniel rubbed his eyes. "Why didn't you mention any of this while Mariah was here?"

She stopped short of saying she didn't trust her. "She seems rather attached to her theory. I think we need another opinion. I have a friend who's a biblical archaeologist in Israel. He's one of the best in the world. It would be good to get an objective point of view."

"Really? Who?"

"Ezra Harel."

"Ezra Harel is your friend?"

"Well, we haven't spoken in years. We were in grad school together at Cambridge. Why? Do you know him?"

"We met once. Brilliant guy but a bit of a pompous ass."

A hint of a smile played upon her lips. "That's Ezra. But his instincts are spot-on. If anyone can crack the language in this scroll, he can."

"Bad idea. The Saudis would never stand for an Israeli entering their turf. They'd throw that scroll in the fire before letting Ezra Harel get a hold of it."

"Why do they need to know?"

"Are you crazy? A well-known Israeli scientist using Israeli resources to decipher an ancient scroll that may well have originated in Israel . . . How do you think you're going to keep that one under wraps?"

"Ezra is very discreet. He would do this as a favor to me."

"Okay. Let's suppose he does and finds out the scroll has biblical significance. Where do you think his loyalties will lie—with you, his grad school buddy, or with his country?"

"Why don't we cross that bridge—"

He put his hands out. "Stop right there. We're not going to cross that bridge. We're not even going down that road. Okay?"

She was calm, but all the frustration that had been mounting since her arrival in Saudi Arabia was bubbling to the surface. "No. It's not okay. We are in trouble here. And we need answers. The nationality of the person giving us those answers is immaterial. The truth knows no borders."

"Don't be so naive. You're talking about two nations that hate each other. If you hand deliver an artifact found on Saudi soil to the Israelis, all kinds of shit will hit the fan. If it's what you think it is, the Israelis will lay claim to it faster than you can say shalom. They will demand it be repatriated, which will infuriate the Saudis. The Saudis will claim jurisdiction over it, and it will be a full-scale war. I'm not getting caught in that political crossfire. And neither are you."

Sarah stiffened. Her father would have called her naive and forbidden her getting caught in the middle of a conflict. She would not stand down for a man. Not this time.

"I must not have heard you properly, because for a moment, it sounded like you were telling me what to do."

He ran a hand through his disheveled hair and exhaled loudly. He started to say something but instead turned away, obviously trying to get his temper under control.

Sarah added, "Let me just say this. Before becoming a field archaeologist, I took an oath. I swore that I would, above all else, seek the truth behind the facts. My first obligation is to that oath. You, of all people, ought to know that."

"Oh, believe me, I know it. And normally I would agree with you. But this is different."

"How so? Because this is *your* project? Because *you* have so much at stake here?"

He stepped back. "I consider this a partnership. What you do impacts me and vice versa." His voice rose. "If you go through with this, we may as well pack our bags now, because we certainly won't have a job here. Or in any Arab state, for that matter. Is that what you want?"

Surely Daniel knew the only reason she accepted the assignment was for the opportunity to work alongside him. She chose him because they shared the same principles. For the first time, she considered she might have made a mistake.

"A job?" Emotion crept into her voice despite her best efforts. "Is that why you think I'm here? Must I spell it out for you?"

He looked down and closed his eyes. His face was twisted into a look of pain. "Please. Don't."

She was shaking. She didn't want to say what she was thinking, but she had no choice. "If you're so worried about losing this job, I will act alone. I resign."

He looked up with a start. "Don't do this, Sarah. Please reconsider." He put his hands on her arms and squeezed. "You're my partner. I need you."

"You need me on your terms." She pulled out of his grip. "I won't forsake who I am. Not even for you."

He let his arms drop, a silent plea in his eyes.

"Good-bye, then," she said.

"No way." He took a step toward her, standing so close she could feel the warmth radiating from his body. "There's no good-bye for us."

She felt the clutches of regret hold her in place. But at that moment, she had to separate herself from him—for both of their sakes. She turned and walked out of the lab, averting her gaze from the blinding Arabian sun.

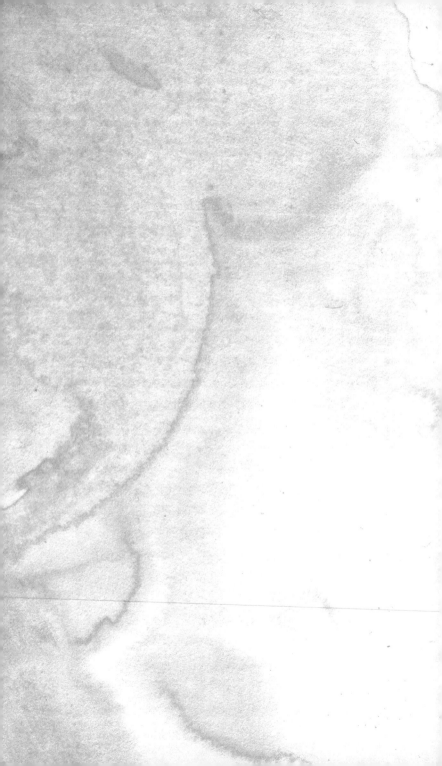

Chapter 11

*A*fter ten months in the desert, with practically no contact with the developing world, it felt strange to drive through a bustling metropolis like Tel Aviv. It was Sarah's first time in the city, but her melancholy wrestled with her usual excitement about exploring a new place.

As she traveled north on the Ayalon Highway, she gazed absently at the scenery, a mixed bag of concrete multifamily buildings that architecture forgot and modern towers of glass, concrete, and steel with angles sharp enough to shred paper. At midday, the highway was a jumble of cars, motorcycles, and groaning trucks that belched black smoke as they accelerated. The interchanges, great mazes of asphalt ribbons surrounded by high concrete walls, were choked with exiting traffic accompanied by a sound track of blaring horns.

She tried to concentrate on navigating the unfamiliar road, conscious she was surrounded by drivers who considered rule breaking a sport, but her thoughts kept traveling back to her last exchange with Daniel. Her resignation was not a knee-jerk reaction to an argument or their failure to see eye to eye on the Ezra issue. It was the final expression of a frustration that had silently been festering inside her for months.

She blamed some of it on herself. In all those months, she could not bring herself to ask why Daniel had pulled away. Once again, her proper upbringing had shielded her from being truly and unashamedly human.

She wanted more than anything to engage in a complete, no barriers partnership with Daniel. It was why she joined him in Saudi Arabia in the first place. But she could no longer invest in a stock whose value was spiraling into the abyss.

Yes, she told herself, it was best to walk away. But there was no denying the massive void her actions had left. She had considered it might be liberating to be unattached to an institution or a partner, but instead she felt disconnected, like an apparition floating between worlds she could not claim as her own. She pulled herself together as she took the Rokach exit toward Tel Aviv University.

She parked the rental car and footed it across campus to Ezra's office in the Gilman Building. She walked past the Cymbalista Synagogue and marveled at its iconic architectural manifestation of squaring the circle. Being on a university campus, particularly one with such a reputation for innovation, always stimulated her. A glimmer of excitement, the first since the confrontation with Daniel, began to materialize in her mind. She had high hopes for Ezra's contribution to the project, even if it was risky to ask for his help. What mattered was not the means but the end: decoding an ancient mystery with potentially explosive ramifications.

At the door of Ezra's office, she took a deep breath and raised her hand to knock. Before she had the chance, he opened the door.

"I felt your presence," he said, his lips curved into a crooked smile. "Shalom."

She relaxed at the sight of him. At that moment, when she felt so alone, it was good to see a face connected to the past. "Hello, Ezra."

He kissed both of her cheeks. "As you were when first your eye I eyed, such seems your beauty still."

She recognized the line from a Shakespearean sonnet and nodded her thanks.

He looked down. "But, alas, look at me."

He had definitely aged. Though he had just turned thirty-nine, his thick, black hair was already woven with threads of silver, as was the short beard that covered his jaw and the hollows of his cheeks. His intense brown eyes were framed by spiderlike lines, and the space between his eyebrows was engraved with a deep groove that made him look permanently worried. He was still as slim as he was during grad school but now was sporting a small paunch, indicating that these days he was more devoted to academia than fieldwork. As unconcerned with his appearance as ever, he wore a faded red button-down with the sleeves rolled sloppily above his elbow and too-baggy khakis held up by a brown leather belt she actually remembered from ten years ago.

He showed her in, his eyes riveted on her as she walked. His office was so cluttered Sarah had to move a stack of books and papers from a chair so she could sit down. Bookcases lined two of the walls, each shelf crammed with books that were arranged helter-skelter. His desk was crowded with more books and mountains of papers, some spilling out of overstuffed folders, others loose in towering stacks.

All around the room were various artifacts and framed certificates of recognition. Sarah's eye stopped on an incantation bowl inscribed with spiraling Hebrew letters and a coiled serpent rendered in fading brown ink.

"Third century," he said. "Magic bowls like that were buried under houses in the Levant to ward off evil spirits."

She turned her attention to him. "Ezra, I know your time is precious, so I will get straight to the point. I'm here to ask your opinion about something. We have unearthed, within the remains of an old caravan in a valley near Qaryat al-Fau, a remarkably well-preserved papyrus scroll. It was buried beneath the sand dunes and only recently exposed after a series of major sandstorms. Long story short, we've dated it to the tenth century BCE—your area of speciality—and we have reason to believe it originated in Israel."

He leaned back in his chair and tapped his fingertips together. "A papyrus scroll, did you say? Dating to the tenth century? I find that hard to believe."

"Oh? Why's that?"

"Come on, Sarah. You know very well that if anything was recorded during those times, it was inscribed on stone or ostraca. Papyrus didn't exist at the time."

"Not here, it didn't. But it did in Egypt. Egyptians were writing on papyrus since the third millennium BCE."

"So your theory is that this papyrus of Egyptian origin mysteriously appeared in the Levant?"

"Maybe not so mysteriously. We must piece the rest of it together, and then it may make more sense."

"Fine. I'll play. So where is this scroll now?"

"At the al-Fau site, at least for the moment." She pulled a silver memory stick out of her backpack. "It's all right here."

He accepted the device. "I'll have a look, but I'm limited as to what I can do without the actual artifact. You know that."

"I'm not sure it's in the cards to have it shipped here. The Saudis are pretty territorial."

"That's a shame. But we're not going to change

seventy years of history, are we?" He inserted the stick on the side of his laptop and hunkered in front of the screen. "All right. Let's have a look."

Sarah came around to his side of the desk and stood behind him. "Basically, what we're looking at here is a papyrus scroll, dimension ten inches by fourteen inches. Our C-14 lab in the US has dated it to twenty nine hundred years BP, plus-minus forty. The language, as you can see—"

"Late Egyptian hieratic. Most interesting. It's so rare to find a long text from that period. I assume you've had this translated."

"Yes, by one of the profs at King Saud. Mariah Banai. Do you know her?"

He looked off. "Name sounds familiar . . . but I can't say I do. Doesn't matter. What did Miss Banai have to say?"

Sarah directed Ezra to another document and waited as he read Mariah's translation.

When he finished, he clicked his tongue. "Interesting. If you don't mind, I'm going to have my own people run a translation, in case they have a different interpretation of it."

"Of course. How quickly can you have it done?"

"I can put them on it right away. Should only be a few days. I will call you the minute it comes in." He raised a thick, black eyebrow. "Then we can discuss it over drinks and dinner."

She was genuinely flattered by his interest, even

though she didn't share it. "You never quit, do you? All right. I accept your invitation. In the meantime, take a look at this." She pulled up the screen with the digital map detailing the impression of the bulla. "On the scroll, there was a faint mark here"—she pointed to an area in the center on the back of the scroll, then another area near the scroll's edge—"and here. I figure that's a bulla impression."

"Right on. I take it the bulla was long lost?"

"When we found it in situ, the scroll was rolled up and secured with a cord. No bulla."

"What kind of cord?"

"Linen twine. Nothing out of the ordinary."

"Did any of the clay from the bulla survive?"

"Indeed. This is where it gets interesting. We tested minute particles, and the lab identified the clay's origin as Jerusalem. So we know it was at least sealed in Israel."

He nodded thoughtfully. "We'll want to take another look at that. Not that I don't trust you and your American lab."

"Always a skeptic."

"I'm a biblical archaeologist. Comes with the territory."

"Well, here's something for you to debate." She pulled up the screen showing the digital map in highest resolution. "I've used some advanced imaging techniques—similar technology that NASA uses—to raise this impression from the dead. I've got a read on it."

Ezra's brow furrowed as he read, "Seshet Irisi, in service to the queen. Are you sure?"

"I'm very confident, yes. But you're welcome to try it yourself." She held his gaze. "Any idea who Irisi was?"

"A female Egyptian scribe, writing in Jerusalem? History certainly doesn't name such a figure. Neither does the Bible, not that it matters. You and I both know the Bible is not a history book."

"Still holding to the minimalist view, eh?" She knew the answer. Ezra let the stratification speak for itself—no matter how controversial the conclusions. It was an all-science, no-faith approach that was causing ripples within Israel's spiritual community and fueling the ire of fanatics.

He looked at her without answering. He turned back to the computer and pulled up the screen showing the hieratic text. "Something is bothering me. How can this script be so intact? If it's truly a tenth-century document, the ink surely would have faded or rubbed off."

"Exactly! A charcoal-based ink, such as would be used at the time, would not be fast. Unless—"

"There's something else in it."

She smiled. "Spot on." She pulled a small specimen cup out of her backpack. "I've taken the liberty of scraping a small amount of the ink so we can test it."

"Finally—a physical specimen." He held up the thimble-sized cup and looked at its contents, which were barely visible with the naked eye. "All right. Let me put this under the glass and see what I come up with. Give me a few days—until, say, next Friday?"

"Sure. Why not?"

"Good. Then let's meet next Friday at Jojo. Dress down; it's a pretty casual place."

"Well, that's fortunate since I left my dancing frock at camp."

He chuckled. "Your sense of humor has improved. Saudi Arabia must agree with you. Though I can't for the life of me see how."

Sarah's thoughts traveled back to Qaryat al-Fau and Daniel. She willed herself to push any lingering sentiments out of her mind and move on.

Jojo was a long, narrow room tucked inside an alley near the port. One wall was a mosaic of exposed brick in shades of green, red, and sand; another was covered in peeling sepia wallpaper with a fading vine motif, on which were mounted two antique bronze sconces with exposed bulbs that cast their flickering saffron light on young, animated faces. Every seat was occupied, and the din of conversation bounced off the walls and concrete floor. It took Sarah a moment to focus through the haze of cigarette smoke.

Ezra was sitting at a table for two in the far corner, tapping away on his phone. He was wearing the same baggy trousers he had a few days ago, with a white oxford shirt badly in need of ironing. A half-spent bottle of Goldstar beer was in front of him.

Sarah sat opposite him and gestured to the waitress across the room for another bottle of Goldstar. "So," she said, "any news?"

He finished sending a text and put his phone down. His face was pinched, as if he was worried about something. "Yes, actually. Quite a bit."

"I'm all ears."

He rubbed his forehead as he looked down at some notes, written haphazardly on loose sheets of paper. "All right. Let's start with the translation. Your people at King Saud weren't that far off. We basically get the same thing, with a couple of minor disparities in the language. The biggest difference is one line they left out." He leafed through the papers until he found the one he was looking for. He pulled it out of the stack and put it in front of her. "Here. You remember this part about the temptress. Well, before the line 'She is redolent of myrrh and good spices' and so forth, there is another line that reads, 'She dwells in the darkest depths of the valiant king's fortress.' They totally missed that."

"Do you understand any of it?"

He held her gaze for a few seconds, as if weighing his answer. "Let me come back to that."

The waitress delivered the Goldstar and the tab. Sarah attempted to pick it up but Ezra snatched it away. "My darling, you may be the one with all the money, but around here we don't do things that way." He paid the woman.

Sarah lifted her bottle. "Cheers, then. What else do you have?"

"The most interesting thing has to do with the ink. I looked at it under the scope. Of course, it was coal based; there was no disputing that. But there were also flakes of something else."

"Gold?" she asked, attempting to confirm a theory that had been floating in her mind. She believed a metal, such as gold, mixed into the charcoal would make the ink fast.

"Close. Copper."

She sat back. "Of course. That makes even more sense."

"Right. So I had the particles tested, expecting the composition to match the profile of trace copper found in Timna, which was an Egyptian mining area dating back to the Neolithic Period."

"Sounds like a logical connection. And did you verify it?"

"No, actually. It matched Khirbat en-Nahas."

A wrinkle formed on Sarah's brow. She tapped her lips with a loosely closed fist.

Khirbat en-Nahas was an ancient copper mine in an arid field in southern Jordan, in the area referred to as Edom in the Hebrew Bible. The mines had been dated by early archaeologists to the Iron Age, but an international expedition recently revisited the site, digging deep beneath the surface to find smelting debris that dated one of the mine's strata to the tenth century BCE. The dating, along with objects found on the site and the sophisticated digital mapping the crew employed, led to a tantalizing theory: that Khirbat en-Nahas was the site of King Solomon's legendary copper mines, which were tapped during the building of the first temple in Jerusalem, around 950 BCE.

"In a way, it makes sense," he said. "There is evidence showing the Timna mines were not in use in the tenth century BCE. But if you buy the new chronology, Khirbat en-Nahas was."

She leaned forward. "Okay. Let me weigh all the facts here. We have an Egyptian papyrus written in hieratic text by an Egyptian female scribe. The copper used in the ink and the clay used to seal the scroll can be traced to Edom and Judah. The letter was written by a man, supposedly to his son, yet the scribe claimed she was in service to the queen. Are we to assume a royal connection here?"

"An Egyptian ruler would have access to resources from a neighboring country, such as Israel. So it's not impossible."

"Let me run something else by you. The scroll was kept in an alabaster box that was inscribed with a winged, human-headed lion. We found the same symbol on a pot of honey inside one of the saddlebags. Is there any way to determine whose insignia that was?"

"The winged animal motif was used widely in Egypt

and the Near East. It was a symbol of power and guardianship. Any number of rulers would have used it. What are you getting at?"

"Exactly my point: perhaps it wasn't an Egyptian ruler at all."

He crossed his arms. "Go on."

"What if it was an Israelite or Judahite king with ties to Egypt?"

"Let me guess. You have a theory."

"Well, the staffer who turned out to be a traitor claims the scroll is a map pointing to a certain treasure of Jezebel. Curiously, the same theory was put forth by Mariah Banai. What do you think about that?" She scrutinized his reaction.

He paused. "Doesn't sound right."

"Why?"

"Aside from the fact that there is nothing to substantiate the biblical tales, you mean? But let's assume for a second the story in the Bible is true. Jezebel, the wicked queen, did not believe in the Hebrew God. If you study the language in the scroll, it is obvious the person who wrote it was a Yahweh worshipper. The references to angels and the five-pointed star give it away. Those were symbols embraced by the Hebrews, not Baal worshippers."

"Spot on. My take on it is quite different. Remember I told you the artifacts were buried with a caravan lost, probably to a sandstorm, in a treacherous valley." She pulled a spiral notebook out of her backpack and turned to a rendering. "I drew this from memory. The saddle itself was taken by Al Murrah rebels. I'm not much of an artist, but this is a fairly accurate representation. What do you make of it?"

"The textile pattern is Sabaean."

"That's what Danny said."

"Daniel Madigan? You call him Danny?" He rolled his eyes. "How positively quaint."

"Be serious, Ezra. My point is, we're likely looking at a Sabaean caravan returning home from a trade mission. We've already dated the remains to the tenth century BCE, and we have evidence suggesting the scroll may have been written by a monarch." She turned to the next page in her notebook. "According to the original Coptic version of the Kebra Nagast, a portion of a royal caravan perished in a sandstorm while returning to South Arabia from Jerusalem. It was the rear of a supposedly five-hundred-camel caravan accompanying the Queen of Sheba on a months-long journey across the desert."

"Anecdotal." His tone was clipped.

"I know it is. But it makes you think, doesn't it? What if there's some truth to the biblical accounts of the Queen of Sheba and King Solomon? What if her caravan was carrying back treasures from his kingdom—including a message to his son?"

He took a long drink, finishing his beer. He signaled

to a waitress to deliver another. "Listen. There is no real proof of the existence of either of those two figures. If you understand the concept of minimalism, you know where I stand on the Solomon issue. If he existed at all, he was a tribal chieftain who didn't have the level of influence, power, or wealth the Bible claims. Nor was he literate enough to compose a message such as this."

"Maybe he wasn't literate enough to write it, but his scribe was. Remember, he was married to a daughter of Pharaoh Psusennes II. The queen would have brought her own scribe to chronicle her travels to her new homeland."

He waved a hand dismissively. "Biblical rubbish. I don't believe a word of it."

"At least allow for the possibility."

"I think the whole thing is preposterous. Perhaps we'd have a more complete picture if we had access to that valley. But after what happened this afternoon, I suspect that won't be anytime soon."

"What do you mean? What happened this afternoon?"

"The heist."

She had no idea what he was talking about.

"Are you telling me you don't know?"

The heist. She went numb. "Wait. Back up. What's this about?"

"According to the news reports, the archaeology department at King Saud sent a courier, escorted by a staff member, down to Qaryat al-Fau to pick up the scroll and bring it to the university for safekeeping. I guess there was an earlier attempt to steal it?"

She nodded, her jaw tight with worry.

"Well, the courier picked up the scroll but never made it back to the university. The truck was found in a ditch on the side of the highway. The King Saud staffer had been shot. Single bullet between the eyes, at close range. The scroll was gone and the driver too. They think the driver pulled the trigger. What nobody knows is who exactly was driving the truck. The description of the suspect does not match the description of the driver the courier company sent. That person, the original driver, is nowhere to be found. But the story is still unfolding." He sat back. "I swear I thought you knew."

Sarah buried her face in her hands. Everything was beginning to make sense. If the text contained a message from Solomon, the artifact would be one of the most significant finds in biblical archaeology, proving conclusively that the legendary king existed. This could be the one piece of evidence the world needed to connect the biblical accounts of Solomon to solid facts.

That alone was reason for various parties—archaeologists, historians, theologists, fanatics—to want to get their hands on it. But who among them would kill for it?

She looked up. "Did the reports say anything about Danny?"

"All I heard was, as of tonight, the site was closed

until further notice and all the crew was gone."

She looked away, her eyes misting.

"You know," Ezra said, "that rugged brute does not deserve you. But if it means that much to you, I can make a few calls to my sources and nail down his coordinates."

"That would be brilliant." She sighed. "I'm sorry. This was a bit of a shock."

"I don't get it. If you are the lead archaeologist of the al-Fau expedition, how is it you weren't informed?"

"I resigned just before coming here."

"Oh. The plot thickens. And why did you do such a thing?"

"It's complicated. I don't want to go into it."

"Never mind," he said, waving a hand. "The take-away here is someone does not want the scroll's message revealed to the world."

She was listening to only half of what he said. Nervous energy had proliferated inside her, causing her thoughts to dart to and fro. She picked up her phone to send a text to Daniel but thought better of it. If someone was keeping tabs, she didn't want to give away his coordinates—or her own. She stuffed her notes into her bag. "I've got to go."

He grabbed her wrist. "Wait a minute."

What was he doing?

"I can't believe I'm saying this . . ." He looked around nervously. "Years ago, there was a ring . . . supposedly

King Solomon's ring. It was stolen from a small temple in rural Poland. I think this is a load of bunk, but there is a reclusive rabbi who knows a lot about it. Uri'el Ben Moshe. He was heading up the Polish temple when it was raided and burned down."

Sarah's face brightened. "Where is he now? I should like to talk to him."

"I figured you would. He left Poland after the temple was destroyed. He's back in Jerusalem now, keeping a low profile; teaching, mostly. His students revere him."

"Fine." She stood from the table. "I'll leave tonight."

He stood after her. "Hold on. He doesn't speak much English and, from what I recall, your Hebrew couldn't even get you a taxi. I'll go with you."

"No, Ezra. I want to go alone. Please understand."

"Suit yourself. But just for the record, I believe you're on a wild-goose chase. You won't be able to prove any of this. There is no scientific evidence, and I highly doubt any will turn up."

"All the same, I'd like to do it my way."

"You always have before." He looked her up and down. "I don't get you, Sarah. Are you inordinately ambitious . . . or just plain stubborn?"

She didn't answer him. She didn't expect him, a high-minded scholar with a narrow focus, to understand her unwillingness to turn away from intuition. That didn't make her less of a scientist than Ezra, just a nontraditional one.

He followed her out the door.

Outside, she turned to him. "Please keep our conversations to yourself. At least for now."

"Let me explain something to you. You can't keep this quiet. As of this afternoon, that scroll has been stolen. It's already hit the regional press. Soon it will be international news. Everyone will know about it anyway."

"Lives are at stake here."

Some passersby turned to look at them.

She took a deep breath and lowered her voice. "Whoever has this scroll is ruthless. He torched the al-Fau site, he systematically dismantled the expedition, and he killed a university escort in order to get his hands on that object. We must keep our moves quiet, or we'll be next."

He smirked. "I don't remember you being so tough. You were always a bit of a pushover, albeit a charming one."

"A lot has happened since then. Listen, I'd best be off. Don't forget to make those calls."

"I said I would . . ."

She gave him a quick peck on the cheek. He tried to put his arms around her, but she quickly slipped into the blur of pedestrians and streetlights.

The long walk to her hotel helped Sarah clear her mind. Her plan was to check out immediately and head east to

Jerusalem so she would be in the holy city at first light. There was no time to waste. In fact, it was a race; she just didn't know what was at the finish line.

Daniel was constantly on her mind. He already had been shaken by the events leading up to this day. How devastated must he be feeling now? Guilt clawed at her for leaving him at such a critical moment—for a reason no better than her wounded pride. She was desperate to know where he was. The thought of losing his tracks maddened her.

A few blocks away from the three-story, 1920s brick building where she'd been staying, a text came through.

I have your answer.

She was thankful Ezra had the sense to not call her mobile or give too much information in a text.

She ran the rest of the way and used one of the public phones in the lobby. He picked up on the first ring. "Ezra." She caught her breath. "Talk to me."

"It wasn't easy," he said. "None of my usual sources knew anything. So I had to eat my pride and contact my ex-girlfriend, Yael, who's Israeli military police. The things I'll do for you."

She sighed impatiently. "And?"

"She trolled through airline reservations and found him booked on a flight that left at eight o'clock tonight. Your friend's off to Delhi."

Unable to utter a word, Sarah stood there, slack-jawed and numb. The blood drained from her face as she recalled Abdul-Qadir's words.

India . . . Varanasi . . .

Daniel was going into the dragon's lair.

Chapter 12

At midday, Varanasi was swarming like a beehive, just as Daniel remembered it. The streets were flooded with traffic of every stripe, from motor to animal. There were no traffic lights, no apparent laws. Halting everything was a flatbed loaded with six rows of crates stacked four high. Hitched in front of it, a white ox had buckled to its knees, refusing to budge in spite of its driver's repeated whippings and profanities. The animal just sat there, moaning in protest, oblivious to the fact that it had stalled three lanes of traffic.

The motorists who were stuck weren't any too patient. They leaned out of their windows, or exited their vehicles altogether, shouting advice to the ox-cart driver and calling him a clueless country bumpkin. The only ones getting through the mire were the moped riders, who wedged their way between cars and camels and rickshaws and sacred cows.

One rickshaw cyclist stood on the pedals, taking in the commotion like it was live theater. His body was thin as a yardstick, covered in a dirty, haphazardly wrapped sarong from which protruded two legs so bony that all the sinew was visible. His head was covered in a striped *dupatta* tied into a loose turban. He turned around to his passengers, smiling to reveal an incomplete row of red-stained teeth. He spat a wad of betel paste onto the dusty pavement.

"This ox finished," he said, bobbing his head. "No more work today."

Daniel sat up under the fringed, robin's-egg-blue vinyl canopy and handed the man a few rupees. "Thanks for the ride, my friend."

Daniel and Abdul-Qadir stepped off the rickshaw and wove their way through stalled traffic to the sidewalk, which was choked with idle onlookers and small-time vendors.

"You sure you know where you are going?" Daniel asked in Arabic.

His companion looked around Varanasi's chaotic maze of streets and alleys and compacted ramshackle buildings. "This is the place. I was here to receive martial arts training. Disgusting. We have some dirty old towns in Saudi Arabia but nothing like this."

Daniel silently agreed. He had been to India several times, and each time he had to get used anew to its chaos, filth, and raging poverty. People flocked here from all parts of the country. Varanasi was to the Hindus what Jerusalem was to the Jews, the Muslims, and the Christians. According to Hindu belief, it was the home of Lord Shiva in ancient times and, later, the place where Buddha meditated and imparted his wisdom upon his followers. The stretch of the Ganges that lapped Varanasi was believed to have the power to erase all sins, and that alone was reason for Indians to make the pilgrimage here.

"So which way?"

Abdul-Qadir shrugged. "All I remember is that it was close to the river." He paused. "And there was a silk shop next to it."

"Well, that could be anything." Daniel pointed toward the east. "River's that way. Let's go."

They walked along a cracked sidewalk.

Parked in front of faded storefront window displays, flat wooden carts proffered betel leaves and paste for chewing. Emaciated men sat on reed mats, their backs against the peeling plaster of the buildings, doing nothing. They had no work, no home, no prospects; their lives were confined to the four-by-five mats they used for sitting, sleeping, and the rare meal.

Just before reaching the river's edge, Abdul-Qadir recognized one of the Hindu temples and pointed north. They ducked into an alley, away from the mass chaos of the main drag. The path was lined with storefronts and merchants touting everything from the famous Varanasi silks to hair oil. Sandalwood incense burned everywhere, perhaps to mask the fetid smell of human waste emanating from the open-air urinals.

A preteen boy, unwashed and missing both of his thumbs, tugged on Daniel's khaki cargo pants and begged for a rupee.

Daniel refused, knowing fully that tossing the boy a coin would mean a swarm of beggars coming out of the cracks. He ignored the persistent urchin for almost ten minutes.

In India, beggars were everywhere, but not all were soliciting money. Some simply wanted a helping hand. One man, reduced to skin and bone and so steeped in his own waste that flies were buzzing around him, lay on the pavement in a fetal position, raising a feeble hand to passersby. He was dying. His fellow men ignored him, some even stepping over him. Daniel recoiled at the callous display even if he knew the purpose of it: it was the man's karma to die in this way, and no one dared interfere with it.

Daniel and Abdul-Qadir turned toward the east and continued through the residential area. The alleys were paved with uneven, rough-cut stones and the path was so narrow that the two could not walk beside each other without brushing shoulders. The buildings on either side were crumbling, yet lace curtains hung in the windows and stenciled artwork decorated doorframes. Commercial signs, mounted outside narrow strip shops, interrupted the rows of residential buildings as ersatz merchants peddled anything that would earn them the day's meal.

Abdul-Qadir stopped at one of the corners and looked around. "Yes. This is the right place. We are very close."

Daniel narrowed his eyes. Though Abdul swore on his mother's life that he would lead him to his British patron, history told Daniel to proceed with caution. No one was to be trusted. In this convoluted game, it seemed everyone was out for himself.

Or herself. The memory of Sarah's abrupt departure flashed in his mind. He resented the way she left, with blatant disregard for him and for their shared mission. He'd considered her a part of him and thought she'd felt the same. The thought of her approaching Ezra Harel about their find felt like a betrayal. He pushed it out of his mind.

"You'd better be right," he said. "Because I meant what I said."

If Abdul could lead him to the right place without a tip-off, Daniel would drop the charges against him. If the plan was botched, Abdul would pay dearly, even if Daniel had to exact retribution with his own hands. It was a huge gamble, and he knew it. But it was the only way to gather intel about the enemy and shed light on his sinister intentions.

"Yes, boss, yes," the diminutive Arab said. "This is the right path. Come this way."

Daniel followed, anticipating a confrontation. They walked for another fifteen minutes, seemingly in circles, through the labyrinthine old city.

They finally came to a doorway that matched the picture in Abdul's memory. It was a double door, freshly painted sky blue, with no knob but only a brass knocker in the shape of Shiva's open hand. Next door was a silk shop, just as he had described it, with rows of brightly colored *dupattas* embroidered with gold thread hanging from the eaves.

"You know what to do," Daniel said. He slipped into the storefront of the silk shop until he was out of view and nodded to Abdul-Qadir.

The Arab pounded the brass knocker three times.

No one opened, but a voice came through the door, asking in Hindi who was there.

Abdul stepped in front of the door. "Let Mister know Abdul-Qadir is here," he replied in English. "He will want to see me."

After a silent moment, the door clicked open.

Abdul stepped inside, and the door closed.

Daniel gave Abdul-Qadir a few minutes. While waiting to be received, he was to crack the door open and place a piece of putty into the doorframe latch to prevent it from self-locking.

Listening from the other side of the door, Daniel heard the two men walk away. He stayed put long enough to ensure no one else was there.

He made his move. Staying clear of the door camera's range, he slipped a paper-thin magnetic rod into the crack separating the two doors and moved it around until the strong magnet attached onto the metal dead bolt plate. He pulled gently, and the door yielded.

He stood in the shadows of the dark foyer and surveyed the place. Two steps led down to a grand-scaled salon with twelve-foot ceilings. A shaft of light emanating from glass doors illuminated the furniture: a single sofa loosely draped with a white sheet and a round pedestal table inlaid with mother-of-pearl. On the far right of the room, a spiral staircase led to a second level. Directly ahead, ornate carved wood arches framed the entrance to a small courtyard garden. Abdul-Qadir waited alone outside, shifting his weight and tapping his fingers.

To Daniel's left and right were corridors leading to other parts of the house. Abdul had told him of a meeting room somewhere along that axis. He stepped toward the right, surprised at how dark it was. If there were any windows, they must have been tightly shuttered. The place smelled stale, as if it hadn't been opened in a long time, and was punctuated with the vague fragrance of spent plumeria and patchouli incense.

The first two rooms were unlocked. He pushed the doors open to find completely empty spaces. He continued to the third room, the last along that side of the corridor. The door was locked. He looked around for any sign he was being watched and reached inside his pocket for his lock-picking tools. He inserted a long hook pick and a tension wrench in the lock, popping it open on the first try.

He winced as the door creaked, then slipped inside the dark room and waited with his back against the wall, listening for potential company. After three minutes or so, silence was still with him. It seemed he was safe—at least for now.

In the pervasive darkness, Daniel could make out the silhouette of a square table in the center of the room with a single chair next to it. Papers were strewn about the table's surface. He approached for a closer look. He took a penlight out of a pocket and pointed the narrow light stream across the papers.

On some were incomprehensible inscribed diagrams. They appeared to be the embryonic scribbles of an engineer contemplating a network of sewage conduits. Others were sketches—and quite good ones—of animals: lions with gaping jaws, mythical sphinxes, eagles with outstretched wings. Daniel remembered the passage in the scroll text about the temptress' menagerie. Then he saw a topographic map of the Judean Desert and the Dead Sea. He studied it, noting the circles around certain elevations of the desolate terrain. Next to the map was a sketch of something that looked like the entrance to a cave. He committed it all to memory.

Just as he was preparing to leave, he noticed a business card at the bottom of a stack of papers. Daniel slid the papers aside to reveal the name on the card: Alastair Bromley, MP. It wasn't an official card, but rather a calling card with Bromley's name and British phone number. No address, no affiliation other than the title—Member of Parliament—at the end of his name.

Daniel slipped the card into his pocket and, satisfied with the information he'd gathered, began to make his exit. He left the room, locking the door behind him so as to not raise any suspicion. He moved stealthily down the corridor, scanning the area for any threat.

He stepped into the foyer and lunged toward the door. The knob did not turn. It was locked, and he tensed up as he realized the putty on the latch was no longer there. He fumbled for the dead bolt.

A beefy hand gripped his shoulder, buckling his left knee. He regained his composure and thrust an elbow behind him, connecting with his pursuer's midsection. Daniel tried for the door again, but the man wrapped a muscular arm around his head, immobilizing him.

Daniel knew it was a matter of time before the man's reinforcements would come. With all the strength he could muster, he kicked his attacker's shin and broke free.

The man, a stout, turbaned Indian wearing a dhoti wrapped in the style of harem pants and no shirt, growled and hurled himself at him.

Daniel tried to block him, and they locked arms. His biceps burning from the effort of overpowering him, Daniel pushed the Indian against the wall. Distant footsteps warned him to act quickly. He drove a punch into the man's midsection, doubling him over. An elbow to the trapezius sent his opponent to the floor.

A half-dozen surly Indians entered through the front door. Daniel darted down the left side of the corridor and into the door at the end, hoping it led to an exit. He closed the door behind him. With the double latch, he bolted the door to buy a little time. He turned and came upon a second door that was locked. He scanned the lock hurriedly and drew his tools, confident he could breach it.

He worked quickly, heard the lock click, then pushed the door open. He found himself standing at the entrance to a basement. A bead of sweat slid down the side of his face.

As the men pounded on the door behind, he hurried down the stairs. In the darkness, he heard trickling liquid and turned to see the faint outline of a wall fountain. He pulled out his penlight and searched for an exit.

On the far end of the room was a gate framed by two carved stone jambs. They were crowned with a frieze depicting various scenes unclear in the dim light. Two pillars flanked the gate, and in his mind he made a loose connection to certain Egyptian tomb entrances.

He ran toward the gate in the dark but collided with

something massive and solid. Clutching his hip bone in response to the pain, he pointed the light on the mass and saw an altar of some sort, on which sat a heavy stone bowl. He glanced inside the bowl. Dark, red liquid. He inhaled the pungent scent. It was indeed blood.

Who was he up against?

His heart pounding, Daniel bolted toward the gate. Thick brass latches on the top, bottom, and side held it firmly in place.

The door at the top of the stairs came off its hinges and crashed to the ground. Six men, some wielding clubs and knives, stepped over it and made their way down the stairs.

Daniel quickly released the latches and opened the gate. He instinctively brought his forearm to his eyes, guarding against the sudden burst of daylight. There was only a narrow ledge outside the doorway, and beneath it a vertical seven-foot drop to the Ganges. The river was cloudy with refuse, untreated runoff, and debris from the dozens of burning ghats lining its edges.

With heavy footfalls close behind, he jumped feet-first into the water, eyes wide open as he sank like a missile to its murky depths. He looked over his shoulder and, through the fog of filth, made out the figures of two men.

A trained cave diver, Daniel was at an advantage. He propelled underwater. His pursuers kept pace at first, but one quickly fell behind. Daniel turned to see the pale, determined face of a young blond man, about five feet behind him and gaining.

Daniel swam faster, knowing he had no more than sixty seconds before he had to surface for air. The young man trailed close behind him, like a shadow. The water pressure crushed his chest like the jaws of a vise. Time was not with him; he had to begin ascending or risk running out of oxygen.

As he made his way to the surface, Daniel felt a sharp jab on his right thigh. He looked down and saw a stream of blood leave his body in slow motion and form a red cloud in the river.

His pursuer, knife glinting in his hand, was now next to him, glaring at him with hard blue eyes. Daniel grabbed his knife hand and bore down on his wrist with a python grip.

Eyes bulging, the man slowly opened his fingers and the knife slipped out of his hand and spiraled to the river-bed. With his lungs now begging for air, Daniel pushed his attacker away with a kick to the gut and made his bid for the surface.

He surfaced with a gasp, swallowing waste-infused Ganges water as he tried to right himself. He looked around for the blond man and saw his head emerge at a comfortable distance. He swam toward the riverbank, aware he was still being followed.

The Ganges was buzzing with activity. On the cloudy gray water, hundreds of boats bobbed. Some were long abandoned. Some were piloted by men angling for contaminated fish. Others carried dead bodies, wrapped in red silk and tied to stretchers, that for religious reasons could not be cremated and had to be committed to the river.

At the river's edge, thousands of pious Indians gathered to perform their ablutions and make offerings to the gods in the form of small, blossom-filled cups or garlands of marigolds. Women did their laundry at the riverbanks, pounding clothes against the stones and laying their saris to dry on the steps, like giant silk ribbons in a rainbow of colors.

Bent with exhaustion and feeling the violent throb of the knife wound, Daniel exited the river at last. He stumbled onto the stone stairway that cascaded down to the water. Even here, in a city where no sight ever was shocking, people stopped and stared at the foreigner who came out of the water, soaked to the bone and bleeding.

His T-shirt and cargo pants were stuck to his body, and his hair clung to his neck and shoulders. He left a trail of water and blood as he made his way up the steps, causing people to step aside in bewilderment and horror.

After he reached the top of the stairs, he darted into one of the alleys and, ignoring the pain, ran in the direction of the main road, praying he remembered the way. He turned and saw his pursuer hurrying up the steps. He limped through the narrow alley, knocking several pedestrians against the wall or to the ground in his hurry.

He turned a corner, only to run into the hind end of a cow moving slowly through the maze. He turned around, searching for a different ingress, and noted the assassin was gaining ground.

Knowing the blocked path was the shortest way out of the maze, he crawled between the legs of the sacred cow as the animal bellowed. Women pressed their young children to their bosoms, and toothless beggars nodded their encouragement as he blasted past grimy storefronts, makeshift temples, and crumbling houses toward the street, where he planned to lose his pursuer in the eternal traffic.

His instincts were correct. At the top of the alley was the main road, choked as always with vehicles and wandering animals. Daniel spotted a free bicycle rickshaw in the distance and ran toward it. He stuffed a wad of crumpled, wet rupees into the driver's hand.

"Get in the back," he said, pointing toward the canopied seat. "I'm driving."

As the blood from his stab wound trickled steadily, soaking his pant leg, Daniel pressed the pedals, maneuvering the rickshaw through tight traffic as other drivers decried his lack of patience.

He scanned the street for his adversary and saw no trace of him. "Which way to the train station?" he called back to the bemused rickshaw driver.

The Indian pointed left. "About one mile, two maybe."

Daniel found his clearing in the traffic and, gritting his teeth, pedaled furiously to Varanasi Junction.

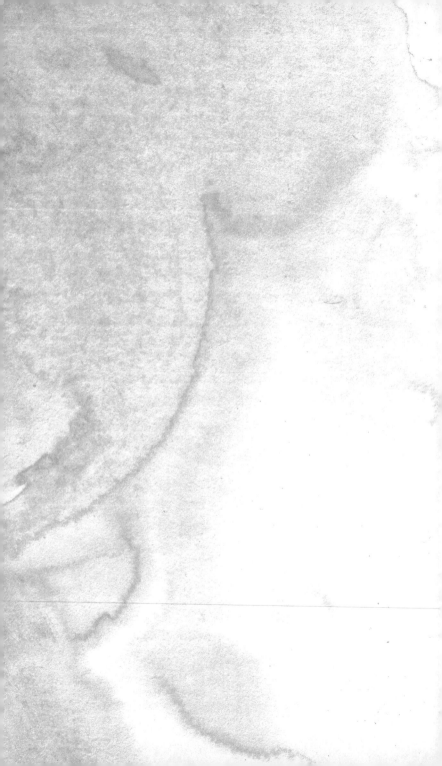

Chapter 13

Trent Sacks lay faceup on the massage table, moaning with pleasure. The young man with the clear blue eyes delivered a few final strokes, firm yet gentle, to his master, concluding the deep-tissue massage that was part of Sacks' nightly ritual.

When he finished, he pulled the white silk sheet midway up Sacks' torso and laid a gentle hand on his chest. "Shall I bring you some tea?"

"Thank you, Angus." Sacks stroked the young man's forearm with a feather touch. "You fought bravely today."

"I regret he got away."

"No matter. You proved your loyalty by pursuing him to the end." He closed his eyes and inhaled deeply. "I will take that tea now."

"Yes, my lord."

Without bothering to dress, Sacks stood and picked up his phone. He dialed the number, making note that it was going on five in the evening in Birmingham.

"What took you so long?"

"We had a little visitor," Sacks said. "Daniel Madigan made his way here."

"Madigan? How is that possible?"

"Our Arab informant played a double game. He came here to bring us the computer files, presumably. But he was not alone."

"I trust Madigan didn't see anything?"

"I'm afraid he did. He was down in the cavern. My people caught up to him immediately and chased him out into the river. They wounded him, but in the end he slipped away."

The man cleared his throat. "What about the girl?"

"We have reports that she left al-Fau prior to the courier incident. We have cause to believe that she and Madigan have gone their separate ways."

"Good. Their alliance is falling apart. But neither is to be trusted. You must know each of their whereabouts at all times. And when the time is right—"

"I shall eliminate them."

"Yes. But do be careful. The girl is Weston's daughter. Under no circumstances are we to raise suspicion. Do you understand?"

He swallowed hard. "Completely."

"Good. Now what about the scroll?"

"It has been delivered safely and is in my possession

as we speak."

"So we are ready for phase two."

"Indeed we are," he said. "We leave at dawn. But first, there is a small matter I must see to."

"Very well. I shall expect the next dispatch from the site." A brief silence hung between them. "You have done well, my son."

"Thank you, Father," Sacks answered in a breathy whisper. The line went dead, and he turned off his phone for the evening.

Angus entered the room with tea and Sacks' freshly pressed *sherwani*—the formal garb of aristocratic Indian men.

Sacks took a sip of the rose tea.

Angus kneeled and held the slim drawstring pants open so Sacks could step into them. He raised the garment to his waist and tied the strings securely. He held open the long brocade frock coat, whose soft white silk was embroidered with silver thread at the cuffs and collar, and Sacks slipped his arms in. Angus buttoned the jacket from the high collar down to the midthigh.

Sacks tossed back his silken black hair and let it tumble down his back. His face hardened, and his heart blazed with hatred. He turned to Angus. "Take me to him."

The two walked down the long, dark corridor to an isolated room on the east side of the building that Sacks had hidden away from the rest of the house by installing a secret door. Because he couldn't find the right technicians in India, he had flown in American contractors and employed them over several weeks to ensure the system worked to his satisfaction.

It was a very important addition to his fortress, for it was there he stashed the library of books and artifacts vital to his mission. But today, the room worked equally well as a prison.

Sacks walked to the fireplace and adjusted the candlestick on the mantel to unlock the mechanism. He then placed a code into a flat-panel display, and the flue and firebox separated from the wall in one piece. Unwilling to exert himself unduly, Sacks stepped back and let Angus push the structure to the side to reveal the doorway.

Angus entered the room first. He stopped before the man lying on the floor with his hands and feet bound with steel chains. In a loud, ceremonious voice, he announced, "Hail the Righteous Trent Sacks."

Sacks walked slowly into the room, his hands clasped in front of his chest. In his expensive white *sherwani*, with his raven hair cascading over his shoulders and down to the middle of his back, he knew he looked imposing and regal. It was his intent. He wanted to put forth the image of a lofty, untouchable being—a king of sorts—to underscore Abdul-Qadir's disloyalty.

The imprisoned man looked at his captor, on whose face he gazed for the first time, with eyes so strained they looked like they were popping out of their sockets. His dark face was covered with the mist of perspiration as he awaited his fate. He didn't try to fight his shackles, trembling in them instead.

Sacks was satisfied that Abdul-Qadir's terror was complete. He looked around the room at the locked cabinets that contained the biblical artifacts he had amassed with great effort during the past decade—inscribed ostraca, bullae, scroll fragments from the caves of Qumran, and the most prized possession of all, the al-Fau scroll—and seethed anew at his informant's incompetence. Not only had the Arab botched the first attempt to reclaim the scroll, but he had engaged in the worst kind of betrayal—bringing the enemy to his doorstep.

Yes, he thought. *He deserves the Lord's judgment.*

Calmly, and without looking Abdul-Qadir in the eye, Sacks spoke. "Do you know what you have done?"

Abdul-Qadir was tongue-tied as he tried to deliver the words.

Sacks turned to face him and, with a voice so loud it echoed, he demanded, "Speak."

The Arab averted his eyes and sobbed softly.

"Very well, then." Sacks pushed a button on the side of a cabinet.

Within seconds three of his men appeared, standing at the doorway and ready to carry out their duty.

Angus handed him a bundle of silk strips and a roll of electrical tape.

Sacks kneeled next to Abdul-Qadir and stuffed the silk into his mouth. "This cloth symbolizes the mantle of God, which you have defied."

The captive man protested with muffled, panicked cries as Sacks pushed the silk farther and farther down his throat. Sacks tore off two pieces of electrical tape and placed one over Abdul's quivering mouth, the other over his open eyes, frozen in panic. The prisoner moaned and flailed like a wounded animal on the throes of expiration.

Sacks stood and wiped his hands of Abdul-Qadir's filth with a silk handkerchief. With a ceremonious tone, he quoted from the book of Jeremiah. "'I will punish you according to the fruit of your doings, saith the Lord: and I will kindle a fire in the forest thereof, and it shall devour all things round about it.'"

The three Indian men entered the room holding a stretcher and yards of red embroidered silk. They took up Abdul-Qadir's thrashing body and laid it onto the stretcher, tying his limbs and neck securely to the posts until he was completely immobilized. As the Arab issued muffled screams of horror, the men proceeded to wrap his body, from head to feet, in the blood-red silk.

Sacks held his head high and inhaled deeply, satisfied with the men's handiwork. "Dispose of him," he commanded and walked out of the room.

With Angus at his heels, he walked up the spiral staircase to an empty room with a big window overlooking the

Ganges. Silently, he waited in front of that window until his men exited the building holding the stretcher. He watched as they loaded Abdul-Qadir's bound body into a twelve-foot motorboat and launched it into the river. It was a flawless plan: no one would question such an incident in Varanasi, assuming the body on the stretcher belonged to a snake-bite victim or a pregnant woman or other unfortunate soul whose remains could not, according to Hindu belief, be eliminated by burning.

The three executioners maneuvered the boat into the middle of the river, as far away as possible from other traffic, and lifted the stretcher on its end. Sacks imagined with delight Abdul-Qadir's stifled cries of desperation as his body was released into the depths of the holy Ganges.

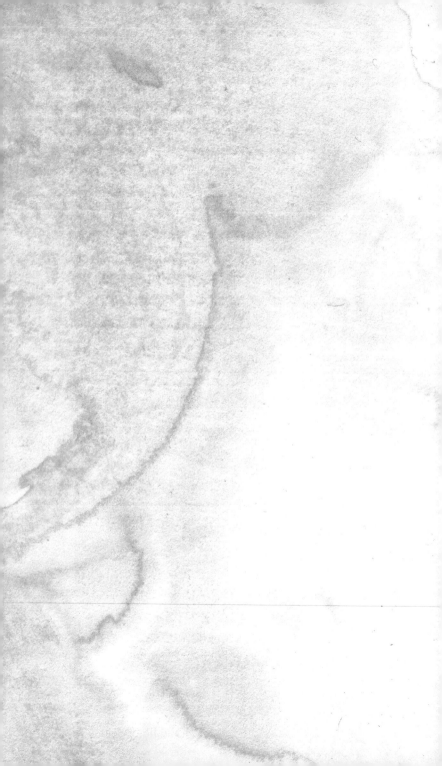

Chapter 14

Daniel woke with a start. He rubbed his burning, tired eyes and emerged from the fog of near-comatose slumber. What had startled him from deep sleep was a dream about Sarah. He saw her standing in the Briton's cavern, smeared with the blood inside the ceremonial bowl on the man's altar, arms outstretched in a plea for help.

Even though his wounded ego prodded him to forget her, he couldn't help worrying. If Sarah pressed on—and he was certain she would—this man would not hesitate to eliminate her.

The thought chilled him. He sat up on the hard bed. The paint on the ceiling was peeling, revealing a layer of black mold beneath. The wall was pockmarked with holes and cracks no one had bothered to fix. A foggy mirror hung above a decrepit vanity table. The connected bathroom was mildewy and smelled faintly of the city's sewage.

Daniel had spent the night in a guesthouse in the

heavily trafficked Janpath area of Delhi. He'd chosen this district teeming with people of every nationality so he could move incognito as he regrouped. Before entering the enemy's retreat, he had given Abdul-Qadir the address of the guesthouse as a meeting point. But that was before everything had gone so wrong.

The plan was to have Abdul distract the others while Daniel snooped around to get any information that would help him track down the scroll—and learn more about the man who had singlehandedly sent his world crashing to the ground. He wasn't supposed to be caught. And even though he managed to escape, he wasn't sure Abdul would be equally lucky.

Daniel originally intended to wait in Janpath for a couple of days, giving Abdul-Qadir a chance to join him. If there was no sign of him, he would have no choice but to assume the worst. Now he thought it best to exit as soon as possible. After all, Abdul had already proven his capacity for playing a double game. Who was to say he wouldn't give away his coordinates?

A chill traveled down his spine as he reconstructed the previous day's events in his mind. That house was both long-abandoned and technologically sophisticated. It was obvious no one lived in it but used it only to carry out operations. And that basement . . . Daniel had worked among the ruins of ancient worship rooms during his time in Egypt and had encountered similar altars and gates believed to lead into the realm of enlightenment.

And yet this was materially different. In the ancient world, such rooms were far more ornate, often bearing the likenesses of gods and employing elaborate instruments of worship. The Varanasi basement was stark, almost Zen-like. Daniel had noted in the entire room a single source of light, directly above the altar, and wondered if this could symbolize the ineffable light of God. The blood, which could have been animal or human, obviously was a sacrifice of some sort, pointing to two possibilities: the manner of worship was either satanic or ancient.

His thoughts turned to the gate that led out to the Ganges. He called to memory the triangular frieze above the doorway. He faintly recalled two male figures, one stepping on the body of the other in a victorious stance, holding something in his hand that was too small and blunt to be a weapon.

David and Goliath. The man lying on the ground was twice the size of the victor. And that object, which did not look like a traditional weapon, could easily have been a sling.

He rubbed his forehead, trying to find the sense in the disparate pieces. The connection to Israel, first hinted at by the analysis of the clay traces on the scroll, was becoming more palpable. The topo map in the locked study was of an area to the west of the Dead Sea—the Judean Wilderness. The Old Testament contained tales of David hiding from the mad King Saul in Judean caves before being crowned king.

He reached for the wet trousers draped over a chair and pulled out of a pocket the business card that had been buried beneath the maps and sketches. It was still damp from the unexpected swim in the Ganges, and part of the phone number had flaked off. Daniel wondered what business a member of the British Parliament could have with that thug. He knew who could shed some light.

With some effort, he put weight on his injured leg and hobbled into the fetid bathroom. He looked at himself in the cracked mirror above the sink. He looked like he had not slept in days. The creases on his forehead seemed deeper than usual, and his eyes were dulled by pain and exhaustion. The dark growth across his jaw and throat was growing ever thicker. He ran his fingers through his coarse, uncombed hair. His appearance was a mirror for his mood: battered, unsettled.

He splashed some cold water on his face. Ready or not, he had to face the day.

Delhi was as crowded, polluted, and loud as ever. Daniel was grateful that it was autumn and a pleasant chill had replaced the pervasive mugginess that usually cloaked the city. From the streets came a cacophony of horns, the loud mufflers of motorized rickshaws, the gruff acceleration of cargo trucks, and shouted profanities. The smell—a miasma of gasoline fumes, burning oil, and black-smoke emissions—was equally offensive. He had come to regard it not as an affront but as part of the local color.

He stepped inside one of the ubiquitous public call offices—known simply as PCO. It was no bigger than a closet, with three computer stations and a phone booth the size of an MRI tube. Daniel got a code from the shopkeeper and went inside the booth, closing a loosely hinged Plexiglas door behind him.

He looked at his watch. It was about seven thirty in the morning in London. He scrolled through the address book in his phone for the number, then dialed it on the archaic Indian phone. The distant double ring brought memories of Europe and of her.

Sir Richard picked up on the third ring. "Weston here."

"Richard," Daniel said, not bothering with the honorifics, even though one was a titled aristocrat and the other hailed from a mountain backwater. "It's Daniel. Daniel Madigan."

"Madigan. What a surprise." Sir Richard's tone was cheerful. "Where in God's name are you?"

Daniel was relieved. He had not spoken to Sarah's father since the confrontation in Brussels, when father and daughter had cut off all ties after a spectacular showdown of wills. Against his orders and the rigid viewpoint of the Establishment, she had exposed the transgressions of a company with political ties to the crown.

It was the first time in her life Sarah had defied her father to such a degree, and he'd punished her dearly for it. Daniel had watched Sir Richard walk away, stonehearted, from his only child, sending a clear message: if she wasn't willing to play by his rules, he would disinherit her.

Daniel knew how that must have wounded Sarah. His own father had walked away from the family when Daniel was young.

But unlike his father, who never finished high school and preferred the bottle to a steady job, Sir Richard—the respected politician Lord Weston—was an educated, reasonable man. His own father's bad behavior he could put down to ignorance; Sir Richard's was far more sinister. Even though he had reservations about the man's character, he preferred not to make an enemy of him. "Calling you from Delhi," he said.

"You are in India? Whatever for?"

"Long story," Daniel said, looking about the small room and the street beyond. "I don't have time to explain. Listen, I'm hoping you can help me with something."

There was a brief silence. "All right. Go on."

"Alastair Bromley. Do you know him?"

"Bromley. Yes, of course. He's in the Commons. Why do you ask?"

"Okay. Is he on any committees? Is he championing any bills?"

"He sits on Foreign Affairs and is on the Quadripartite

Committee on Arms Export Controls. He's a bit of a *liberal* chap," he said with obvious contempt.

"Interesting. Any idea what his background is?"

"I don't know him well . . . I do know he's from the North. Edinburgh, I think. He's CEO of a small but rapidly growing manufacturing company called Advanced Electronic Solutions. They make instruments and components for naval ships. The Royal Navy is their biggest client."

"So we're talking military defense."

"That's correct." Sir Richard's tone turned skeptical, even suspicious. "And of what importance is this to a cultural anthropologist?"

"I can't really go into it," Daniel said. An explanation would have been counterproductive. The last thing he needed now was for Sir Richard to become implicated by association. And he didn't want to tip him off to the dangers facing his estranged daughter.

Sir Richard, ever the diplomat, asked his question another way. "And how is your expedition going, old boy? Carrying on swimmingly, I should hope."

Daniel didn't want to lie. Sir Richard could learn the truth with some snooping. "Right now we're on hold. We had a little fire, and we're just trying to rebuild from the damage."

"Oh?"

"It's nothing, Richard. Situation's under control."

Sir Richard was quiet a moment. "And Sarah?"

Daniel weighed his reply. Despite the falling out between the man and his daughter, Sir Richard must have still cared about her. "She's in Israel, consulting a biblical archaeologist about an object we dug up."

"Israel. Fascinating. And you're in India."

"Listen, Richard, I'm running out of time on this calling card . . ."

"Why don't you call me back from your mobile? I do wish to finish this conversation."

"I'll try you again later. Gotta go. Good talking to you . . . as always."

Daniel hung up and exhaled. Perhaps it was a mistake calling him. Another misstep.

He sat at one of the computer stations and looked up Advanced Electronic Solutions, hoping for any nugget that would point to a relationship between Bromley and the enigmatic, wealthy Englishman holed up in Varanasi. As expected, the company website offered nothing but propaganda. But a few scattered news reports shed a little light on the company's plans, if not those of Bromley himself.

There were two Daniel found particularly interesting. The first was a report of a pending merger between AES and the American aircraft electronic systems manufacturer Apex Avionics. Apex was a supplier of GPS navigation, missile guidance systems, and countermeasure dispenser systems for military aircraft. Notably, Apex supplied components to the US Air Force but also sold to foreign governments, including Saudi Arabia and Egypt. Considering the client base, the merger would make AES a major player not only in the British defense industry, giving giants like BAE Systems a run for their money, but on the international stage as well.

What he found equally intriguing was a reference to an AES subsidiary, EastCorp, a small but innovative electronics company based in Jerusalem. That company, a magnet for young, talented Israeli scientists, had become known worldwide for its advanced radar countermeasures. Components manufactured by EastCorp were used mainly by the Israeli military, but contracts were being penned between the company and other nations.

Daniel found nothing immediately questionable about Bromley—what little press there was about him painted him as upstanding. But the more he dug, the more references he found to his voting record, which underscored Sir Richard's comment. *He's a bit of a liberal chap.* In one particularly telling case, Bromley had voted in favor of exporting smart—self-destructing, cluster—munitions, a highly lucrative category. That was back in 2005 as part of a heated debate that ultimately resulted in the British government's decision to eliminate some types of cluster munitions from its arsenal. Indeed, the entire world jumped on that bandwagon, and by 2008 there was a worldwide ban on cluster bombs.

There were other such cases pointing to Bromley's appetite for arming versus disarming. Daniel filed that information away and shifted his focus to the intel he'd gathered in Varanasi.

He paid the attendant and stepped out into the chaotic sights and sounds of Delhi. He hailed a rickshaw—a motorized, three-wheeled two seater painted in blocks of yellow and grass green—and asked the driver to take him to the University of Delhi.

The university library was as crowded as every other place in Delhi. Students occupied all the chairs, and more stood around the computer stations and tables or leaned against walls, glancing at books. The aisles were choked, and the reference desks were stacked seven deep with students waiting to ask questions. Daniel wondered how they functioned with such little personal space, though he realized this was all they'd ever known.

He walked upstairs to a mezzanine area that was slightly quieter. A young library worker in a bright blue sari was putting books away.

"I'm looking for any maps you might have of the Judean Desert in Israel," he said to her.

She took a step backwards, clearly unsure what to make of the limping foreigner and his unusual question. "Maps are in the reference area, behind the desk. I do not know if we have any that match that description."

He winked at the girl, which elicited a look of equal parts bewilderment and intrigue, and walked to the map section. He found two volumes of interest—a cartographer's rendition of biblical Israel and Judah and a set of topographic maps of modern Israel. He looked inside the latter first.

Daniel recalled the areas that were circled on the map—both were in the wild, arid terrain of the Judean Hills rising just above the Dead Sea, north of Masada. That was the southern edge of the Judean Desert, which sat between the sea and the Judean Mountain range to the west. The area was basically a complex of craggy escarpments, but it also was rich in caves, including the caves of Qumran, where the Dead Sea Scrolls were famously found by Bedouins in the 1940s. It sat atop a major aquifer that flowed from the mountains into the Dead Sea, feeding the springs of the Ein Gedi Oasis.

He had a flashback to the mysterious line from the scroll—*I wander shoeless in the desert, searching for my beloved*—and was now almost certain this was the desert the author spoke of. He looked for a free computer and noticed a student getting up from one of the stations. He quickly sat down and called up the first book of Samuel from the Old Testament—the Hebrew Bible. He scrolled to the part about David fleeing the madness of the reigning King Saul.

*And it came to pass, when Saul was returned from fol-
lowing the Philistines, that it was told him, saying, Behold,
David is in the wilderness of Engedi. Then Saul took three
thousand chosen men out of all Israel, and went to seek
David and his men upon the rocks of the wild goats. And
he came to the sheepcotes by the way, where was a cave; and
Saul went in to cover his feet: and David and his men remained in the sides of the cave.*

Daniel checked the map of ancient Israel for the location of the Ein Gedi wilderness in biblical times. It was
the precise spot referenced in the map he found in Varanasi—a vast, rocky plateau above the oasis, a place more
suitable for wild goats than humans.

Sarah's theory was beginning to ring true.

If the scroll pointed the way to a biblical artifact,
it was possible that somewhere in that realm of ancient
caves and windswept hills lay one of the most significant
archaeological finds of modern times.

Daniel knew exactly what he had to do.

Chapter 15

It was six in the morning when Sarah arrived in Jerusalem. The light of day had not yet cast its warm glow over the land, and the city, a compacted jumble of old stone structures and ancient ruins surrounded by modern buildings, was suffused in the steel-blue hues of early dawn. Only the gilded crown of the Dome of the Rock, the Muslim shrine that looked down upon the old city from the top of Temple Mount, glittered golden, seemingly radiating a light of its own. The dome's brilliance, assured by an outer layer created with eighty kilos of gold, was never extinguished, shining like a beacon to the faithful at all hours of the day.

Sarah parked outside the walls of the old city and entered on foot through the Dung Gate, on the southwestern edge of Temple Mount. The masonry gate, a structure that had been constructed, destroyed, and reconstructed over the centuries, welcomed visitors through a modest arched passageway. Its ramparts hinted at the city's history of fortification against the bloody sieges that inevitably came upon it. Such was the fate of a city deemed holy and claimed as God's kingdom on Earth by not one but three religions.

She came to the Western Wall—the Jews' infamous Wailing Wall—and took in the activity as dawn broke over the city. She stood at an appropriate distance, respectful of those who came to worship. The ancient structure, a relic from the second temple period that was curiously left intact by the Romans who destroyed the temple above it, was sacred to the Jews. Every day the wall heard their prayers.

At first light, the pious had already gathered for their morning devotions. Some stood close to the wall, yarmulke-covered heads leaning on the ashlar masonry stones; others stood or sat a few steps back in quiet contemplation. A group of men cloaked in *tallitot*—white, fringed prayer shawls with black and neutral-colored stripes—stood with heads bowed, reading scriptures. Their faith was palpable, and their worship had a quiet, humble quality, more a lament than an exaltation.

Rabbi Uri'el Ben Moshe lived in the Jewish Quarter, at the foot of Temple Mount just behind the Western Wall. He did not lead a synagogue, possibly because he was entering his eighth decade and had tired of the politics of organized worship, yet he had a following. His teachings, delivered mostly through books and word of mouth, made him one of Judaism's most respected spiritual leaders.

He also had a group of faithful students who regularly came to his home for spiritual guidance and in-depth study of both traditional and mystical Jewish texts. It was through one of these students—an acquaintance of Ezra—that Sarah found the rabbi's address.

Daylight had not yet penetrated the stone alleys of the Jewish Quarter. Activity would not begin in earnest for another couple of hours, so Sarah was practically alone as she wandered the cobbled streets. At that hour, a ghostlike quiet had befallen the stone arcades, and she could hear her own footfall as she climbed the steps to her destination.

Everything here—the cobblestones, the buttresses, the modest buildings made of dressed stones the color of sand—seemed to be of the earth. The few bursts of color, mostly storefront signs and awnings, were incongruous, violating the ancient quality of the place. Israeli flags hung on poles or were draped from open windows, reminding everyone whose home this was.

Sarah walked beneath a series of flying buttresses connecting one side of the alley to the other. She passed through a notched archway that led to a courtyard, in the midst of which sat a lone olive tree. As the sun's first rays crept over the buildings that enclosed the tree like a stone fortress, the play between light and shadow gave life to the monochrome scene. She regarded the tree's silvery leaves, its twisted trunk's textured bark. Regardless of the tumult the city had faced through the ages, the olive tree persisted, a silent witness to the past, enduring in spite of man's impositions.

She continued through a path that led to another series of steps. The narrow alley at the top of the steps was the one she was seeking. An almost forgotten strip on the edge of the Quarter, it was walled in on one end, so that the only ingress and egress was the small stone staircase. There were a few doors along the alley, all of them residential. She looked for the number and found it on a weathered wood door with rusted iron hardware. She tapped the heavy iron ring knocker lightly on the door so the sound heard inside was gentle, not aggressive.

Three minutes passed, and no one answered. Sarah knocked again. After a long moment, a voice came from the other side of the door.

"State your purpose," a man said in Hebrew.

Her Hebrew was limited, but she attempted it anyway. "Rav Ben Moshe, I come seeking guidance. I am an archaeologist." Unable to find the words in Hebrew, she continued in English. "I need your help deciphering an ancient riddle."

He cracked the door open and peered at her from the shadows. "You want spirit to answer where science falls short?"

She was surprised he spoke English. "Something like that, yes."

He opened the door and gestured for her to come in. The rabbi was a good four inches shorter than Sarah's five-ten and looked shorter still since his shoulders were hunched. His hair was pure white and pulled back in a bun at the nape of his neck. A simple black yarmulke capped the back of his head. A wiry white beard fanned out from his face and grazed his collarbone. He wore a white shirt covered with a wide-sleeved, black wool long jacket that was wrapped across his chest and tied at the waist with a rope belt. He led her inside. Though he walked using a cane, his step was spry and confident for a man his age.

They entered a sitting room. Steadying himself on his cane, he sat down with some effort on an aging olive-green velvet sofa draped at the back and arms with embroidered textiles.

She sat on the edge of a chair opposite him.

"Forgive my skepticism," he said in heavily accented English. "Archaeologists and rabbis don't exactly see eye to eye. Especially in this country."

"I can't apologize for my profession, nor is it my intention to disparage yours. But I do hope we can begin from a place of mutual respect."

She could feel his eyes probing her for any trace of insincerity. It was the age-old dilemma of living in a place so intensely contested: nobody could trust anyone or take a thing at face value. In that regard, they weren't so unlike each other.

"I want to speak to you about a biblical figure. King Solomon."

He adjusted his spectacles. "One of my favorite subjects. What is it you want to know?"

"We have uncovered a scroll we think may be authored by him and executed by one of the scribes in his court—an Egyptian woman."

"A woman. That's very fascinating indeed."

"Precisely my thinking. According to her seal, she was in service to the queen."

"Pharaoh's daughter?"

"Presumably, yes." She leaned forward. "We have no proof that any of this is accurate. This is only a theory of mine. I am hoping you will help me either advance that theory or discard it."

He twisted the ends of his beard. "I'm sure I don't have to tell you the world is utterly lacking in artifacts relating to Solomon. And every time something surfaces that could be attributed to him, it disappears just as quickly. Very curious, isn't it?"

Her face tightened. She probed for the facts behind his veiled statement. "What do you mean?"

He waved off her question. "Tell me what you want to know."

"The minimalist position is that Solomon, if he existed at all, was ruler of a small tribal hinterland, not the empire of biblical testimony. The wealth, the wisdom, the wives . . . it's all a myth designed to perpetuate a legend of Davidic entitlement. As a biblical scholar, what do you think?"

"In our faith, young lady, Kings Solomon and David make up a significant cornerstone. We pray for the day the one with Davidic blood running in his veins will rise up and bring peace to the world. As for what I think of the archaeologists who hold to this minimalist view, I pity their souls. It is a terrible thing to not know spirit."

Despite her putting forth the minimalist counterargument, Sarah did not personally believe it. Though she was far from a woman of faith, years of experience had taught her there were questions science alone could not answer. "How do you interpret the biblical stories about Solomon?"

"The story of Solomon is presented very differently in the books of Kings and Chronicles. In Chronicles, he is practically deified. In Kings, he is presented as a flawed man who began with a strong faith but ultimately went astray. If you are asking what I think . . . I believe the Kings version is closer to the truth."

"And the temple?"

"The Bible says he built the temple. I believe it is so."

"Even though no proof whatsoever has been found?"

The rabbi smiled serenely. "A land like Israel is full of proof that has never been found. Her soil holds answers you and I can't even fathom." He pointed in the direction of Temple Mount. "What lies beneath the Mount? Do you know? Will you ever know? I know you are an archaeologist and cannot take anything on faith, but you must allow for the possibility. Your science is far from perfect."

"I wouldn't be here if I didn't allow for the possibility."

He bowed slightly. "Point taken."

She took a notebook out of her backpack and turned to her notes. "I'd like to read you something, and I'd like you to tell me if it resonates with the Solomonic vision in your own mind. May I?"

He gestured for her to continue.

She read from the text. "'My son, the dusk of my life is upon me. I wander shoeless in the desert, searching for my beloved. I have been blessed with riches and wisdom and wives aplenty, but now, as my youth withers and my powers fail me, I seek solace in her breast.'"

Rabbi Ben Moshe shifted his gaze, looking at nothing in particular. After a long silence, he said, "In addition to what we know from the Bible, there are mystical texts that contain clues about Solomon's life and times. The latter are full of metaphors and philosophical arguments. They're not meant to be accepted as written but rather to urge the reader to think multidimensionally in his search for spiritual truth. I say this as a preface, because I want to reference both to answer your question."

"This is why I came to you," she said, aware of his reputation for controversial exegesis of the Bible and his profound command of the midrashim—the rabbinic literature dedicated to the underlying significance of biblical texts.

"The part about wandering in the desert does appear in various texts, from the Kabbalah to the Quran," he said. "The legend says that he was deposed from the throne because of his sins and wandered as a pauper for forty days. Depending on which version of the story you believe, he was either absolved of his trespasses and returned to the throne or he died a commoner in anonymity."

"What do you think?"

"My position has always been that Solomon was a man of God but not godlike. He was given power at a young age and grew up on the throne. He had wisdom, but he had weaknesses too. He struggled . . . and triumphed . . . and failed. Like all men, then and now. In his time, wandering for forty days would not have been out of character for a king who was very much defined by his faith. He very likely chose to wander the desert—shoeless, as you say—to come to terms with his own spirituality. By all accounts, from the Bible to the apocryphal texts, he had strayed. Wealth, power, and pleasures of the flesh had blinded him to his true purpose. He could easily have left the palace one day, with nothing but the tattered clothes on his back, and gone to find himself."

"What desert might he have gone to?"

"Nobody knows this. But it was probably one in close

proximity to Jerusalem. The Judean Desert, most likely."

"We found this scroll buried in Saudi Arabia, on the edge of the Rub' al Khali." Sarah knew it was a long shot, but she asked anyway. "How could it have gotten there?"

He shrugged. "I couldn't say."

There was no easy answer to the question that gnawed at her mind. "Could he have given it to Makeda, the Queen of Sheba, when she came to visit him in Jerusalem? Could she have been carrying it, along with other gifts, in her caravan?"

"It is possible, I suppose."

"Are you aware of a story in the Kebra Nagast that says Makeda and Solomon had a son? Supposedly, she gave birth to that child, Menelik, during the long ride back home."

"Of course I know the story. It is said he built a second Jerusalem in Ethiopia." He squinted behind his spectacles. "What is your point?"

"Rabbi, the scroll makes several references to a divine secret and to a treasure. I suspect that doesn't mean material wealth but rather a trove of knowledge—something Solomon knew and wanted to pass on to his son— perhaps his son Rehoboam, who succeeded him on the throne, or perhaps . . ."

"His illegitimate son with the Queen of Sheba." The rabbi shook his head. "I couldn't comment on that. But to your point about treasure, if something was worth hiding, it wouldn't have been gold. Wealth was temporal; it came and went. What endured, and what was worth preserving, was something granted by God—a covenant, for example. That's why the Ark of the Covenant has been moved and hidden so many times over the millennia, and why still no one knows where it is."

She agreed in theory but did not believe in a divinely granted covenant. Her instincts told her that, whatever this treasure was, it was the work of man. But there was no time for such philosophical debate, particularly since it almost certainly would lead to impasse.

"Let me read you another passage, if I may." She read from the translated text. "'The orchard is profuse with fig, the vines heavy with grape. When my lover's face appears from the shadows, all mysteries are revealed. Her beauty illuminates the path and the dark stones, and I follow, powerless to resist. What power hast thou over me, O fair nymph? And she saith, All that is hidden I will show thee, all that you hunger for I will feed to thee, but only if thou art faithful. Come with me now to the ramparts, under the gaze of the mountain, and partake of my love, for when the rooster crows I will be gone, but thou will have all that thou desire.'"

When Sarah looked up, the rabbi was leaning on his cane with shaking hands. His gaze was distant, his skin pallid.

Worried that his health was failing, she stood. "Are you all right? Can I get you some water?"

He pointed to the chair. "Sit."

She did, unsure what was going on.

"Where is this scroll?" Despite his agitated look, his voice was quiet and calm.

She sighed. "It's been stolen. A courier had come to collect it for delivery to King Saud University, only he never made it there. The lorry was found on the side of the highway, and the university escort had been murdered. The courier and the scroll were gone." Her eyes scanned his face, reading his reaction. "I should like to know what you are thinking."

The rabbi looked away. "He has returned."

"Who has returned?"

He turned to her, his face now stern. "Young lady, if you know what's good for you, you will abandon this. Otherwise, your fate could match that of the university escort . . . or that of my followers."

She was surprised. She had gone there looking for guidance—not a connection. That was an unexpected twist she was determined to learn more about. "Hear me, Rabbi. Since this scroll surfaced, we have had nothing but calamity. Our crew has been poisoned, the site we were studying was damaged in a fire during which men were horribly injured or killed, and now, with the theft of the scroll, the expedition has been shuttered and my partner and I are practically fugitives." Emotion crept into her voice as she recounted the events of the past weeks.

She took a deep breath. "If you know something about this madman we are up against, I beg you to tell me."

Rabbi Ben Moshe fell into silence. The mist in his eyes shimmered as the morning light came in through the window. Finally, he spoke. "About six years ago, I was living in Poland, a small town in the north, in the middle of nowhere. There stood a modest synagogue that was built entirely by hand by a group of Jews fleeing the Crusades in the twelfth century. There was nothing remarkable about the stones that were used to build it—except for one. It was an ancient stone rumored to have come from Jerusalem, which had been passed from hand to hand by those who knew it was sacred. It had survived centuries of diaspora and persecution because of this organized attempt to keep it hidden. Only certain members of the rabbinate knew about it."

"I assume that includes you."

"Yes. It was the reason I went to Poland in the first place. We had lost the rabbi who was in charge there, and I was chosen to take his place."

"And what is this stone? Why is it sacred?"

The rabbi looked around nervously. He leaned into his cane and spoke softly. "Our tradition holds that it was one of the stones used in the temple of Solomon—the first temple built in Jerusalem. According to an unwritten legend, this stone was wedged into the ramparts around Mount Moriah—the fortress that protected the temple.

It was inscribed with a simple image: two jagged peaks depicting a mountain."

Come with me now to the ramparts, under the gaze of the mountain. Sarah felt the familiar tempest in her gut as she considered the possibility of a connection between the message in the scroll and an actual object dating to the period of the first temple. If it were true, the ramifications would be enormous. The two artifacts together could point to the existence of a temple in Jerusalem during Solomon's reign—something that had eluded historians and archaeologists to that day, sparking fierce debate between the academic and theological communities. But that stone, like the scroll, was likely lost. As Ezra had said, the synagogue in Poland had been raided and burned down.

She knew the answer before asking. "This stone . . . where is it now?"

"Before I tell you, let me give you a little background. When the Babylonians destroyed the temple in the sixth century BCE, a priest took the stone and hid it. Since that day, it had been in the possession of the men and women who were closest to God. We don't have the exact chronology, but legend says the stone was carried out of Jerusalem sometime in the early twelfth century, soon after the Crusaders captured the city. It was entrusted to a woman—a descendant of the long forgotten House of David—who feigned love for one of the Crusaders and left with him when he returned to Europe."

"Were all the keepers of the stone members of the Davidic dynasty?"

"No. It started out that way, but by the thirteenth century all traces of Davidic heirs were erased. Killed, mostly, or gone into hiding to avoid persecution. The Jews have faced difficult times"—he waved a hand—"here, and everywhere. It hasn't been easy to hold on to our history."

"I understand the synagogue was burned. Did this have something to do with the stone?"

A sorrowful look descended upon his face. "Yes. Or, more to the point, with the object hidden within the stone."

Sarah remembered Ezra's comment about the ring. She studied the rabbi's face. It was pale as sailcloth, his eyes full of unease. She didn't let on she knew; instead, she read the rest of the passage. "'Our love is a perfect circle forged of earthly matter but anointed by celestial grace. Its mystery unfolds and, lo, there is rapture in the heavens. Give to me thy chest of treasure and I will give thee the key that unlocks it.'"

"This text," he said, "is a reference to that object. It was a ring—the ring of the king."

According to a legend she'd always dismissed as the fantasy of medieval occultists, King Solomon used a magical signet ring to communicate with the beyond realms. "Are you referring to the Seal of Solomon? The ring with supernatural powers? I've always thought that was invented."

He smiled. "The king had a ring. The rest of that nonsense was invented. As were a lot of things about Solomon. If you think about it, he was probably the most controversial person in history. Everyone has a version about who—and what—he was. Wise man, great monarch, builder of empires, voracious lover, idolater, magician . . . Sounds more like the makings of a Hollywood film than Judahite history, no?"

"Indeed. This ring, then . . . was simply a ring?"

"Well, not quite. The last line you read me was the most significant. The ring was meant to be a key that unlocked a manuscript left behind by Solomon. That is what the unwritten history says." He paused to take a deep breath. "It is also said that the manuscript and the ring together have unspeakable power. They are to be brought together only by the messiah."

Sarah had so many questions. Scientific method discounted factors such as an oral apocryphal history. But she held evidence—an ancient scroll lost in a distant desert—that some of that history might be true. She suspected the manuscript the rabbi spoke of and the treasure referenced in the scroll were one and the same.

"What can you tell me about this manuscript?" she asked. "Do the apocrypha speak of its contents or give a clue as to its whereabouts?"

"Not of its contents. That is a mystery unsolved since

ancient times. As for its location, all we know is that it is meant to be somewhere in ancient Judah. My guess is that it is very well hidden. I doubt someone would stumble upon it, as was the case with the Dead Sea Scrolls."

"We may have a hint," she said. "What do you make of this? 'She dwells in the darkest depths of the valiant king's fortress.'"

"The valiant king would not have been Solomon. Solomon was not a warrior, nor was he known for his valor. That would have been David, his father."

"So his fortress would be his palace."

"Maybe . . . maybe not. In ancient times, the word 'fortress' was not used quite as it is today. Its meaning would be closer to 'stronghold' or 'cave.'" He rose with some effort and walked out of the room. He returned a few minutes later holding a copy of the Hebrew Bible.

She stood and helped him take a seat. She sat next to him on the sofa.

"Let me read you something." He leafed through the book and stopped to read. "'And David went up from there, and he stayed in the strongholds of En-gedi. And it was, when Saul had returned from following the Philistines, that they told him, saying, "David is in the Desert of En-gedi." And Saul took three thousand picked men from all Israel, and went to seek David and his men on the Rocks of the Wild Goats. And he came to the sheepcotes on the way, and there was a cave, and Saul went in to cover his feet, while David and his men were staying at the end of the cave.' Depending on which translation you use, the 'wilderness of En-gedi' is also called 'the stronghold of En-gedi' or the 'fortresses at En-gedi.' It was where David hid with his men while he was being hunted by Saul. That's one reference to a fortress where David dwelled. There are others—"

She interrupted him. "No. That's the one. I'm certain of it."

"How can you be?"

A single word within the scroll text had given her a clue. "Balsam," she said. "In the same passage, there is a specific reference to balsam. Ein Gedi is one of the few places in the Holy Land where balsam is grown."

"Even so," he said, "Ein Gedi is a vast wilderness. The network of caves on the plateau above the springs is rather considerable, and some of those caves are deep and complex. Searching for a buried artifact there could take years. And it sounds to me like time is not on your side."

Sarah knew the rabbi was right. But if the scroll really was a map pointing the way through metaphor and allegory, she was confident she could pick up the crumb trail left by King Solomon so many years ago. All that remained now was to get to Ein Gedi and let the place speak to her. It wasn't scientific or even rational, but her instinct told her it might just work. She needed to know one last thing.

"Rabbi, there is something I must ask. When the synagogue in Poland was razed, what became of the stone?"

"It was taken. No one has seen or heard of it since."

"Any idea who was behind the fire?"

"Oh, yes." A bitter smile crossed his lips. "It was a British fellow. Said his name was Asher, but who knows if that's the truth. He had come to Poland to study under me, or so he said. He stayed there less than two weeks before the incident."

Sarah started. Another connection. Everything pointed to the same person being responsible for both fires—and both thefts. "How can you be sure he set the fire?"

"Witnesses. A village couple, out walking their dog late at night, saw someone dousing the place in gasoline. The man went back in the house to call the police and then brought out his binoculars for a closer look. By the time the police arrived, the place was already up in flames and he was long gone. But the villager was able to identify him as a lanky fellow with long, black hair worn in a ponytail. Not too many people in rural Poland matched that description."

A chill raked Sarah's flesh as she recalled the fire at the Qaryat al-Fau site. She could still smell the stench of gasoline and the foul smoke. And she could never forget the words etched onto the charred earth. "Was anything left behind? A message?"

He looked at her quizzically. "No . . . nothing was

written, if that's what you mean."

"I ask because a message was left at Qaryat al-Fau. It said, 'The army is coming. Let no man stand in the way of the judgment.' What could that mean?"

"The army? God's army?" He stroked the ends of his white beard. "The 'judgment,' in Judaism, refers to a time when all Jews will be called back to Israel. It's part of the messianic prophecy."

"Could that be what we're looking at here? Someone acting out that prophecy?"

"Your guess is as good as mine, young lady. But whatever it is, no good can come of it." He steadied himself on his cane and stood. "I must go now; I have a student coming in. It's been a most illuminating morning." He put a hand on her shoulder. "I like to think good triumphs over evil, but that's not always the case. I think you know what you're up against. Just watch yourself."

Sarah lowered her head and took his gnarled hand in both of hers, silently conveying her thanks. His gentle touch warmed her, made her feel strong. Her trepidation was overshadowed by her determination to unravel one of antiquity's great mysteries. The answers waited for her in the untamed heart of the Judean Wilderness.

Chapter 16

*E*in Gedi had retained its rugged character of biblical times. In the lower plateaus along the banks of the Dead Sea, the place was quite fertile, with date palm orchards, waterfalls, and springs fed by two rivers—an oasis in the midst of a rocky realm.

Sarah stood at the edge of one of those springs, her thoughts overtaken by the murmur of rushing water. Silvery threads of water cascaded down a vertical rock face carved into symmetrical horizontal layers by the hands of time. Emerald-colored vegetation clung to the crags, a reminder that even in the harshest conditions life triumphed.

It was almost dusk. Sarah knew the perils of climbing in the dark, but she had no choice. Ein Gedi was no longer deserted, as it was in the time of David. The place was now teeming with tourists and dotted with their hotels, restaurants, and bars. There was even a kibbutz with a botanical garden and a spring water bottling facility.

But that was worlds away. Where she was going, signs of human habitation were almost nonexistent. Only the most intrepid souls made their way up to the high plateaus and into the forbidding network of caves.

She ascended a well-worn trail on the side of the waterfall, using the plentiful handholds on the porous limestone. At the top of the trail, she surveyed the terrain to the west. A series of arid peaks and valleys obscured the horizon line: the lithic wilderness of the Judean Desert.

The rock, glowing like fired iron in the afternoon light, betrayed the trials this wild outpost had endured. From Roman occupation to Jewish rebel revolt, the place had persevered through it all, the blood on its soil evanesced by the hot, dry breath of a cruel sun or washed away in the freak floods that often befell the region.

That rocky realm, hostile as it was, was her destination. She walked in that direction until the sun, a massive golden orb intersected by threads of magenta cloud, began its descent behind the mountaintops. Sundown came swiftly to this place, and soon the rocky wasteland would be shrouded in darkness. It was dangerous to be in the desert, among the wolves and leopards, at night. But climbing in the dark here, where the drop-offs were precipitous and came without warning, was practically suicidal.

Sarah was not without worry. Though she trusted her abilities, she did not know this terrain. She felt a pang of loneliness. The last time she attempted a hazardous night climb, in the Ethiopian backcountry, she was not alone. Had she been, she might not have survived it. She lowered her head and pressed her eyes shut. *What have I done?*

In leaving the al-Fau expedition and Daniel's side, she had put emotion before reason. Like the Judean Wilderness, for her that was uncharted terrain. She was alone, a ship adrift in a rushing river of peril without ballast, without an oar. And so, she imagined, was he.

There was no time for regrets. She clenched her jaw and took a deep breath. Whatever the consequences of her actions, she would own them. She had always relied on her own wits and hers alone before he came along; she would do so again.

She reached inside her backpack for her headlamp and strapped it on. She continued walking along the plateau until she reached a series of chalky cliffs, sculpted into eerie, face-like forms by the winds of the ages. She pulled out her sit harness and stepped into it, clipping on her rope using a figure eight knot. She pushed an anchor into the rock and slipped the rope through.

Sarah was well aware of the dangers of rope soloing without a partner to belay her. In the craggy cliff country of the Tuwaiq Escarpment, Daniel had trained her on the advanced technique of self-belaying. She didn't think at the time she'd have to use it.

In the absence of someone keeping friction on the rope, the risk of a long, unprotected fall was great. The impending darkness compounded matters.

She fastened a self-belay device to her harness, tying the rope into it in a clove hitch. Her heart pounded as she jammed her foot into a toehold and took the first step up. Light was diminishing fast. She raced up the cliff so she could get to the top before nightfall and examine the surroundings.

Inserting a series of anchors through which to pass the rope, she negotiated the sheer face faster than she should have. Just below the cliff ledge, her upper body muscles burned as she held onto the rope with one hand, anchoring with the other. With both feet in toeholds, she let go of the rope and grabbed the ledge. With teeth clenched, she pulled herself up. She suppressed a loud groan, lest it echo off the canyons. The last thing she needed was for the night predators to hear her.

On the top of the cliff, Sarah stopped to catch her breath. By now the sky was an abstract painting of magenta plumes on a violet canvas, with flecks of gold above the darkening mountaintops at the horizon line. The rocky landscape beneath her feet was shrouded in shadow. Only the highest peaks reflected the sun, red-hot tips in a sea of gathering blackness.

With a pair of binoculars she scanned the rugged terrain, hoping to spot the network of caves carved into the rock faces. She knew the Judean Desert was rich in caves, some of which had been occupied by shepherds and rebel warriors during biblical times, others by refugees in wartime as early as the first centuries of the Common Era. Archaeologists had explored several of these, and their research had borne fruit in the form of sarcophagi, papyri, tools, and vessels. The cave she was looking for, however, had almost certainly been overlooked by her colleagues. She had a hunch the wise king would not have made it too easy.

In the distance, along a cliffside beyond a ravine, three openings in the rock looked like the features of a face. These caves were fairly inaccessible—one would have to climb the rock in order to reach them—but their construction appeared man-made. She hypothesized these were carved out of the rock by Jews seeking strongholds during the Bar Kokhba revolt against the Romans. The fortress where the valiant king dwelled—David's hiding place in the tenth century BCE—would have occurred naturally.

She lowered her binoculars. Nothing was apparent to her. She was sure that was by design. That was why the scroll was written, after all. It was to be a map, though its destination points were marked not by diagrams but by words meant to be understood by only those who believed.

Under the darkest cloak of night the temptress appears.

She waited. Here, on top of a cliff above the high plateaus, the world came to a standstill. Nothing stirred in the desert—even the hyrax and ibex that often scampered among the rocks were nowhere to be found. The air was inert, without so much as a whisper of a breeze to freshen it. She inhaled the fragrance of ancient earth. It was dry, dusty, and vaguely sulphuric. In the utter silence, she was one with this wild land.

The sun completed its journey beneath the dark silhouettes of the mountains, leaving a streak of gold in its wake. Within moments, the indigo veil of night covered the sky and the evening star appeared, flickering like a flame in the *sharav*. The dunes and canyons of the Judean Wilderness melted into a shapeless black mass.

Sarah faced east. The moonrise was her only hope for distinguishing detail in the darkened landscape. The air grew frigid. She shivered and gathered her knees to her chest. She was dressed in a long-sleeved, lightweight wool T-shirt with a polypropelene thermal layer beneath and black climbing pants—hardly enough to keep out the night chill. She would have to stay on the move to keep warm.

The first trace of luminescence appeared behind the mountains. Like a nymph revealing herself slowly to an adoring lover, the full moon rose an inch at a time, growing more and more brilliant with every increment. A halo surrounded the sphere of pale golden light as it ascended the inky sky. It was so close she could discern the faint outline of craters and valleys on its pockmarked surface.

At last it showed its full face. It was bigger and more swollen with light than she had ever seen it. The Hunter's

Moon. For a fleeting moment it hung above the horizon like an ethereal promise.

A wolf howled in the distance.

Sarah had only a few minutes to find what she was seeking, which would be revealed only while the moon wore its gossamer golden veil.

She is redolent of balsam and good spices, and her fingers are dusted with gold.

With binoculars, she scanned the illuminated landscape, slowly turning three hundred sixty degrees. Facing northwest, she stopped and lowered her binoculars. For a moment, she forgot to breathe.

A cliff, by day like any other, was rendered surreal by the light of the ascendant moon. Three limestone protrusions were brushed by golden light, glowing like ancient, twisted fingers against a backdrop of shadows. At the base of the cliff grew a lone tree, no taller than a shrub, with woody branches and scant leaves. *Commiphora gileadensis.* The famed balsam of Ein Gedi.

Midway up the cliff, between two of the protrusions, was a small opening that easily could be overlooked as an ordinary fissure in the rock. But she knew better. This was it: the fortress of one king and the hiding place of another.

The fine hairs on her arms stood on end. She could only imagine what secrets lay inside its stone confines.

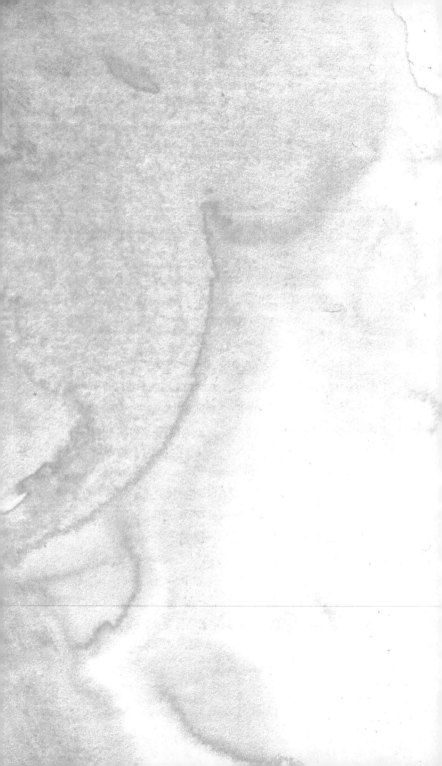

Chapter 17

The cliff was not easy to reach. Sarah mapped out her route, estimating the journey would take the better part of the night. She had to ascend to the high plateau, then cross the undulating expanse of rocky terrain en route to a deep ravine above a dry riverbed. On the other side of that ravine was the cliff and, presumably, the cave she believed it housed.

The moon, now a brilliant white disk hovering higher in the sky, granted a silvery luster to the bleak wilderness. A play between shadow and fragile light made the distant mountain range appear like a lunar landscape. She was grateful for the extra illumination; it was a boon in this treacherous, unforgiving country.

She rappelled down the lookout with relative ease, which boosted her confidence in her self-belaying ability. When her feet hit the ground, she gathered up the rope and anchors and placed them in her pack. She would need them again to descend the ravine and reach the opening on the cliff face. She fastened the chest and waist straps of her pack, adjusted the elastic band binding her thick blonde locks into a ponytail, and launched into a slow jog across the gradually ascending surface of the moonlit plateau.

A pair of wolves took turns howling. The sound issued from the top of a nearby rock formation but reverberated throughout the limestone bowl. Her heart rate quickened.

She stopped jogging when she reached a stretch of boulder-strewn terrain that trailed off into dips and rises—the land equivalent of cresting waves. She moved gingerly between the boulders, careful not to rouse snakes or scorpions or other cantankerous desert dwellers. She was amazed at how much flora grew in this part of the desert. Shrubs sprouted between the rocks, making the arid land appear impossibly fertile. There was water somewhere. Though two rivers—Nahal David and Nahal Arugot—flowed through Ein Gedi's canyons, they were quite far from where she stood. She wondered if some of the springs could be hidden underground.

Negotiating the peaks and valleys in this stretch of the desert slowed Sarah down considerably. There was no way to hurry through the undulating sea of petrified sand and limestone. She tried to find a meditative rhythm but she was too restless. So close to unearthing King Solomon's promise, she was powered by adrenaline and driven by an irrepressible desire to find answers to long-forgotten questions. Her senses were fully engaged. She felt alert, strong, alive.

At last she came to the edge of the ravine. Hands at her waist, she caught her breath after the physically demanding trek that had taken several hours—far longer than she'd calculated. She looked at her Timex and saw it was going on three o'clock. She had about three hours of darkness to complete her reconnaissance. She had to move quickly.

She studied the pitch of the ravine. It was near vertical and dropped almost two hundred feet to the canyon floor, where the rivers of antiquity once flowed. Illuminated by the moon's pale light, the rock face appeared as menacing as any she'd encountered. The tightly packed layers of hard limestone, blown raw by the desert winds over the millennia, were bleak and hostile. On the plus side, the texture of the rock afforded some hand- and footholds. But one wrong move could result in nasty injury.

Sarah knotted the rope onto her harness and tugged to make sure it was secure. Her plan was to top-rope, which was the least risky of her solo climbing options. She anchored the summit line around a boulder on the ledge. She questioned whether it was sturdy enough and decided not to rely on it completely. With her back to the drop, she stepped off the ledge, carefully holding onto the line, and climbed down about twenty feet to set her backup anchor. She screwed two hexes into the rock and attached carabiners to them. Then she passed a length of cordelette through the carabiners, bringing the ends together in one central point. That would serve as her belay station.

She tied her backpack to the end of the rope and let it drop. The weight would help the rope feed. She tugged on her anchor point, ensuring it was bombproof, and began to descend. She felt every muscle of her upper body engage as she tried to control her movements by holding the rope while trying to wedge her feet into cracks in the rock. Her vantage point was limited to what was in front of her: her rope, the integrity of the rock, the next foothold. There was nothing to do but take it a step at a time—and trust.

Knowing she was working against the clock unnerved her. She looked behind her, careful not to throw herself off-balance. She couldn't see the bottom or judge distance. She went back to work.

Despite the cliff's rich texture, footholds were not always available. In places, the rock was tightly stacked with no cracks. Sarah had to make do by using the slight protrusions in the rock as steps. It was folly on two levels: it wasn't as secure as a foothold, and it made her work harder, spending her reserves.

She managed to descend a good portion of the face—judging by the distance to the top of the cliff, she figured she was at least halfway down—before her legs started to feel shaky. She was feeling the effects of trekking through the night and solo climbing with scant visibility in particularly forbidding terrain.

"Just a little while longer," she whispered. Gritting her teeth, she said the words like a mantra. "You can do this."

The next few steps were strained. Her heart was beating faster now. Her muscles burned. She found a small ledge in the cliff face and stepped onto it, resting against the rock. She closed her eyes and caught her breath. The limestone felt cold and rough against her face. She breathed in the dry dust and chalky scent of the rock.

She opened her eyes and looked over her shoulder toward the cliff that was her target. She thought about the rabbi's words: *The ring was meant to be a key that unlocked a manuscript left behind by Solomon. That is what the unwritten history says.* The possibility of finding that manuscript gave her a sudden burst of energy.

She always had been nourished by the prospect of a magnificent find, something that could alter the way people perceived history, that could give credence to legend, that could shatter or bolster beliefs. It was the *raison d'être* of the archaeologist, the reward for all the mundane and mechanical undertakings that defined the profession. It was, perhaps, a romantic notion, but she ached so much for a game-changing revelation that she went all in to pursue it.

Conscious that time was running out, Sarah stepped

off the ledge and launched into the remainder of the descent. Her newfound energy was an illusion. Though she was mentally charged, physically she was too fatigued to continue safely. She knew it but had no choice. She counted on her mind to compensate where her body fell short.

She descended another thirty feet before feeling what climbers called "Elvis leg"—the uncontrollable shake of lower limbs due to overworked muscles. She pressed on anyway.

It was a mistake.

When she attempted to step into the next crack, her legs gave out completely and her foot slid off the rock, throwing her body off balance. In a desperate attempt to hang on, she grasped at the rock but missed. Her feet and hands lost all purchase, and she fell feetfirst into the void.

She knew her self-belay device would lock, preventing her from plummeting too far. But something went wrong. She heard the whirr of the device attempting futilely to do its job.

She was freefalling.

With all the strength she had left, she lunged toward the cliff, slamming against the rock. The effort jettisoned her headlamp, so now she was without light, but it slowed her momentum, giving her better control.

She clawed at the rock and was able to slow herself further. As she slid along the face, the exposed limestone scraping her skin, she was finally able to grab hold, ending the plunge that surely would have killed her. Gasping, she hung in the darkness, holding onto the rock with both hands.

She looked over her shoulder and watched the light of her headlamp, small as a pin's head, sail toward the ground. Judging by the time it took the object to reach the canyon floor, she surmised the distance was about fifty feet. She was so close.

She looked at the time again. It was almost five o'clock. One more hour of daylight. She had to ignore her throbbing muscles and give it one final push. She positioned her feet on the rock and slowly rappelled, her legs trembling with fatigue.

By the time she got to the ground she was exhausted and shaken. She looked up at the face she had just descended. In the waning moonlight it looked like an impenetrable wall, a rampart guarding the secrets of a kingdom.

Sarah gazed across the ravine at the cliff with the three fingers. Without the golden illumination of the rising moon, it looked nondescript, a rock formation like any other. Had she seen it in this light, without guidance from the scroll's enigmatic words, she never would have paid attention to it. Now she knew with every fiber of her being this was the right place.

She was eager to explore the rock for an opening. She needed her headlamp. She looked around for any trace of its light, but there was none. She figured it was turned off, or broken, by the impact. She reached into her pack for a penlight. Head down, she swept the blue light beam across the dark canyon floor. She searched the cracked, thirsty soil of the ancient riverbed but found nothing. She pointed her light to the shale along the dried river's banks. Nothing again.

Without looking up, she kept walking along the bed, slowly moving the light across what seemed like a thousand pottery shards. She heard a faint rustle, like something was crawling across the shale. She stopped and kneeled for a closer look. She pointed the light to her left, then slowly turned toward her right. Something was there.

Her light stopped on a man's boots.

She froze.

A male voice said, "Looking for this?"

Chapter 18

Sarah slowly looked up and saw a black-bearded, curly-haired man dressed in sand-colored fatigues. An Uzi was slung on his shoulder, and her headlamp dangled from his hand.

"Who are you?" Her voice trembled.

His robust laughter echoed off the rocky bowl. "You scared?" His face turned as expressionless as the old stones. "You should be."

She stood. She took a deep breath and said nothing.

He tossed her headlamp on the ground next to her feet. "I think you ought to come with me." He spoke English with a harsh accent that led her to believe he was Israeli. "The boss doesn't take kindly to intruders."

"Intruders? The Judean Desert wasn't private property, last I checked."

"Shut up and walk." He pointed to the path with his Uzi and walked behind her.

With the man following so closely she could hear the rustle of his fatigues, Sarah walked at a brisk pace. The desiccated soil crackled beneath her feet. Her eyes darted to and fro, registering the characteristics of the landscape and making a mental trail she hoped she would use later.

Who was this man? Where was he taking her? Who was his boss? She had a hunch everything was connected. The rabbi's Asher, the fire at Qaryat al-Fau, the theft of the scroll, and this. She shuddered when she thought she might soon face the mastermind of so much evil in a place so desolate no one would ever hear her scream.

A warbler twittered, heralding the dawn. Soon the sun's rays would crack open the darkness. She bit her lip. Her plan had been thwarted—at least for now.

She heard the man behind her strike a match. The smell of tobacco smoke surrounded her.

She spoke over her shoulder. "Do you have another one of those?"

"A smoker." He chuckled. "Here." Gun pointed at her, he stopped and offered her a cigarette from a crumpled soft pack.

She took it. He struck another match and lit her cigarette. In the faint match light, she noticed his leathery skin and hard eyes. Despite the gesture, she knew he was not the friendly type. She nodded her thanks.

"So." She inhaled the smoke. "Do you have a name?"

"Hassan." He pointed to the path again.

She kept walking. "Where are you taking me, Hassan?"

"To the rig."

"Rig? What sort of rig?"

"Enough questions," he barked. "You'll know it when you see it."

Sarah followed the path along the riverbed until it turned into a narrow passage between two sheer rock faces. She looked back at Hassan. He threw his cigarette butt to the ground, not bothering to extinguish it, and jutted his chin toward the passage.

The path was covered with shale and fallen bits of limestone so parched she could smell the dust raised by every step. In the dark, she could not see more than a few feet in front of her—the distance illuminated by Hassan's flashlight—so she walked slowly. Terrain like this was notorious for causing ankle injuries; she couldn't risk it.

Somewhere behind them, the sun was rising. She could see the first signs of day on the rock, whose peaks gradually turned rosy gray as the sun gazed upon them. The light eventually seeped down into the canyon, lifting the shadows and revealing the elemental texture of the rock. On both sides of the chasm, the layers of compacted sediment mirrored each other so well it looked as if the rock had been torn asunder by a particularly violent earthquake hundreds, maybe thousands, of years ago.

As they walked, the passage widened and Sarah could see the outside edges of the rock. They were approaching a wide ledge at the end of the path, beyond which was the misty outline of a mountain range and the lavender sky.

She stopped at the edge and looked into the valley below. Her body stiffened as she realized something was down there. She squinted for a closer look. Could it be?

She turned to Hassan. "Is that what I think it is?"

He smirked. "You'll know in a few minutes." He pointed his weapon at her. "Let's go. They're waiting."

Chapter 19

The sound of the pneumatic drill boring holes into the earth was deafening. Like a giant's heartbeat, the rhythmic thumps thundered across the peaceful valley. In the midst of the thirsty ground stood a derrick about fifty feet tall, a lone beacon in a sea of sand and shale. Holes that had been previously dug and had come up dry littered the earth's surface, giving the place the appearance of an ancient boneyard.

Oil. The promise of an underground reservoir was recently whispered to Israel, which, despite its location in the midst of the world's most oil-rich nations, depended on others for its own supply. Though no one had struck the mother lode yet, a handful of companies claimed the Judean Desert held millions of barrels scattered across its shale fields.

Sarah stood motionless, trying to wrap her hands around it. She recalled reading a few years ago that exploratory drilling in the desert had been approved, but she also knew the locale was sensitive, from both an archaeological and environmental viewpoint. According to the reports, the Council of National Parks and Nature Reserves had approved the initiative on the condition that any damage caused by drilling would be repaired. Seeing this rig and the violence with which it attacked the earth, she doubted this was possible.

"This way," Hassan yelled over the roar of the machines.

They walked past a scattered fleet of heavy equipment to a temporary structure with concrete block walls and a sloping tin roof. A big window commanded one side of the building, allowing the inhabitants to watch the action away from the ear-splitting commotion.

Hassan held the door open and motioned to Sarah to enter. Three men, all dressed in some variation of the khaki fatigue theme, were inside the building. One was talking in Hebrew on a military-style two-way radio. Obviously there was no mobile phone reception this far from civilization. The other was behind a computer, working on some graphs. The third, a pale-skinned man with spiked blond hair, wearing a tight black T-shirt and fatigue cargo pants, faced the window, hands clasped behind his back. He turned toward the door.

"Well, then," he said in a British accent. "What have we here?"

"Bit of a night climber," Hassan said. "I found her

rappelling down Hell Rock in the pitch black."

So that menacing cliff face has a name, she thought. *How appropriate.* "Listen, I'm only a recreational rock climber—"

"Are you, indeed?" The British man stared at her with a mocking grin. "That's not the way I understand it."

She cocked her head. "Oh? Then please enlighten me. What is your understanding?"

He walked slowly toward her, stopping a few inches away. He crossed his muscular arms in front of his chest. "Seems to me you've been snooping around. Perhaps you're on a bit of a mission. Isn't that so, Dr. Weston?"

She went numb. How could he know her name? What could this rig possibly have to do with her mission? She scanned the room, looking for anything that would help her make the connection.

"Let me be plain," he continued. "Your presence here is not welcome. We have important work to do, you see, and we'd rather do it in private."

She narrowed her eyes. "Why? Do you have something to hide?"

He laughed. "Quite the contrary, Doctor. Our little setup here is quite legal. But how rude of me. I haven't even introduced myself." He extended his right hand. "I am John Ridley. I work for a British company called Royal Petroleum. As a subject of Her Majesty, you might even know of it. We are in partnership with Judah Oil and Gas, which holds the license for exploration in this area."

She didn't take his hand. "Your operation is of no consequence to me. And just as you have a right to be here, so do I. I demand you let me go."

"I don't think you understand." He turned to the man with the two-way radio. "Akim, see what he wants to do with her."

For all his bravado, Ridley was obviously not the one calling the shots.

With his back turned to them, Akim muttered something into the radio. Sarah couldn't tell if he was speaking Hebrew or English, nor could she hear the voice on the other end of the device. She felt a gnawing sensation in the pit of her stomach.

With a snap of his head, Akim motioned to Ridley to join him. The two stood in the back corner, whispering to each other. Then Ridley turned to Sarah. "It appears he wants us to take you to him." He walked to her and scanned her from head to toe. "You may leave your pack here."

She gripped the straps. "This is my property. I have every right to take it with me."

She felt the tip of Hassan's Uzi on the back of her head. With a soft sigh, she let the backpack drop from her shoulders.

"Hands up," Hassan barked.

She cooperated.

He patted her down. "She's clean."

Ridley smiled sideways. "Good." He bent down and picked up her pack. "The only thing you'll need where you're going . . . is luck."

Chapter 20

Through his dark green aviators, Daniel scanned the landscape rolling past below. Though it was a monumental expanse with endless peaks and valleys, there was a sameness to it. The eroded faces of mountains and cliffs had such a similar stratification he thought they were flying in circles.

According to the topo map he'd found in the Varanasi study, this was the right place. Deep in the heart of the Judean Desert, it was probably two days' hike from the banks of the Dead Sea and well beyond eyeshot of the casual tourist. Somewhere in this vicinity was the cave he was searching for—a sheer cliff with a midface opening camouflaged by three rocky spires. The sketch he had found and burned into his memory was explicit. There would be no mistaking this rock formation when and if he would see it.

So far, however, it eluded him. The helicopter he had

hired in Tel Aviv had now been circling the desert for almost an hour. He looked at the pilot, a young Israeli with an Army haircut and a permanent snarl. Both his arms were tattooed from wrist to bicep.

Daniel adjusted the mouthpiece on his headset. "How much longer?"

The pilot stared dead ahead. "Half hour max. I still have to get back to Tel Aviv."

Daniel sat back and was suddenly aware of the copter's vibration and the rhythmic drone of the blades, reminding him of the urgency of the situation. He weighed his options. He could land there and continue on foot, but considering time was of the essence, that would be inefficient. He could have the pilot circle one more time, hoping this turn would be different. Or he could have him descend below the standard helicopter fly zone. That would give him better visibility but also would present the risk of being heard or seen by the enemy camp, which surely was on the move.

He drew circles in the air with his index finger. "Let's circle round one more time."

Without acknowledging, the pilot banked the chopper to the left.

Daniel raised his binoculars and looked out the curved windscreen of the cockpit. He studied every inch of the rocky landscape as the chopper glided past but still could not locate the cliff. Time was running out.

He watched an ibex scramble down a bank of boulders and remembered the biblical passage. *Then Saul . . . went to seek David and his men on the rocks of the wild goats.* He followed the animal with his eyes and saw it stop at a diminutive tree and nibble at the leaves. He sat up. *The balsam tree.*

Before he had a chance to look closer, the helicopter had flown past the area. He turned to the pilot. "Go back."

The pilot turned the helicopter in a tight circle.

"Good," Daniel said. "Now hold steady." He surveyed the cliff marked by the balsam tree. It matched the sketch perfectly.

Now he needed a place to land, far enough from the site that no one would detect his presence. He quickly scanned the surroundings and noticed a flat patch in the distance. He estimated it was about three miles away. "Over there," he said. "Bring 'er down."

The pilot flew to the makeshift landing pad. As he descended slowly onto the earth, the air from the rotors blasted the shale below and raised a maelstrom of dust. The skids touched down roughly, jostling pilot and passenger. The pilot gave him the thumbs-up for exit. Daniel shook his hand and ducked out of the craft, walking in a wide arc to avoid the rear rotors. A roar filled the air as the copter took off again, and Daniel hoped the commotion didn't mark him.

A helicopter wasn't an unusual sight in that part of

the desert, as several flew overhead daily to offer tourists a bird's-eye view of the wild heart of Judea, a forbidding wasteland where they wouldn't dare venture on foot. A landing, however, wasn't so common. It was the risk he took to get to the site more quickly. He had already lost quite a bit of time in India with delayed flights and red tape. He could not waste another minute.

He strapped his backpack on and walked at a brisk clip in the direction of the site. The autumn air was mercifully cool, even if it was bone dry and choked with dust. The familiar sensation felt more like a comfort than an annoyance. He glanced at the sky to check the trajectory of the sun and noted that it was hovering above the western horizon. It was just as he'd planned it: complete the technical portions in the waning daylight and enter the cave under cover of night.

His estimate of three miles between the landing zone and the cliff face was almost dead-on. But it was a hard three miles. He had to negotiate a field of boulders and seemingly endless undulations in the landscape, which slowed him more than he would have liked. By the time he got to the edge of the ravine, dusk had cast its blue-gray light upon the fields of stone.

He surveyed the pitch. It was near vertical but nothing he hadn't met before. He decided the easiest and safest way to descend was to secure a top rope and rappel down. He looked at the rocks on the top of the ledge, but none looked stable enough to be bombproof. There were certainly no trees anywhere in sight. He would have to create a three-point anchor on the rock face.

He pulled his equipment out of his pack. He strapped on his harness and tied one end of his rope onto it, keeping the length of the rope in a loop hanging from his shoulder. Using the few available handholds, he carefully free-climbed down to a spot where he could balance himself long enough to set the anchor. He let the rope fall into the void and noted that it wasn't long enough to get him to the ground. He would have to repeat this step midway down the rock.

He wedged two cams between cracks in the rock. He knew this was the best equipment for the limestone surface, which could be weak in spots and crumble under extraordinary pressure, such as that placed by a downclimb. He then connected slings and carabiners to the device, to which he affixed his rope. He was ready.

With light diminishing around him, Daniel kicked off the rock and lowered himself steadily. A blast of cold wind swept across the canyon, announcing the frigid temperatures that would descend upon the desert with nightfall. He'd grown accustomed to the peculiar cold of the desert and welcomed it. It was bracing but not assaulting, more sweet than bitter.

As he walked backward down the cliff, he noticed climbing equipment crammed into the rock. There was no sign of rust or age on the biners, indicating someone had climbed down this face recently. He looked toward the ground for any sign of human presence but it was too far below and light was scant. He might not have been alone in this desolate place.

Daniel's goal was to arrive first at the site and have an opportunity to explore before his opponent made his move. But that was looking less likely. He considered the now all-too-real possibility of a confrontation. He didn't shrink from it. After all this monster had done to decimate the al-Fau expedition, after the arson and the terrorism and the theft of a potentially monumental piece of history, facing him down, man to man, would be a privilege.

That thought fueled him, and he continued descending. About midway down the face, he saw another anchor. It had been compromised. One of the hexes had not been securely placed and had come off the rock. The climber's rope was still affixed to the contraption. He picked it up with his right hand and examined it. It looked and felt strained, so he presumed a fairly high fall factor.

He let it go and continued along his own path, picking up the pace. He was eager to get to the ground, where he could better assess any imminent threats.

Working quickly, he inserted a second anchor into the rock face and reattached his rope. He now had plenty of length for the remainder of the descent. Confident in his equipment, he fed himself a long piece of line and ran down the cliff with catlike agility. He was on the ground in no time.

Daniel gathered his rope around his arm in a figure-eight loop and stuffed it into his pack. Catching his breath, he looked around. The place was perfectly still as the dark hands of night embraced it. The black cliffs towering skyward closed in on him like Scylla and Charybdis, but a silver moonbeam illuminated his path down the center of the canyon. He was grateful for it, since he planned to use no artificial light. He had to be as stealthy as possible.

Bent at the waist, he darted to the other side of the ravine and, with his back against the rock, skulked toward his destination. Every few steps, he stopped and listened. A breeze carried the distant howl of a lone wolf calling to his pack.

Where the call of the wolf filled others with dread, it comforted Daniel. It was the one thing he remembered fondly from his youth. He grew up in the mountains of Tennessee, the son of a struggling single mother and a deadbeat father who left the family early on and never resurfaced. On his thirteenth birthday, Daniel grabbed a shovel and a hoe and went to work in a clay quarry to bring in some money and help his mother with the mounting bills. It was there he discovered a love for the earth and the mysteries it hid beneath elemental layers of rock and soil—a passion that never left him.

As dusk cloaked the Great Smokies toward the end of his workdays, the wolves' howls sounded across the range as they attempted to reunite. During those days, as he stood at the portal of manhood, he used to imagine the depth of the bond that tied the wolf to its pack and longed for just such a connection, something he'd never known in his broken, dysfunctional family.

To that day, he made the same association. Bolstered by the cry of the animal to which he felt such a kinship, he edged forward. Adrenaline surged through him as he neared the cave that might elucidate an ancient mystery. His need to know masked the anxiety about what—or whom—he would find there.

When the cliff came into full view, he stood at a distance to plan his next move. The face was craggy enough that an experienced climber could ascend it without equipment.

So far, so good.

He located what he believed was the mouth of the cave, a small opening that looked more like a fissure than an entrance.

He looked in every direction. All was still, encouraging him to proceed. He edged toward the cliff and stopped behind the balsam tree.

Autumn's cool breath drifted through the ravine, making the leaves of the tree quiver. From the corner of his eye, Daniel noticed an object hanging from a low branch and did a double take.

A chill rippled through him as he realized what it was: the Tibetan prayer beads he had given Sarah a year ago in Ethiopia.

Again he heard the solitary wolf howl.

He clutched the beads and looked up the cliff face.

She was in there. And she was in trouble.

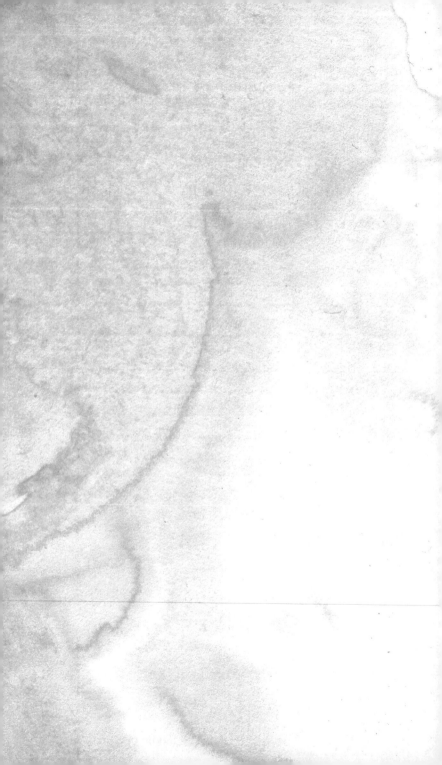

Chapter 21

"Here. Put this on."

A small-bodied, bearded Indian man with his hair tied into a tight black turban handed Sarah a buoyancy vest and an oxygen tank. She accepted it reluctantly. "What's this for?"

"No need to get ahead of ourselves, is there? Just accept and take what comes."

"Spare me your dime-store spirituality. I have no need for it."

He snarled. "Lady, it would be in your best interest to keep your mouth shut. Now do as I said."

She slipped on the vest and watched the Indian sort through a bag of diving gear. He pulled out a regulator and a mask and tossed them at her feet. "Hope you know what to do, because I don't have time for a lesson."

He put on his own BCD and attached a regulator to his tank. They were going diving.

Sarah looked around the cave. The only water she could see was a small, seemingly shallow spring about twenty feet below the ledge on which they stood. Obviously, there was a bigger pool beneath it. She wasn't particularly fond of the water, and the idea of diving, which she'd only tried once, years ago, filled her with dread. She closed her eyes and took a deep breath to calm her racing heart.

"Ready?" he barked. The word echoed in the hollow limestone womb.

"Oh, do shut up," she whispered behind her teeth as she fiddled with the regulator, trying to remember how to attach it.

He walked to her and snatched it from her hands. "Give me that. Idiot." With deft movements, he attached and tested it. "Works fine. Put it on. We're wasting time."

She did as he commanded. A small part of her wanted to push him off the ledge and run for it. She wasn't sure whether it was decency or fear that didn't allow her to do it. She slipped on the mask and inhaled a breath of oxygen.

The Indian pointed to the water. "We'll be descending to that spring. You'll follow my lead. There is a chute beneath the water's surface that leads to a reservoir. We're going to the far end of that reservoir. It's a long dive." His gaze traveled down her body. "The water's cold. Very cold."

She kept a straight face though she felt shaky. She nodded.

"Okay. Let's do this." He clambered down the jagged

rock to the bottom of the cave. Before entering the water, he put on a pair of fins. He turned to her. "Sorry. Only have one pair." He lowered his mask, put the regulator in his mouth, and adjusted the computer on his wrist. He handed Sarah a flashlight and gestured to her to enter the water first.

She lowered herself into the spring and tensed when she felt the frigid water on her limbs. The Indian was wearing a dry suit, but she was in her climbing clothes. It was going to be an uncomfortable journey.

The water was so dark it was like diving into black ink. She tapped on her flashlight, which emitted an eerie blue beam. She pointed it around her. She registered the nubby bottom of the spring and estimated they were floating in twenty feet of water. To her right was the entrance to the chute, a darkened, barnacle-encrusted maw with jagged rock teeth. They entered single file, he behind her.

Their flashlights flooded the narrow cave with a blue glow. In the otherworldly light, the twisted, gouged rock looked like the set of a sci-fi movie. Sarah could hear her breath rise and fall through the regulator. Her limbs tingled from the cold, and the sensation slowed her down. She forced herself to pick up the pace. Uncomfortable as it was, she knew that the longer she spent in that water, the higher her chances of hypothermia.

In places, the cavern narrowed so much that a diver could barely fit. It was as if they were swimming through a vise clamping down on intruders with heavy stone jaws. The shapes around them were remarkable. Gnarled rock spires, like teeth of a prehistoric beast, rose from the cavern floor while thousands of tiny stalactites rained from its roof.

Sarah was beginning to lose feeling in her fingers. She opened and closed her fists to restore sensation, but it was too far gone. Her palms felt prickly, and she could not feel the tips of her fingers. Fear gripped her. The smell of rubber from the mask was pervasive. Every sound—the gentle swooshing of water as they passed, her own breath—was amplified as if heard through a PA system. She fought against a rising tide of dread to stay calm. A panicked breath could deplete oxygen in no time.

She inhaled slowly and steadily. In her adrenaline-riddled consciousness, she realized for the first time the air in the tank was preheated. That would keep her from succumbing to the effects of the cold, or at least prolong the inevitable. Then she became aware of what she was wearing. Wool and polypropylene stayed warmer when wet than other fabrics. Had she been wearing cotton, which could rapidly drop body temperatures when soaked in cold water, she probably wouldn't have stood a chance.

These realizations calmed her and helped her stay focused as they swam toward a narrow vertical portal in the midst of a dark womb.

It led to a pool so wide and deep it could have been

an ocean. Sarah shone her light in every direction and saw nothing but water. Her companion launched into the liquid void and signaled to her to follow.

It was like swimming in an abyss. There was no shelf, no coral, no sea life—just the eternal darkness. Sarah felt a strange serenity that bordered on euphoria. There was something delicious about floating in nothingness, with no indication of a beginning or an end, no awareness of direction. Rational thought melted away like salt in water and all that remained was the assault of random images. Her eyes registered everything with sharp clarity, but her brain did not process it. Perception and awareness gave way to instinct.

It felt like the very beginning of life.

Or the end.

She felt two hands under her arms and her head rise above the water's surface. At that moment, her face felt like it was hit by a thousand icicles. She tried to focus ahead but could not tell what she was looking at. The hands pulled her across the water, then let go. She closed her eyes and floated, unaware of place or time.

The hands grasped her again and pulled her backward. She heard the sound of agitated water. Her chest felt like a block of ice had been set upon it. She had no control of her legs. A strange sound—a crunching, almost—filled her ears and the heavy mass of her body came to a standstill. The regulator fell out of her mouth, yet she was able to breathe. She turned to her side and rested her cheek against a hard, dry crust. She felt something warm hit her back. Sleep weighed on her eyelids, and she could not fight it. She drifted away to a state between wakefulness and dreaming, where she was haunted by the raw imagery of her subconscious depths but unable to interpret it.

A hand shook her violently. "Wake up. Wake up and face him."

She opened her eyes with great effort, suddenly aware she was covered with blankets. Her awareness was slowly returning.

"There. Up on the ledge."

She looked up and saw a male figure standing about ten feet above her, illuminated by a terrible halogen spotlight. She blinked to focus. He was dressed in a shiny black wet suit that revealed all the contours of his lean body. His face was as pale as the moon, his expression composed but hard. Pin-straight raven hair hung over his shoulders.

"Good evening, Dr. Weston," he said in a proper English accent. "You're just in time."

Chapter 22

Two young men grunted as they leaned into crowbars, trying to get the boulder to budge. It was a massive stone, probably eight feet tall by six feet wide, and it wasn't going anywhere. Behind the men was a panoply of tools, diving gear, watertight cases, and at least a dozen oxygen tanks.

Sarah sat up. "Who are you?"

He smirked. "Don't you know?"

"Asher."

"I see you've met the rabbi. He really ought to keep his mouth shut. What else has he told you about me?"

"Nothing I didn't know already. I've seen firsthand the sort of destruction you leave in your wake."

He stepped off the ledge and made his way down the rocks to the small shore on the reservoir's edge. Arms folded across his chest, he stood over Sarah. "Name's Trent Sacks. You and I, Doctor, have rather a lot in common."

She looked up at him. "I very much doubt it."

He squatted in front of her and met her gaze. His slate eyes were so full of hatred she had to look away. He clutched her wet hair and pulled her head back. "You have no idea whom you're talking to, do you? Well, soon you will." He let go abruptly, making her head jerk forward. "Everyone will."

"It's giving way." The British-accented voice reverberated off the cave wall.

They both looked up at the ledge, where a young man with tousled blond hair stood.

"Well done, Angus," Sacks shouted up. He turned to Sarah. "What we have in common, Dr. Weston"—he nodded toward the boulder—"is what's behind that stone. And we both know it's a game changer. The proof the world needs to confirm King Solomon's existence—and the legitimacy of the Bible." He stood. "That's eluded archaeologists all these years. But not you. You were determined to be the one whose name goes down in history."

"Don't presume to know my motivations, Sacks."

He shook his head. "My dear, I know the human condition. The frailty of the human spirit. People are weak. Give them half a chance and they will succumb to worldly temptations like fame or glory or money. It's pathetic, really."

She stared at him. "That has nothing to do with me."

"Doesn't it?" He lifted a hand to his chin. "I suppose

you're going to tell me you have higher ideals. That you aren't guilty of wanting to be first to the finish line."

She didn't answer.

"Tell me this, Dr. Weston. When was the last time you spoke to your so-called partner?" He looked up at the ledge and gestured to the blond man.

Angus threw an object down. She saw something glinting in the halogen light but didn't realize what it was until it hit the ground.

"This is the knife that was used to teach Daniel Madigan a lesson when he broke into my property."

The thick, angled blade of the hunter's knife wedged into the shale. Sarah's lower lip trembled.

"Haven't you anything to say?" Sacks asked calmly. "Are you not interested in his welfare? Is your personal ambition the only thing that matters to you?"

"Bastard. How dare you?"

He spat on the ground. "You are like all the rest of them. You have no morals. You merely hide behind a curtain of righteous principle. You would have the world believe that you're willing to put your own life on the line to rescue these relics in the name of history"—he bent to pick up the knife by its black handle—"when in reality all you want is your name in lights. Perhaps even your reputation back, because that has been rather tattered, hasn't it?"

He squatted in front of her and slowly ran the blade from her sternum to the underside of her chin.

She was shaking, partly from fear, partly from rage.

"Well, I say you must be punished for your sins."

The sharp tip of the blade stung her skin. Warm liquid trickled down her throat. She kept her eyes fixed on his. She had never felt the killer instinct before that moment. She wanted to strike him, to make him feel pain. Could that monster truly have harmed Daniel? She didn't believe it—or didn't want to. She couldn't let the thought enter her consciousness; it would unravel her.

He stood and pointed the knife at her face. "On your feet."

With awkward movements, she slowly stood. Sensation had not fully returned to her legs.

"I suppose you want to know why I've brought you here."

She didn't speak or change her expression.

"No? Well, I will tell you anyway. I make it a point of pride to know my enemies before I eliminate them. And you have been a particularly interesting case study. The crusading archaeologist. The maverick who would risk everything." He shook his head. "At first I thought, such lofty goals. But then I realized it's easy to put everything on the line when you have nothing left to lose. No one cares about Sarah Weston. They've all backed away from you, haven't they? Your institution, your colleagues, your father . . ." He smiled slyly and hissed out the words, "Even Madigan."

She clenched her fists and looked away.

"What's the matter? Truth hurt?" His sinister laugh thundered inside the limestone womb. "Take heart, Dr. Weston. I am a generous man. I want you to bear witness to what I am about to uncover. I want the long-buried manuscript of King Solomon to be the last thing you'll see. Consider it my Judas kiss to you before I leave you to your fate."

Still recovering from a hypothermic state, Sarah wasn't thinking clearly. She found herself getting sucked into the vortex of his odium, struggling to break free. It obviously was what he wanted: to make rage fester within her so as to weaken her character and prove she was inherently wicked. She wouldn't let him get away with it. "Who are you, really? What do you want?"

He offered a tight-lipped smile. "A good question. Very well, then; I shall tell you. I am a descendant of a long line of kings. To put it plainly, I am the sole living member of the Davidic dynasty from the bloodline of King Solomon. The final heir, if you want. That was a distinction I shared with my older brother, until he had a rather unfortunate accident. He was a pilot, you see, and one day his instruments failed. The police suspected foul play"—he looked away—"but could never prove it."

"You beast," she whispered. "You killed your own brother?"

He smirked but did not answer. He pointed to the boulder. "Whatever is in there is my inheritance from my ancestors. I am the rightful owner, and I am here to claim what is mine. And the way I see it . . . you are an intruder and a thief in my house. And for that you shall be judged."

"Judged? By a murderer? And who's going to judge you, Mr. Sacks? Or are you above it all?"

"Though your sins are like scarlet, they shall be as white as snow; though they are red as crimson, they shall be like wool." His voice resonated like that of an evangelist. "If you are willing and obedient, you will eat the good things of the land; but if you resist and rebel, you will be devoured by the sword. For the mouth of the Lord has spoken."

Sarah recognized the passage from the book of Isaiah. She was starting to put the pieces together. The biblical references, the supposed Davidic pedigree, the quest for the Solomonic treasure, even the message that was left on the ground at Qaryat al-Fau. This man had intentions far more sinister than she'd originally imagined.

"We have passage," Angus called down.

Sacks closed his eyes and inhaled, his face suddenly serene. "At last." He reopened his eyes and addressed Sarah. "Let us see what lies in Solomon's cave." He motioned toward the ledge. "After you."

Sarah's heart pounded with equal parts anticipation and apprehension. On the one hand, she lived for such moments. On the other, the odds of surviving the experience were stacked against her. Sacks had already put his cards on the table. Considering he'd proven himself capable of anything, she had no reason to believe he was bluffing. All she had now was her own ingenuity. But was it enough to beat him at this deadly game?

She made her way up the craggy limestone to the overhang. Sacks' men had moved the boulder just enough to expose a gap.

She met their eyes briefly. The first was a young man with the beauty of a Romanesque statue, smooth skinned and pale as his master. His eyes, clear as blue topaz, were two empty pools in which life did not dwell.

The second was an Arab with taut skin the color of black tea and wet black hair tied loosely at the nape of his neck. Around his waist, tied with a leather belt, was a curved *khanja* sheathed in embossed silver with a black stone on the handle. Her gaze lingered on his face, and he smirked ever so slightly. She read the message in the glinting onyx eyes that had haunted her since the night of the blaze: *We meet again.*

When Sacks stepped onto the ledge, both men bowed deeply. He gestured for them to rise. "I believe you've met Sa'id, the heir apparent who will lead the Al Murrah savages into a new dawn."

Daniel had been right; the al-Fau arsonist was the tribal amir's son. Sarah looked away, sickened by the realization.

"We have lit the torches, my lord," Angus said.

Sacks stood before the gap with his head bowed. After a long moment of silence, he looked up and unzipped his wet suit. He slipped it off his shoulders and down his hips, and stepped out of it completely. He wore only a pair of black, low-waisted Lycra leggings of mid-calf length.

Sarah winced at the sight of his body. Hairless and imbued with a gray pallor, it had a corpselike appearance. A life-size asp, rendered in ink so intricately that its pattern and scales were remarkably realistic, was coiled around his torso. The inference was not lost on her. In antiquity, particularly in dynastic Egypt and North Africa, the asp was both a lethal snake and the symbol of royalty.

He gave the thumbs-up to the Indian, who stayed behind to guard the entrance. He turned to her. "Angus and I will enter first. You will follow. Sa'id will be behind you, so mind yourself." Angus offered him a handgun and Sacks tucked it inside his pants, letting the handle rest on his midriff. He nodded to the others. "We are ready."

They entered single file through the narrow opening. Inside the mouth of the cavern, the ceiling was so low they had to bend at the waist. Iron torches hanging on either side cast golden light on the striated rock. The walls radiated a wet chill. Shivering, Sarah hypothesized some of the water from the reservoir ran beneath the cave floor.

The mouth opened to a wider chamber whose structure was barely discernible in the wan torchlight.

"There are more torches here," Angus announced. He proceeded to light them. The original straw stuffed into the torches was too moist to light, so he wrapped it with shreds of cloth. The smell of kerosene filled the cave as he ignited the makeshift wicks.

As each torch was lit, more and more of the cave came into view. The interior was almost tubular, like an orifice. Overhead, stalactites formed a curious sheet pattern, like a petrified waterfall frozen in mid-drop. The quivering flames of the torches cast deep shadows on the ancient limestone, and the cavern seemed to come alive as the light bounced off the walls.

At the very end of this chamber was something that stopped Sarah in her tracks. On the wall was a painting of two winged lions facing each other, a more elaborate version of the symbol on the alabaster box. The painting was rendered in charcoal and decorated with sheets of gold. The charcoal was fading, and much of the gold had rubbed or peeled off; however, the artist's original intent was still visible, and it was glorious. On a rock shelf beneath the painting was a quintet of bowl-shaped, patinaed brass censers, which would have been lit in ceremony.

"Magnificent," Sacks whispered.

Sarah cringed. He didn't have the right to proclaim anything in this cave magnificent or to sully such an important moment.

He looked at his men. "This was an altar of offering

to Yahweh." He used the ancient Hebrew name for God. "The royal lions are the symbols of the king. We are in the right place."

The chamber veered toward the right. Sacks, with Sarah and his team in tow, followed the passageway. The short path stopped abruptly at a lip. They could not continue, nor could they see what was beneath them.

Though she was chilled to the bone, Sarah felt the warm flood of anticipation. Fear evaporated, and all that mattered was what she was about to encounter.

"Shine the floodlight," Sacks ordered.

Angus reached inside his pack and removed a heavy light with a base. He secured the base on the ground, then pivoted the light toward the chasm and clicked it on. White fluorescent light flooded the space.

Sarah gasped. She could not move. Not in her wildest imagination had she ever conceived this.

Chapter 23

Below the lip on which they stood was a niche in the rock that appeared manmade. The exposed layers of sediment betrayed the fact that the stone had been intentionally quarried to become a hiding place, a vault to protect its precious cargo.

Tucked inside this stone hollow, the object emitted a radiance so dazzling Sarah was transfixed. Carved in the shape of a miniature amphitheater, the structure consisted of six steps, each adorned with gilded statues. At the apex of the staircase sat a carved wood armchair.

King Solomon's throne.

Could this truly be the mechanized throne referenced in the biblical texts and the midrashim? Was it not stolen by the Babylonians, along with the rest of the temple treasures? Had it not eventually made its way to Egypt and then to Persia before vanishing and being reduced to legend?

And most importantly, who buried it here? Could it

have been the king himself, after he'd been stripped of his potency and left to wander the desert? Was this internment the very purpose of his wanderings?

She was so mesmerized by the object she began to descend toward it, forgetting she was in the company of others, until a strong hand grasped her forearm, stopping her.

She turned to meet Sa'id's burning gaze. He tightened his grip until she grimaced with pain, then let go.

Sacks dropped to his knees and bent forward until his forehead touched the ground. In a reverent tone, he muttered something Sarah could not comprehend. She assumed it was a prayer and was grateful she could not make out the words. Even the most sacred offering would sound abominable issuing from his mouth.

With a single fluid movement, he stood and brushed past her as he made his way down a set of eroded stone steps that appeared to be hewn by the hand of man. Obviously the dubious staircase was a passage between the throne room and the altar above it. This chamber, it seemed, was more than a hiding place. Some form of worship likely was carried out here.

The rest of the group followed Sacks down. He stood in front of the throne with eyes closed and arms outstretched. He was motionless, silent, an apparition floating between the worlds of the living and the dead.

Sarah focused on the throne. The steps were wide, smooth, and the color of milk. She was almost certain they were carved of ivory. Each tread was flanked by life-size sculptures of beasts overlaid with gold. On the first step was a lion, mouth open and baring sharp canines, ready to shred its next victim. Opposite the lion was an ox with head bent sideways so as to display its gleaming horns, which spanned three feet in width.

The next step was the dominion of the wolf. Shoulders raised above its head, the predator was frozen in stalking position. Opposite the wolf was a sheep whose pointed face and spindly legs protruded from a golden fleece so intricate it looked lifelike. Its expression was serene, its stance relaxed, as if it wasn't threatened at all by the wolf's imminent attack.

On the third tread, a tiger reared on its hind legs, front paws outstretched like it was ready to pounce. Its face locked in a teeth-baring snarl, the wild cat faced a sitting camel whose hump was loaded with a cargo of ornate boxes, presumably holding precious spices.

Next came the eagle and the mountain cock. With wings spread so wide they formed a canopy over the tiger below, the eagle exposed its massive talons and parted its beak in a terrible expression. The mountain cock sat on a branch, with its beak pointed to the sky and its prolific tail feathers opened in the shape of a flamenco dancer's fan.

On the fifth step was a demon, a foul creature with the legs of a hoofed animal, a barbed tail, and the claws of a raptor. Long horns protruded from its head, and its bearded, contorted face looked like a cross between a goat and a bat. Opposite it, a seated man, wearing only a loincloth and a turban, held a scroll—probably the Torah.

The final step was commanded by two birds: a dove and a sparrow hawk. They faced each other with wings outstretched as if they were readying to fight. Curiously, the birds were not flanking this step but rather were in the middle of it, making it impossible to reach the top without stepping over them.

On a pedestal at the apex of the structure was the king's throne. The sides were carved in the now-familiar shape of the winged lion and leafed in gold. The lions' eyes were malachite; their fangs were ivory. The high back of the chair was engraved with a tree on whose branches were written seven names in ancient Hebrew. On two finials on the very top sat two eagles.

Sarah could hardly believe her eyes. What for so long had been relegated to legend actually existed—and fit the biblical description almost to the letter. If this object indeed dated to the time of Solomon, the ramifications of such a find would be huge. Corroborating passages in the Bible brought theologians a step closer to proving it was a book of history, which cemented the people's belief in the teachings and their faith in the prophecies—as well as Israel's claims in the Holy Land.

But actually proving the story of Solomon would have profound impact, for it was the very foundation of messianism. The messiah for whom the Jews waited was to come from the tree of David via the branch of Solomon.

The thought rattled Sarah. She regarded the man standing before the throne. Could it be?

With eyes closed and palms up, Sacks chanted in a monotone that seemed more medieval than ancient. He raised his arms higher, and for the first time she noticed a tattoo inside his left wrist: a cross with scalloped points and a wheel in the center, inscribed with symbols she did not comprehend. Below it was tattooed the word *Magus*. The symbol was familiar, but she could not place it.

"God almighty, who hast created all things and who hast given us the power to know good from evil, thy holy name be worshipped. O Lord, grant the success of this experiment to your humble servant, and let all truth be revealed through thy Holy Seal. Amen."

Delivered by a man who did not distinguish between worship and crime, the words sounded profane. Sarah recognized the dangerous mentality of justifying the most horrible deeds in the name of a higher power. It was the hallmark of evil.

Sacks lay prostrate on the ground with legs together and arms out. His ashen body formed the shape of a cross. Angus and Sa'id stood on either side of him, chanting.

Obviously, he had bought these men's loyalty rather handsomely. Whether they believed in his brand of spiritualism or not, they certainly embraced the part. Even

Sa'id, an Arab of Bedouin descent whose people looked to Allah and accepted a very different prophet, seemed to buy into Sacks' rhetoric.

What had he promised them? Money? Power? A place in history?

Sacks stood, and Angus approached him. With head bowed, the acolyte held up a box. The master reached inside and took up its contents, a rough-hewn iron ring encrusted with four stones.

Sarah's eyes widened. The ring of the king.

She recalled what Rabbi Ben Moshe had said: *The ring was meant to be a key that unlocked a manuscript left behind by Solomon. The manuscript and the ring together have unspeakable power. They are to be brought together only by the messiah.*

She was revolted by the realization that this monster believed he was the anointed one. And just as he was ruthless in claiming the first of the objects that would grant him that power, he would have no qualms about eliminating anyone standing between him and the manuscript. She suddenly saw her fate written on the walls of that cave. She was trapped, with no way out.

Sacks slipped on the ring and put his hand on Sa'id's shoulder. "My dear pupil, it is time to ascend the staircase. Remember: faith is key. If you believe, you shall be unharmed."

Sa'id bowed and approached the throne. He seemed

apprehensive as he prepared to meet the first step, as if he was trying to summon his wits.

Sarah recalled the biblical passages about the mechanism of the throne. It was to be ascended only by the king; any impostor would fall victim to the golden beasts. According to legend, Pharaoh Necho, the Egyptian ruler who killed King Josiah of Judah, claimed the throne along with the other treasures of the palace but did not know how to operate it and was made lame by the strike of the lion.

Sa'id must have known that story, for he chose to ascend the staircase from the right side—the side of the ox. Just as he stepped up, his weight triggered the mechanism and the ox rushed forward, impaling his midsection with its horn. Sa'id wailed like a cat in heat.

The animal jerked its head, driving the horn deeper until it exited through his back, and threw its victim a good five feet into the air. Sa'id's body landed with a thud and rolled twice before coming to a halt in a supine position. His midsection drenched with blood, the man flailed and gasped for air. His arms were outstretched and shaking as he begged someone to come to his aid.

No one did.

Sarah raised both hands to her mouth and fought the instinct to gag. Terrified, she looked at Sacks. He was immovable, expressionless, his gaze nailed to the throne. She shut her eyes tightly; she could no longer watch.

The gasps stopped.

"That was unfortunate," Sacks said. "It is as I thought. The throne yields nothing."

Sarah half opened her eyes and saw that Sa'id was no longer moving. That bastard. He'd sacrificed one of his own without emotion or mercy. Bile rose to her mouth.

Sacks turned to her. "And now, my dear, it's your turn. Let's see how clever you really are."

She gritted her teeth. "Why don't you just turn your gun on me? Because I'd rather die than be your pawn."

"I don't think you understand." He walked toward her, stopping a couple of inches away from her face. His tone was calm. "This choice isn't yours to make. This is something that is willed from above. I know it's hard for you to comprehend that God is at work here and that I am his instrument."

"God? You just killed a man. And he's only one in a string of many. Does your god condone that?"

He inhaled deeply. "Sa'id died honorably, in service to the anointed one."

"You disgust me. Do you really think you are the one? Have you not read the scriptures you claim to uphold? The anointed one you speak of is to be a man of extraordinary virtue, a man who shows mercy and wisdom and leads the people into an era of peace. You've done nothing but kill and destroy."

"Now, now, Dr. Weston. None of that was for sport.

It was necessary in order for me to claim what was duly mine." He scoffed. "What am I doing explaining myself to you? You haven't the moral or spiritual foundation to speak about such matters."

"Mashiach"—she used the Hebrew word for messiah—"will not judge by what he sees with his eyes or decide by what he hears with his ears; but with righteousness he will judge the needy, with justice he will give decisions for the poor of the earth. He will strike the earth with the rod of his mouth; with the breath of his lips he will slay the wicked."

"I see you've been coached. It's too bad you don't understand a word of it. Let me do you a favor so that you do not die an ignorant sinner. Mashiach will arrive when the world is at its most wicked—which, as we both know, is now. True, in the messianic age there will be no war, but in order for the messiah to arise and gather the exiles of Israel, nations to the north must be subdued. A war will be waged, but the northern enemy shall be crushed and the great nation of Israel will be feared. Israel will know prosperity through new technologies that will make her self-sufficient—namely oil and natural gas." He smiled broadly. "It's all part of the plan, my dear."

"I don't understand. What war?"

"Suffice it to say that our friends in Lebanon will soon be up in arms about a certain territorial dispute. But their military prowess will be no match for

Israel's—particularly with the advent of some sophisticated new weaponry, courtesy of the British. But you shouldn't be concerned with such things. After all, you won't survive to see it."

"Aren't you forgetting something, Mr. Sacks? The pivotal concept of messianic prophecy is the building of the third temple. How do you intend to do that, exactly?"

He walked toward her and stood so close she could feel his breath as he spoke. "Let me make something clear. I am forgetting nothing. I have devoted my adult life to the study and fulfillment of the prophecies. The temple will be built."

"And what of the mosque on Temple Mount?"

He laughed. "That's incidental; the smallest of my challenges. The question you should be asking is, 'How will you build it?'"

"All right, then. How?"

"Ah, but that's why we're here. I will say no more. Why spoil the surprise?" He lifted her chin with his index finger. "Perhaps you'll find out for yourself. If you're worthy."

Sarah jerked away. "Don't touch me."

A storm rose in his slate eyes. "You dare to address me in such a manner? Have you no idea whom you're disrespecting?"

"Oh, I know exactly. You have no respect from me."

He struck her face with a backhanded blow. She fell to the ground. He stood over her with fists clenched, his black hair hanging like raven's feathers around his face. "Get up this instant and ascend the throne."

Her face was hot. "Do your own bidding."

He pulled his handgun out of his pants and pointed it at her head. The snake tattooed across his chest appeared to be slithering as his muscles rippled. "Perhaps you didn't hear me. I said, get up this instant."

"No." She spat at his feet.

With a snarl, he pulled her up by her hair. As she stumbled to her feet, he pushed her against a cave wall and pinned her back with his forearm. Hand trembling, he pushed his gun against the middle of her forehead. "I ought to kill you here and now."

She struggled to break free from his unexpectedly strong grip. A bead of sweat trickled from her brow despite the damp cold. "What's stopping you?"

"It's all you deserve. But I am feeling benevolent, so I will give you a second chance. The choice is yours. Will you meet the challenge of Solomon's staircase?" He dug the gun's barrel into her forehead. "Or will you die?"

She shifted her gaze toward the king's throne.

He clicked back the safety.

She could die by his hand, or she could roll the dice. "I'll do it."

He relaxed his grip. "Good." Gun still pointed at her head, he took one step back. "Now let's go. There is much to do."

If she successfully ascended the staircase, she would be handing him a victory. Chances were he would kill her anyway. She glanced about the cave for Angus. She hadn't heard or seen him in a while. She looked into Sacks' loathing eyes.

She was running out of choices. She planted her foot into Sacks' midsection with all her strength.

He fell backward but sprang to his feet. The gun fell from his hands, but he did not bother to pick it up. With a fresh surge of rage, he started after her.

She ducked, managing to dodge him a couple of times, but he was too fast, too strong. He pinned her to the ground and wrapped his hands around her neck in an iron hold.

She choked.

"I thought you were smarter than that, Doctor. You have squandered your opportunity to live." He bore down on her throat.

The weight on her windpipe rendered her breathless. Her eyes watered from the pain. She dug her fingernails into his forearms, but he was unfazed. Every second that passed weakened her. She was losing the battle.

"Let her go, freak."

Sarah felt Sacks' grip loosen, and she gasped for air. Through the haze, she saw Daniel standing over Sacks with a gun pointed to the back of his head.

Chapter 24

"Get up slowly. No funny business."

Sacks complied. "Well, well. He lives. I was hoping you'd bled to death in Varanasi."

"That would've been convenient, wouldn't it?" Gun pointed at Sacks' face, Daniel stepped toward Sarah and offered her a hand.

She took it and let him pull her to her feet. His hand was warm even though his hair and clothes were soaked through.

After their last exchange and his abrupt departure from Saudi Arabia, she feared she'd seen the last of him. Now, as he stood next to her again, she had found more than an ally at a critical moment; she'd found the deepest kind of strength, the one that could come from only true human bonds. His presence charged her, amplified her. For the first time since meeting Sacks, she felt like she had the upper hand.

"Angus!" Sacks called for his acolyte.

No answer came back.

"He can't hear you," Daniel said. "He had a little accident. Walked right into a full oxygen tank. Put him out cold."

Sarah looked about and spotted a body lying on the far side of the cave. Angus was indeed unconscious, his torso and hands wrapped with climbing rope.

"And don't bother to call for your Indian friend," he added. "He came after me in the water. Let's just say he's not a very good swimmer."

Sacks glared. "So what do you plan to do, Madigan? Kill me?"

"Oh, no. That would be too easy. I reckon you can help us."

"Really? Please. Do enlighten me as to your grand plans."

"We're here for the same thing you are. Difference is, we're going to walk out with it and you're not." He nodded toward the throne. "Somewhere in the king's throne is the treasure referenced in the scroll. But someone has to tame the beasts. I figure that's you."

"Impossible. The throne yields to no one but the king. The beasts cannot be tamed, only appeased . . . with blood."

"'If thou art the chosen one, she will reward thee with a treasure unlike any other, forged by the whispers of angels and guarded by kings for all eternity.'" Sarah repeated the words of the scroll. "If you are who you say you are, what have you got to fear?"

Sacks glowered at her, then at Daniel. "I am not accustomed to taking orders. The answer's no."

"Are you prepared to accept the consequences?" Daniel said.

"My dear fellow, there is nothing you can dish out that I cannot take. Do your worst."

"Very well, then." He pointed the gun between Sacks' eyes and put pressure on the trigger.

Sarah tensed. She read an unfamiliar hostility in Daniel's expression that bordered on detachment. She wanted to believe he was bluffing. But was he?

She would never find out. Sacks swung around and kicked the weapon out of Daniel's hand. It spun across the floor and came to rest more than ten feet away.

Daniel grabbed Sacks' shoulders and squeezed. Sacks delivered a blow to Daniel's midsection, but Daniel did not let go. The bulging veins on his temples betrayed a determination fueled by loathing.

Sacks reached for Daniel's shoulders and dug in.

In obvious pain, Daniel released his grip first, driving an elbow hard into Sacks' bicep. It did nothing. Hooking his leg behind Sacks', he upset his balance enough to gain an advantage. With a groan, Daniel toppled his opponent, and the two rolled on the ground.

In her periphery, Sarah detected movement across the cave. Angus was coming to, struggling to break free from the rope that bound him. Perspiration trickled into her eyes, stinging them. She darted to pick up the handgun.

In the midst of the struggle, Daniel turned to her. "Do it, Sarah."

She shook her head. She didn't have enough confidence in her marksmanship to hit a moving, entwined target. Not to mention, she could not take a life, not even one so brazenly evil.

Daniel had Sacks pinned to the ground. Jutting his head toward the throne, he shouted, "Go!"

She realized he meant for her to ascend the staircase. A chill rippled through her like snowmelt trickling over river stones. She looked at the magnificent ivory and gold structure, then at Daniel. She nodded.

She approached the throne nervously. She regarded the first step, where the ox still was frozen in attack position, its horn stained with fresh blood. She closed her eyes.

Beware, brethren, for she will trap thee and feed thee to her army of beasts.

Did she have it in her?

Her thoughts turned to King Solomon. How little she—or anyone, for that matter—knew of him. He was one of those rare, venerated figures in history whose legend had surpassed the truth. She summoned her instincts from deep in her core. Though everything had become so convoluted and steeped in enigma, her gut told her Solomon was not a malevolent king. He was not deliberately trying to kill; he was merely protecting something from the clutches of infidels.

The realization gave her new resolve. She knew the first step was the deadliest, designed to deflect the impious. She needed to avoid it at all costs. She took a few steps back to get a running start. She ran in the direction of the ox and jumped over it, landing on the second step next to the sheep.

Her weight triggered the mechanism, and the wolf lifted its head, exposing fangs capable of shredding flesh. In the split second before it lunged forward, she lurched onto the third step.

In her haste she didn't realize she had stepped onto the path of the rearing tiger. She screamed as the animal's massive razorlike claws rapidly approached her. It was the last thing she saw before being toppled to the ground.

"What in the world would you do without me?"

Her heart pounding in her throat, she looked up at Daniel, who had hurled his body onto hers to move her out of harm's way.

"Good question," she said, breathless. She looked down and saw Sacks lying on the ground. "What happened?"

"Right hook to the side of the head," Daniel said, scanning for threats as he stood. "He's out for now, but we don't have much time."

She stood next to him. "Three more steps and we're there."

"You know what to do."

"I think so." She glanced at the eagle on the fourth step. "'Her eagles will deafen thee with their cries.' Be prepared."

"The scroll says, 'He who is pure of heart and gentle of manner can tame her beasts and possess the fruit of her womb.'" He put his hand on her shoulder. "Whatever you do, don't lose sight of that."

She nodded and stepped up, hands tightly cupped to her ears. Daniel followed.

As predicted, the eagle let out a high-pitched shriek that could shatter glass. Sarah's eardrums vibrated. She lowered her head and grimaced. Even in the silence that followed, the eagle's diabolical cries reverberated in her mind.

Two more steps to go.

On the fifth step, where the demon sat opposite the man holding the Torah, she knew what to expect. She crouched and crawled onto the step. She looked up and saw the demon's sharp, forked tongue whip out of its mouth. Had they not been warned by the scroll, they would have been skewered. As the demon's tongue struck the head of the seated man, the Torah scroll fell out of his hand.

Sarah knew that was not by chance. She weighed her next move. The sixth and final step, occupied completely by the dove and the sparrow hawk, was a challenge. There was nowhere to step and, therefore, no clear way to ascend to the king's seat. She glanced at Daniel, crouched by her side. He looked as bewildered as she felt.

Only he who is pure of heart . . .

She considered the symbolism of the dove in Judaism. Used widely in the ancient texts, most notably in the Song of Songs, which was attributed to Solomon, the dove was a symbol of the nation of Israel. White doves were sacrificed routinely in the temple of Jerusalem as symbols of purity before God. Sarah studied the wings of the gilded bird, barely open as if preparing for flight. One of its talons was completely open, the other curled.

She picked up the tiny effigy of the Torah. Its width was about the same as the space inside the curled talon. Knowing the significance of the Torah to the Jews, she took a chance. With trembling hands, she slipped the scroll inside the dove's talon.

It worked. The mechanism rolled into motion, and the dove stretched its wings and lifted off the ground. With its free talon it captured the sparrow hawk, presumably signifying Israel's victory over its enemies, and together they slid to the edge of the step, leaving a clear path.

"Clever girl," said Daniel. "I knew you could do it."

She exhaled. They ducked under the demon's extended tongue onto the final step and proceeded up to the ornate seat that was King Solomon's throne.

She looked around cautiously. "Beware of the serpent," she said. "Somewhere here there is a snake or snakes that 'will coil themselves around thy foot and paralyze thee.'" She scanned the chair. "I don't see anything."

"They might be guarding the treasure," he said. "Whatever the treasure is."

She studied the throne. How magnificent it was to her eyes. The carved eagles on the very top of the throne were like sentinels guarding the seven Hebrew words, which she recognized as the names of the patriarchs and matriarchs—Abraham, Isaac, Jacob, Sarah, Rebekah, Leah, and Rachel—etched into the chair back. The winged lions on either side of the seat seemed to be watching her with their malachite eyes. She wanted to touch them but did not dare betray the memory of the great king.

"Check it out." Daniel pointed to a tile on the floor, covered by two coiled golden asps facing each other. "There are your snakes."

"That's got to be where the manuscript is."

"The manuscript?"

"The treasure that Solomon spoke of had nothing to do with gold or riches. It's a cache of knowledge he apparently went to great lengths to hide. According to the mystics, it's meant to be found only by the messiah."

Daniel looked over his shoulder at Sacks' immobile form, then at Sarah. "He thinks he's the messiah?"

She nodded. "That's what makes him so dangerous."

He rubbed his forehead. "Now it adds up."

"What?"

"Not now. We have to figure out how to open that tile

before Sleeping Beauty over there wakes up." He looked around. "There's got to be something . . ."

She pointed to a round indentation in the chair's right arm. "Wait. What's this?"

"Bingo. That looks like a lock mechanism."

"Right. All we need now is the key." She bent to study the indentation carefully. She noted four slight grooves within the circle. She looked up slack-jawed, suddenly putting the pieces together. "The ring. We need the ring."

Daniel reached inside his pocket. In his scraped, bloodied hand he held a small iron object with four embedded gemstones. "You mean this?"

She smiled. "Daniel Madigan, you are a genius."

"I know." He winked. "Do you want to do the honors?"

She held out a palm. He put the ring in her hand and closed her fist. The object felt rough against her skin and heavier than she expected. She thought of Rabbi Ben Moshe. What pain and sacrifice had gone into concealing this relic from the gaze of common man, only to have it yanked away by someone so wicked. Holding it in her hands felt like a vindication for all the men and women who had risked everything to keep the secret.

She walked to the throne, placed the ring inside the indentation, and turned. She heard a soft click.

Daniel, who was standing over the tile guarded by the gold asps, gave her the thumbs-up. "We're in."

She stood beside him and saw that the snakes had

uncoiled and retreated and the tile had detached from the floor. It was the only thing separating them from an ancient truth, and all they had to do was lift it. Sarah felt the gravity of the moment. Her mouth felt dry, her hands shaky. *The manuscript and the ring together have unspeakable power.* The words of the rabbi rang in her ears, and she hesitated.

"Sarah? What's wrong?"

"Nothing. I'm ready."

Together they lifted the marble tile, which appeared to be four inches thick and eighteen inches square, and heaved it aside.

Daniel wiped his brow. "That must weigh eighty pounds. How did they get it here? Or any of this, for that matter."

Sarah did not answer. She stared at the contents of the box the tile had hidden. There was a papyrus scroll, several pages rolled loosely together. The ancient paper was the color of straw with honey-colored striations, and its edges were uneven. It appeared almost identical to the scroll buried in the Valley of the Wind.

Daniel lifted the scroll and examined it carefully without opening it. He handed it to her.

She felt ashamed for ever doubting his sincerity. Only a man of honor and character would hand her that moment rather than claim it for himself. She carefully unrolled the fragile document.

It was not what she was expecting.

"Wow," Daniel whispered. "Is that what I think it is?"

She did not take her focus off the papyrus. She leafed through the sheets—five in all—and gasped at the familiar diagrams. The first two contained the outline of a building with walls of remarkable thickness, a series of alcoves and chambers, and a facade delineated by columns. Another contained rudimentary drawings of details—a menorah, the capital of a column, cherubim. On another was inscribed a detailed plan for the altar of fire, presumably where animal sacrifices were to be burned along with spices, releasing the scent of singed flesh and perfume unto the heavens.

The last page was a sketch of a chamber with which Sarah was not familiar. She made a mental imprint of the round, colonnaded structure and its vessels of water and fire, noting the metaphor of the four elements.

"These are blueprints." She glanced at Daniel. "The plans for the first temple of Jerusalem."

He let out a long breath. "That's a hell of a treasure."

"It is, indeed."

Sarah and Daniel looked back in unison.

Behind them stood Trent Sacks. He lifted his right hand, and the blade of the hunter's knife shimmered in the lantern light. "Thank you for making my job easier. And now I must ask you to step aside."

Sarah remembered the handgun in the waist of her trousers. She reached for it.

"I wouldn't do that if I were you, Dr. Weston." Sacks glared. "I'm far quicker with a knife than you are with a gun. If you want to test me, go right ahead."

She glanced furtively at Daniel. His brow was furrowed, his jaw tight.

"Stand up." Sacks pointed the blade at her.

She did as told, hoping Daniel had her back.

Sacks yanked the handgun out of her trousers and pointed it at Daniel. "Now carefully put down the scroll. You are polluting it with your sinful hands."

She tried to think of her next move, but her options were few. He had been a formidable opponent, even unarmed. Now he held two weapons.

Reluctantly, she put the scroll inside the box.

"Good. Now come to me and face your judgment."

She looked at Daniel and tried to read his thoughts. Perhaps it was a fool's hope, but his glance told her to create a distraction.

"Now," Sacks bellowed.

She walked toward him and stood where he pointed, at the edge of the staircase. The sight of him, pale and sweating, repulsed her.

He licked his lips. "You have served your purpose. And now"—he pushed her with his forearms—"you must die."

The force sent Sarah tumbling down the middle of the staircase, various components of the structure slicing and bruising her skin, shapeless forms of gold and ivory rushing past.

She hit something at the bottom of the staircase. She rolled onto her back and looked up to see the blond man staring down at her with cold blue eyes. He turned his gaze toward Sacks and raised his hand. Sacks threw the gun down at him, and he caught it in midair. He pointed the barrel at her.

Horrified, she watched the scene at the top of the throne.

Sacks held the knife to Daniel's throat. "I have a score to settle with you, Madigan. You have been a thorn in my side every step of the way." He dug the knife into his jugular.

Daniel groaned, his face twisted in pain.

Sarah tensed. "No," she whispered.

"On your knees, heathen," Sacks ordered.

Daniel complied.

"Now reach into that box and hand me the scroll."

Loathing in his eyes, Daniel lifted the scroll and placed it at the feet of his enemy.

Without breaking eye contact, Sacks bent to pick it up. Then he took one step back and reached for the arm of the throne. As he lifted the ring out of the lock mechanism, the beasts slowly began moving toward their original position. He slipped the ring on and held the knife high above his head. He pointed to Daniel, who was still on his knees.

"What have you to say to your redeemer?"

Daniel spat. "Go to hell, pal."

With a roar, Sacks plunged the knife toward Daniel. Daniel caught Sacks' wrist and held it back, trembling.

"Angus!" Sacks let the manuscript roll down the staircase to his partner and dug his fingers into Daniel's neck.

Sarah could barely breathe as she watched.

With their arms locked, they struggled to the edge of the staircase. Sacks pushed his opponent, and the two of them rolled down the staircase as the gilded beasts were still moving.

They fell against the tiger's claws, and Sarah heard a faint shredding sound. As they tumbled down the remaining steps, she saw the bloody lines across Sacks' bare back. The rest was a blur until their masses came to a halt at the base of the staircase.

Daniel pinned Sacks' arms with his knees and held the knife to his throat.

Sarah exhaled.

Angus pointed the gun at Daniel. "Let him go."

"No, Angus," Sacks said calmly, his eyes trained on Daniel. "He won't do it."

Daniel was breathing hard. His hand shook as he drove the knife into Sacks' skin.

"You pathetic bastard. You don't have the guts, do you?"

Daniel's jaw was clenched. He clutched Sacks' hair with one hand, holding his head still, and lifted his knife arm above his head. With a primal cry, he drove the weapon downward.

Sacks' eyes grew wide as the blade plunged toward him.

Sarah clasped her mouth to muffle a scream. She watched, horrified, as Daniel's knife came down. Instead of driving it into Sacks' throat, Daniel sliced off a thick strand of Sacks' long black hair. He tossed the tuft aside, dropped the knife, and got to his feet, panting as he turned away.

Sacks stood and composed himself. "Coward. Don't you know you are no match for the power of the anointed one? Nothing you can muster can stop the plan that has been set in motion by God himself. We are talking about the destiny of mankind. A worm like you can't stand in the way of that." He barked out the words, "I ought to make you bow before me and beg for mercy." He took a deep breath and spoke again in a calm tone. "But I am a benevolent lord. I forgive you. You may die in peace knowing that." He spoke over his shoulder. "Angus? Are we ready?"

"Everything is packed, my lord."

"Very well, then." He held Solomon's manuscript to his chest and shot them one final, blazing stare. The four smooth stones of the iron ring, wrapped around the bony middle finger of his right hand, glowed with an inextinguishable fire. "Let us make haste."

Angus held up his gun. "Shall I eliminate them?"

"No," he said, turning to leave. "Let them rot."

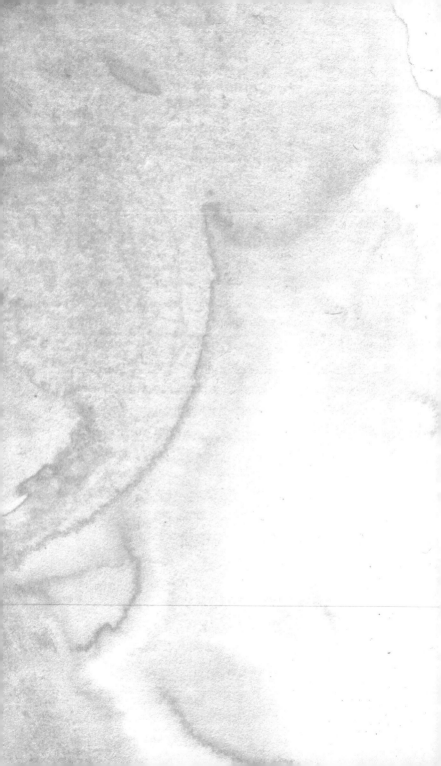

Chapter 25

"Damn it to hell!"

The word *hell* bounced off the limestone walls, echoing with varying degrees of intensity and mocking Daniel like a demon. He kicked the ground, dislodging a few loose pebbles.

Sarah placed a hand on his shoulder. "I wouldn't have done anything differently."

He yanked away. "I was weak. It's unforgivable."

"Don't punish yourself for being human."

"Being human works only when you're faced with another human. That guy's an animal. He didn't deserve to live."

"That's not for us to decide."

He shot her a pained look. As usual, she was right.

"Problem is," she said, looking around the stone cavern, "we're trapped. They've taken all the oxygen tanks."

He glanced at the throne. The beasts had returned

to their original positions, and the structure radiated opulence and serenity, as if nothing had happened. But something had. Without the very thing it was designed to guard, the throne was nothing more than a splendid shell, a spectacle betraying the wealth and prowess of ancient Israel's united monarchy.

Once again, Sacks had won. That weighed heavily on Daniel's mind. No matter how much he invested, how much he risked, he was defeated, time after time, by this despicable enemy whose malevolence knew no bounds. His stomach turned at the thought of Sacks posing as the messiah. His delusions of grandeur and his perceived permission from God made him the most brutal kind of foe: one who fancied himself both righteous and invincible.

At least he had let them live. Daniel swore he would make him regret it.

"Danny?" Sarah broke his contemplation. "What's on your mind?"

He regarded her absently as his thoughts gelled into a vague theory.

"All right, then, I'll tell you what's on my mind," she said. "Before you got here, Sacks revealed a bit of his plan. He spoke of a war in which the northern enemy, presumably Lebanon, will be crushed. It was almost as if he was personally putting the wheels in motion to spark that war."

He was intrigued. "How's that?"

"He said something about a territorial dispute and

about oil and natural gas. Interestingly, he is somehow affiliated with a drilling rig not far from here. Not sure how . . . or why."

"Did he say anything else? Did he mention a British company named Advanced Electronic Solutions?"

She shook her head. "No. But he did say something about winning the war with the help of some sophisticated new weaponry, courtesy of the British."

He snapped his fingers. "That's it. Advanced Electronic Solutions is an instruments and components manufacturer for Her Majesty's naval ships. The AES folks have recently gotten in bed with the Americans and have added military aircraft electronics to the mix. And AES has a subsidiary in Jerusalem that is the world leader in advanced radar countermeasures, mostly for the Israeli military."

"How do you know all this?"

"When I paid the creep a visit in Varanasi, I snuck into his library and found some maps and sketches, which is what led me here. But I also found a business card for a guy named Alastair Bromley."

"Bromley? The MP?"

"That's the one. Bromley is the head of AES and apparently pretty pro-weapons." He left out the part about gathering intel from her father. He didn't need another fight now. They both had to be calm if his exit plan was going to work. "The way I understand it, he stands to benefit greatly from a conflict in this region."

A wrinkle formed between Sarah's brows. "Something else has been bothering me. Did you happen to notice the tattoo on Sacks' left wrist?"

"Vaguely. Things were moving pretty quickly." He searched his memory. "A cross of some kind?"

"Right. It was a type of rose cross inscribed with all sorts of symbols, and beneath it was the word *Magus*, which of course means sorcerer. It has to be related to a secret society."

"This guy is definitely into some sort of voodoo. As I was trying to escape in Varanasi, I walked into a basement that was obviously used for rituals. It was odd: a darkened room with a single spotlight above the altar, where a bowl of blood sat. There was a fountain on one end and a doorway on the other. Pretty damn creepy, if you ask me."

"The knife," she said, as if she had just had an epiphany. "That was no ordinary weapon. It looked just like a knife used in the dark arts I once saw in a museum exhibition."

That was a promising clue. "What was the exhibition of? Think."

She looked down and rubbed her forehead. After a long moment, she looked at him. "The Order of the Golden Dawn. It's a society of magicians founded in England in the nineteenth century. The exhibition was of the implements and ciphers used by members—adepts, I believe they're called—to practice ritual magic. The knife with the angled blade and the black hilt was, as I recall, used to strike fear in the spirits."

The stab wound was healing, but the pain was still fresh in his mind. He felt it anew as she described the knife. He downplayed it. "Sounds like a bunch of hocus-pocus to me."

"Right. But for the people who live and die by these esoteric traditions, it's all too real."

"So we're looking at an occultist with messianic ambitions who is plotting a conflict that could set the Middle East ablaze." He stroked the prickly stubble on his jaw. "I think we have our work cut out for us."

"Sure, if we could only get out of here."

"Well, we're not going to sit around here and wait to die, I can tell you that." He started toward the exit. When he realized Sarah wasn't following, he called back, "Let's go."

"Go . . . where? The only way out of here is through that spring. That can't be negotiated without oxygen."

"I've got a plan." He winked. "Trust me."

She looked back at the throne. "Give me a minute."

She approached the Arab's corpse and removed the belt and silver *khanja* from around his waist. She met Daniel with the objects in hand. "This might come in handy later. Now all we have to do is leave here alive." She tightened the belt around her hips and shoved the blood-stained knife behind it. "Lead the way."

Sarah and Daniel stood at the edge of the spring. This part of the cave was pitch black. Without artificial light, the water seemed an infinite pool of ominous blackness.

A distant hum pierced the silence. Daniel instinctively held his arm out in front of Sarah and engaged his senses to gauge potential threats. The echo cheated his ears, and he couldn't identify the sound or where it was coming from. When the din grew progressively louder, it became clear it was the beating of wings—scores, then hundreds. As the unseen invaders drew nearer, their collective winging thundered like a cannonade in the limestone womb. Then it grew fainter until it stopped, and all that remained was a soft sigh as the water trembled from the breeze the creatures stirred in their wake.

"Bats."

Daniel nodded. "They're coming back to their roost. Day must be breaking."

"Where are they coming from? There has to be another opening."

"You got it. You don't think I actually swam the length of this abyssal sea, do you? I had to find a shortcut."

"But how did you know?"

He chuckled. "I'm a cave diver, honey. I have seen grottos like this a hundred times. I could tell by the amount of water it was much deeper than it looked. Besides, they left some diving gear. That was a dead giveaway. So I climbed around and looked for another way in. I found a chute on the backside of the cliff. It's still a long swim, but it's doable."

She sighed. "I don't know, Danny. I'll try, but . . . underwater distance swimming was never my sport."

He couldn't read her expression in the darkness, but he heard the trepidation in her voice. He squeezed her forearm. "You'll be okay. And by the way"—he pulled the mala beads out of his pocket—"you almost lost these."

She was silent for a moment. He could hear the soft clicking of the beads as she presumably wrapped them around her wrist. "Thanks, Danny."

He heard her breath rise and fall rapidly and realized how vulnerable she was at that moment. He felt an overwhelming need to protect her. "Ready to go diving?"

"There's no reason to delay it, I suppose. Let's go for it."

They inhaled deeply and dove into the inky water. Daniel recalled it was a short swim through utter darkness to a clearing where a shaft of light came through an opening in the rock. He clicked on the green light of his waterproof watch and checked the reading on the compass. On the way in, he'd swum in a northwest direction. Now, he pointed his body in the opposite direction to find his way out.

The light of the watch went off and for about sixty seconds, he could not see a thing. He was relieved to feel Sarah's subtle movements beside him. He didn't let on, but he was genuinely worried about her ability to execute a free ascent. Aside from being an experienced cave diver, he had had the benefit of underwater training during his time in the Navy; she had no such advantage. He knew he'd have to keep a close eye on her.

As they emerged from the dark heart of the reservoir, a sunbeam pierced the water, creating a light tunnel they could follow all the way to the water's surface. Daniel had timed it on the way down: it had taken about two minutes to descend, but the ascent would take slightly longer. He turned to Sarah, and she gave him the thumbs-up.

He set the pace as they swam upward, knowing that ascending too fast could be lethal. He exhaled continuously, ensuring optimal lung volume, and could see she was doing the same.

Almost there, he repeated to himself. It was something between a mantra and a delusion.

By the time they were halfway to the surface, he was feeling heaviness in his lungs. Despite controlled exhales, he was running out of breath. They were cutting it so close.

Sarah was no longer beside him. She began to fall behind, and he wondered if she was in trouble. He glanced back at her. Her movements seemed normal, if slower, and her expression was calm. He felt a pang of concern but pressed on.

Seconds later, he felt the crushing sensation that told him he was seriously running out of time. He was relieved to see the water's surface. A few more strokes and they'd be there.

He looked back. Sarah had fallen farther behind. Her movements were haphazard, and she looked panicked.

Fear wrenched Daniel's gut. He turned and swam down to her. Her lips were tightly sealed but were beginning to turn blue.

He remained calm as he weighed his options. Only buddy breathing could get a stressed diver out of such a jam, but without so much as a pony bottle of air, there was no way to perform it.

Her eyes looked vacant.

Or was there a way? Desperate, he pulled her close to him and placed his lips on hers, forming a tight seal. He exhaled half of his remaining breath into her mouth, grateful she was lucid enough to receive it. He backed away and watched her reaction. She nodded faintly. He put his arm around her waist, and together they negotiated the remainder of the ascent.

Their heads pierced the water's surface, and they gasped loudly in unison. Daniel held up Sarah's convulsing body as she coughed to expel the water from her lungs. He held on to her and swam to the nearest rock outcropping.

Muscles burning, he grasped the notch of a boulder at the water's edge and with a groan lifted his own body and hers onto dry land. She crumpled to the ground, coughing violently and shaking. Wet strands of hair stuck to her forehead and cheek, dripping onto the rocky ground.

Exhausted from the effort, Daniel collapsed on top of her to warm her. It was too close a call. A few more seconds and they wouldn't have made it. He wouldn't take the gift of life for granted. He'd use it to stop that monster once and for all.

Chapter 26

Sacks stood on the deck of the eight hundred–foot drillship *MedStar*, wrapped in a long black parka. His black hair, shorn just below the ear on his right side, hung beneath a black wool skullcap. He'd left it uneven on purpose. It was his badge of honor, a reminder of how close he had come to perishing. That he emerged alive and victorious confirmed his invincibility. He was indisputably the chosen one.

The Israeli flag whipped wildly as a stiff winter wind howled across the Mediterranean Sea. The waves heaved, slapping the sides of the massive gunmetal-gray ship. Thanks to its sophisticated dynamic positioning system, the vessel hardly moved. Only the cranes on its deck swayed and groaned.

As big as three football fields, the ship was an engineering marvel. Similar in appearance to a tanker, it was a self-contained drilling rig with a massive derrick in the center and a moon pool in its hull, through which the drilling equipment was deployed, reaching thousands of feet beneath sea level to access subsea wells. On the bow of the ship was a helideck used to fly in supplies and transport personnel.

The *MedStar*, the pride of the Royal Petroleum fleet, gave the operator, Judah Oil and Gas, the benefit of mobility, as it was able to explore more of the ocean's floor than traditional fixed oil platforms, thereby bypassing dry holes and zeroing in on the most promising areas. In the race to find oil off Middle Eastern shores, something in which several nations had a stake, time was of the essence.

In the eighteen months since its arrival in Israel, the *MedStar* had explored acres of seabed and had identified three spots of interest. The first two had come up dry but the latest, fifty miles west-northwest of Haifa, had the most potential, with an estimated reserve of four billion barrels. It also was the most controversial, as it was located dangerously close to the Lebanese border.

Sacks regarded his operations engineer, a rotund, middle-aged Scotsman with a ruddy face and a repulsive skin condition that spread a peeling white crust across the folds of his nose, chin, and forehead. "I'm growing impatient, McConnell. How much longer before we have a hit?"

"There's oil in this hole; that you can be sure of. But

it's deep. We're already at six thousand feet and nowhere near it."

"I see. What's your best estimate?"

"We'll probably go eight, eight-five before we hit a vein." He pushed back the sleeve of his flannel jacket and looked at his watch. "We should be there by first of December, maybe earlier."

"Good," Sacks said calmly. "Sixty years and four hundred holes, each of them dry. It's time Israel gets its piece of the pie . . . and we make history."

"Whatever you say, boss."

"Get back to work. I expect to hear good news sooner than later."

McConnell rubbed his gloved hands. "We'll do our best."

Sacks' phone vibrated. It was the call he was expecting. He dismissed McConnell and watched him walk toward the derrick.

He engaged the video call. The familiar face—long, narrow, and pale as his own, with a vaguely sour look—flashed on the screen. The worry lines crept up his forehead, calling attention to his receding silver wisps. His eyes, dull pools the color of swamp water, had the vacant, detached look of a mercenary. Sacks recognized himself in his father's antiseptic gaze and instantly felt validated. "Good morning, Father."

"You look awful. What's happened to your hair?"

"I had another run-in with Madigan. He tried to

plunge a knife into my throat and missed. But not to worry. He and Sarah Weston are no longer a threat."

A spark flickered in his eyes. "You killed them, then."

"No. I couldn't risk their death being connected to us. I abandoned them in the cave with no possible way out. When—and if—they're found, it will look like they went snooping and got trapped inside." He smirked. "Such a terrible accident."

"I hope this time you're right. We can't afford any more mistakes." His face was expressionless, but his tone was stern, like a reprimand. "Now listen carefully. I was just on with Bromley. All weapons systems are go. All we need now is a provocation."

Sacks' heart skipped a beat. This was his chance to redeem his past disappointments; he was determined to execute flawlessly. "Leave it to me. I already have a plan."

He riveted his gaze on his son and spoke through his teeth. "The success or failure of this operation is dependent on you. Do not let me down." His face relaxed and his tone turned sweet. "Remember: you are the chosen one."

His father's facile duality was one of the qualities Sacks admired in him and one he strived to emulate. He felt a wrench deep inside, a hunger of sorts. "Father, it's been a year. When will I see you?"

"If our plan works, Son, we'll have all the time in the world." He smiled as if he was privy to some secret. The screen went black.

A frigid gale blew up, making Sacks' lips feel as cold as a dead man's. He closed his eyes and imagined the embrace of his beloved father when all was said and done. It wouldn't be long now.

He looked up at the derrick, which easily was as high as the Eiffel Tower and twice as wide. New pipe was being added as the drill reached deeper and deeper inside the earth's core. Judah Oil's Israeli crewmen yelled over the cacophony of clanging machinery and whistling wind.

Though his crew was multinational and even included a couple of hungry young lads he'd recruited from the Bedouin tribes, Sacks trusted the Israelis to carry out the most sensitive operations. Not only were they the best in the business, but they also had a vested interest in the operation's success. They knew all too well what oil meant to their country: independence, at long last, from the OPEC oppressors who held their economy hostage, and an unprecedented level of wealth and power for the state.

It was high time Israel was restored to the glory of ancient times. The prophecies said that day was coming. God, speaking through Ezekiel, had made this promise to the Jews: *I will settle you after your old estates, and will do better unto you than at your beginnings: and ye shall know that I am the Lord.* Israel had prospered during its beginnings, under King Solomon. But that was nothing compared to the prosperity it was about to know. And Sacks was the one who would deliver God's promise to the people. And when he did, there would be no doubt as to his power.

He walked toward the bow and stepped up the perforated metal treads of the stairwell to the helideck. He gave the signal to the pilot of his Bell 407, and the rotors roared to life. He inhaled the cold air and glanced east. Fifty miles away, he could see the shores of both Israel and Lebanon, two identical specs on the horizon, though in reality so different.

He smiled. Everything was going exactly according to plan.

Chapter 27

"Sarah. Wake up."

The hard knocking on her hotel room door rattled Sarah out of deep sleep. Every one of her muscles ached, and her lungs felt as if they'd been pinned beneath a boulder. It had been two days since they'd returned to Jerusalem, but still she had not recovered from the ordeal in Solomon's cave. She attempted a deep breath. "I'll be right there."

She threw on a fleece and opened the door. Daniel was standing on the other side, holding up a handful of papers. "Got the DNA results," he said, a little too cheerfully.

"So quickly?" She was surprised. Hair analysis usually took a couple of weeks.

"Had to call in a favor with my friends at the lab. I told them it was a matter of life and death, and they treated it like a criminal case."

"It's not too far from the truth. So what's it say?"

He glanced over her shoulder into her room. "Are you going to invite me in?"

"Sorry." She stepped aside to let him pass and locked the door behind him.

He didn't bother to sit. She couldn't blame him. The only chair in the room was coming apart at the hinges and buckling. In fact, everything in the room had an air of decay—the mattress was lumpy, the light blue paint was peeling, the bedding was spotted with unidentifiable stains, and the entire place smelled of mildew. It suited her just fine. The lower the profile they kept now, the better.

"For starters, I got a real name on him. Trent Robert Ashworth. I ran a quick background on him and found his next of kin." He thumbed through his papers and read from one. "Father is James Ashworth III; mother Agatha, maiden name Patton, deceased aged fifty-two; brother Harry, deceased aged thirty. Sacks apparently was his maternal grandmother's maiden name. The Jewish heritage came from his mother's side, though he wasn't brought up in the Jewish faith. He converted to Judaism at eighteen."

She tapped her lips with her forefinger. "Why does the name James Ashworth III sound so familiar?"

"Because he's the founder and CEO of Royal Petroleum, based in Birmingham. Big money."

That piece of information was like a floodlight in the abyss. "So that rig in the Judean Desert—"

"Was his. I didn't have time to look into Royal

Petroleum's holdings, but I'd bet the farm that's not the company's only drilling concern in Israel."

She sat on the edge of the bed. "So that's his plan."

He sat beside her. "What's his plan?"

"When we were in the cavern and he revealed his messianic delusions, I asked him how he planned to go about the building of the third temple, which is one of the mandates of the messiah. I reminded him a mosque stands on Temple Mount. He laughed it off, as if the Arabs were merely ants he could flick off his shoulder. He hinted at plans to engage them in a conflict . . . and what better thing to fight about than oil?"

"That would cause a major international incident. A jihad the scale of which the world has never known."

"Yes, but that's exactly what he wants. He said that in order for the messiah to usher in an era of peace, as prophesied in the Bible, there first has to be a full-on war. There is already a territorial dispute over oil and gas between Lebanon and Israel. This just might be his leverage to rouse conflict. My guess is he wants the Lebanese to strike, so that Israel, with the help of advanced weaponry procured from the British, can crush them."

"No way. What about Syria? Iran? They will join the game faster than you can say Allah."

"Right. It's part of his plan. Spark a major conflict and have Israel, with the help of the West, emerge victorious over its ancient enemies. Don't you get it, Danny?

He's acting out biblical prophecy."

Daniel stared at her, as if trying to digest the words. "Were you able to find out anything about the Golden Dawn?"

"I researched the symbol on Sacks' wrist—the Rose Cross Lamen. The symbols on it are Kabbalistic in origin and apparently represent every universal truth. But they also can be traced back to the time of Solomon, particularly to the first temple. In fact, many of the magical practices of the order are based on Solomonic rituals. There is something called 'the key of Solomon,' which is fundamental to the order's beliefs. It's the template for the medieval occult practices members of the original Golden Dawn had adopted."

"I'm not up on my dark arts. What is this key?"

"It's an old Hebrew manuscript found in Europe in medieval times. Supposedly, it was written by King Solomon. But if you ask me, that's bollocks."

"What's in it?"

"It's a numbers and letters theory. The numbers represent the spirits of the divine order—the virtues and powers of the universe, if you want. The numbers are then translated into talismans and symbols, which can be combined in different ways to make the spirits and angels speak. It's a bit out there."

"So that's what he's doing in that dark dungeon of his: invoking the spirits and pumping them for information." His voice was laced with irony.

She crossed her arms. "You think his insight comes from the beyond?"

"I've read about some of these so-called magicians. Their insight doesn't come from the beyond but rather from the stuff they're inhaling. They use various hallucinatory substances to enter an altered state. Then they claim they've been spoken to." He tapped his fingers together. "My guess is he has a network of informants. If we play our cards right, we should be able to use that against him."

She glanced at the nightstand, where Sa'id's silver-sheathed knife lay. "I think I know how."

He checked his watch. "Hold that thought. We have to be at the university in twenty minutes."

Ezra Harel showed Sarah and Daniel inside one of the research institutes at Tel Aviv University. He led them to an area used only by faculty. A library of reference books and textbooks lined three walls of the room, while computer stations and work areas occupied its center. A wall of floor-to-ceiling glass overlooked the university campus, a complex of green spaces and concrete buildings sprawling below.

"You should be able to find what you're looking for and then some," Ezra said. "You will have full access to all university research archives and some of the world's most sophisticated databases, which include everything from public records to government documents. If it's not here, either it's classified or it doesn't exist."

"Thanks for doing this," Daniel said.

"Anything for Sarah."

Blushing, Sarah glanced at Daniel, who turned away.

"I'll leave you to it, then," Ezra said. "Call if you need anything."

When he was out of the room, Sarah said, "Look, Danny, about Ezra—"

"Forget it." His tone was clipped. "Let's get to work."

She felt a vague tightness in her chest. She wanted desperately for the lingering friction between them to vanish, but she knew it would hang there, mocking them both, until they had an honest, perhaps painful, conversation. She started to say something but stopped herself. It wasn't the time.

They sat at their respective workstations and went to work. She began by researching Royal Petroleum, hoping she'd find clues as to the company's involvement in Israel and its ties to Advanced Electronic Solutions.

James Ashworth III had been president and CEO since the company's inception in the seventies. At the time, it was called British Isles Energy Group. It was co-founded by Ashworth and a partner, Charles Bellows. Bellows had served as president until 2005. The same year, Ashworth's eldest son, Harry, was killed in a plane crash in the Scottish highlands. Was there a connection?

What was behind Bellows' departure? The official

company statement said only that the president had retired—no detail given. She found it odd that the company had issued such a curt statement about one of the company's founders. She decided to dig further.

She came across an article in the local daily. The reporter had gotten hold of some memos from Bellows to Ashworth, in which Bellows advised strongly against investing in Israel, stating that such a move would alienate the Arabs, whose support they could ill afford to lose. At a minimum, he'd noted, volatility in the region could result in tens of millions in lost revenues.

In another, even more strongly worded, memo penned six months later, Bellows recommended against a pending initiative to drill in the eastern Mediterranean because maritime boundaries had never been agreed upon. He'd blasted Ashworth's proposal to partner with Israeli company Judah Oil and Gas, saying such a move would be catastrophic to the company's relations with the client governments of Jordan, Syria, and Iran.

So Bellows had seen the handwriting on the wall. That's why he'd stepped—or had been forced—down. According to the company records, he received twenty-five million pounds in cash but turned down that much more in stock options. A chill raked Sarah's skin. Was he bought off? Did he leave the stock on the table because he considered it dirty money?

"Sarah," Daniel called. "Come check this out."

She walked to his station and pulled up a chair. "What have you got?"

"Sacks has managed to stay remarkably clean. There is no criminal record on him; not even so much as a parking ticket. I even checked into the brother's death, thinking he might be implicated. It was deemed an accident. There was nothing suspect, according to the reports."

"That's consistent with his story. The police never could prove anything."

"Maybe not." He pointed to some text on the screen. "But take a look at this."

Sarah read aloud. "'The full amount of Harry Ashworth's trust fund, with an estimated value of five hundred million pounds in cash, securities, and property, was transferred to Ashworth's youngest and only surviving son, Trent. In an unusual move, Trent Ashworth was named both a trustee and a beneficiary of the fund.'" She turned to Daniel. "So that's how he gets his money."

"It gets better. After the fund transferred, young Trent proceeded to liquidate all property and kept the cash in numbered accounts throughout Europe."

She frowned. "I don't get it. Why would Ashworth give his son, who was twenty-something at the time, full discretion of those funds? That's not standard procedure in families with such wealth."

"Maybe it was a moment of weakness for a grieving father. Or maybe"—Daniel called up a new screen—"Trent had something on his dad."

Sarah felt a wave of nausea rise within her as she read the 1995 report from the Department of Children's Services, alleging that Ashworth was sexually abusing his youngest son, then fifteen. Both the younger and the elder Ashworth had denied allegations and, in the absence of proof, the charges were dropped and the file closed. The case was never reopened.

"This is just a theory," Daniel said, "but I wouldn't be surprised if both father and son have been keeping that dirty secret all this time. That would explain the carte blanche with the trust fund."

Sarah's forehead tightened as she considered the emotional impact of such a relationship. It would not be the first time this kind of trauma unhinged or hardened someone to a criminal state of mind. "How did the mother die?"

"I hadn't gotten to that." He turned back to the computer and called up one of the screens, then another, scanning the text for a revelation.

She leaned in and read too. Something caught her eye as he scrolled down. "There. Stop."

He zeroed in on a link to Agatha Ashworth's obituary. He clicked.

The obit offered nothing of a reason for her demise. "Typical of the British upper class," she said. "Reveal as little as possible and state only the positive. Should have known."

Daniel did another search and found a link to a

Birmingham Post article dated 1998. That was what she was looking for. She read the contents of the short piece and stood upright.

Sacks' mother had committed suicide. According to the article, she had gone to visit a friend in London but never returned. Her bloated, cyanotic body had been spotted a fews days later, floating in the Thames. It was December 1997, just before Christmas. Though there was no note, the police had deemed it a suicide.

Sarah shivered. Thoughts of her own experience with suicide came rushing forth, uninvited. Snapshots of her mother, floating like an apparition in the spent gardenia bubbles, taunted her. She turned away.

Daniel placed a gentle hand on her shoulder. He knew her story. His quiet gesture gave her a moment to snap out of it and get back to business.

She took a deep breath and picked up the conversation. "I suspect Sacks also had something to do with Ashworth's insistence on entering into a pact with Israel against his own lieutenants' better judgment. His long-time partner, Charles Bellows, left the company straight after the announcement that Royal was investing in Judah Oil and Gas. He was staunchly opposed to it."

"Judah Oil . . . that's the company that holds the license for the Judean Desert exploration."

"Yes, and a lot more. They also operate offshore platforms in the Mediterranean and are exploring the oil-shale fields southwest of Jerusalem. They are sitting on potential reserves of billions of barrels of oil, to say nothing of all the natural gas. That's all being done with Royal Petroleum money and equipment."

"So what's Sacks' role in all this?"

"When I was taken to the rig in the desert, it was obvious he was calling the shots. So I'm guessing he's running the local operation for his dad. The curious thing is I haven't been able to find anything listing him as a company employee or board member. All his activity for Royal Petrol is under the radar."

Daniel clicked away at the keyboard as he formulated a new search. Moments later, he called up the most recent Judah Oil and Gas annual report and navigated to the page listing the board of directors.

T. Robert Ashworth, vice president.

His name was near the top of the list of directors. Suddenly, it was all very clear to Sarah. He was flying under the radar at Royal Petroleum because he wanted the credit to come to him via Judah Oil. That was the only way the Israelis would accept him.

"Do me a favor," she said. "Look up Judah's concerns in the Mediterranean."

Daniel's search showed two natural gas platforms and one drillship, the *MedStar*, all located off the coast of Haifa.

Her suspicions were roused. "Any way you can get me

the coordinates for the *MedStar*?"

"Doubtful. We might need to consult the military for that one."

She raised an eyebrow. "I'll be right back."

She returned to her station and, still standing, dialed the number.

"Archaeology. Harel."

"Ezra, I need you to find something for me. I need the exact coordinates for a ship that's prospecting for oil in the Med. It's called the *MedStar*, and it's operated by Judah Oil and Gas. I also need to know whether or not it's stationary."

"You want me to call Yael."

"Would you mind?"

"If I ask any more of her, I will have to start dating her again."

"Thanks, Ezra. You're the best." She hung up and sat at the computer desk, collecting any information she could find on the individual she believed could help them.

Twenty minutes later, the call came. Sarah picked up on the first ring. "Hello?"

"I tell you, she still loves me."

"So you have my coordinates?"

"You just cut right to the chase, don't you?" Ezra sighed. "All right. Yes, I have your coordinates. North thirty-three degrees, three minutes; east thirty-three degrees, twenty-five minutes, fifty-three seconds. And yes, it's stationary. Has been for about a week."

"Brilliant. Cheers, Ezra." She hung up and mapped the coordinates on a GPS site. It was as she thought: fifty miles west-northwest of Haifa, just shy of the Lebanese border. Disputed waters.

Daniel walked over and stood behind her chair. "Anything interesting?"

"I should say." She swiveled around to face him. "It appears the *MedStar* is drilling as we speak, in an area that's bound to cause upheaval."

A look of concern crossed Daniel's face, and she knew they were thinking the same thing. It was time for a little trip to England.

Chapter 28

Sarah drove a hired Land Rover up the gravel driveway as the late-afternoon sun filtered through the beech trees, casting a pattern of confetti-like shadows on the ground. It had just rained, and the drops clinging to the brown leaves and grasses shimmered and danced like mythical fairies of the wood. She lowered her window and smelled the freshness of wet earth.

The sound of gravel crunching beneath her tires reminded her of weekends at her family manor in Wiltshire, a time so long lost it had ceased to feel real. As a girl coming of age, she had ridden horses on bridle paths through similar country. The innocence of those days would forever be marred by what she'd secretly heard on a fall day much like this one so long ago.

As she'd ridden through the woodland toward the clearing, she'd heard voices. They were loud, combative, churning with rancor. She'd halted her horse and listened.

"How could you be so heartless?" she'd said. "I've sacrificed everything for you. I've given up my career, my country, my very identity. All so you could throw me out on a whim."

"A whim? Is that what you think?" he'd shouted. "Take a good look at yourself, Alexis. You are a common addict. It's all the gossip in London. Frankly, you embarrass me."

"You son of a bitch. All you can think about is your place in society." There was a faint sob. "What about Sarah? She's twelve years old. No child that age should have to go through a divorce."

Sarah had frozen. *Divorce.* She knew her parents had fought on occasion, but she'd never fathomed this. The word had not even settled when the final blow came.

"I'm sure you'll look after each other," he'd said.

"What do you mean?" Her mother had sounded surprised. "She's just entered boarding school at Brighton."

"I've already pulled her out. You are taking her with you to Connecticut." He'd paused, surely to let the gravity of his decree be felt. "She's just like you, after all."

Sarah shook off the unwelcome memory. The first breath of winter in England had a way of sobering her. There was a vague frost in the air, the harbinger of the snows. Yet the sun persisted, reveling in the last vestiges of fall before surrendering its light to the solid gray clouds that gripped the sky during the bleak winter months.

She parked on the motor court and made her way to

the front door. Charles Bellows' country house, perched on five acres along a lake in Hertfordshire, was an impeccable nineteenth-century Georgian built of red brick with painted wood accents. Ivy crept up the facade, its leaves withering as the cold settled in. Four white columns supported the portico guarding the glossy mahogany door with the brass knocker.

Sarah knocked. She was not expected, but she suspected the gentleman of the house might see her anyway. She knew from her research that he was at home, recovering from knee replacement surgery.

A plump, pink-cheeked housemaid cracked open the door. "Yes?"

"I am here to see Mr. Bellows. Sarah Weston is the name."

"Is Mr. Bellows expecting you, ma'am?"

"No."

She started to close the door. "Well, I don't think—"

"This will introduce me." Sarah held up an envelope. "Give it to him."

The maid looked at Sarah suspiciously.

"Please."

"Wait here." She took the envelope and shut the door.

Sarah checked her phone, on loan from Tel Aviv University courtesy of Ezra, for word from Daniel. No text had come. She wished they hadn't divided, but there was no other way. Time was running out.

The maid returned to the door, opening it wide. "Mr.

Bellows will see you."

Sarah stepped inside and slipped off her Barbour coat, then handed it to the maid. As she waited for the girl to return from the coatroom, she studied the surroundings. The house was far less traditional than its exterior suggested. The foyer was arranged like a gallery. In the center, beneath a Chihuly art glass chandelier, sat a white leather bench. The walls displayed an impressive assortment of contemporary art, some American, some Chinese.

She followed the maid down the east hallway, past a collection of contemporary photography. She recognized a couple of Skrebneskis that appeared to be the original silver gelatin prints.

The maid motioned to her to wait. She opened the door. "I have Miss Sarah Weston, sir." She held the door open for Sarah to enter and took her leave.

Charles Bellows sat on an armchair, one leg resting on an ottoman. He was a man nearing seventy, she'd calculated based on his career history, but looked far younger. He had a full head of gray hair, parted neatly on one side, and his green eyes were alert and full of life. His fit physique suggested he still enjoyed a daily game of tennis.

"Hello, Miss Weston. You'll forgive me if I don't stand."

"Please," she said. "No need for such formalities."

"Please have a seat." He pointed to a black leather sofa facing the marble fireplace.

She sat on the corner nearest to him and looked at

the dancing fire before addressing him. "Thank you for seeing me."

"For the record, it wasn't because of this that I accepted your visit." He held up the envelope containing an op-ed piece from the *Jerusalem Post* in which the writer sang the praises of oil exploration in the Mediterranean, specifically mentioning the *MedStar*. "I know who you are. And I know your father."

She felt a knot rise to her throat. She should have expected it. She couldn't move in such circles in England and avoid the association. Her name, and everything attached to it, followed her, regardless of how vehemently she tried to shed it.

"My father and I aren't speaking. Just so you know."

"That's a shame. I've witnessed firsthand what the acrimony between father and child can do." He looked away. "It can be very ugly indeed."

"Mr. Bellows, I'm here because I need your help." She waited for him to face her. "I'm an archaeologist, as you no doubt know. My partner and I have made some significant discoveries . . . but we haven't been alone in our quest. A person with whom you're very familiar has been shadowing our steps. Or perhaps we've been shadowing his."

Bellows stuffed some tobacco into a pipe and lit it. He puffed twice, releasing the smoke slowly. It smelled of toasted hazelnut and vanilla. "Do go on."

"Trent Sacks. You know him as Trent Ashworth."

He shifted slightly in his chair.

"He has taken an obsessive interest in these relics, so much so that he has left a trail of blood and destruction. He holds in his possession a set of ancient blueprints for the building of the temple of Jerusalem. Aside from being crucial to Judaism and to the recording of the history of mankind, these have a significant spiritual meaning. The temple, as you know, is to be built by only the Jewish messiah." She crossed her legs and leaned in. "Trent Sacks believes he is that man."

He shook his head. "Trent Ashworth is very ill. He should have been locked away ages ago. If I were you, young lady, I'd stay very far away."

"All the more reason to stop him. He is igniting the fuse that will cause the region to explode. The *MedStar* is drilling in the eastern Med, in waters claimed by both Israel and Lebanon. That is bound to lead to conflict. He has confessed his motive: to spark a war. And he's well on his way to doing it."

"What does any of this have to do with me?"

"No one knows the inner workings of Royal Petroleum better than you. I need you to tell me what it's going to take to stop him."

"My dear, there is no stopping him. The only one who could put the brakes on that operation is his father. And he won't do it."

"Why not?"

"I can't discuss it." He looked away. "I'm sorry."

"Has he threatened you? Or bought your silence?"

He turned to her with a steely gaze. "That is quite enough." He looked at the door and called, "Fiona!"

"It's a matter of life and death, Mr. Bellows. Too many people have fallen to his sword already. And it's nothing compared to the carnage that might ensue. Now is the time for transparency, not secrets."

The maid opened the door. "Yes, sir?"

"Show Miss Weston out, Fiona. We're quite finished."

Sarah looked at him coldly. "You walked away from the truth once. And now you're doing it again. What does that make you?"

"Smart."

She stood, staring at him until he turned away. She walked toward the door.

He called behind her. "Oh, Miss Weston?"

She faced him.

He held up a folded newspaper. "You might enjoy reading this."

She walked to his chair and accepted the paper. Their gazes locked for a moment, and she swore she saw encouragement in his bright green eyes. Without another word, she followed Fiona to the front door.

Outside, Sarah shivered and zipped up her coat. The temperature had plummeted as dusk settled into the countryside outside London. She got into the Land Rover and fired the ignition. She unfolded the paper and read the headline of a small article below the fold.

Judah Oil and Gas Chairman Found Dead

She put a hand over her mouth. Then she noticed the handwriting on the paper's margin.

Gadebridge Park, 22:00 sharp.

Chapter 29

Daniel looked at his reflection in the mirror before leaving his hotel room for the evening. He was clean-shaven and dressed in an expensive navy three-piece suit he'd rented for the evening. He adjusted his platinum-colored tie and smoothed the matching pocket square. He hadn't worn slacks, let alone a suit, in a decade. But if he were to be taken seriously at tonight's event, he had to look the part.

He had the doorman of the 41 hail a black cab. He sat in the back and gave the driver the Belgravia address. He looked at his watch: nine. The party had started an hour ago, but he knew the main players wouldn't be arriving until later. He looked out the window and watched central London roll past. He indifferently regarded the orderly traffic around Buckingham Palace Gardens and the bright lights of Victoria. His mind was fixed on a singular task: getting to Alastair Bromley.

The cab stopped in front of the white stucco house on Upper Belgrave Street. "Here you are, lad," the driver said. "Fancy party, eh?"

Daniel smiled tensely and paid the driver. The windows of the three-story townhouse were bathed in light, and he could see activity behind the panes as guests made their way through the house and to the roof garden. He walked up the steps to the landing and rang the doorbell.

When the footman answered, he presented his calling card, which was engraved simply with *Daniel Madigan, PhD.* The footman acknowledged his welcome with a slight bow and showed him inside.

The lady and lord of the house were greeting guests at the doorway of the parlor. There was endless chitchat, much of it in pretentious, high-pitched voices, and he was reminded why he had chosen the solitary life. He was so bored by scenes such as this, but he was also good at pretending when he had to.

When his turn came to greet his hosts, he extended his right hand to the husband, a potbellied man with salt-and-pepper hair and untrimmed black eyebrows that were combed upward. "Lord Strathmore. Daniel Madigan. I am a guest of Lord Weston."

His wife cut in. "You need no introduction, Dr. Madigan. We're thrilled you could join us."

"Lady Ashley." He raised her right hand to his lips. "Enchanted."

She slipped a hand into the crook of his arm. "Dear, I'm going to introduce Dr. Madigan to a few people. You'll be all right here, won't you?"

Lord Strathmore waved his approval and continued greeting his guests.

Daniel leaned down and said, "My friends call me Danny."

"Danny. How absolutely charming."

He smiled at her. She was a lovely fiftysomething woman with a serene face framed by a blonde, teased bob. She wore a salmon-colored, long silk dress with a sheer capelet over the bodice and a panoply of diamond jewelry.

"Tell me, Danny, when can we expect another film from you? Everyone so enjoyed your documentary about that city in the Saudi desert . . . Oh, dear. I'm afraid I can't pronounce the name."

"Qaryat al-Fau." He kept up the volley, though in reality he couldn't be less interested in empty cocktail banter. He scanned the room for familiar faces but saw none.

Lady Ashley stopped in front of a trio of women sipping champagne and gossiping. "Ladies, may I present Daniel Madigan . . ."

In his periphery, he caught a glimpse of Sir Richard going up the stairs.

"Danny, this is the Baroness Strongwater, Lady Cybil of Bainbridge, and Penelope Millstone, daughter-in-law of the prime minister."

"Delighted to make your acquaintance," he said in his most charming Tennessee drawl. "Now if you'll excuse me, I do have some business to attend to."

He took the stairs to the roof, which had been landscaped to resemble a formal garden in miniature. A fountain at the center was surrounded by hedgerows in long planters. Trees lined the perimeter, framing views of Hyde Park and Mayfair. Tiny white lights contributed to the magical atmosphere.

A brisk breeze carrying the promise of winter braced him. He ordered a scotch at the bar and made his way through the crowd. He approached Sir Richard from the back and greeted him with a firm slap on the shoulder.

Sir Richard turned to him. "Daniel, old chap. Lovely to see you."

"Hello, Richard. Thanks for inviting me."

"Not at all. Though for the life of me, I don't know why you insisted on coming tonight. If I do say so, the place is full of stuffed shirts."

"I have my reasons for being here."

"I have no doubt." He sipped his brandy. "Tell me, are you here alone?"

"Yes."

"And where is my daughter?"

"She's safe. That's all I'll say."

"I trust you're looking after her."

Daniel chuckled. "Sarah doesn't need me, Richard.

She's perfectly capable of taking care of herself. In fact, she's saved *my* hide a couple of times."

Sir Richard scoffed. "You Americans are always exaggerating."

"Richard, your daughter is the most competent and fearless woman I know. The only difference between you and her is"—he nodded toward the crowd—"she doesn't subscribe to all of this. Give her a chance. You might just see someone familiar in her."

An uncomfortable expression on Sir Richard's face told Daniel he understood the implication. Before the title and the public office, Richard Weston lived in the high plateaus of the Himalayas among the ethnic tribes of Nepal, studying and recording their culture for the Royal Geographical Society. At the end of a seven-year mission that had yielded groundbreaking research, he'd returned to England and shed his explorer persona for good. Something told Daniel he harbored a vague regret and resented Sarah for having the courage to embrace the life he did not.

"I like you, Madigan." Sir Richard did not attempt to mask his irony. "You're not afraid to speak your mind. Even if you are spectacularly misguided."

Daniel let that one go. He hadn't come for a spar. If anything, he needed Sir Richard's cooperation. "Listen, Richard, about that favor I asked you for earlier."

"Oh, yes—Bromley. Are you sure you want to meet that scoundrel?"

"I'm sure." He glanced toward the far side of the garden. "Isn't that him?"

"Indeed." He took another sip. "Shall we?"

Daniel followed Sir Richard to the edge of the roof, where Bromley was conversing with another man among the kumquat topiaries. He was younger than Daniel had expected. He looked to be in his late forties, a slim man about his own height with graying chestnut hair and brown eyes. The corners of his mouth pointed downward in a permanent frown.

Daniel stayed back as Sir Richard approached Bromley. "How are you, Bromley, old chap?"

"Hello, Weston. Never better."

"I understand business is going swimmingly. What's this I hear about a big deal with the Saudis?"

"The Saudis don't need us. The deal was with the Lebanese. We just sold them some missile guidance systems. Standard defense equipment."

Daniel's ears perked up. So Bromley was selling to both sides. Sir Richard caught his eye, and Daniel gestured to him to continue.

"The Lebanese or Hezbollah?"

"We don't sell to terrorists, Weston. You know that."

Sir Richard winked. "Not that you know of, anyway. Lebanon is a can of worms, if you ask me."

Bromley shrugged. "Their money is as good as anyone else's. I don't question their motives."

Daniel nodded to Sir Richard.

"How rude of me. I'd like to introduce you to an American friend." He gestured to Daniel to join him. "Alastair Bromley, meet Daniel Madigan. He's recently finished up a project in the Middle East."

Bromley went pale.

Daniel smiled and extended his right hand. "Pleasure to meet you, sir." He exaggerated his accent and down-played his knowledge. He didn't want to let on he knew who Bromley was. "How do you fellas know each other?"

"Bromley here is an MP," Sir Richard said. "We both work for Her Majesty's government. You'll excuse me, won't you? My presence is demanded elsewhere."

As Sir Richard walked away, Bromley's gaze remained on Daniel. "What sort of work do you do in the Middle East?"

"I'm an anthropologist. I was heading up a dig in Saudi Arabia, but we ran into a bit of trouble and had to shut down." He took a swig of his scotch. "The Middle East is not for me. I've moved on."

"Really? I'm fascinated. What sort of trouble?"

"Let's just say it was getting real . . . competitive. Too many people after the same things." He shook his head. "I let them duke it out. Fighting's not in my nature."

Bromley forced a smile. "So where to now?"

"Back to the States. Leaving Saturday. I'm going to take a sabbatical, figure out what to do next."

Bromley waved his right forefinger. "Now I recall your name. Qaryat al-Fau, no?"

Daniel smiled broadly. "That's right. Good memory."

"Of course. You're the one working with Weston's daughter." He looked around. "So where is she?"

Daniel looked surprised. "Sarah? I have no idea. We've gone our separate ways. Lovely girl but"—he leaned in—"too much of a maverick for my liking."

He smirked. "So I hear."

Daniel looked over Bromley's shoulder and waved. "Say, I'd love to stay and chat, but I see an old friend. Would you mind, Mr. . . . Remind me your name again?"

"Bromley. The Right Honorable Alastair Bromley."

"You have a good night now." He shook his hand and made his way to the group of ladies entertained by Lady Ashley.

The women greeted him enthusiastically and folded him into their conversation about travel. He nodded politely but couldn't focus on what was being said. Their chatter was like the buzzing of bees. At the first opportunity, he made up an excuse about early-morning meetings and headed for the door.

Chapter 30

*I*n the icy chill of late November, winter had already settled on Gadebridge Park. So many of the trees had lost their leaves that the woodlands looked twisted and eerie in the blue shadows of the waxing moon.

Sarah glanced at her Timex. It was a quarter to ten. She walked along the serpentine banks of the River Gade, trying to calm the anxiety that needled her. Was Bellows sincere in his request for a meeting? Was she walking into a trap?

To make matters worse, she hadn't heard at all from Daniel. She worried about his plan to meet Alastair Bromley, not least because he was to enlist the help of her father. She'd insisted it was folly—he was putting himself squarely in the path of peril and potentially implicating her father—but he'd have none of it. His goal was to distract the enemy, and he swore the best way to do it was to casually drop word about his plans and to demonstrate his alliance with a high-ranking politician.

Her thoughts traveled to the article she'd read earlier. The news of the death of Judah Oil's chairman shouldn't have come as a surprise, particularly since T. Robert Ashworth was named his successor. Now Sacks was well positioned should Judah strike oil in the Med. He would take the credit and look like the undisputed hero. His plan was coming together flawlessly.

The dried leaves crunching under her feet were profane shouts in the utter stillness of night. She felt like the only creature stirring in the quiet village of Hemel Hempstead. A gust of wind whistled through the bare trees. A few feet away, beneath a willow tree weeping over the river, she detected a slight movement. She walked in that direction.

Charles Bellows was standing beneath the thinning canopy, leaning into a cane. He wore a long black leather jacket with a gray hoodie underneath and faded jeans. He had the look of a young man despite his advancing age and limited mobility.

She stopped in front of him. His face was hidden in the shadows of the cascading branches. She nodded a greeting but waited for him to speak first.

After a long moment, he did. "Sarah, do you know why I asked you here?"

"You couldn't talk in your own home."

"That's correct. When I walked away from Royal, I

pledged my silence in exchange for my family's safety."

"Silence . . . over what?"

He looked toward the river. "So many things . . . I couldn't even begin."

"I read the reports from the Department of Children's Services."

He turned to face her and took a step forward. His face was in full view now, and she could see the lines of concern in his forehead. "James Ashworth and his son have a unique relationship. Trent is an extremely intelligent, highly functioning delusional psychopath. That young man ought to be institutionalized; instead, he's enabled. His father has taken advantage of his illness to further his own means."

She glanced at him. Did he mean what she thought he did? "Are you saying it was James Ashworth who hatched this plan?"

"I am, indeed. He wanted to prospect for oil in Israel for years, but the board would not have it. So he went about it a different way. Knowing it would feed Trent's delusional disorder, he paid a genealogist to trace a bogus bloodline." He pressed his lips together and looked away.

She exhaled sharply and could see the warm mist of her breath. This was a twist she did not expect: the enemy was not one man but a full-on machine.

Bellows continued. "The most heinous act of all was James' manipulation of his son's fragile emotions. In spite of the abuse, or perhaps because of it, Trent worships his father with a pathological love. That's how James can use him as a puppet to do his bidding."

Sarah was sickened. As much as she despised Sacks, she understood the reality of his condition. People with delusional disorder were marked by a powerful, all-consuming belief in their delusions but no other symptoms of insanity. If they acted out their delusions, nothing could stand in their way—not reason, not decency, not the law. And they were particularly hostile if they sensed someone did not believe them.

The perpetrator was also the victim. Though some part of her pitied Sacks, she knew he had to be stopped, for there was no limit to what he would do to play out his fantasy. "Tell me something, Mr. Bellows. What convinced the board to finally buy into James Ashworth's propaganda about Israel?"

"Two key voting members—his son Harry and I—were out of the way. The rest could be convinced or bought."

She urged him on. "Did he ask you to step down, or was that your own choice?"

"I was getting threats. At first, I ignored them. Then one day, my young daughter was kidnapped on her way home from school. The captors didn't make demands of money. The note merely said, 'You know what you must do.' I resigned from the company, and she was returned to us the next day. Since then, I vowed to forget Royal

Petrol and keep quiet. It was hard, after pouring myself into that company for so many years, to stop caring. But I knew the consequences."

"And Harry?"

He paused. "There's something I have been carrying around with me for some time now, and it's been heavy on my conscience. I will tell you what I know, but I won't go public with it. You have to figure out some other way to make it work for you."

"I'm listening."

"While I was president, I was an unofficial mentor to Harry Ashworth. He'd come to me with all sorts of issues and I'd help him work them out. He was a fine young man . . . smart, talented, incorruptible. He was the natural choice to succeed me as president. Not only did he understand the business in an almost instinctive way, but he'd also brought in a flurry of new accounts. He was unstoppable, really.

"The trouble started when he began looking into the deal with Judah and was rather outspoken about pulling out of Israel. It wasn't so much the oil exploration he was opposed to; it was this new partnership with Advanced Electronic Solutions. He didn't see why the Royal Petrol ships needed such sophisticated combat systems."

The words struck Sarah like a lightning bolt. "Wait. Are you saying the drillship *MedStar* is equipped with a weapons system?"

"It isn't common knowledge but, yes, it's true. It has rather elaborate computers and radar to detect oncoming attacks and defend itself against them."

"Defend itself . . . with missiles?"

He nodded. "Harry fought that for the better part of two years. He and his father would bicker at board meetings, and it was painfully obvious they didn't see eye to eye. Then one day, Harry came to see me. He was a pilot, so he flew his plane to Sardinia, where I was vacationing. I will never forget that meeting. He was a wreck. He was paranoid his father was out to silence him, and he feared for his life."

"How could he have known?"

"He overheard a private phone conversation, in which his dad was saying things like 'I want him eliminated' and 'This must be watertight; no one can suspect anything.' He surmised that his father was talking about him. A week later, his plane went down over Scotland. He was on his way to give a lecture to a group of students at St. Andrews University."

So it was a conspiracy. Sarah trembled involuntarily. "Trent confessed to me, when he thought I'd never again see the light of day, the instrument panel on Harry's plane was sabotaged. It only appeared to be an accident."

"The ironic part? It was all done with Advanced Electronic Solutions technology."

Her eyes widened. "What? How do you know this?"

"According to the reports, the instruments failed due to a computer glitch. That looked random to investigators, but I know better. I know what AES are capable of. They reprogram navigation computers all the time, though usually to achieve different ends."

"So this is a hypothesis of yours."

"I have proof."

She grasped both of his arms. "You must tell me."

He looked over one of his shoulders, then the other, then back at her. "Shortly after our talk in Sardinia, Harry returned to London. A few days later, I flew back on my own plane. As I walked across the tarmac at Biggin Hill Airport, I happened to walk past Harry's plane and noticed it was being worked on. I registered the technician's face, though I didn't know him at the time. After the accident, I became suspicious, so I did a bit of research. And indeed, that man was an AES contractor. Not an employee, per se, but someone who had worked on several major projects for the company."

She dropped her hands. "And you never said anything?"

A bitter expression crept on his face. He looked away. "To my eternal shame, no. I never did. I was too afraid to."

"It's not too late. You can still expose them."

"Sarah, if I come out with this, my entire family will be at risk. They sent that message loud and clear by kidnapping my daughter. My own life is one thing, but endangering them . . ." He looked down. "I mustn't think of it."

She understood his reservations but pushed him anyway. In a short list of allies, he was her biggest hope. "So you'll just sit back and watch the death toll rise. Is that it?"

"What choice do I have? Tell me."

"There are so many whistle-blower programs. Surely your family can be protected."

"And live in anonymity in some remote village in Finland? Away from everything they hold dear? Their lives would be ruined, and they would resent me forever."

She was incredulous. "So you're saying your own comfort outweighs your moral responsibility. If you think you can live with that, then I have nothing more to say."

He looked at her pensively for a silent moment. "I'll think about it. I'm sorry I can't readily give you the answer you want to hear. Perhaps I'm not as brave as you."

She softened. "I find that being brave is far easier when you're convinced you're doing the right thing. This is the right thing, Mr. Bellows." She looked into the depths of his green eyes and sensed his regret. "I do hope you'll change your mind."

She turned away and walked along the riverbanks toward the park's exit. Her mind was so overloaded from everything she'd heard that she felt too numb to think of the next step. The questions swirled in her head like wraiths, too restless to settle. What had Harry known that cost him his life? Why would a company like AES engage in illegal activity that, if uncovered, could shut its doors forever? And what kind of man would exploit his son's mental illness?

The moon reflected on the surface of the Gade, illuminating the ripples on the water as a brisk breeze blew. Sarah's hair danced across her face. She pushed back the errant strands. Dry leaves floated toward the ground in a slow aerial ballet. She checked the time; it was past midnight. Daniel would be back by now.

She waited until she was in her car to dial his number.

He picked up on the first ring. "How did it go?"

"Quite well, I must say. I am just back from a rendezvous with Bellows. He was too paranoid to talk at his home."

"All right. I'm all ears."

"For starters, he handed me today's paper, folded to an article about Judah Oil's chairman dying in an apparent drowning. He was found in the bottom of his pool last night. The report said it was a cardiac event."

"Let me guess—"

"Right. Sacks was named to succeed him."

"One more notch on his scoreboard. What do you want to bet Judah is getting ready to announce an oil discovery?"

"That's what I'm afraid of, too. It gets worse. The *MedStar* apparently is equipped with a weapons system. What do you suppose they plan to do with that?"

"Exactly. Did Bellows give you anything we can use against Sacks?"

"Perhaps." A vague paranoia courted her. She looked

out the driver's window into the shadows. The bare trees clawed at the night with gnarled wooden fingers. The serpentine river cutting through the woodland shimmered like a premonition. She shook it off and continued. "He did confirm Sacks is deranged. His father has planted his delusions. Get this: he paid off a genealogist to tell Sacks he was King Solomon's descendant, knowing fully he would act out that delusion to the end. Sacks truly believes he is the most important figure of our times, when in reality he is his father's operative. James Ashworth is using him to strike big oil in Israel through any means, with the ultimate goal of controlling a portion of the Middle Eastern supply. It is the height of evil."

"Wow." He exhaled slowly. "This is valuable intel, but it won't help us nail him. We need something we can prove."

"How about this? They apparently conspired to have Harry killed. According to Bellows, Harry heard his father talk on the phone about a hit. He feared for his life and said as much to Bellows, who was his friend and mentor. This is where it gets complicated." She paused. "A programmer for Advanced Electronic Solutions was working on Harry's plane just before it went down."

There was a long silence on Daniel's end. "Are you sure about this?"

"Bellows saw him."

"That's perfect. Can he give a positive ID on him?"

"He knows what he looks like. But he won't talk. He's

skittish because his daughter was kidnapped once, and he fears for his family's safety."

"Oh, come on. We're talking murder here. How can he keep quiet?"

"Fear is a powerful motivator," she said. "Tell me about your evening."

"It took a whole lot of acting, but I believe our mission was accomplished. Your dad made the introduction to Bromley, as planned."

Though Sarah knew this was the only way to get to Bromley quickly, she had mixed feelings. She didn't want to involve her father, but mostly she didn't want to endanger him by association. "How much does my father know?"

"He doesn't know anything. He was just doing me a favor. I asked him to introduce me to Bromley, so he took me as his guest to this party full of politicians and society types. Beyond that, he has no idea. But he's a smart man. He suspects something's up."

"And what was Bromley's reaction when he saw you?"

"He went white as rice. I think I was the last person he expected to see. I'm sure he thought you and I both died in that cave. The good thing is, he doesn't realize we know who he is. So I just played dumb. I told him you and I had parted company and I was through with the Middle East and heading back to the States."

"Brilliant. Do you think he believed you?"

"Sure seemed that way."

"So now what?"

"I'm guessing he'll be tracking my movements, so I have to make good on what I said. I'll fly to the States while you work on the next part of the plan. Then I'll meet you in Jerusalem."

A sense of foreboding seeped in. "You will be careful, won't you?"

He laughed, but there was a hint of nervousness in it. "Don't worry about me. You just stay under the radar and get yourself to Israel safely. Everything will be just fine."

"I'm not sure I believe you. But thanks all the same."

"Don't mention it. Get some rest now, Sarah. Another big day tomorrow." He paused. "You sure you want to do this?"

Her next move was a risky one. Success could earn them a valuable ally. But failure could be catastrophic.

"Yes," she said. "I'm sure."

Chapter 31

At one in the morning, Sacks stepped onto the balcony of his two-story apartment to feel the energy of the thunderstorm raging outside. Wind gusts pushed the sheets of rain off their vertical course, whipping them into a frenzy. Distant lightning pierced the starless Jerusalem sky.

He rather relished the sensation of the cold rain pelting his bare skin. He felt the liquid needles hit his face and chest, exposed beneath an unbuttoned white linen shirt. He squinted through the deluge toward the Old City. An amber light, like fire, bathed the stone fortress, making it stand out like a jewel in the jumble of buildings and lights that was modern Jerusalem. The golden orb topping the Dome of the Rock glowed white-hot at center stage, impossible to ignore.

A faint smile crept across his lips. The moment was nearly his. No longer would the heathens lay claim to

Mount Moriah and the foundation stone of the world. No more would they tarnish the Holy of Holies that once held in its breast the very word of God. The time had come for the Jews to reclaim what was rightfully theirs. He would soon hand his people that long overdue victory, and he would live forever.

His phone vibrated loudly against the glass top of the dining table. He stepped inside the groin-vaulted salon and walked barefoot across the golden limestone floor. He looked at the phone's caller ID: *Private*.

He picked up but did not speak.

The caller spoke first. "I ran into an old friend tonight."

"And who would that be?"

"I was at a soiree in Belgravia with members of the Conservative Party. Imagine my surprise when I was introduced to Daniel Madigan."

He started. "What? Impossible."

"Oh, I assure you it's possible. He stood before me in the flesh. Last I heard, he and the girl were left to die in a cave without egress." He paused. "What happened?"

Sacks' gaze darted about the room as he tried to come to terms with the shock. "They must have escaped somehow."

"You should have done the job right the first time," he barked. "You should have never left them there alive."

His nostrils flared; his jaw tightened. He was not accustomed to being spoken to in that manner. Through his teeth he said, "When you address me, you speak with respect. Do you understand?"

Bromley said, "Let me remind you who has the upper hand here. Without me, none of your tawdry plans could come to pass. So I will speak as I choose. Am I clear?"

He did not deign to respond. His eyes burned with loathing. He despised Bromley's aggression even as he depended on it. Had Sacks' father not brought Bromley to the table, and had their mission not relied on his unorthodox arms deals, Sacks would have broken ties with that arrogant prick long ago. He needed him, but he didn't trust him.

"Good. Now listen to me carefully. Madigan mentioned he's headed back to the States tomorrow—alone."

"What about her?"

"We'll deal with her later. For now, I want him out of the picture."

Sacks paced the room. "I couldn't agree more. He has a habit of turning up at the most inappropriate moments. In fact, I'm not convinced he was at that party by accident. You spoke to him. Do you think he suspects?"

"I don't, actually. He's a bit of a buffoon. Had no idea who I am, let alone what I'm capable of."

"So he said. He's far more dangerous than he lets on. And so is she."

"All the more reason to move quickly. And this time, it can't be a mere warning. I have already placed a call to my favorite airplane technician."

Sacks stopped in his tracks. Thoughts of his brother's flawless assassination galloped into his mind. He liked the idea of a repeat performance. "I see. And what exactly are Madigan's flight plans?"

"He's flying private. He's taking Weston's plane to New York. I checked. He's the only passenger on board."

"And Lord Weston?"

"He flies in the morning to Moscow on a diplomatic mission. He'll be on one of the government planes with a group visiting Russia and the Stans. He'll be gone a good two weeks."

Sacks walked to the balcony doorway and watched lightning illuminate the eastern horizon. A crack of thunder added to the symphony of hissing wind and violent rainfall. "Very well, then. I shall coordinate everything on my end."

"Remember: no mistakes."

Sacks smiled. "No mistakes."

Chapter 32

Dressed in a simple black djellaba and a black-and-white plaid hijab, Sarah sat in the back of the jeep, trying to tune out the cacophony of shrill Arabic music and the loud voice of her driver, who was talking incessantly on his mobile phone. It was a long way from Riyadh to the desert, and she'd hoped the drive would give her time to gather her thoughts. Instead, she felt more agitated than ever.

That was due partly to the conversation she'd had before boarding the plane to Saudi Arabia. She'd phoned Johann Marlowe, the chief adept for the Hermetic Order of the Golden Dawn for the past twenty years, offering him a glimpse into the Solomonic texts they had unearthed in exchange for information on his former pupil.

Marlowe, who typically kept a low profile, had been intrigued by the blueprints for King Solomon's temple. For the Order, Solomon was a guiding light, a foundation for philosophical doctrine and an inspiration for worship rituals. She had counted on that to open doors, and it had.

The chief had been surprisingly forthcoming on the subject of Trent Sacks; it was clear there had been some bad blood. She replayed the conversation in her mind.

"Trent joined the order about ten years ago," Marlowe said. "There was a real fire in him. When he was merely an initiate, he pored over everything ever written about the magical arts. He didn't talk to many people; he hardly slept. His passion bordered on obsession. But he knew his stuff, and he became quite good at conjurations. Three years ago, he reached the post of Magus, the second highest rank within the third order of the Golden Dawn. That's when he became volatile . . . drunk with power. He was no longer part of something greater. He was his own entity, and he did what he wanted without adhering to the teachings."

"What was it he wanted?"

He paused. "This is a little difficult to explain to someone who is not a believer."

"I have an open mind."

"Let me see if I can put everything into context for you. Much of what we do is communication with spirits. We invoke, and we evoke. In invocatory magic, we call forth higher spirits—mostly angelical beings. In evocatory magic, we summon lower beings or demons, primarily to interrogate them. The latter is very dangerous, as the person doing the summoning must be extremely strong. Any crack in his faith can provide a portal for the demon to enter . . . and do irreparable damage."

This was foreign territory for Sarah. She tried her best to follow without passing judgment. She needed to understand Sacks' *modus operandi*. "Are you saying he . . . evoked demons?"

"He considered himself a Solomonic magician. The great king, as you probably know, was renowned for his ability to communicate with both angels and demons. It was the latter that caused his spiritual downfall. If you've read some of the Arabic literature, and even the Talmudic texts, you might have seen references to the demon king Ashmedai, whom Solomon captured, imprisoned, and forced to work in the building of his temple. But Ashmedai was cunning and eventually robbed Solomon of his ring and his power and cast him out to wander the desert as a pauper. Some believe Solomon triumphed and was restored to the throne; others believe he died in that pitiful state, steeped in the sin of his vanity and arrogance. Trent was highly influenced by this story. He was determined to be a master of the demon world, to avert his own spiritual downfall."

"You speak about him in the past tense. I assume this means he is no longer part of the Golden Dawn?"

"That's correct. His interpretations of the teachings became sinister. As he focused more and more on evocations, he became increasingly distant—reclusive, even. He engaged in some rituals our order never condoned. He blatantly disregarded the masters, as if our opinion was of no consequence."

Sarah suspected he was referring to the dark side of the magical arts. "What sort of rituals?"

"Blood sacrifices. We've never practiced them and never will. In fact, we vehemently oppose them."

She knew Marlowe wasn't referring to Sacks' mere elimination of people who'd gotten in his way. These were formal, deliberate sacrifices, offerings to the heavens. It was his way of desecrating and destroying enemies—and showing how far he would go for his god.

Sensing she had his trust, she probed further. "Mr. Marlowe, Trent Sacks has stolen the Solomonic treasures, and I fear he will use them with ill intent. Is there anything you can tell me about rituals or legends surrounding this manuscript or the ring of the king?"

"The ring," he whispered. "The masonic instrument . . . so it does exist."

Sarah's pulse quickened. "The ring is an instrument? How does it work?"

"Unfortunately, we don't know. There are enigmatic references to Solomon's Seal throughout the texts but no concrete data on what it looks like or how it works. It has always been thought that if one is in possession of it and that person has had magical training, he would know what to do."

The masonic instrument. Somehow the ring was to be used to measure, level, or center during the building process. That was why it was imperative to possess both the ring and the blueprints: one was useless without the other.

Rabbi Ben Moshe would know about this. She would pay him another visit—but first, she had a delivery to make.

The driver propped an arm onto the seat back and turned around. "Here you go, lady. This is the place."

Sarah gazed out the window at the desolate corner of the Empty Quarter. The jeep had come to a standstill on a dirt road cut through the desert. The golden sand dunes, blushing pink in the morning light, stretched toward infinity. In the distance, a thicket of palms and some meager 'asal shrubs provided reprieve from the harsh conditions.

The semipermanent settlement of the Al Murrah stood on the fringes of the oasis. "Wait for me here," she told the driver as she stepped out of the jeep.

She slipped a woven bag over her head and across her chest. She inhaled the dry, hot air, which carried a sort of ache. It wasn't so long ago she had been digging a few miles away from this very spot. Yet the al-Fau days were already behind a closed door in her mind. She had a strong premonition she would never go back, and the thought disturbed her. For the first time in her life, she had nowhere to return to, no compass in the wilderness. The rational part of her, the part she trusted, was terrified. But she could not silence the voices that told her to fight on, regardless of what might come.

Even in December, the desert baked at a steady ninety degrees. In the silence of the sandy realm, she could hear the swish of her cotton djellaba as she walked toward the encampment. Though time was of no consequence here, she was keenly aware of its passage. Every minute that ticked away was a reminder that the enemy was gaining ground.

Sarah walked quickly to the Murrah settlement.

Two women carrying water greeted her with suspicious looks.

She bowed her head. "I would like to see the amir," she said in Arabic.

The two women looked at each other, then at Sarah. They didn't regard her with distrust but with curiosity, surely wondering what a woman with blue eyes and fair skin was doing in their midst, dressed in a black robe like them, speaking their language.

One studied Sarah with shining brown eyes, the only part of her face not hidden by her black headdress. She nodded toward the far side of camp, where a gray-and-brown-striped tent was set up.

Sarah knew it wouldn't be easy to gain audience with the leader of the tribe. In the patriarchal society of the nomads, women and men were segregated, and a woman's opinion didn't register as heavily as a man's. She clutched her bag. She hoped the object inside would convince the amir to at least hear what she had to say.

Outside his tent was a group of young men, sitting cross-legged in a circle, drinking coffee. She stood at a nonthreatening distance and waited to be spoken to.

"What is it you want, woman?" one asked.

"I bring news of the amir's son."

"Say what you have to say, and take your leave."

"No." She tried not to sound disrespectful, but her independent spirit seeped in. "I must speak to him privately. It is a grave matter."

They mumbled something among themselves, and one of the men stood. "Wait here."

He disappeared into the tent. A few moments later, he reemerged and gestured for her to go inside.

With her head lowered and hands clasped, Sarah entered in silence.

"Approach." The voice was deep and gravelly, like a lifelong smoker's. The amir sat on a pile of woolen pillows, thumbing a string of amber beads. He was dressed in black, his head wrapped in a red-and-white keffiyeh secured at the crown with a black band. His face was the color of milk chocolate and carved with the lines of hardship. A graying beard hung to his sternum.

Sarah knew the only reason he allowed a woman to

enter his tent was the connection to his son. She thought it only fair to disclose who she was. "Your graciousness is great, Amir. May I introduce myself?"

"I know who you are." He clapped his hands loudly. "Sit."

She sat opposite him on the worn carpet.

Not a minute later, two masked women entered with a small plate of dates and a bowl of white, frothy milk they placed in front of Sarah. She conveyed her thanks with a slight bow and took a sip of the sweet milk, still warm from the camel.

"The men tell me you have news of my son," he said. "I have not seen him in many days."

"I saw Sa'id in Israel, inside a cave in the Judean Wilderness." Her voice was confident, unapologetic. "He was with the Englishman. I was their prisoner."

The amir's dark eyes narrowed. "Go on."

She had already measured her words. The Al Murrah elders were honorable, forthright people who appreciated the truth without embellishment. "The throne of King Solomon of Israel and Judah was in that cave. The Englishman ordered Sa'id to ascend it so he would not have to face the danger himself." She lowered her eyes. "Sa'id was killed instantly, gored by the horn of a golden ox. I saw it happen."

"Lies," he bellowed. "How dare you bring such blasphemy into my house?"

She reached inside her bag and pulled out Sa'id's *khanja*. The curved part of the sheath was bent, and there was a telling gash in the handle. She placed it gently in front of the amir.

The chief scooped it up and examined it, then held it close to his heart. Sorrow overtook him.

Sarah gave him a moment, knowing her next message would enrage him. The Al Murrah prized loyalty above all else. In return for a betrayal—by one of their own or an outsider—they would exact revenge, no matter how long it took or how far they had to go. It was part of the *sharaf*, the Bedouin's honor code.

"The Englishman betrayed Sa'id, Amir. He used him with no regard for his life. He didn't even go to his aid as he lay dying. I don't know what he has promised you, but you can count on this: he will break his promises before it's over."

The amir inhaled sharply. "His pact was not with me. I am of the old order, and I opposed an alliance with a foreigner. Sa'id insisted. As my soon-to-be heir, he was granted certain privileges. He went forth with the partnership because it would mean jobs for our young people. 'They are tired of being camel herders,' he said. 'They want a new way of life.' Our end of the bargain was to hand over the artifacts found in the valley."

"What sort of jobs did he promise them?"

"Oil. He has rigs in the Rub' al Khali. Some of our

men work for him there. Some he has taken to other parts of Arabia."

"Do you know where?"

"No. But we can find them. Word travels swiftly among our people."

She knew that to be true. Nomadic tribesmen communicated across the desert, utilizing messengers and strategically lit fires. In this way they could reach other tribes, miles away, to warn them about impending dangers like sandstorms or raids. The system, employed since ancient times, was taken seriously by all the tribes and thus had never failed.

"I pray you will find justice for the death of your son." She bent forward until her forehead touched the carpet.

"Rise."

She met his gaze. The anguish had left his eyes, now replaced by a terrible wrath that carried one of the inviolable laws of the desert: you do not cross the Bedouin.

She had accomplished what she'd gone there to do. She stood and exited the amir's tent, walking past the gawking tribesmen and women who'd stopped what they were doing in vigilance for their leader. She felt their stares as she left the settlement and hurried toward the car that waited to take her to the airport.

Chapter 33

Beyond the porthole window of the Royal Jordanian jet, Tel Aviv looked especially bleak on this December morning. Thick clouds the color of old parchment hid the sunlight, casting a gray hue on everything below. The rain came down soft and steady, misting Sarah's window with droplets that streamed down the Plexiglas like tears.

The plane taxied to the gate, and a symphony of beeps sounded across the cabin. As the flight attendant made the deplaning announcement, Sarah turned on her phone and checked for messages. There was nothing, not even a note from Daniel, who probably would be en route to New York by now. It was nine in the morning Tel Aviv time. She put the phone in her jacket pocket and exited the plane.

The terminal was packed, as usual. She walked toward the exit through a sea of faces, all detached and insipid, like apparitions. Her phone vibrated against her hip.

She answered.

"Sarah . . ." Ezra's voice sounded choked, distant. "I am so sorry."

She could barely hear him. She placed a hand over her other ear. "Sorry . . . for what? What's happened?"

There was a brief silence. "You mean you don't—? Where are you?"

"I just landed in Tel Aviv. Walking through Ben Gurion now."

"Stay where you are. I'll be right there."

She was puzzled, almost annoyed. "What's going on?"

She looked up and caught a glimpse of the newscast on a television monitor. She could not hear the words of the Israeli anchor over the clatter of the terminal, so she tried to read the Hebrew characters superimposed on the screen.

Crash of Flight 43

The next image was of a sea she could not identify. Wreckage from a broken wing and fuselage was floating on the water. Then, Luton, one of the London airports, was cued up, followed by a hangar and the image of an intact jet. She recognized it instantly: a Dassault Falcon 900, the Weston family plane. She froze beneath the monitor. People bumped into her, jostling her.

"Sarah? Are you there?"

The photo of her father flashed on the screen. She dropped the phone.

A young man picked up her phone and handed it to

her, saying something in Hebrew she did not register. She could hear Ezra's voice emanating from the device.

"I'm here," she said. "I just saw."

"I'm on my way. Stay put. I'll meet you at the El Al lounge."

Her hands were shaking as she tapped the phone screen to hang up. Instinctively, she dialed Daniel's number. As she suspected, it went straight to voice mail: he was still in the air en route to New York. She felt detached from her body as she walked to the lounge, thoughts and emotions barraging her.

At the lounge, she paid the attendant the day rate and went straight to a computer to read the developing story. There was frustratingly little information. It said only that the flight was en route to the United States when it crashed over the Atlantic. No word about the cause or survivors.

She called her father's office. His secretary did not pick up, and her voice mail was full. Sarah called his flat in London and the country house in Wiltshire. No answer at either. She tossed the phone onto the coffee table and rested her head on her palms.

The photo of her father on the screen of the Israeli newscast haunted her. Everything felt so surreal, like she was experiencing it from a parallel universe. Could he really be gone? In a way, she'd lost him long before. Her mind went into rewind mode, replaying scenes from the past, episodes she had tried so hard to forget.

She saw herself at sixteen, on that dreadful night just after New Year's. She was on break from her all-girls boarding school in Wallingford, Connecticut, and staying at her mother's home in New Canaan.

First there was the phone call, around one in the morning. Sarah wasn't trying to listen, but the walls between their bedrooms were thin and her mother's voice was loud, almost a shriek. She was sure she was under the influence. She could hear only her side of the conversation.

"I don't give a shit about your tennis game, Richard. I'm tired of being put off by you . . . Listen to me. The money is running out. I can't keep it together anymore. The bills from Choate alone are killing me. You're going to have to . . . What? No, I haven't. There's nothing out there. I'm in the city practically every week, auditioning . . ." There was a series of sniffles.

Sarah cringed. She knew her mother, who'd had a brief acting stint in Hollywood before meeting Sir Richard and moving to England, had been trying to resurrect her career. Too many years had passed and too many wrinkles had descended, and the rejections were piling up.

"How could you do this? This is your child, for heaven's sake. You can't cut us off like this . . . Richard? Richard!"

She heard a growl, then the sound of broken glass.

Sarah had tried knocking on her mother's door, but there wasn't an answer, only the sobs of despair. She'd made the fateful decision to let her be.

Around five in the morning, she jolted awake, suddenly remorseful. It was the first time she'd felt intuition overtake logic. She went to her mother's door again, knocked, got no reply.

She entered. The bed was unslept in. The mirror of the vanity had been shattered. She was overcome by dread.

"Mum?"

There was no answer. The bathroom door was cracked open and a strip of light shimmered in the dark. She walked toward it.

She stood outside the bathroom for a moment, listening to the silence, letting the door shield her from what she feared she might find on the other side. She slowly pushed the door open, squinting at the sudden brightness.

"Mum, are you here? You okay?"

She stepped inside and scanned the room. There was a faint smell of gardenia. Her eyes stopped at the bathtub. An empty rocks glass sat on the shelf behind the tub.

Terrified, the teenage Sarah approached. From beneath the water, her mother's pallid face stared at her with open but vacant eyes. She was fully made up with crimson lips and heavy eyeliner, a beautifully painted shell. Her long, wavy locks floated around her head like a golden halo.

Sarah let out a wail that disintegrated into sobs. She steadied herself on the tile wall as her knees buckled, and she slid to the floor, unsure of what to do. She felt abandoned, desperate, immobilized. And so very guilty.

Her father did nothing to ease her anguish. On the day of the funeral, he pulled her aside. "Sarah, what's happened is terrible, but you mustn't brood. It does nothing for your character. You must look forward now."

That sort of prescience eluded her. At that moment, she wanted only to be comforted. "Daddy, I'd like to come back to England."

"Not yet. You have one more year at Choate. I want you to finish."

"But I hate it. And I'm all alone here."

"You are no longer a girl, Sarah. You must be strong. Has this incident taught you nothing? Despair is for the weak. And weakness"—he paused—"has dreadful consequences."

That was the last time he ever spoke of the "incident." Sarah was left to wade through the bog of her emotions alone, with no compass and no map. Not only did he offer no branch of encouragement; he pushed her farther in by deriding her despair.

By all accounts, she should resent him. She didn't. Somewhere in her latent mind, he was still her daddy. She didn't want his approval and certainly not his fortune; she wanted him to put down his guard long enough to admit his foibles and shortcomings and to accept her despite hers.

The prospect of that ever happening was drifting

away like wreckage in the cold Atlantic. She reminded herself there was no confirmation of her father's perishing in that crash. As long as there was hope, she would cling to it.

She felt a hand on her shoulder and looked up with a start. Ezra was standing over her, talking on the phone.

"Can you get the manifest?" she heard him say. He lowered the phone. "I'm talking to a friend who works for IAA. Couldn't get anything from the media, so I thought I'd go straight to the source." He returned the phone to his ear. "Yes, I'm here."

She watched his brow furrow as he listened. He nodded and muttered, "Okay," a couple of times.

She stood and crossed her arms. "What is he saying?"

He lifted a palm and continued listening. "I see. Okay, great. Call me back." He hung up. "Good news. Your father wasn't on that plane. His name was registered on another flight that left today for Moscow."

She dropped her head. "Thank goodness."

"There was one passenger on the Falcon. He's trying to find a name. He'll call when he does." He stroked her hair. "You all right?"

She nodded. "Did your friend say what the cause of the crash was?"

"They don't know yet. They won't put any theories out there until the black box is found and they conduct an investigation."

"What about the pilot?" She worried about Branford Welles, who had piloted the Weston planes for the past twenty-six years and was practically family.

"They're looking for survivors. There is always a possibility . . ."

She looked away. In the shock of the news, she hadn't even considered what now seemed obvious. Her blood went cold.

What if . . . ?

Ezra's phone rang once. "Adam. Talk to me."

As he listened to his IAA contact, Sarah's thoughts turned to the thugs who sabotaged Harry Ashworth's plane. Could they be sending her a warning by bringing down her father's jet? Would they really go that far?

"What? Are you sure?" Ezra looked pale. He shifted his gaze downward. His expression was blank. He whispered, "Shit."

"Ezra? What is going on?"

He hung up and stared at her. His brow was wrinkled, and his frown lines were pronounced beneath his silver-streaked beard.

She had never seen him look so concerned. It alarmed her.

He took a deep breath. "The plane was en route to New York. The name on the manifest was Daniel Madigan."

His words hit her like a wrecking ball. She felt like she was suffocating.

"Sarah, I am so sorry."

"No . . ."

With a pained look, he nodded.

She pounded his chest. "No . . . no!"

Ezra grasped her forearms and pulled her close. She struggled against his embrace, but he held on. "Shh . . ."

A choked wail escaped her lips, and she unclenched her fists. She crumpled into his arms, her body quaking violently with sobs.

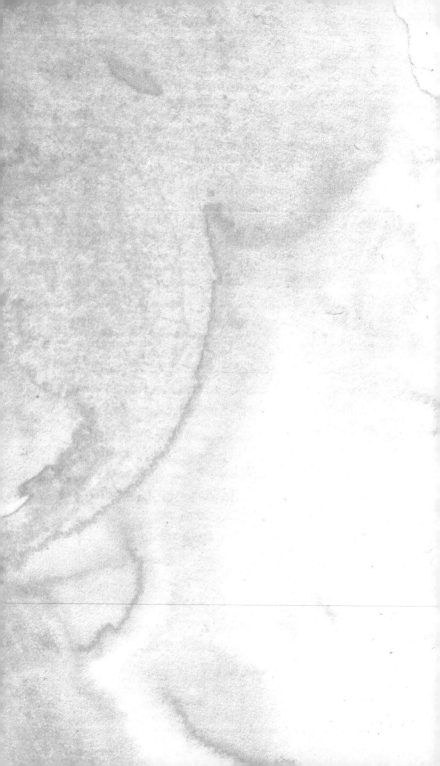

Chapter 34

Sarah woke up on Ezra's sofa, still dressed in the chambray shirt and faded jeans she'd worn during the flight the day before. Her head felt heavy and detached from her body, likely the result of the tranquilizers Ezra had procured for her the previous day. She rubbed her stinging, swollen eyes.

Day was dawning beyond his living room window. The steely sky was streaked with wisps of rose gold, and pale light filtered through the undressed window. She scanned her surroundings. Ezra's house was as messy as his office, with stacks of books and magazines on tables and all over the floor. And yet there was a homey smell to the place. She thought she detected the scent of cinnamon.

She had been sleeping for a long time. The last thing she remembered was being curled up on that sofa, steeped in a bitter brew of despair and anger. The tranquilizers softened the edges but did not take away the dark reality.

Her chest felt tight as she considered Daniel's death. She refused to accept it. She told herself there wasn't conclusive evidence. His body had not been found.

She was certain of one thing: this wasn't an accident. It was plain to her now that Alastair Bromley had mobilized his assassins after meeting Daniel at the party. Considering her conversation with Bellows, she should have realized this was a very real possibility and warned him. Why did she not see this coming? Why didn't she stop him from flying?

"Good morning." Ezra walked into the living room holding a tray with a coffeepot, two mugs, and a coffee cake. "How are you feeling?"

"Like hell. You?"

He poured the coffee and handed her a full cup. "Not bad, actually. Guess what's all over the Internet this morning?"

She stared at him blankly as she took a sip of the strong, black coffee.

"News from the wreck site," he continued. "The pilot has been found alive."

"You're joking."

"Not at all. He was unconscious and hypothermic, but he had a pulse. They've taken him to hospital in critical condition."

"Ezra, that is amazing news. It means Danny—"

"Could be alive too." He rested a hand on her forearm. "But I don't want you to get your hopes up. That water is really cold. The fact the pilot survived is a miracle."

"He's the most resourceful and capable person I know. If anyone could survive something like this, he could."

He gave her a tight-lipped smile. "I hope you're right."

She knew it was a long shot, but she believed in Daniel's abilities. Obviously, the plane did not explode or come apart in the air, or Branford never would have survived. There had to have been a water landing. Which meant there was still a chance. "I have to talk to Branford."

"There is no way. The Pope himself couldn't get to Branford now. First of all, he's battling for his life. Secondly, he's under tight security because of the investigation. It's going to be that way for weeks."

He was right. There was no way Scotland Yard would let Branford talk to anyone before a full inquiry was launched. She'd have to think of another way to confirm the cause of the crash and come closer to exposing Bromley and Advanced Electronic Solutions. She would like nothing more than to put that murderer behind bars.

But if there was one thing the crash underscored, it was that she needed to stay in the shadows. She stood and fetched her backpack and coat.

"What do you think you're doing?"

"I have to go. My presence here puts you in danger. I can't have that."

"Wait. You're not saying someone was targeting Daniel?" Ezra looked bewildered. "And you're next?"

"That is actually what I'm saying." She sighed. "There is so much you don't know."

"Seems to me you need an ally right now. Why don't you at least tell me what's going on? I could help you."

"Believe me. The less you know, the better off you are."

He walked to her and put both hands on her shoulders. "You don't worry about me. I've got a pretty good safety net. Now . . . how can I help you?"

She thought about it. She couldn't tell him everything—it would put him in danger—but she could tell him this. "King Solomon was real, Ezra. His throne is buried in a cave in the Judean Wilderness. It was the hiding place for a manuscript of immeasurable significance to our profession." She paused. "It contains the plans for building the original temple of Jerusalem."

His eyes widened. "Where in the desert? We can send a crew."

"I can help you get to the throne. But the manuscript is no longer there. It has fallen into the wrong hands, I'm afraid."

"What? Who?"

"The man who is hunting us down. He has designs on Temple Mount. His plan is to build the temple anew."

"That's preposterous. Temple Mount is untouchable. Besides, only Mashiach can build the third temple."

"Exactly."

"You don't mean—"

"He is very deluded, but he's also very powerful. There's nothing this man won't do to further his goal."

"So what do you plan to do?"

She slung the backpack over her shoulders. "I'm going back to Jerusalem. I'll hide there until he's ready to make a move."

"And then what? You'll ambush him? Be real, Sarah."

"Well, I can't sit back and do nothing. If he goes through with his plan, it will mean disaster on a vast scale. The least I could do is try to block his moves."

"With what resources? You're not thinking clearly."

She brushed past him on her way to the door.

He followed her. "Let me at least go with you."

"You can help me far more by staying here. I need you to help me figure out something. The plans are meaningless without knowing the true unit of measurement—the one that was used to build the original temple. I need any information you can give me on that."

"Guess all that talk about the old king's wisdom wasn't just bunk."

"Anything but. My theory is Solomon foresaw the collapse of the united monarchy. He saw signs of it during his reign and knew it was a matter of time before the temple was destroyed by Israel's enemies. So he left the plans behind for his son, or the son of a son, but withheld a critical piece of information for fear the plans would fall into the wrong hands. In his eyes, there was probably no more heinous a crime than the unworthy building a temple to God."

"You'll forgive me if I remain skeptical. But for you . . . let me see what I can do."

"Just keep it tight. This guy has sensors everywhere."

Ezra walked her to the door. "If you change your mind, just text me. I'll bail you out of trouble anytime."

She gave him a peck on the cheek. "Thanks for everything, my dear friend. I'll be in touch."

She closed the door behind her and stood alone in the dark corridor. She no longer felt fear. She was ready to face down the enemy, regardless of consequences.

On the train from Tel Aviv to Jerusalem, Sarah was needled by unshakable anxiety. She wasn't sure whether she should attribute it to the lingering effects of the drugs or to her own growing sense of despair.

She checked her phone for messages. She had called and texted Daniel's number so many times, clutching onto the hope she'd somehow receive a reply, that it was beginning to feel pathological. Be it by intuition or plain denial, she could not accept his death.

She was no stranger to the cosmic injustice that cut large lives short, brutally ripping them away from those who loved them before good-byes had been said or amends had been made. For the living, it was a minefield of regret that exploded into a personal hell.

She went through it once, when her mother died, and it was nearly her undoing. She attempted then to detach from the pain completely, running from the false pity of polite society to places where no one knew her name or her story. There, among the silent stones, she could control her world.

That state of benign numbness was hers for years until circumstances stoked the fire that lay in cinders.

It was Daniel who had helped her find her way. He hadn't let her get away with her girlish fantasies of being a feisty loner, instead coaxing the passionate woman out of her protective fortress so she could fight for her ideals. By letting her be an individual yet stubbornly refusing to leave her side, he'd helped her understand strength and interdependence weren't mutually exclusive concepts.

It was his gift to her, and she'd never even thanked him for it. The thought of never seeing him again, of so many words left unsaid, made her chest ache.

She rubbed her eyes, then looked out the window. The hilly landscape of the Israeli countryside, plugged with trees whose thinning leaves trumpeted the advent of winter, rolled past so quickly she didn't have time to contemplate its beauty. It was a reminder of the fragile nature of the moment—how quickly it could fade if she wasn't careful to notice.

She rolled her phone between her hands, summoning the courage to make the first move. *Yes*, she thought.

It's time. She called up the dial-pad screen on her phone and entered her father's mobile number. She remembered every digit, even though she hadn't called him in a year.

There was a pause, then the familiar distant double ring. She had practiced what she would say to him given the opportunity. She also knew he wouldn't pick up if he didn't recognize the number.

Voice mail.

"It's Sarah. I am so sorry about what's happened." She sighed, aware of the double entendre. "Please ring me. I should like to hear from you." She gave her temporary mobile number.

She was sure he wouldn't call. She'd seen it time and again: when he fell out with someone, he closed the book and didn't reopen it. But these were extraordinary circumstances. Perhaps, for once, he'd find some measure of compassion in that cold soul of his. It was worth a shot, if only for her own satisfaction at having tried.

To distract herself, she scanned the Internet news sites. She began with the usual British sources—BBC, *The Guardian*, *The Times*—and moved on to a few American newspapers and blogs. It was more of what had dominated the news for years: internal unrests, mass shootings, economic troubles. The stories were the same; only the settings varied. These sorts of reports had become so frequent that they had bred among the populace a general numbness bordering on apathy. It was a dangerous state of mind, this rampant dismissal of world events as noise.

Perhaps that was what Sacks was counting on. At a time when news was so consistently bad that people were anesthetized, there was a collective craving for something profound. The coming of the messiah, the promise of peace: the time was never more right.

She called up the *Haaretz* news site and read the Breaking News ticker across the top.

05:01 | Hundreds die in clashes in north Syria.

06:56 | US claims Iran is within months of completing nuclear weapon.

As the next headline flashed onto the screen, Sarah sat up. The blood drained from her face.

08:29 | Developing story: Oil found in the Mediterranean.

Chapter 35

ootsteps echoed across the marble floor of the long corridor leading to the boardroom. Sacks felt uncomfortable in his costume—gray suit with wide pinstripes, French-cuffed white shirt, and lilac silk tie—but no one would know it by his confident gait as he traversed the headquarters of Judah Oil.

He was about to lead his first board meeting as chairman, and he liked the idea of beginning with fireworks. He was the only one privy to the latest bit of news from the Mediterranean oil rig, and soon he would parlay it into an historic announcement.

It was only yesterday he'd come back from the new drilling platform. While the sea churned around them, the waves swelling and rolling as the wind and rain picked up, Sacks had given specific instructions to his foreman.

"What's our position, McConnell?"

"It's as we discussed: just south of the test site," the

foreman had said. "We have no choice. If we shift any farther north, we'll be in the trouble zone. You don't want that."

"No, we don't want that. But we want to strike the vein in the sweet spot."

"From our position, it won't be as easy, and it might take longer, but we can do it."

"Longer? How much longer?"

"Weeks, months maybe." He shrugged. "Best I can do."

"Is that so? Well, I say we can do better. I want you to go directional."

McConnell's plump face looked as if he'd just bitten into a lemon. "Boss . . . that's illegal. We'll be stirring Lebanon's tea."

Sacks smirked. "I expect you and the crew to work into the night getting the rig ready. I want to be in production within a week. You let the men know I will compensate them amply."

"A week? What's the bloody rush?"

Sacks clutched McConnell's shoulder a little too hard. "You are not here to question. You're here to follow orders. Am I understood?"

The man nodded.

"Good." He released his grip. "Carry on. And remember, there can be no delays. I will be back in a week's time to announce we have a show."

As he recalled the conversation, Sacks took a deep breath and let his face relax into a smile. The time drew near. Soon, all the years he'd devoted to study and all the family wealth he and his father had invested would be rewarded. All was in place for the grand finale—all, that is, but one thing; and that, too, would be his in time.

He stood outside the door of the boardroom and heard the chatter within. He smoothed his hair, held tightly in a ponytail, and turned the knob decisively. He entered the room with the flourish of a politician.

Voices were hushed; one by one, bodies rose from their seats.

"Please." With a serene smile, Sacks looked at the faces around the room. "Be seated."

He sat at the head of the table and removed a laptop from his briefcase. He connected it to a projector, which he turned on. "Ladies and gentlemen of the board, first let me say thank you for your confidence. I will do my utmost to lead this fine organization into the recognition and prosperity it deserves. As you already know, I am passionate about oil exploration and believe the future is right here in Israel." He captured the gaze of each man and woman in the room. "That future is now. What has long been a personal conviction, the mission of this company, and a dream of Jews everywhere, is about to become reality."

The room erupted in applause.

He waited for the clapping to subside. "I called this special meeting to share some news, so I will come straight to the point."

He cued up a presentation, beginning with images of the newly constructed semisubmersible platform that served as the permanent hub of Judah's offshore drilling operations. This rig was their best option for accessing the oil reserves, now estimated at twenty-five billion barrels and sitting at a depth of seventy-nine hundred feet, while withstanding the inclement weather that plagued the Med all winter.

Resting on four massive cylinders attached to submerged pontoons, the structure looked like a city of the future. A three-story building housing the Judah operations crew overlooked the deck, a multilevel stage on which sat the main derrick, four cranes, hydraulic lifts, pumps, engines, and a jumble of yet-to-be-dispatched pipes.

"As of this week, our platform is complete." His voice was clear and confident. "The crew there is fast-tracking the work. Others are laying claim to our discovery. But," he shouted, "*we* will prevail."

There was more applause. He quieted the room with his upraised hands. "Our testing has yielded the results we had hoped for. There is both quantity and quality on this site, and we are perfectly poised to tap into it." He displayed an animated diagram of the proposed drilling route. It did not show the horizontal directional line he'd instructed McConnell to deploy but rather a multilateral path that reached into several pockets of oil. "If you will note, the oil sits at a depth of almost eight thousand feet and is concentrated in several layers. Our proprietary drilling techniques give us the advantage of reaching multiple layers in a fraction of the time it would take other companies. The men assure me we will be in production within a week, showing the first evidence of an estimated twenty-five-billion-barrel reserve."

A silver-haired man at the opposite end of the room raised a hand. "This multilateral route you are proposing could be very sensitive from a geopolitical or environmental standpoint. We should consult someone from Ocean Energy Management. We don't want any trouble—"

"I have that situation under control." He recalled how easy it had been to grease the top officials. Their willingness to be on the take was yet another confirmation that men, even the ones who waved the flag of morality, were iniquitous and in need of salvation. "The president of OEM sees absolutely nothing wrong with what we're doing. Should there be an outcry, he will publicly come out in support."

He called up a photo of the *MedStar*. "While it is perfectly within our right to be here, it also is a reality we will be staunchly opposed by Beirut. I fully expect an attack, and we should all be prepared for it."

A middle-aged woman, one of few Americans on the board, leaned forward. "What is your plan for this, Mr. Chairman?"

He smiled. "Our ship, the *MedStar*, is stationed outside

the platform for a reason. It is equipped with highly advanced countermeasures for just such an event. There is nothing our enemies can serve that we cannot defend ourselves against." He paused for emphasis. "Nothing."

The woman seemed skeptical. "What if they strike elsewhere? These headquarters, for example, or our rigs in the desert. Or, worse, a public place."

He'd expected that question. "It has all been considered. I have personally met with high-ranking officials in the Ministry of Defense and explored this scenario. The government fully supports our efforts and will do whatever is necessary to defend this discovery. No one can take this oil from Israel. Every drop of it is ours."

"Hear, hear," one director said.

Another stood and applauded. Others followed suit.

Sacks stood and clasped his hands in front of him, taking in his colleagues' approval. "My friends," he said as the room quieted, "our time has come. Israel will know prosperity as never before." He raised his glass of water. "To you."

"And to you," said the vice-chairman, a former Israeli politician, "for leading us here. I think I speak for everyone in the room when I say we owe so much of this to you and Royal Petroleum. Without your resources, guidance, and perseverance, we could not have come this far."

"Hear, hear," sounded across the room.

Sacks bowed his head in false humility. "This is the

Lord's miracle. It is a new era for Israel. The era of prosperity"—he lifted his gaze to the sky—"and peace. Selah."

He adjourned the meeting and spent a few moments shaking hands and accepting congratulations. He then gathered his things and walked to his office on the other side of the building.

He locked the double wooden doors and walked to the bank of windows overlooking the concrete and glass teeth of downtown Tel Aviv. From his vantage point on the twenty-second floor, the skyline seemed old, tired, in need of renewal. He tapped the number into his mobile phone.

"All systems are go. I want you to leak to the press we are running a directional line north."

"I will happily do that," said the female voice on the other end of the line. "And shall I pack my bags?"

He smiled. "By all means. Meet me in Jerusalem tomorrow. We have some cleanup to do, and then we'll be ready for the show of shows."

"Are we sure Madigan is dead?"

"Oh, yes. It's been several days now, and no trace of a body. No one could survive that frigid water for that long."

"What about . . . her?"

"She's a major part of our plan, so we must be sure she walks into the trap. I know exactly how to make her come out of hiding. I will use her own nature against her."

"Sounds intriguing. Please do tell."

"All in due time, my dear. All in due time. You just

prepare yourself for the ritual cleansing. The time draws near, priestess. Soon you will fulfill your life's purpose."

"I am at your service, my lord."

He tapped the phone off and smiled. His flesh bristled as he considered the events of the coming days. He looked to the sky and recited a silent prayer of thanks to his forebears. At long last, his time had come.

Chapter 36

At the train station, Sarah slipped into a taxi and headed directly for the Old City. She was reeling from the report in *Haaretz*, which confirmed her worst fears: the oil vein struck by the *MedStar* was the tip of a significant reserve, and more than one nation was laying claim.

Turkey, Cyprus, and Lebanon all were disputing Israel's right to the find. Like everything else in the region, the maritime borders in this part of the Mediterranean were not black and white. Nations that failed to agree on anything certainly could not agree on this. In the past, it was a problem that lay dormant. But now that trillions of dollars and a hefty measure of power were on the line, old vendettas were awakened.

Of the three, Hezbollah, the leading party in Lebanon's coalition government, had issued the most threatening statement: "The Jews are nothing more than thieves. If Israel continues to tap into Lebanon's resources without regard for the people to whom those resources rightfully belong, we are prepared to take drastic action. We will do whatever it takes to protect our assets."

This wasn't the first time such threats had been made. When Israel had claimed a huge natural gas field discovered off its northern coast a few years before, Hezbollah leaders cried foul. Already Arab rage was simmering; the addition of this highly lucrative find was enough to make it boil over.

The article stated that the UN would intervene to help define the boundaries and reach a solution acceptable to both parties. Since the UN was driven mostly by the West, chances were it would support Israel's claim but ask the government to share the wealth with its neighbor to the north. The solution would be designed to keep the peace, which was of the utmost importance to the US and its allies. But in the eyes of Israel's mortal enemy, it wouldn't be viable. The issue was less about profit sharing than about control. The nation sitting on top of twenty-five billion barrels, and possibly more, was the one wielding all the power. Historically, all that power had belonged to Arab states. To have Israel suddenly outside the circle of oil dependence could mean diminished diplomatic relations between the Jews and the Arabs. And that could be disastrous to the fragile state of peace in the region, which would have a ripple effect worldwide.

Sarah shuddered at the thought. Any attempt by the

West to settle the conflict was almost certain to be met with violence. Hezbollah's band of well-armed terrorists would not sit on the sidelines and accept a UN decision. Lebanon had too much to lose. Like Israel, Lebanon had never had its own gas or oil reserves and had depended on its neighbors for its supply. With a soaring debt level and economic crisis on its hands, Lebanon stood to benefit significantly from such a windfall.

What better reason to wage war?

"Stop here," Sarah told the driver. She paid and entered the Old City through the Zion Gate.

It was late morning, and the city was buzzing in spite of the cold. That suited her just fine. The more faces she could disappear among, the better. She had already disguised herself with a long, black *sheitel*—the wig intended to cover the hair of married Orthodox women—with bangs that nearly covered her blue eyes. Over the *sheitel* she wore a long scarf tied at the back of the neck. Her conservative dress consisted of an ankle-length, gray skirt and a long wool sweater over it. She blended inconspicuously into her surroundings.

She hurried through the alleys of the Jewish Quarter and arrived at the familiar wooden door. She tapped the iron knocker and waited, her head bowed and her gaze darting.

A young man came to the door. "State your purpose."

"I must see the rabbi," she said in Hebrew.

"The rabbi is with a student now." He started to close

the door.

She held the door back with her forearm. "It's an urgent matter. Tell him Sarah Weston is here."

Without saying anything, he closed the door.

Sarah waited, trying not to look nervous as she checked her surroundings for any unwelcome presence. It was only a few minutes, though it felt far longer, before the young man returned and let her in.

"Rabbi Ben Moshe asks that you wait in the salon. He will be finished shortly."

She didn't bother to sit. With arms crossed, she paced as she waited. She was too agitated to stay still. So much had happened since she last sat in that salon. She felt the sharp stab of grief as she pondered how much she had lost.

"Sarah Weston." A soft voice came from the shadows of the hallway. "What a nice surprise."

As he stepped into the light, Sarah walked toward him. She was surprised at the emotion that flooded her, as if his mere presence meant deliverance from the quicksand of evil in which she was slowly sinking. She grasped his hands and looked down, unable to speak.

"You seem distraught. And this disguise . . . Dare I ask what's happened?"

She took a deep breath and looked up with clouded eyes. "I met him, Rabbi. I met the man who razed your synagogue. His name is Trent Robert Ashworth. He believes he's the Davidic heir—Mashiach."

"Why does the name sound familiar?" He averted his gaze. "There was something in the news."

"He was recently appointed chairman of Judah Oil and Gas. His family own Royal Petroleum in England. The two companies have partnered in oil exploration in the Judean Desert and the Mediterranean. You may recall seeing reports about a recent discovery offshore that is highly controversial."

"So he's behind it."

She nodded. "The worst part is, this plays into his plan. He aims to bring unprecedented wealth to the Jewish state, fulfilling some ancient prophecy."

"'And of Asher he said . . . let him dip his foot in oil.' Deuteronomy. This must be why he went by the name Asher all those years ago. He has been plotting this for a while."

"It's been at least ten years by our accounts. And his plan seems to be coming together rather nicely. He is purposefully drilling in an area contested by several nations, including Lebanon. It is his intent to use the oil as a wedge between Israel and Lebanon. He wants to spark a war from which he will deliver the nation. It's complicated, but let's just say he's thought of everything, including arming the Israeli Air Force and Navy with sophisticated weaponry and countermeasures. Even with the help of Syria and Iran, Lebanon wouldn't stand a chance."

He stroked his white beard. "These are presumably the events preceding an era of peace. I suspect he will then rise as the rightful Davidic heir, holding the ring of Solomon."

"And the manuscript. It was, as we thought, buried in a cave in the wilderness outside of Ein Gedi. The words of the scroll guided me there. Trouble was, he got there before me."

"The manuscript. So you have seen it."

"Yes. It is a set of blueprints for building the temple of Solomon."

His eyes grew wide, magnified behind thick, round spectacles. He was speechless.

"His ultimate goal is to build the third temple on Temple Mount. Just as the prophecies command." She squeezed his hands. "I need your help, Rabbi. Do you know anything about the ring as a masonic instrument? Could it hold the key to building the temple?"

He stood straighter and took a deep breath. He scanned her eyes for a long time but said nothing.

She read into his silence. "Please," she whispered. "It's our only weapon."

After a long moment, he spoke. "There is a legend that has been told to one man per generation."

Though she was sure of the answer, she asked, "Are you that man?"

He nodded.

She was beginning to understand. It was why he had been a recluse all his life and why he had been sent to

Poland. It wasn't the temple he was guarding but the secret buried within its stone walls. "Who else knows?"

"I alone." There was no hesitation in his voice.

"I need you to tell me what you know. Anything that can be used to stop him."

"The original unit of measurement is contained within the ring. But it isn't obvious unless you know the riddle of Solomon." He extended an open palm.

"I don't . . . understand."

He withdrew his hand. "It must stay this way for now. I've taken an oath. To break that would be to sin against God. Only on my deathbed can I pass along the knowledge."

She knew nothing she could say could sway a man of such powerful faith. It felt wrong to try to wrestle it out of him. "In that case, I'd better be going."

"Why don't you stay here? My people will protect you."

"No. It would be a mistake. I'm quite sure they're after me."

"All the more reason to hide."

"Yes, but I must do it on my own terms. I mustn't endanger anyone else. Too many have—" She lowered her head and shut her eyes.

"As you wish. But know this door is always open to you."

She looked up. "Rabbi . . . what do you do when you lose what you love most?"

He took a step toward her and put a hand on her

shoulder. "Death is part of life. It is not to be feared or despised, no matter how unjust or untimely it may seem. Those who are taken from us dwell in a higher place . . . the world to come. They are not tormented; we are. Only when we realize that life does not end with death but merely takes on a different form do we liberate our own souls. Mourn, by all means. But then let go, for that is the ultimate love."

A tear escaped from the corner of her eye. She felt a flood of emotion and let out a quiet gasp.

He squeezed her shoulder. "Be brave, child. They can't kill us. They can silence our voices, but they cannot claim our spirits."

"I wish I had your faith."

"You may not believe in the almighty God, but you have a covenant of conduct that is in tune with the divine. There will be more trials ahead. You will be called upon to question that covenant." He leaned closer and looked at her over his spectacles. "Do not do it, regardless of what happens. Stay the course even if all seems lost. It is the only way you can claim victory."

She smiled weakly. His words penetrated, but she still felt an immense sense of loss. "It may ultimately not be within my power, but I will do what I can to throw him off course. I promise you that."

He regarded her pensively. "May I ask you something?"

"Of course."

"Are you doing this to claim an eye for an eye?"

In her weakest moments, the answer was yes. But it was more than that. Like it or not, she possessed this knowledge, and with that came the responsibility to act. Her covenant of conduct, as he called it, did not permit her to look away. "I'm doing it, because no one else will."

Chapter 37

For the week of purification preceding the grand invocation, Sacks retreated to his lair in Varanasi. He was in self-prescribed isolation, for it was only through the complete abstinence of human company he could center his being in preparation to receive wisdom and instruction from Solomon, history's most powerful king.

He took a sip of detoxifying tea—the only nourishment permitted during the ritual fast that was to last seven days. The tea was a carefully formulated brew containing persimmon leaf for a natural dose of sugar, blood-cleansing Indian cayenne, a host of obscure Chinese herbs to purify the organs, and stimulating roots to compensate for the lack of sleep. For this particular experiment, the body was nothing but a conduit for the transmission of knowledge. It was imperative that it be immaculate.

He changed into a long, white habit and slowly descended the steps to the basement. He heard the steady trickle of water as he entered the dark cave of the art. It immediately soothed him. He stood at the entrance with eyes closed for several minutes, letting the soft murmur chase any impure thoughts from his mind.

He had become a master at harnessing his thoughts and controlling emotion. Even after six sleepless days and nights required to fulfill the sacrament, he was focused. Communicating with Solomon could only be achieved after severe self-discipline.

He opened his eyes and blinked rapidly to adjust to the darkness. He touched a switch on the wall and a stream of blue light projected from the ceiling, illuminating the center of the room. In the midst of the blue veil stood the altar and all the implements required for the series of conjurations that would prepare him for the main event.

He approached. He opened a blue velvet case and removed the golden talisman he had one of the goldsmiths in Varanasi fashion to his specifications. Shaped like a teardrop and hanging from a chunky chain, the amulet was carved on one side with the ancient Hebrew names of the divine presence. On the opposite side was a maze of intertwined geometrical shapes signifying the order of the universe to which the wise king held the secrets.

Sacks slipped the amulet around his neck and let it dangle close to his heart. He felt his arteries pulse with anticipation. He unsheathed a sword with a black leather handle inlaid with three tiger's-eye cabochons and held it high. "By the name of El Shaddai the almighty, I call upon this consecrated sword to serve and protect its master in the operation that is to follow."

He pointed the sword downward and inscribed upon the concrete floor three straight lines: the triangle of the art. He lit a censer containing frankincense nuggets and juniper bark and watched the smoke billow forth. He placed the censer inside the triangle along with a round black mirror.

He stood two feet away from the triangle and, with the same sword, carved a circle around himself. He placed the sword back on the altar and stood dead still inside the circle, which was designed to separate and protect him from the unexpected, for anything could happen within the triangle of the art.

With arms raised, he intoned: "Solomon, Solomon, Solomon. Thou who have gazed upon the divine face and have won the omnipotent one's favor, step from behind the celestial curtain and manifest thyself before this humble servant of the almighty. O Solomon, sage and benevolent king, thou who hast been chosen to build the temple of glory, thou who restored the earthly kingdom to goodness and perfection, step down to the lower heavens and guide Yahweh's chosen son.

"Solomon, Solomon, Solomon. Keeper of secrets and sentinel of heavenly mysteries, hide not thyself. Thy presence, a manifestation of the divine, is the supreme liberator from human folly and the beacon of the righteous. Step forward from the mists, O Solomon, and reveal the mystery of thy instrument, for its time has come."

Sacks paused and fixed his gaze on the scrying mirror, looking for any evidence of a manifestation. The mirror shone black, devoid of any imagery. Frustration crept into his being, and he fought hard against it. According to the prescribed formula for invocation of high spirits, a series of minor visions should precede the grand revelation. But so far, he had been rewarded with nothing.

He reached toward the altar and took up a sharp-bladed poniard. He rolled its carved silver hilt in his hand, feeling the weight of the instrument. Despite its slender blade, it was substantial. He held the poniard upright, tip pointing toward the sky, in front of his face. He inhaled deeply again and again, letting the fumes of the frankincense and juniper purge his mind of earthly thoughts and desires. The sweet smoke, a combination of dry earth and fragrant wood, made him lightheaded. He continued to inhale until he felt himself transported to a different realm.

He heard an indistinct voice inside his head, like a reverberation against a metal drum. Encouraged, he continued: "Solomon, Solomon, Solomon. Thou who art like a vessel containing all the virtue of all the ages, who art the keeper of the heavenly light, who knoweth the future just as thou knoweth the past, step into the triangle and let me gaze upon thy face. With this dagger do I defile the eyes of the serpent as an offering to thee. Humble is the gesture and paltry the blood in the face of such greatness."

Sacks leaned his head toward his shoulder, letting his long hair tumble away from his neck to expose the head of the serpent permanently inked onto his skin. The creature's terrible face was frozen in a hiss, its forked tongue resting just beneath his ear. He was intimately familiar with the anatomy of the sacred snake. He knew the position of every scale, every curve, every feature.

He pointed the sharp tip of the poniard toward the nape of his neck and moved it slowly across his skin until the blade reached the intentionally scarred area that defined the serpent's eye. With a fast, decisive jab he thrust the blade into his flesh.

Hot blood gushed forth, trickling down his neck and spilling onto his white robe. He could see the deep red liquid saturate his shoulder and inch down his sleeve. The open wound burned and throbbed. He gritted his teeth but held perfectly still. He inhaled the fragrant smoke once more.

"Solomon, Solomon, Solomon. O exalted king, descend on fiery wings and open the eyes that have been blinded. Strong is the faith that calls you forward into the rolling swells of sacred smoke. The wisps become thy flesh and the shadows thy countenance. Come now swiftly as thunder and gently as the wind and cast thy holy gaze upon the chosen."

He kneeled and, with his bloodied poniard, stirred the smoldering nuggets inside the censer. The smoke issued forth profusely. He looked into the black mirror and saw the brume gather on its surface like storm clouds on a night sky. In the mists he saw a vague form, like the face of a man. He held his breath as anticipation gripped him.

As the perfumed smoke billowed, the shape became more distinct. He saw the face of a youth with tumbling black curls, half-opened eyes, and a serene smile. A vision of the monarch at the dawn of his reign: it was more than he'd hoped for. He did not dare blink lest he miss a precious millisecond.

Then the apparition spoke. "Before the full moon rises, the secret will be held by the godless. Only through the ultimate sacrifice on the threshing floor of Araunah will you come to possess it."

Chapter 38

*F*ive days had gone by since she'd arrived in Jerusalem, and still there was no sign of activity from Sacks' camp. The calm before the storm: she was certain of it.

She adjusted her *sheitel* in the mirror. Her reflection startled her. She had become gaunt and pallid, her fair skin devoid of its usual rosy glow. Her eyes were lackluster and encircled by dark shadows. She looked so much older than her years, thirty-seven to the day. How had everything gone so wrong?

She looked at the mala beads Daniel had given her, which she wore faithfully around her wrist. It was her only connection to him now. The crew on the site of the Falcon's crash had given up the search for survivors and the black box. The water was far too frigid for anyone to survive this long, they'd said. And the Atlantic was too turbulent in mid-December to allow for a proper search of the depths, where the black box likely lay.

She felt profoundly alone. She closed her eyes and saw Daniel's face—the sculpted lines of his bone structure, the amber-flecked brown eyes, the crooked smile that at once encouraged and challenged her. She recalled his words to her when they were in Paris.

"You're a tough little lady. You don't give yourself enough credit. You may be a product of the upper class, but you're nothing like them. You don't do what you do to keep up appearances or because the Establishment expects it. You do it because your conscience compels you to. Your father, your people—they don't have soul like you do."

It was the first time they'd made love. That seemed so long ago, so far removed from her here and now. She missed him so much, it ached deep in her bones. Even if it cost her everything, she would try to vindicate him. She owed him at least this.

She sighed and looked around her room. The exposed, stacked masonry walls were closing in on her. She had been hiding within the confines of the Lutheran guesthouse, like a wounded animal in its cave. Beyond a window covered by a filigreed metal grate, she gazed upon the walled garden and its stone beds planted with palm trees and its greenery dotted with the occasional winter flower. She took it as an invitation.

She stepped out of the room and through the garden to the streets of the Old City. She had no plan; she just needed to be swallowed up by the frigid afternoon. She walked along the cobbled streets, avoiding the gazes of passersby. A cold blast of wind whistled through the stone arcades. She raised her heavy woolen wrap over her head and draped it across the lower half of her face, leaving only her eyes exposed.

She walked until she saw a dark, tiny café with a fireplace. She ducked in and ordered an Americano. As she waited for it to be made, she gazed absently at the graffiti on the walls and at the exposed concrete floor, which was stained with espresso no one had bothered to clean, letting it form artful patterns instead. Above her head hung an elaborate, if aging, crystal chandelier, its muted light reflected on the crackled surface of an old Venetian mirror hanging above the fireplace.

She took a seat at one of the six tables. There was only one other person in the room, a college-aged woman with several piercings and spiked red hair, bent over her laptop. She seemed so carefree in comparison to Sarah, whose nerves were strung tightly. She was frustrated by the dead ends she had encountered on so many fronts. Her father had not replied to her numerous messages. The pilot was still in intensive care and therefore off-limits. And Charles Bellows, whose alliance she desperately needed, was incommunicado, underscoring his position on coming forth with evidence against Advanced Electronic Solutions.

Two men sat at the table behind her. She could hear

one of them open a laptop and click the keys. Though the men spoke Hebrew softly to each other, she could hear their conversation.

"So when did she call you?"

"A week ago."

"And you didn't put anything up?"

"No, man. That's a serious accusation. We don't want to spark an international incident without substantiation."

"Did you call the authorities?"

"Of course I did. I told them I was going to write something but wanted to give them the heads-up first. So today Feinstein called me and said it was true. The crew of the *Sufa* confirmed it."

The only Feinstein she knew of was Aluf Benjamin Feinstein, commander of the Israeli Navy. *Sufa*, the Hebrew name for storm, must have been a submarine. These two men likely were journalists or bloggers, and high-profile ones at that. Not everyone had a direct line to the head of the Navy. She listened more actively.

"Who was this woman anyway? And how did she get that kind of information?"

"Don't know. Said her name was Mary, but that was probably a fake name."

Sarah held her breath. Was this woman a potential ally . . . or a plant?

"Anyway, it doesn't matter," he continued. "What matters is she was right. The story is the location of the well, not who tipped me off." He tapped the keys. "Listen to this: 'Judah Oil and Gas's announcement it had discovered a massive oil field beneath the surface of the Mediterranean became controversial this week as drilling began in earnest. The semisubmersible platform located about fifty miles off the coast of Haifa has reportedly installed a horizontal directional line, tapping a well several miles north of the rig. Directional drilling is standard practice in the industry and is considered legal if the wells are located within the maritime boundaries of the country whose flag is flying on the platform. In this case, however, that is not clear. According to a government official who does not wish to be identified, Judah is drilling in territory long claimed by Lebanon.'"

"Wow. Do you think it's a good idea to publish this? It's going to stir the pot in a big way."

"I'm a journalist, Abi. It's my job to stir the pot."

"But the reaction . . . I don't even want to think about it. What did the head of Judah have to say?"

"I have been calling for a week. No response. Tell you who did respond, though. Gilad Blum from Ocean Energy Management. He sounded outraged. He mobilized a research team to look into it. His pronouncement could either make or break the Judah operation. He should be calling me any day now. So what do you think? Should I hit *send*?"

"As if I could stop you."

The two men chuckled.

Sarah's heart hammered against her rib cage. It had begun.

Chapter 39

Early the next morning, Sarah left the guesthouse and walked outside the Old City gates to look for a taxi. She had not slept all night, weighing her next move. She was convinced she had to get to Gilad Blum and tell him what she knew. If he had the power to make or break the operation, as the journalist had suggested, she wanted him on her side.

She stepped inside the taxi and gave the driver the downtown Jerusalem address. On the way, she checked the *Jerusalem Post* website on her phone for the latest news. The journalist's story had been posted the previous evening and had already amassed almost two hundred comments. The excerpt she'd heard him read to his friend was there, verbatim. She read the full text, which included a timeline of the oil-centered conflict between Israel and Lebanon throughout history and at the end noted a link to a new report.

The Oil Conflict: OEM's Reaction

So Blum had commented. She tapped the link. It was a short article, posted less than an hour before, stating Ocean Energy Management's position on Judah's drilling practices. Remarkably, the agency found no wrongdoing. Blum was quoted saying, "Judah Oil and Gas has had a history of integrity and runs one of the cleanest and safest drilling platforms in the business. Even so, we scrutinized the operation thoroughly. The drilling line is within Israel's borders, and we see no reason why the company cannot maintain its current course."

Sarah's brow furrowed as she read the words. Blum sounded like a spokesman for Judah rather than the environmental and ethical watchdog he typically was. It didn't make sense. Then she read on.

"Hezbollah leaders issued a statement yesterday, blasting the Judah initiative. 'The people of Lebanon will not stand for this bold-faced rape. Those resources belong to the Lebanese nation, and anyone who challenges that can expect a retaliation.'

"When informed of this, Judah Oil officials issued a statement of their own. 'Judah Oil and Gas will not bend to threats. This discovery is a gift from God to the people of Israel, and we will not walk away from it.'

"Judah Oil chairman T. Robert Ashworth, whose reclusiveness has rendered his identity a mystery, said in the statement, 'Ezekiel 36:11 tells us, *I will settle you after your old estates, and will do better unto you than at your beginnings: and ye shall know that I am the Lord.* The time has come for this ancient prophecy to be fulfilled. This is the dawn of a new age for Israel. Prosperity, power, and peace. I will personally see that these are delivered to the people. As for enemy threats, I say let them come. We are ready.'"

She cringed at the provocative words. Hezbollah would be infuriated.

The taxi was four blocks away from the OEM headquarters and stuck in traffic. Horns blared and impatient drivers yelled profanities, yet nothing moved. The road resembled a used car lot with a surplus of inventory.

"I will walk from here," Sarah said. She paid the driver and exited the taxi.

She threaded her way through the stopped cars, whose bumpers nearly touched. She stepped onto the sidewalk and walked briskly, constructing in her mind the conversation she would have with Blum should he agree to see her. It seemed futile at this point to try to sway him from a position that appeared so firm in the media. But she had come this far and had to at least make the effort. She was running out of options.

She was a little more than a block away from the building when a massive blast thundered in her ears. The force of the explosion sent her tumbling across the sidewalk and slamming into the wall of a building. She lay there in the fetal position, arms over her head as more blasts shook the earth, and watched the horrific scene unfold.

Charred pieces of metal and shards of glass floated through the air, seemingly in slow motion. People scattered like ants in a rainstorm, bloodied and screaming. Some were not so lucky. Bodies lay on the street, some mutilated beyond recognition. She watched a shoe, foot still within, hit the windshield of a car parked near her. She fought the gag reflex. The smell of singed flesh was everywhere.

The epicenter of the explosions was a bus, now hollowed out and smoldering. The cars around it were picked up like toys by the force and landed atop other vehicles nearby. One of the overturned cars was on fire.

The dust and panic from the explosion hadn't even settled when another detonation followed, this time inside the building housing the OEM headquarters. First, there was a deafening boom that made the sidewalk quake, then the crackle of shattered glass from the blown-out windows. A suited man plummeted from the third floor. Sarah turned her head, unable to watch the moment of impact.

Ocean Energy Management was being taught a hard lesson.

Sarah heard the piercing wail of a siren. Unable to get through the stalled traffic, the fire engine had straddled the sidewalk to get to the scene of the bombings. The truck parked a few yards from her. A dozen firefighters went to work as their chief barked orders. It was a well-oiled operation, as they were used to responding to such incidents.

Another fire engine and several police cars followed.

As they struggled to put out fires and rescue the injured, Sarah kneeled and then stood on trembling legs. She clutched her chest as she caught her breath. Her ears ringing from the blasts and the desperate cries of people in distress, she left the chaotic scene and walked toward the Old City. It was far away, but so much the better. A long walk would, she hoped, give her time and space to process what she'd just witnessed.

Fifteen minutes later, her phone rang. A familiar number flashed on the caller ID. She answered. "Ezra?"

"I saw the news. Tell me you're nowhere near that blast."

"I saw it happen."

"We all live in fear of these moments."

"I'll be fine." She shuddered.

"Listen, Sarah. There's more. Around the same time the bombs went off in Jerusalem, an underwater missile was sent to the Judah platform. Gift wrapped from Lebanon."

She stopped. "What? Did it strike?"

"No. That's the remarkable part. The missile was a Russian-built Shkval, probably sold to Iran and handed to Hezbollah by the Iranians. It has long been thought that there are no good countermeasures against such a weapon. Turns out the *MedStar*, which is still anchored nearby, is armed with its own missiles and countermeasures. The ship's crew was able to track the missile with sophisticated radar and redirect it. It struck the hull of the Lebanese sub that launched it."

"Bet Hezbollah aren't too happy about that. I think we can safely expect another attack."

"Especially since the new Judah chairman is being pretty cocky about it."

"What do you mean?"

"He's a one-man band playing the tune of salvation. It's all over the news."

"Has he come out of hiding?"

"No way. He's keeping his identity tightly under wraps. He's building a mystique around himself, and it's working. Just here at the university, there's a group of students protesting this morning, waving all sorts of anti-Arab signs. It's a mess."

Cold drops of rain sprinkled her face. The sidewalk became pockmarked with tiny wet spots, then larger ones. She ducked under an awning and watched the water crash down. "Any luck figuring out the measurement unit?"

"Yes and no. What we're looking for is the exact measurement of the ell, which predates the biblical cubit. Even though scholars have come to a sloppy agreement about the ell, the truth is no one knows how long it really was. To complicate matters, there were two ells. The earlier one was the one used by royalty."

She snapped her fingers. "Yes. Something similar was done in Egypt. The royal ell was the unit used to construct the pyramids at Giza. Given Solomon's connection to the Egyptians, he surely would have used the same standard."

"Trouble is, since the first ell was replaced by a latter one, which was more commonly used and later became the cubit, its length remains a mystery. If we knew the exact width of the *tefah*, we might have something."

"*Tefah* . . . the breadth of a palm."

"Yes, that was the lowest unit of measurement for building."

She recalled the rabbi's words: *It isn't obvious unless you know the riddle of Solomon.* He'd held his palm open: a hint, surely.

"And believe me, I've looked everywhere, even consulted a couple of trusted sources," Ezra continued. "Interestingly, your friend Mariah Banai from King Saud surfaced as one of the experts on Iron Age measurements."

She was jolted from the stream of her thoughts. "You called Mariah? How could you?"

"Take it easy, Sarah. I didn't mention specifics. We had a philosophical conversation, nothing more. Your name didn't even come up." He paused. "You are so tightly wound. You're downright paranoid. Where's the genteel girl I know?"

"How can you demand that of me, after all that's happened?"

"Perhaps too much has happened." He paused. "Sarah, maybe it's time to give this up. You are one woman, albeit a fierce one, against an entire organization of greedmongers and assassins. You can't win."

She blinked back tears. She feared he was right. "Maybe not. But what would I be if I didn't try?"

"Alive. You have too much to offer the world to blow it all on a revenge mission." His tone softened. "It won't bring him back."

She looked through the sheets of rainwater tumbling from the sloped aluminum awning. A grainy pewter film had covered the buildings, the umbrella-toting pedestrians on the sidewalk, the tightly packed traffic. It was like a scene captured in a daguerreotype. It matched her gloomy mood.

"Sarah?" Ezra interrupted her reverie.

"I'm here."

"Every station is reporting breaking news. Ashworth has issued a response to the Judah attackers. Listen to this: 'Today the unthinkable happened. A terrorist organization targeted a private company with the sole aim of destroying its infrastructure and murdering dozens of innocent people. We will not stand for this. We proved it by defending ourselves against a deadly attack, and we are prepared to do it again. In the interest of defending Israel's God-given right to claim this precious gift, we will respond aggressively and we will win, for any war against Judah Oil and Gas is a war against God's will. If the Arab terrorists dare to challenge our sovereignty, we will strike where it hurts most. That is a promise.'"

"He's provoking them. He wants them to strike again so he can retaliate in a big way."

"According to this report, he's calling himself 'God's messenger' and 'the oil prophet.' The guy's a lunatic. And people are playing into his madness. Apparently, there are pro-Judah demonstrations all over Israel." He paused. "I've got a call coming in. Let me ring you back."

Sarah hung up and took a deep breath. Despite the storm, she was too restless to wait. She charged into the frigid deluge toward the Old City.

Minutes later, a text message came in. She jolted when she saw her father's number. She stopped in the midst of the downpour and opened the message.

It wasn't from him.

Your father is safe—for now. His fate is up to you.

She froze. Sacks was waging a war of emotions, the kind she was ill-equipped to fight against. He was systematically taking away everything she cherished, leaving her with no defenses.

She closed her eyes, suddenly aware of how sodden and cold she was. Her enemy was closing in, and she knew precisely what he was after.

Chapter 40

The clouds cleared just as the steely dusk was overtaken by darkness. Sarah sat in a crowded Internet café at the edge of the Christian Quarter, her gaze alternating between a computer screen and the television monitor hanging above her head. The anxiety in the room was palpable. A good fifty people, tourists and locals, were watching the latest reports about the oil conflict.

Earlier in the day, another suicide bomb had gone off, this time near the British Embassy. Twenty-two people had been killed or injured. Hezbollah had claimed responsibility for the incident, stating there would be more severe action if the West did not intervene and stop Israel's "illegal activity."

The British Prime Minister condemned the bombing, ordered all official personnel evacuated, and urged all British subjects to leave the region. The conflict was escalating, as Sacks had warned it would.

Conversations buzzed all around her. Two American girls were panicking about their futile attempts to find airline tickets out of Tel Aviv. All flights were booked for the next two weeks. A group of Israelis loudly hailed Judah Oil's resolve to stand its ground, speaking particularly fondly about the "balls" of the "oil prophet."

The websites flashed images of demonstrations all over Israel, where people waved banners with such statements as "Hands off our oil!" and "Ezekiel's prophecy is now." Clearly, Sacks' Bible-pounding approach was striking a chord with the people.

Sarah knew he was readying for his next move. She mulled again Solomon's scroll, the words of which were emblazoned on her memory.

The orchard is profuse with fig, the vines heavy with grape.
When my lover's face appears from the shadows,
All mysteries are revealed.
Her beauty illuminates the path and the dark stones,
And I follow, powerless to resist.

It was now clear to her this passage was a reference to the moon. It would rise above the city, illuminating the dark stones of the walled compound and revealing all mysteries. Whatever Sacks was up to, she was certain it would take place tonight, as the full moon ascended, somewhere in the Old City.

The obvious place was Temple Mount. Would he dare? The Chief Rabbinate mandated that no person enter the sacred place. Somewhere on that hill was once the holy of holies, the most hallowed earthly place before God. Because no one knew its location for certain, the entire area was forbidden ground. Entering it defied the laws of the Torah. Surely Sacks didn't think the faith community would embrace him after so grave a trespass.

She scanned the online news sites. Something caught her eye on the home page of *The Times* in the Latest News ticker across the top: "Electronics tycoon detained."

She clicked. The story had just been posted and was still unfolding. The two-paragraph article said only that a credible anonymous informant had contacted the newspaper with proof Advanced Electronic Solutions had engaged in illegal activities. It didn't mention specifics, presumably because no official arrest had been made. It said only that, following a tip from *The Times*, AES chairman Alastair Bromley had been summoned by police for questioning.

Had Bellows stepped forth at last? It was a pale light in a dark horizon.

She shifted in her chair, too restless to keep still. She began tracking the story online when her attention was commanded by the television monitor hanging on the wall. The news station was running an interview with a political analyst when the anchor interrupted to announce breaking news.

"We just got word," she said, "that tonight reclusive Judah Oil and Gas Chairman T. Robert Ashworth will make his first public appearance with a major announcement for the Israeli people. We have Judah spokesman Alexander Bateman on the phone. Alexander, good evening."

The room went silent.

Pulse quickening, Sarah sat up.

"Good evening."

"So the chairman is ready to come out of hiding. Tell us what we can expect from this announcement."

"Well, this is not something I am at liberty to reveal. I can only say that Mr. Ashworth will deliver a live webcast shortly after midnight and that his announcement will be a momentous revelation."

The web address was superimposed on the screen.

Sacks was readying to announce his inheritance of the Solomonic manuscript and ring and his intent to build the third temple. Sarah was sure of it. *Shortly after midnight.* She glanced at her watch and saw it was already after nine. She didn't have much time. She stood and put on her coat.

"Alexander Bateman, thank you. And speaking of coming out of hiding, our next guest is speaking publicly for the first time in nearly ten years of self-imposed exile. Beloved Rabbi Uri'el Ben Moshe spoke to correspondent Ari Grossman by phone earlier today. Let's listen."

A small black-and-white photo of Rabbi Ben Moshe, probably taken twenty years before, flashed on the screen. Sarah froze.

"Rabbi, the events of the last few days have been disturbing, to say the least. Threats, bombings, territorial disputes. Seems like we have the makings of a holy war. What do you make of all this?"

"Let me be clear about one thing." The rabbi's shaky voice crackled on the telephone line. "I rejoice with every one of my countrymen at the notion of Israel finding oil. But there is something fundamentally wrong about taking it with a sword. We really don't know who has rights to those wells. We say we do; they say they do. Until an independent body can decide the boundaries once and for all, we should not be charging forth. That is a blatant provocation, and it can only end badly."

"Judah's chairman, T. Robert Ashworth, says this discovery is worth going to war over. Your thoughts."

"I am an advocate of peace. I believe certain lofty things are worth fighting for . . . freedom, for example, or the right to worship. But to put innocent lives at risk over something we're not even sure we can claim, why, that's just criminal. As for this Mr. Ashworth, his rhetoric is blasphemous. He is claiming to be the conduit of certain biblical prophecies by fulfilling God's promise to the people of Israel. Ordinary men should not make such claims. We should be asking ourselves, what does he stand to gain on a personal level?"

"What do you think he stands to gain?"

"Let's just say people are seduced by power and by the

idea of being chosen. That leads to all sorts of illusions, all of which are dangerous."

"What is your spiritual advice to the people?"

"Know the laws of the Torah. Believe only in the word of God, not of false prophets."

"Are you saying Mr. Ashworth is a false prophet?"

There was a brief silence. "That is what I am saying, yes."

Sarah cringed. On a chessboard with few remaining pieces, his provocative statement was a desperate move. The rabbi obviously thought this was the most effective, if not the only, way to make his case to the masses and even to members of the religious community, who were increasingly pledging their support to a charlatan.

The interview went off the air, and the anchor came back on. "It will be interesting to hear Rabbi Ben Moshe's reaction to the latest developments. Ari Grossman will speak with him about Ashworth's announcement, so be sure to tune in or follow us on Twitter for live updates as this story develops."

As if synchronized with the news report, a text came through on Sarah's phone.

If you want to see your father alive, go to 4 Hakara'im St.

The rabbi's address. She hurriedly gathered her things and bolted out the door.

Chapter 41

*H*iding behind a woolen shawl draped over her head and across her face, Sarah strode toward the Jewish Quarter. She wanted to run but couldn't risk drawing attention to herself.

After walking ten blocks, she was breathless yet felt supercharged. She knew what she had to do. She was taking the biggest risk of her life, but it was paltry in light of everything at stake.

She ducked beneath the stone arches of the alleyways that would lead her to the rabbi's house. The silent stones were bathed in the faint golden light of the streetlamps, their texture punctuated by shadows. With furtive glances, she searched the faces around her. Old men sat on chairs outside cafés, carefree and idle as infants. Lovers walked arm in arm, oblivious to anything but each other. She did not register any threats.

She walked past the same lone tree she'd noticed

when she first came to the Old City. In the floodlight of the rising moon, its bare branches looked like old, gnarled fingers imploring the heavens. Something floated in the darkness and Sarah felt the familiar kiss of ice on her face. She held out an open palm and watched the snow flurries land on her fingerless glove. It rarely snowed in Jerusalem. She took it as an omen.

She was practically alone in the alleys along the far side of the quarter, where the rabbi lived. She gazed over her shoulder through the falling snow and saw no one. She slipped into the dark alley and stood beneath the overhang at the rabbi's door, evaluating her surroundings. There was a light inside, though the curtains were drawn. She looked around the alley and didn't see a soul. She rapped lightly on the door.

A minute passed; there was no answer. She put her ear to the door. She picked up some muffled sounds, perhaps even voices, but could not be sure what she was hearing. Warmth radiating through her, she raised her fist to knock again and noticed the door was cracked open. She bit her lip as she turned the knob and entered the dark foyer.

She stood still, listening, her heart pounding in her ears. There were definitely voices, though she could not make out the words. The house was dark save for a single light coming from the other side of the hallway, likely from the library.

She proceeded down the darkened corridor. Her

footfall made the old wood floor creak.

"Who's there?" she heard a man call out in Hebrew. It was not the rabbi's voice.

Footsteps came toward her. Gripped by fear, she slipped behind an armoire. In a mirror hanging on the opposite wall, she saw the reflection of a man, probably thirtysomething and Israeli, looking up and down the hallway.

"Damned rats," he growled and went back inside the room.

She rested her head on the wall and exhaled.

She heard the rabbi's voice but could not hear what was being said. Encouraged, she stepped into the hallway and tiptoed quickly toward the light. She peeked into the open doorway and gasped as she realized what was going on.

"So this is how you intend to enter the kingdom of heaven? By worshipping a phony and killing a man of God? Shame on you." The rabbi, tied to a chair, glared at an armed man standing over him.

"Kingdom of heaven?" The man roared with laughter. "You think I give a damn about that? The only thing I worship is a suitcase full of cash. Now shut up and give me what I came here for."

"You'll get nothing from me."

Sarah hid behind the doorframe and watched from the crack of the half-opened door.

The man raised his gun to the rabbi's forehead. "I'm losing patience. This is your last chance. If you want to live, give me the cipher of the ring." He dug the barrel in. "I'm waiting."

Sarah was stunned. Sacks knew the rabbi held the riddle of Solomon.

"You will wait for eternity. Take my body, if you must. It means nothing. Only the soul matters, and that you cannot extinguish with your gun. The secret you seek, you're not worthy of. Therefore, you cannot buy it—at any price."

"Then you give me no choice." He clicked the safety.

Sarah looked frantically around the space. A heavy crystal vase sat on a console opposite the doorway. She snatched it, pushed the door open, and hurled the vase at the assailant.

The vase hit him on the back of the head. The weapon dropped to the floor, and the man fell unconscious over the rabbi. Under his weight the chair, with the rabbi still tied to it, crashed to the floor.

Sarah rushed to Rabbi Ben Moshe's side and heaved the unconscious man off the chair. She went to work on the ropes.

"Sarah, there is no time for that. Listen to me."

She stopped and looked at him. His expression was so serene. He was a man utterly at peace. She envied him.

"That which is five really is one," he said. "Solomon's ancient riddle is now in your hands. He must never know."

Sarah nodded. "But what does it mean?"

From behind, hands gripped her head, snatching the

wig off and pushing her face to the floor.

"She's here," he called out.

There were others—and they knew she was coming. It was a trap.

With her attacker straddling her back and pinning her arms behind her, she lay immobile, head turned toward the rabbi. "I'm sorry," she whispered.

Another man stuffed a large piece of cloth into her mouth. She gagged and her eyes watered, but she did not divert her gaze from the rabbi. His face was the last thing she saw before a bag was slipped over her head. Rough hands turned her to her back and bound her wrists and ankles with coarse rope. Two hands grasped her ankles and two cupped her head. They lifted her off the floor. She kicked but could not break free from their grip. She tried calling for help, but the fabric gagged her.

As she was being carried away, she heard the unmistakable crack of semiautomatic gunfire. Three shots thundered. With the sound still ringing in her ears, Sarah bit down on the cloth and, with all the force in her lungs, let out a scream no one could hear.

Chapter 42

Unable to move even an inch in the confines of her bindings, Sarah could not fight the hired guns who were carrying her through the Old City. To transport her without rousing suspicions, they had rolled her tightly inside a carpet. She was sweating and could hardly breathe.

Sounds outside her woolen prison were muffled, so she could deduce nothing about their intentions. Where were they taking her? Were they delivering her to Sacks or planning to dispose of her altogether? Either way, she was ready to face her fate.

Not being able to see at all or hear well was both maddening and liberating. Her logical side demanded answers to everything, but the impalpable part of her that floated in a purgatory between reality and absolute faith was serene in not knowing.

The men suddenly stopped. They spoke rapid-fire; though she could not hear the words, she picked up on their tone of urgency. They placed her on the ground, none too gently. More voices. It seemed a third man had joined the party. She tried again to wiggle free, but the rope binding her hands and ankles burned her skin. She was immobilized, and there was nothing to do but accept it.

The men hoisted her up again. She felt forward movement, though the men's steps were slower and more labored. Based on the way she was jostled to and fro, she gathered they were walking on uneven terrain. She heard a grunt.

As they turned to the right, she felt her body swing around and rub against something. A wall? The man holding up her head adjusted his stance and got a tighter grip. Her head was lower than her feet now. They were ascending. She could not fathom where they were until they began talking again. Their stifled voices did not trail off but rather seemed contained within a closed space. As they moved, her carpet coccoon hit something again, this time on both sides. She had spent enough time underground to know they were carrying her inside a chamber or tunnel. The thought made her heart race.

Struggling to breathe, she began to feel lightheaded. Perspiration covered her forehead and dripped down her temples. The cotton sack covering her head was soaked through and stuck to her face. She felt as if she would pass out at any moment.

They stopped. The voices sounded again, this time

loud and argumentative, like they were at odds about what to do next. Their indistinguishable words bounced against the walls for several minutes, during which Sarah felt her consciousness slipping further and further away. The last thing she sensed was being hoisted and thrown to the ground. Everything faded to black.

When she came to, the carpet and the sack had been removed, and she was lying in a fetal position on a rock with her wrists and ankles still bound and the cloth gag still stuffed in her mouth. Her clothes damp, she shivered as cold air blew across her skin.

She blinked to clear the clouds from her eyes and looked around her dark prison. In the dim light, she noticed the outlines of columns. She looked up and saw the unmistakable black-and-white marble arches framing the colonnade. She realized where she was. She rolled onto her back with some effort and stared at the gilded, ornate dome, at the base of which were a series of windows. The Dome of the Rock.

Sarah was lying on the sacred Foundation Stone of the world, Judaism's holiest site. This was the rock on which Abraham was called to sacrifice his son Isaac and where Jacob dreamt about the ladder that climbed to heaven. It was on this stone that Solomon built his temple almost three thousand years ago. Believers held that God gathered the earth from this very spot to form Adam. The center of the earth, the origin of all existence.

It was no accident she had been taken there. This was clearly Sacks' intention all along. Whatever his plan was, she was central to it.

She smelled burning incense, an intoxicating blend of sandalwood and frankincense that reminded her of places of worship. A faint chant floated in the space between her and the outer walls of the dome. The sound grew closer, and she realized it was the voice of a woman.

A white-robed, hooded figure approached and stood on the edge of the marble floor surrounding the stone. Sarah could not distinguish a face in the darkness. She blinked rapidly, trying to focus. Teeth clenched, she stared at the shadowy figure and waited.

The cloaked stranger picked up an object from a table, then stepped onto the stone and circled Sarah in a wide radius, stopping five feet away from her head.

There was utter silence.

The stranger stood still for a long moment, as if in prayer, then held up a book.

Opening the book, she began to chant in Hebrew in a deep, ceremonial tone.

Sarah listened to the words. After a few passages, she realized the woman was reading from the Zohar, the Kabbalist texts that examined the mystical side of the Torah.

"Woe when this departs and those phantoms of ember manifest, hissing past, not lingering in place. The living beings darting back and forth . . . Flee to your place! If you soar as high as the eagle, from there I will bring you down."

The voice was hoarse but somehow familiar.

"The earth sprouted. Then air issues and a spark is readied. One skull expanding on its sides, above it brimming dew, of two colors. Three cavities of inscribed letters are revealed in it.

"Black as a raven, hanging over tortuous holes, so that neither right nor left can hear. Here is one path above, slender.

"A forehead does not shine, discord of the worlds—except when the Will gazes upon it. Eyes of three colors—to tremble upon them—bathed in shining milk. It is written: your eyes will see Jerusalem a tranquil abode. And it is written: justice lodged in her."

The words were from the highly enigmatic Book of Concealment, the conclusion of the Zohar. Sarah had never ventured too deeply into the interpretation of these texts, but she did not need to be a Kabbalistic scholar to know this passage referred to the restoration of Jerusalem to the righteous.

The woman closed the book and fell back into silence. From the shadows, another figure cloaked in white appeared, ascending as if rising from the depths of the earth. Sarah recalled there was a natural cavern beneath the Foundation Stone—the so-called Well of Souls—that could be entered via a perforation on the rock's surface.

As the figure walked across the stone, Sarah could tell by the slow, arrogant gait it was Sacks. An acrid taste filled her mouth.

He stopped within her eyeshot. A faint moonbeam shining through an open doorway illuminated his face. His skin was more pallid than usual and his countenance was gaunt. A thin dark beard crept along his jaw. His eyes were dull and distant, the color of ash. He looked like a walking cadaver.

"Tonight is a holy night," he said. "The king anointed by God has revealed himself. The heavens have cracked open." He closed his eyes. "I can hear the strings of the lyre calling for peace."

Sarah wanted to blast his misguided discourse but knew any attempt to do so would only drive the cloth farther down her throat.

"All that remains now is to offer the final sacrifice. The blood of the godless must be shed this night."

Chanting, the woman walked slowly toward the table, placed the book upon it, and picked up another object. She stood a few feet behind Sacks, clutching a dagger to her chest.

Sarah felt as if she'd been dropped in an ice bath. Obviously, the blood he spoke of was her own. Frantic, she tried to maneuver her wrists free of the rope.

Expressionless, Sacks stared at her. He either had

entered some transcendent state or was drugged. He crossed his hands in front of his heart and bowed his head. On the middle finger of his left hand was the ring of Solomon, its four stones glowing in the wan moonlight.

Sarah thought about the cipher of the ring and the rabbi's final words. *That which is five really is one.* There were only four stones, indicative of the four elements. Perhaps it was a reference to the fifth element—the quintessence, the divine, that which could not be seen or touched. Her mind raced across a field of possibilities, stopping at nothing.

As if tapping into her thoughts, Sacks said, "You can still save your soul, if you choose. I know you hold the cipher of the ring. Give it to me, and join the righteous in heaven."

Sarah cast him a caustic stare. *How dare he speak of heaven, peace, and the righteous? Has he no concept of what he has done?*

"I see you need to be convinced." He kneeled in front of her and lifted the ring's gem-encrusted lid so that it balanced on one hinge. He leaned into it and blew.

A powder floated into Sarah's field of vision, and she instinctively closed her eyes tightly. She felt the powder enter her nostrils. It was as if a branding iron had seared her skin. She blinked rapidly, her eyes burning.

The open ring was still pointed at her. Through a cloudy veil, she could see the pentagram engraved in gold on the ring's inner circle. The five-pointed star, an ancient symbol of the divine before it was hijacked by occultists and neopagans for dubious worship purposes.

That which is five really is one. Somewhere within the pentagram's five intersecting lines lay the key to building the temple of Solomon.

Sarah's lungs felt as if they were full of liquid. She heard the shallowness of her breath, tiny gasps of agony. Her eyes were on fire. The toxin was taking effect. She closed her eyes, and the golden pentagram floated in her mind's eye. In the miasma clouding her thoughts, the image became ragged and warped and began to unravel. She reopened her eyes with a start.

Sacks stared at her without emotion. "Do you have something to say?"

She nodded.

She smelled the woody scent of frankincense as his cold hand reached into her mouth and pulled out the gag. "The world waits, Dr. Weston. Soon I will announce the task that has been appointed to me by birthright and divine ordinance. There is nothing you can do to stop it. The Messianic Age is here. The time has come for peace."

"After all you've done, all the people you've murdered, you dare speak of peace." Her words were choked, but she'd be damned if she didn't speak them.

"We make war that we may live in peace." The Aristotelian quote sounded perverse coming from his mouth. "If you look back in history, King David was God's chosen, but he was a warrior. He had to purge the land of infidels so that Israel could know peace." He stood. "His son Solomon could have granted peace to our nation forever, but he faltered in the eyes of God. As the last descendant of the great king, it is my duty to continue his legacy. To grant riches the likes of which Solomon could only dream. To crush our enemies and make them fear us. To reclaim Jerusalem and rebuild the temple that the world may know the one true God. To rule with justice and piety and unwavering faith. That is peace in our lifetime . . . and it is so close."

The woman began chanting again. Sacks spoke over her, his voice so loud it ricocheted off the marble surfaces of the dome. "Only one piece remains . . . the true measuring unit for construction of the temple. The rabbi was bound by oath to pass the cipher to someone before his death. I know he entrusted it to you. Building the temple exactly as Solomon did, which is to say as God commanded, is paramount to our faith. If you choose to take this information to your death, your soul will be eternally damned. If you release it, you will contribute to the greatest achievement of humanity. What will your legacy be, Dr. Weston?"

Sarah's cheeks felt numb, and breathing grew more difficult. She feared the toxin would slowly paralyze her. "If I give you what you ask, why kill me?"

"It has been commanded of me. God spoke through

the great king and asked for your blood. I have to make this sacrifice to prove my faith. Just as God has commanded, so I will do."

"Pathetic wretch. Do you really believe a just god would ask for a human sacrifice?" Her lungs throbbed from the effort of getting the words out.

"Blasphemy," he bellowed. "Was not Abraham asked to sacrifice his son? Did Jephtah not offer the flesh of his only daughter? How little you know about unconditional faith, Doctor. You who bow to the altar of science and the holy grail of the damned . . . you deserve the hell you shall inherit."

"Then do your worst," she hissed. "Nothing will make me bargain with you."

"No?" He nodded to his accomplice. "Not even this?"

The woman reached into a pocket and pulled out an iPhone. She tapped the screen fourteen times: an international call. A double ring issued from the speaker, and a man answered on the second ring.

"Hello, Jerusalem," he said with a thick accent Sarah could not place.

The woman held the phone in front of her mouth and spoke. "Is everything ready?"

"Ready."

She turned the phone toward Sarah. The face of a long-haired, dark-bearded man filled the video call screen.

Sarah lay on her side, face to the cold stone, breathing

shallowly. She could do nothing but watch as the man shifted the phone's camera toward his captive.

Hair mussed and clothes crumpled, Sir Richard sat on the ground with his back against an exposed concrete block wall. His upper lip was swollen, and his cheekbone had been scraped raw. There were dried bloodstains on his open shirt collar. He stared blankly at her through the video screen.

It was the first time Sarah had seen her father so vulnerable. Since her earliest recollections, he had been the impeccable patriarch, always perfectly in control. Infuriating as his untouchable persona was, it had come to define him. Seeing him this way shattered all her childhood illusions and made him, for once, human in her eyes.

She clenched her teeth, but the tears came anyway.

Sacks laughed. "Such a touching moment. Let's up the stakes, shall we?"

The assailant raised a gun to Sir Richard's temple.

Sarah let out a soft gasp.

Sacks turned on his heels, his white robe swaying behind him. He snatched the dagger from the woman's hands and held it out, pointing its tip at Sarah's face. "I have been quite patient indeed. But time is running out. You have a choice to make, Dr. Weston. Will you give me what I want"—he swung the dagger toward the phone—"or will your father join you in hell?"

The message was loud and clear: she couldn't save

her own life, but she could spare his. In exchange for her father's life, she would have to hand a madman the keys to humanity's most exalted kingdom.

"And don't you dare call my bluff." He sneered. "I didn't hesitate to kill Madigan, and I won't hesitate now."

His words were like a crowbar to the knees. Her strength was waning. She stared at her father through the two-way video screen, watching his expression as he heard that Sacks had brought down the Weston plane.

Sir Richard was stone-faced. It was as if he already knew. He locked eyes with his daughter. "Give him what he wants, Sarah."

She shut her eyes tight. Sharp stabs traveled down her spine, making her muscles twitch. Though her body was ailing, her mind was lucid. The choice she was about to make would be with full conscience.

He must never know.

Would she betray the rabbi, and all the men of faith who held the secret before him, to save her father?

She opened her eyes and turned to Sacks. "How can I be sure you'll let him go?"

"You have my word."

There was nothing about him she trusted. She would have to roll the dice.

Images of Rabbi Ben Moshe's face flashed in her mind. Somehow, he knew she would arrive at this crossroads. *There will be more trials ahead. You will be called upon to question that covenant.* His spiritual mandate was without compromise: *do not do it, regardless of what happens.*

Her thoughts traveled to all the biblical men and women who were willing to sacrifice their own flesh and blood in the name of God and wondered what extraordinary faith would bring them to that point. To her, that was a sealed room, completely elusive and inaccessible.

However she might be judged for it, she could not make that sacrifice. "Okay," she whispered through numb lips. "I'll talk."

He dropped his arm, letting the dagger dangle at his side. "I thought you might."

The chessboard was down to the last pieces, and she was out of options. Any move she'd make now would lead to checkmate. She glanced at her father, bloodied and compromised, then at the animal in immaculate white linen.

"It's a riddle." There was a bitter taste in her mouth as she uttered the words: "That which is five really is one."

"What does it mean?"

Sarah struggled to catch her breath. "I don't know."

"Remember the scroll," the woman said. "All is revealed in the king's words. 'The mystery unfolds and, lo, there is rapture in the heavens.'"

He took her cue. "The five points of the star correspond to the five planets that were visible at the time—Jupiter, Mars, Mercury, Saturn, and Venus. When those five converge in the Jerusalem sky, they will form a straight line. The length of the Mosaic cubit." He laughed. "I knew it."

Though Sarah had relinquished the riddle, she'd withheld the nuances—the rabbi's open hand, the subtle but loaded biblical references—that helped her form her own version of the answer. Solomon hid the measuring unit within an ideogram so simple and so straightforward no one would perceive its esoteric value. The five-pointed star on the king's ring would be dismissed as a common symbol when in reality it held the ultimate secret.

The woman was right: the answer was in the scroll. *Go in the direction of the bright star, whose five rays of light point to the one divine truth.*

The star's five sides unfolded into one straight line, revealing the precise length of a *tefah*, or palm, the basic unit of measurement. She couldn't be certain until she put her theory to the test, but she was convinced that was the answer.

Sacks looked toward the top of the dome. "I will do as I said." He directed his voice toward the phone's video screen. "Do not harm him. Wait for my instructions."

He glared at Sarah and dropped the dagger. A metallic clang filled the dome as the weapon bounced twice off the stone. "My hands will not be stained with your blood tonight." He turned toward his priestess.

With head bowed, the woman awaited his command.

"Kill her."

Before the woman in the hooded robe turned off the phone, Sarah caught her father's glance for a second. He looked shaken, bewildered.

"Call into the platform," Sacks told his accomplice. "Make sure all systems are go for the missile launch."

She dialed the number and waited. "There is no answer," she whispered. She tried again. She looked at Sacks and shook her head.

He looked surprised. "They were expecting this call. Bunch of incompetents. Log on to the remote monitoring site."

She tapped and swiped the screen. Her hand froze in midair, and she looked up at Sacks. "The platform burns."

He snatched the phone from her hands. "This is impossible." He swiped the screen a few times. He stopped and looked intently at the images delivered by the remote video cameras. He looked disoriented and downright panicked. "Arab scum!"

He threw the phone to the ground, shattering the screen.

Sarah could see the image despite the cracked glass. The entire platform was engulfed in flames. The massive pyre reached several stories up, its flaming tongues licking the sky. A red-and-white keffiyeh hung from a high pole, whipping defiantly in the stiff winter wind. The banner of the Bedouins. The corner of the fabric caught fire, and the scarf disintegrated in the blaze. The screen went black.

She knew in that instant her plan had worked. The Al Murrah had taken their revenge by setting the rig alight.

With erratic movements that betrayed his rage, Sacks stepped off the rock and walked around to one of the columns, where a rope hung down from the upper level of the dome. He shed his white robe, revealing a loose-fitting white button-down shirt tucked into slim black trousers. His hair was tied back into a tight knot, but two long strands hung around his face. A yarmulke capped his crown. He draped a prayer shawl around his shoulders and began to climb up the rope.

The woman approached Sarah and picked up the dagger. She placed it flat onto her palms and raised it to the sky. "God almighty, exalted ruler of the heavens, source of the ineffable light, savior of the damned, I dedicate this instrument to you that it may be consecrated unto your purpose. Accept this humble sacrifice upon the virgin earth, upon the firmament you alone have laid as the foundation of all things holy. This we offer in the name of peace. Selah."

That voice . . .

With a gesture bordering on theatrics, the robed figure sliced the air with the dagger before holding it in strike position.

Eyes wide and unblinking, Sarah stared at the tip of the blade.

With a primal yell, the woman drove the dagger

toward her heart.

Sarah's muscles burned as she raised her bound arms to block the strike. The knife came down between her wrists, slicing through the rope. Her forearm was cut, but she was free. Mustering what little strength the drugs had left her, she grabbed the woman's ankles, knocking her off her feet.

The dagger fell onto the stone. Sarah claimed it and cut the rope around her ankles. She tried to throw it over the fence surrounding the stone, but her ailing muscles prevented her from tossing it more than a few feet.

The woman jumped to her feet. Her hood was now off. "We meet again."

Sarah stared at her slack-jawed. She should have known Mariah Banai was working for him. It explained everything: the burning of the Qaryat al-Fau camp, the murdered university courier, the scroll's theft, Sacks' intimate knowledge of obscure Hebraic concepts. She was his informant all along.

Mariah laughed loudly. "All this time, you and your idiot partner were placing information directly in the hands of your executioner. How does that feel, Doctor? I would say it's supreme irony."

"Traitor. You betrayed us, the university, your oath as a scholar . . ."

"My loyalty is to my people—their past and their future. My stint with the Arabs was nothing more than a means to an end. I'd long known about the legend of the scroll, which was given by Solomon to his lover, the Queen of Sheba, for safekeeping after her visit to Jerusalem, only to vanish in a violent sandstorm. Then I met the chosen one, and all became clear. We had crew members from archaeological digs all over southern Arabia working for us. We waited for years; then you and Madigan hand-delivered the one object that would change everything."

Sarah looked up. Sacks had climbed to the top of the rotunda and was standing at the base of the dome in front of an open hatch. He ducked through the opening and climbed out.

"What better place to announce the coming of Mashiach than the top of Mount Moriah? The era of peace is at last upon us. Shame you won't live to witness it." Mariah charged Sarah, sending her tumbling onto the stone.

Sarah's muscles and joints had stiffened so much that it required great effort to lift herself up. She ignored the stabbing pain and awkwardly got to her feet.

Her slow movements cost her. Mariah kicked her backwards and stepped onto her throat, pinning her to the ground. Sarah choked under the pressure. She gritted her teeth and tried to pry her opponent's foot away, which only made Mariah bear down harder.

"What's the matter? Lost your strength? I should let you die slowly of tetrodotoxin poisoning . . . but that wouldn't be nearly as much fun."

Sarah's lips were completely numb. A thousand invisible needles pricked her face. Desperately, she looked around her for anything that would give her an edge. There was only the foundation stone, now stained with drops of her blood.

She was losing the battle, but she would not give up the fight. She noticed on the stone's ragged surface a broken piece jutting out near her right hand. She reached for it. It was loose enough to pull out and sharp enough to inflict damage. With all the strength she could muster, she drove it into Mariah's calf.

The woman howled and jerked her leg away.

With a pained grunt, Sarah stood and lunged toward Mariah, knocking her over. Hoping the distraction had bought her time, she hobbled as quickly as she could toward the rope.

She hadn't gotten far when Mariah rose and started after her. Sarah picked up the pace, panting as her heavy lungs doled out scant air. Directly in front of her was a deep perforation on the rock's surface. The hole, an opening into the Well of Souls below the foundation stone, was large enough for a person to fit through.

She looked back and saw her opponent gain on her, then glanced at the opening. There was no alternative.

She turned to see Mariah rush her with a primal growl. Too weak to fight effectively, Sarah crouched in front of Mariah and pushed her legs out from under her. Mariah tumbled into the mouth of the opening, struggling to avoid a fall.

Sarah's arms trembled as she pushed Mariah farther in.

Mariah's legs slid inside the well, and she grabbed hold of the lip. Her face strained from the effort of holding on. "Go to hell, Sarah Weston," she hissed.

A spark of loathing ignited in Sarah's gut. Every ill this woman was responsible for, all her evil intentions, rushed to the forefront of Sarah's mind. All that was left now was to even the score: an eye for an eye.

She forced herself upright. "You first," she said as she delivered one final kick.

A scream pierced the silence of the dome, growing fainter as she plunged.

Sarah looked inside the hole and saw Mariah still conscious and lying on her back on the carpet-lined stone floor of the cavern. Sarah could make out the outline of a broken bone beneath Mariah's robe and figured her tibia had snapped in two. She was alive but immobilized.

Sarah leaned into her knees and attempted to catch her breath.

She wasn't finished yet. She looked up at the dome and estimated the distance she'd have to climb. Even if she had the strength to make it up, it would take everything out of her. But she had to do it, even if it was her last task on earth.

She limped toward the rope, her legs stiff as wooden

beams. She grabbed hold and hoisted herself up. Teeth clenched and eyes watering, she ascended one painful inch at a time. The hair circling her face was drenched, and drops of perspiration trickled into her eyes. Her heart protested violently against the effort.

With one last push, she heaved her body onto a narrow ledge at the base of the dome. She lay there panting and shaking, unsure she would survive the night. She gazed at the painted interior of the dome and tried to distract herself by concentrating on its beauty. It was truly awesome. Intricate glass and tile mosaics in repeating scroll patterns glittered against a gilded wood backdrop, giving the structure a jewel box effect. Islamic religious inscriptions, rendered in black and gold, lined the perimeter. In the center, a golden medallion emitted a muted glow.

A series of arched openings encircled the dome's base. One of those openings was a hatch to the outside. Sarah noticed the faint light of a moonbeam entering the dome and crawled toward it.

A small window connecting the dome's interior with the outside was cracked open. She could hear his voice. She sat with her back to the wall and listened.

"This mount will once again hold in its bosom the house of the Lord," he proclaimed in Hebrew. "Long have we been deprived of the right to worship in the most sacred of places. Long have we been kept out of our own lands, the lands handed to the tribes of the Lord. The time has come to reclaim what is ours. To rebuild the temple and return peace to Jerusalem.

"Only one man can do this. Behold, O fellow tribesmen, the one who is descended from the royal house of David. King Solomon was my forefather as surely as snowflakes crowd the sky this night. The ring of the righteous king, passed by divine intervention to his last surviving heir, is a symbol of the awesome power and the infinite wisdom that shaped this land of ours three millennia ago."

Sarah peeked through the crack and saw Sacks a few feet away. He stood at the very edge of the dome facing a camera mounted on a tripod. As he delivered his live webcast, snow fell around him, landing on his yarmulke and on the *tallit* draped across his shoulders.

He reached beneath the shawl and pulled out a scroll. Solomon's blueprints for the original temple. She cringed at the thought of such an important artifact being handled that way.

Sacks held the scroll up and unfurled it. "Solomon's own words have led me to the most important find of our times—the plans drawn by the great king himself for the temple of Jerusalem. This was his legacy, left for the most worthy of his heirs. He foresaw the destruction that would be wrought by the infidels and knew the temple would vanish in the hands of the wicked. The one who would come to possess Solomon's most sacred manuscript would have the power to rebuild the temple and usher in the era of peace as told in the prophecies." He rolled up the manuscript and held it to his forehead, reciting a prayer.

The time had come. Sarah crawled through the hatch and stood upright. The poison had taken firm hold of her body. Her muscles had contracted into rigid, painful clumps, and every movement required great effort. She felt immense pressure behind her eyes and for a moment thought she would black out. She fought the sensation.

She stood behind Sacks, within view of the video camera. On the ground next to his feet was the remote control for the device. As swiftly as she could manage, she kicked it off the ledge, and it sailed toward the lower roof structure.

Startled, he looked back.

Sarah spoke into the camera. "Believe none of this." Her jaw was tight, distorting her words. "This man is a murderer. Ask him how many people he killed so he can stand here tonight."

"Silence," he bellowed. "This is blasphemy in the eyes of the Lord."

She was relentless. "These artifacts have been stolen from sacred sites. They belong to the people."

He was shaking with rage. He extended an arm and pointed at her. "This woman is the devil. She is godless . . . an empty soul."

She shouted toward the camera. "He's a false prophet. He belongs in prison." The exertion made her gasp for breath.

"Harlot! You cannot block the coming of the messiah. God himself has ordained it, and it shall be so. You cannot stand between the people of Israel and their glory." He swung at her, striking her face and sending her to her knees. "All enemies of God shall be punished. The judgment is upon us." He kicked her shoulder, and she landed on her back inches away from the ledge. "The righteous shall rise, and the sinners shall cower in the face of the Lord." He lifted his arms and gazed to the clouded sky. "God almighty, ruler of the heavens, send now a plague upon your enemies. Paralyze them that they may not rise against you. Take away their breath that they may not blaspheme against thy holy name."

Sarah lay there, unable to prop herself up. Her body was leaden, and she could no longer will it to move. Her heart was beating irregularly. It was a matter of time.

He pointed to her and turned to the camera. "Behold, the miracle of the Lord."

She tried to lift an arm, but it was too heavy.

"And a wolf shall live with a lamb, and a leopard shall lie with a kid; and a calf and a lion cub and a fatling shall lie together, and a small child shall lead them. They shall neither harm nor destroy on all my holy mount, for the land shall be full of knowledge of the Lord as water covers the sea bed. And it shall come to pass on that day, that the root of Jesse, which stands as a banner for peoples, to him shall the nations inquire—"

The roar of a helicopter drowned out his words. Sarah turned her head slowly toward the sound. The bright spotlight of the craft hovering above the dome blinded her, and she looked away.

Sacks shaded his eyes and squinted toward the light. He was clearly stunned by the intrusion.

"Put your arms up and stand with your back to the wall." The command, spoken in English with a heavy accent, came through a loudspeaker.

"What is this?" Sacks shouted, though he could not be heard over the rhythmic rumble of the rotors. "Who are you?"

"It's over, Trent." The voice was different from the first. Sarah detected a northern British accent. "You must turn yourself in."

Sacks' body jolted. "Father?"

"Alastair Bromley was arrested, Son. They know everything. I had to tell them about your illness."

His bottom lip trembled. "Father, no—"

"I've told them you have done all of this without my knowledge and without full disclosure to the company. But I will not press charges."

"How could you do this?" His voice was too soft to be heard by anyone in the chopper. He looked around with jerking movements, as if looking for someone to come to his rescue. His hands trembled. "I have been betrayed."

He kneeled by Sarah and hoisted her body toward the

ledge until her head hung over the void. "Go away, or I will throw her over."

Sarah could not fight. She lay helpless, seeing but barely feeling the snowflakes falling on her.

"Don't do anything foolish, Trent. Turn yourself in now and lessen your burden. Otherwise, they will take no mercy on you."

He looked down, his brow pinched. "Where is she? Where is Mariah?"

Sarah shook her head and struggled to get the words out. "Game's over."

With a growl, he delivered a backhanded blow across her face.

Her head jerked violently, but she did not feel the strike.

"You are doomed to a painful death, whore. It's no more than you deserve." He spat on her face, his glare venomous. He stood and faced the helicopter, shouting the words of a desperate man. "I am the messiah, the twig sprouting from the roots of the stump of Jesse. I am destined to build the third temple on this very spot, and nothing you do can stop it, for it is the will of God. I will bring riches to the people of Israel and independence from their old enemies."

The Israeli cop reclaimed the microphone. "Trent Robert Ashworth, you are under arrest for assassination, arson, sabotage of a public servant's airplane, and illegal drilling practices. Put your hands up. You are surrounded."

"Tell them, Father." The veins on his temples bulged. "Tell them I am the chosen one. The messenger of God."

James Ashworth said nothing.

The Israeli pointed a semiautomatic at him. "Put your hands up or I will shoot."

"Barbarians! You cannot kill me." He stepped to the lip of the ledge and held his arms high. "I am invincible. Do you hear me? Invincible . . ."

He jumped.

Sarah watched as his body, with arms and legs outstretched as if he expected to take flight, plunged into the void. The *tallit*, yanked from his shoulders by the wind, floated down like an open parachute. She closed her eyes just before impact.

She struggled in vain to catch her breath. She looked up at the helicopter, which had descended toward the suicide scene. Everything was a blur in the bright lights. As her consciousness faded, she thought she saw Daniel's face, his long dark hair tousled beneath a black ski cap, his hand outstretched to her as he shouted something.

She was certain his spirit had come to guide her on a journey she was not ready to take. But she no longer had the strength to fight.

She closed her eyes and surrendered.

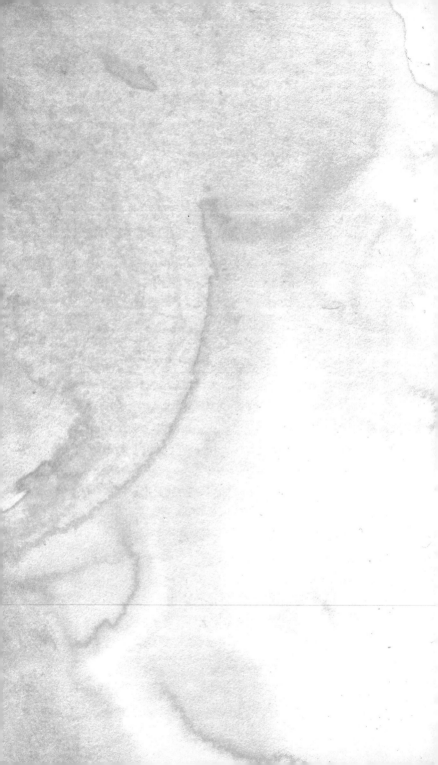

Chapter 43

A steady sequence of beeps pulsed in Sarah's ears. She heard the exaggerated sound of an inhale.

She didn't have to open her eyes to know where she was. It was enough to know she was alive. She tried to move her fingers. They responded to her brain's command, albeit in slow motion. She attempted to shift in her bed but could not. Her body might as well have been made of lead.

She willed her eyes open and regarded the darkened room. There were no windows and no lights beyond the LEDs emitted by the machines she was hooked up to. She heard shuffling and shifted her gaze. A nurse dressed in scrubs and a hairnet sat in the far corner, monitoring his patient on a computer and leafing through a stack of papers.

He swiveled his chair around. He stood and approached her bedside.

As he stepped into the pale red light of the heart-rate

monitor, Sarah realized she knew his face. The hateful blue eyes she'd last encountered in Solomon's cave, deep in the Judean Wilderness, now glared at her.

"At last, she wakes," Angus said. "I've been waiting patiently for this moment."

Sarah looked around the room, noticing a mass on the floor. The naked body of the real nurse lay motionless, shoved against a wall. Her breathing, exaggerated through the ventilator, grew more rapid. She was helpless. She could barely move and could not make a sound.

"Evil whore. Have you any idea what you have done?" He spoke slowly behind clenched teeth. "Because of you, our only hope for peace in the world is gone. Who now can reclaim the throne of Solomon and restore the judges? Who will banish evil and tyranny? Who shall rebuild the ruined cities of Israel and make her enemies shudder? When you killed my master, you ended the royal bloodline and all hope for redemption. That is the gravest of crimes, and for that you shall pay." He bent down and reached under his pant leg, pulling the familiar black-hilted knife out of a holster.

With awkward fingers, she fumbled around her bed. She found what she was hoping for: the nurse call button. She pressed it again and again, hoping someone outside the room would realize it was a sign of distress.

He held the knife above her chest. "I want you to watch as I slice through your sternum and rip out your heart with my bare hands."

She stared at the blade engraved with mystical symbols. The beeps on the heart-rate monitor were faster, more erratic. The ventilator registered shallow, rapid breaths.

He laughed. "Frightened, are you? Good. I want fear to be what you take with you to hell."

She tried to lift her arms. Though some of the feeling had returned to her limbs, her brain still could not will her body to move. Desperate, she punched the call button again.

Angus placed the knife on the center of her chest like a surgeon wielding a scalpel. He licked his lips and shot her a wicked sideways smile. "This will only hurt a bit."

A banging sound came from the other side of the door. Someone was trying to enter but could not.

He did not even turn around. It was almost as if he was expecting them. He pressed the knife down.

The banging became louder and was now accompanied by shouting. They were trying to break the door down.

Sarah heard the ripping sound as her hospital gown yielded to the blade.

Angus remained focused on his task. Pressing the knife firmly against her chest, he glared at her. "I shall avenge him if it's the last thing I do."

She was too numb to feel anything. She watched, helpless, as her own blood spread across her bosom.

The door flew off its hinges and fell to the tile floor

with a crashing sound. Three men entered. Two pushed Angus to the floor and overpowered him. The third came to Sarah's bedside, stuffing gauze onto her chest to stem the bleeding. He called for backup, and a nurse ran into the room. She shot a syringe full of clear liquid into Sarah's IV line.

Everything else was a blur. Nurses and doctors came and went, trying to stabilize her condition. Police officers cuffed Angus and led him out of the room.

As he exited in their custody, he looked back at Sarah with a sinister smirk.

She pressed her head into the pillow and exhaled into the tube. Her peripheral vision registered a figure standing in the open doorway. She turned her head slowly.

Dressed in torn jeans and a black Rutgers hoodie, Daniel met her gaze and smiled.

He was alive. She smiled back with her eyes.

"Sir, you can't be here," said a nurse.

Daniel didn't look away from Sarah and didn't move.

"Sir," the nurse repeated. "This is critical care. You really cannot be here. Please."

He nodded and walked away.

The nurse pressed some buttons on the monitor. "That's the strongest your heartbeat has been all night." She turned toward the doorway. "Who was he, anyway?"

With the ventilator stuffed into her mouth, Sarah could not speak. If she could, she would have said, "The man to whom I owe everything."

The nurse put on reading glasses and wrote something on the chart. "Never mind." She looked over her glasses at Sarah. "I can use my imagination."

Sarah relaxed, letting her mind absorb the revelation that Daniel was with her again. Everything made sense. It was Daniel, not Bellows, who was the *Times'* anonymous source. He had not let anyone know he was alive because he was working under the radar to prove Advanced Electronic Solutions' role in the plane crash. To reduce his sentence, Bromley must have sung about his relationship with Royal Petroleum and the Ashworth men, which led to James Ashworth's detainment and the hunt for his son.

Sarah closed her eyes. It was the first time in months she'd felt safe enough to let go and allow her thoughts to drift untethered in the river of her mind. The words rang in her ears as if Uri'el Ben Moshe were there speaking them.

Stay the course even if all seems lost. It is the only way you can claim victory.

At last, she understood.

Epilogue

*T*he road leading to Solomon's cave looked much different by day. Without the moon casting pewter shadows upon the stones, the landscape looked like an endless patch of parched brown earth, a jumble of peaks and valleys and rock faces sculpted into curious shapes by the eternal winds.

The balsam tree beneath the cave's entrance was the lone reminder that life persisted in this remote place. Its meager shadow, elongated by the afternoon sun, pointed east, where the Tel Aviv University camp had been set up.

Ezra, conferring with two team members beneath a tented canopy, stopped his conversation as his guests approached. "You made it," he said. "I was beginning to worry."

"Helicopter traffic," said Daniel. "It's brutal this time of day."

Ezra turned to Sarah. "How are you feeling?"

"A hundred percent. Surely you don't think a little

poison can slow me down."

"She's lucky she inhaled a small dose of tetrodotoxin," Daniel said. "They were able to get an inhibitor to bind to it. A few more milligrams and it would have been lights out."

"And your father?"

"He was being held by Sacks' thugs in some compound in Tajikistan. Mariah led them to him in exchange for a lighter sentence. He's safely back in England."

Ezra chuckled. "I can only imagine how ill-tempered he must have been."

She smiled. In fact, her father's reaction had surprised her. She'd expected him to blame her for putting him in such a predicament, to chastise her for what he liked to call her "juvenile crusading antics." But he never called, neither to criticize nor to commend. Instead, he sent a bouquet of daffodils to her hospital room.

Though she would have rather had a conversation than an object, the gesture was significant. It was a reminder of the springs of her childhood, when daffodils exploded like a bright yellow carpet on the grounds of their country manor, a time when the Weston family was still intact—before the arguments and accusations, tragedies and regrets.

She interpreted it as a peace offering and, though they still stood on opposite sides of a chasm of silence, she allowed the possibility there might just be a bridge somewhere. Eventually, she thought, they'd find it.

Ezra turned to Daniel. "And you, Madigan. We thought we'd lost you. What the hell happened?"

"The instruments failed. Branford couldn't keep the plane in the air. We landed in the Atlantic nose first and that was when the plane broke apart. We had seconds to get out before it sank. It wasn't pretty."

Though Sarah had already heard the story, she cringed at his retelling of it. They'd had many near misses, but this was way too close. She was still in disbelief he'd made it out of that icy water alive. He'd drifted on an airplane wing in a hypothermic state when a fishing boat spotted him and brought him on board. It was sheer luck.

"Luckily, he was scooped up by some friendly blokes." She turned to Daniel. "Tell him how you convinced them to keep your rescue a secret."

"Actually, it wasn't that hard. One of the guys recognized me from some of my old shows. Said he'd always wanted to be on TV. So I promised him a spot on my next documentary as an extra."

"That, and a couple of cases of Newkie Brown," Sarah said. The three laughed in unison.

"Well, you two will be happy to know that while you were slaying dragons, our crew made significant headway here," Ezra said. "We've located the throne through ground-penetrating radar. It will take a while to get to it, but we are committed. This is beyond huge."

"What do your minimalist colleagues think about that?" Sarah said.

"It's a game changer, no doubt. Everyone's scrambling to come up with new theories." He gazed toward the cave. "Solomon, supreme ruler of the united monarchy. Never did I dream I would see proof of that in my lifetime."

She removed her aviators and rubbed off the sandy film with the corner of her fleece pullover. "And what about the manuscript and the ring? Where are they now?"

"Authorities retrieved the manuscript from the top of the dome. It was turned over to Antiquities. As for the ring . . . it was never found."

"What? But he was wearing it. I saw it on his finger just before he—" She stopped short, disturbed by the recollection.

Ezra shrugged. "They scoured the place. There was nothing. Perhaps it was dislodged at impact."

"Or maybe somebody took it," Daniel said. "It wouldn't surprise me."

"We may never know," Ezra said. "The worst part is, if the ring truly is the measurement unit, the manuscript is meaningless without it." He looked at Sarah. "Isn't that right?"

"If the temple is to be rebuilt as Solomon intended, yes." She considered the irony of holding the cipher, only to lose the object it was tied to. "We were so close . . ."

"Well, if the good book is to be believed, everything

will reveal itself when the time's right," Daniel said.

"False," Ezra said. "We don't sit around, waiting for things to be revealed. We will find that ring. A group of Israel Museum supporters have put up a massive reward. If someone has it, he'd be a fool not to come forward."

"Say you do find it," Sarah said. "Will you know what to do with it?"

"I'm sure we can figure it out. How hard can it be?"

She smiled and put her aviators back on. Perhaps Daniel was right: some things were not meant to be revealed. For the time being, she would keep to herself the knowledge she alone held. Beyond her promise to the rabbi, she knew in her heart it was the right thing to do. "Good luck, then. We must be going."

"What? You just got here. At least stay for supper. I want the crew to meet you. You are legends in their eyes."

"Sarah's right," Daniel said. "We have commitments back in Tel Aviv. Perhaps some other time."

"Suit yourself." Ezra kissed Sarah on the cheek, lingering a little too long. "Shalom, old friend. Don't be a stranger." He turned to Daniel and extended his right hand. "Madigan. Look after her, will you?"

Daniel laughed. "I would if she'd let me." The two shook hands.

Sarah waved and started toward the helicopter.

Daniel caught up to her. "Walk with me."

They walked in silence for a few minutes. Then he

spoke. "What are you going to do?"

"Don't know. Haven't sorted it out yet." Anxiety barbed her gut. She had dreaded this conversation. "What about you? Going back to al-Fau, are you?"

He shook his head. "Nah. I'm done there. I've asked for reassignment."

She was surprised. He had been in Saudi Arabia for so long it had come to define him. "Where to, then?"

"Well, there wasn't much available. They asked if I wanted to get in on the ground floor of a new expedition to Thebes. I'd have to put my team together." He turned to her. "You'd be at the top of my list, of course."

She stopped and faced him. She wanted more than anything to take him up on it. But she wanted to be sure about his intentions. "What makes you think I'd want to go?"

He pushed an errant tendril away from her eyes. He leaned down and kissed her. "Just a hunch."

She hadn't expected that. She felt the blood rush to her pale cheeks and turned away from him, at a loss for what to say. The words came out all wrong. "Well, you shouldn't be so presumptuous."

He smiled. "Why, Dr. Weston, I do believe you're blushing."

She smiled awkwardly and started walking. Her heart was pounding.

She heard him call behind her. "Damn it, Sarah . . .

can't we stop pretending?"

She stopped and slowly turned around. A few feet away from her stood a man who was unequivocally strong yet so devoid of defenses she felt ashamed for putting up her own.

"You may be highly capable," he said, "but you need me. And you know it."

She suppressed a smile. "Your arrogance is staggering."

He ignored the remark, which she meant more as a joke than a jab. He was dead serious. "And I sure as hell need you."

There was no fine print in his pronouncement, no trace of insincerity. His honesty made her walls crumble. She beamed and broke into a belly laugh. It was out of character for her, but it felt true.

He approached slowly. "That's the first time I've noticed you have dimples. You should laugh more often."

He was right. It felt liberating to let go. After so many months of darkness, this was the first shaft of light piercing a seemingly impenetrable gloom.

He slipped his arms around her waist, and she let him pull her close. She felt his warm breath on her cheek as he whispered, "Stay with me, Sarah."

With eyes closed, she lingered for a moment before stepping back and nodding. Without another word, they held hands and walked toward the helicopter.

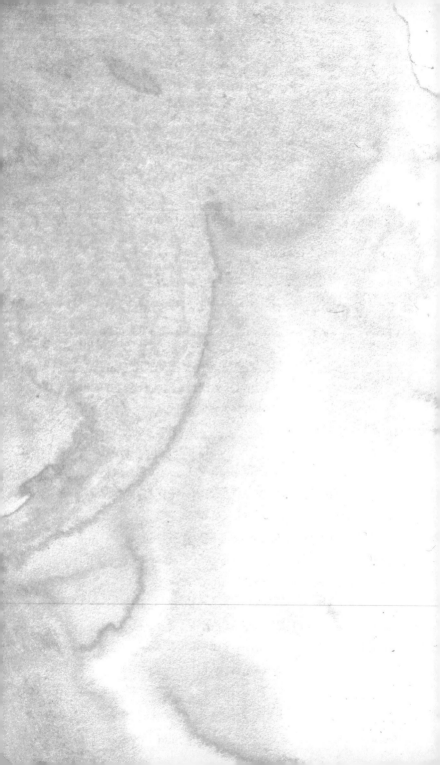

Acknowledgments

My sincere gratitude goes to everyone who contributed to the research process for this book: Rabbis Moshe Scheiner and Avrohom Stolik, for guiding me through the intricacies of Judaism and biblical archaeology; Dr. Tommy Schechtman, for sharing valuable resources; Steve Barry, for contributing to my understanding of rock climbing; the remarkable archaeologists working in Israel, whose bodies of work inspired and informed this story; Julian and Yamit Wood, for clarifying Israeli cultural nuances; Paul Rubio, for contributing research; Ben Simpson, for teaching me a few things about helicopters; my amazing editor, Emily Steele; and Peter Lioubin, my husband, for his patience, insight, and encouragement through every part of the process.

MEDALLION

P R E S S

Be in the know on the latest Medallion Press news by
becoming a **Medallion Press Insider!**

As an Insider you'll receive:
- Our FREE expanded monthly newsletter, giving you more insight into
Medallion Press
- Advanced press releases and breaking news
- Greater access to all your favorite Medallion authors

Joining is easy. Just visit our website at
www.medallionmediagroup.com and click on
Super Cool E-blast next to the social media buttons.

Want to know what's going on with your favorite author or
what new releases are coming from Medallion Press?

Now you can receive breaking news, updates, and more from
Medallion Press straight to your cell phone, e-mail, instant
messenger, or Facebook!

Sign up now at **www.twitter.com/MedallionPress** to stay on top
of all the happenings in and around Medallion Press.

---

m e d a l l i o n m e d i a g r o u p . c o m